Dear Reader,

December is a magical time of year, a time for joy
and fun and love. Phyllis Taylor Pianka brings you
all three in *The Thackery Jewels*, three stories about
three special, high-spirited sisters who take the
London ton by storm.

But although related, all of the girls are unique—as is
their much-married guardian, Lady Udora, who now
only wants to see them all settled in a very proper
way. But the Thackery girls have ideas of their own,
which often lead to mischief and mayhem.

Enjoy each of their adventures in "Amethyst,"
"Emerald" and "Topaz."

The best of the season, and happy reading to all.

The Editor

THE THACKERY JEWELS

PHYLLIS TAYLOR PIANKA

Harlequin Books

TORONTO • NEW YORK • LONDON
AMSTERDAM • PARIS • SYDNEY • HAMBURG
STOCKHOLM • ATHENS • TOKYO • MILAN
MADRID • WARSAW • BUDAPEST • AUCKLAND

CONTENTS

ABOUT THE AUTHOR

The Thackery Jewels collection was inspired by characters in Phyllis Taylor Pianka's previous book, *A Coventry Courtship*. In that story, the heroine, Udora Middlesworth, was left an inheritance, which she believed to be a fortune in gems. Instead, she inherited three wild orphans who turned her world upside down. These orphans make their own debut in *The Thackery Jewels*.

Phyllis Taylor Pianka is the author of 19 novels, many of which were published by Harlequin. This talented author makes her home in California.

Books by Phyllis Taylor Pianka

HARLEQUIN REGENCY ROMANCE
3—THE TART SHOPPE
34—THE CALICO COUNTESS
48—THE LARK'S NEST
80—A COVENTRY COURTSHIP

THE THACKERY JEWELS—Amethyst
Emerald
Topaz

AMETHYST

CHAPTER ONE

MISS AMETHYST THACKERY was less than pleased to see the gilded barouche parked in front of Lily's house when she, her twin sister Emerald, and their abigail, Maggie McGee, were assisted from their full-top cabriolet. Amethyst coiled a burnt-honey curl around her finger and frowned. "I fear we've chosen a poor time to call on Miss Lily. It seems that her odious brother is at home this afternoon."

Emerald clutched the book she had been reading and looked hopeful. "It isn't too late to turn round and return home. I didn't want to come along, anyway. I don't know why Lady Udora insisted that I accompany you, especially since Topaz was allowed to take the air in Regent's Park."

Maggie gave her a speaking look. "Miss Topaz had an invitation from Lord Venable. Sure an' if you'd take your nose from a book long enough to catch a wink from some nob, m'lady would be pleased to let go your leadin' strings, too."

Maggie turned her attention back to Amy. "Lord 'ave mercy! 'Is lordship at 'ome and you wearing a dress that covers you up to 'ere,'' she said, drawing her finger up to her chin. She squinted at her charge. "Aye, and p'raps you could loosen a button or two at the top."

Amethyst sighed. "You know very well that it is not my intention to court his glances. Indeed, I consider him a conceited, overbearing Corinthian."

"A coxcomb 'e might be, Miss Amy, but 'e's already come into 'is title. A viscount is nothin' to fly into the boughs over, even one what's young enough to 'ave 'is own teeth. If 'twas me in your shoes, I wouldn'a be so quick as to give 'im the shoulder."

"I wouldn't have Egan Kimble if he were the Crown Prince. Besides, he doesn't like me above half. I'm Lily's friend, not his, and that's the way I prefer to keep it."

Maggie, seeing the heat rise in Amy's face, gave her a knowing look and simply smiled.

Emerald, who thoroughly understood her sister's penchant for overstatement, wondered at the differences between Amy and herself. Where Amy enjoyed the company of others, she liked nothing better than to keep company with a good book. Her other sister, Topaz, was another story, but then Taz was adopted, so that would account for her adventurous and usually outrageous behaviour.

When the butler showed the twins and their abigail into the second-floor sitting-room, Lily, her black ringlets bouncing, was in transports. She flew to the door and embraced Amy before dragging her over to the settee, where she pushed her down.

"It has finally arrived. I cannot wait for you to see it. Sit there while I fetch it from the armoire."

Amy clasped her hands together. "Your gown for the Drummond musicale! Oh, do put it on."

"Not just that, silly goose." She lowered her voice. "It comes with one of those new bust improvers. Not the wax kind, of course, but this one is stuffed with the finest cotton wool. You'll see," she said before darting into the next room.

Emerald, puzzled by such frivolity, found a comfortable chair by the window and opened her book.

Maggie, sitting a short distance from Amy, raised her gaze to the ceiling. Seeing that Miss Lily was beyond earshot, she leaned forward and whispered, "'Twon't 'elp 'er a bit, you know. 'Er with 'er skinny neck an' short legs."

"Do be still, Maggie. You're far too outspoken. One of these days Lady Udora will turn you out for good, and then where would you go?"

Maggie grinned. "I 'spect I'd find me a rich protector and spend the rest o' my life in bed, instead of behind a hot iron pressing ruffles for you and your sisters."

"Don't be too sure of yourself. You're becoming quite the hoyden of late, and I doubt that any man in his right senses would give you a second glance."

Maggie just tilted her head and smiled. They both knew that as brash as Maggie was, she was popular among the men of her station. Furthermore, Udora loved her and would never let her go. Certainly not until they found someone who could equal Maggie's talent with the brush and comb, and the chances of that were decidedly remote.

At that moment Lily drifted into the room on a cloud of white-sprigged muslin. Although the gown was beautifully designed, it did little to enhance her pale skin...or conceal her unusually long and thin neck. Amy intercepted a wink from Maggie and gave

her a quelling look before she rose and walked round
Lily to get a better view. Lily swivelled her head.

"Well, don't keep me waiting, silly goose. Am I not
the *dernier cri* in this gown? Isn't it the most beautiful material you've ever seen?"

Amy ran a length of the fabric between her fingers.
"It is truly beautiful. So soft and luxurious. The embroidered white roses are adorable."

Lily looked downcast. "You don't like it."

"I do, I do. I just wonder perhaps if you need
something bright to liven it up a bit. To bring out the
colour in your cheeks."

"A shawl? The bishop's blue!"

"Why not the jonquil-yellow Kashmir that your
brother brought back to you from India?"

"Splendid. I don't know why I didn't think of it."

There was a tap on the door. It was Milly, the upstairs maid. "Beggin' your pardon, m'lady. His lordship wishes you and the Misses Thackery to join him
in the library."

Lily wrinkled her nose. "Oh, bother. I know what
he wants. Very well, Milly. You may tell him that we
shall be down directly."

Then she turned back to Amy and Emerald, who
finally looked up. "It's Rupert Effington come to call.
Egan is forever trying to palm me off on some unsus-
pecting individual. He is determined that my come out
will take so that he can rid himself of responsibility for
me once and for all."

Emerald wrinkled her nose. "Rupert Effington?
How dismal! He has a wet mouth. Can you imagine
being kissed by him?"

Amy shook her head in disbelief. "But it has only been two weeks since we made our bows. Surely he cannot be so desperate as to fob you off on just anyone."

"Indeed he can and will give me over to him if Effington decides to offer for me," Lily declared, at the same time stepping carefully out of the new gown. "Egan learned his lesson with my older sister."

"Your sister!" Amy grasped the arms of the chair. "I thought you and Egan were the only living children in your family."

For the first time Emerald's interest was caught, and she marked the place in her book with her finger as Lily continued.

"We might as well be," Lily declared. "Darlene's name has been banned in this house since she eloped to Gretna Green with Johnny Lapwell nearly two years ago."

Amy looked properly shocked, but immediately her gaze softened. "Scandalous to be sure, but, oh, how deliciously romantic! They must have been very much in love. I...I suppose he was unsuitable. A commoner?"

"Worse than that. He is a crackrope sort of fellow, just a yard short of the hangman, so I've heard." She lowered her voice. "A woman I know says she saw them leaving a Grub Street pub and that they live together but have never even bothered to take their marriage vows at all."

"Oh, my dear. How dreadful."

Lily nodded as she slipped into a day dress of cotton brocade. "If Mama and Papa were alive, they would have been horrified. I'm glad they were at least spared that, but I do wish they were here to take over from Egan. He is most overset at having to see me properly wed.''

Emerald frowned. "But why? It's not as if he is pressed for money. Your family left both of you well provided for, or so you've told us on several occasions.''

Lily dimpled. ''I shouldn't tell you this, but I suppose everyone knows. His lordship is quite bewitched by a dancer from the French Corps de Ballet. Eva Delight is her name, though not her real one, I daresay. She has leased rooms in a hotel.''

"Grillon's on Albemarle Street?''

"Good heavens, no. It is far too respectable. She is staying in the Pulteney in Piccadilly.''

Emerald tilted her head. "I read that it has water closets and that the Russian Tsar and his obnoxious sister, the Grand Duchess Catherine, once stayed there.''

Amy ignored the history lesson to lean breathlessly towards Lily. "And your brother goes there to dally with her?''

Lily giggled. "I suppose he does, though he is most discreet. Once I'm safely married off, he can, of course, do as he pleases without concern for ruining my chances.'' She glanced at the tiny gold clock on her night table. "But come. We'd best go down to the library. Egan will be difficult enough without my further antagonizing him.''

Not surprisingly, Maggie was the first to rise. Her shoe-button eyes flashed, giving evidence of the fact that she enjoyed confrontations. She welcomed anything that would add a spark to her daily routine as a lady's maid. The day her oft-wed mistress, Lady Udora, had taken on the guardianship of the three girls, who were jokingly referred to as the Thackery Jewels, Maggie's life had turned in an exciting new direction. Now at last they had made their début, and it was just a question of time until they found suitable matches, for they were all three exceedingly attractive.

She grimaced as she followed them down the wide stairway to the ground floor of the Kimble mansion. Of course Miss Emmy was sure to be a problem. Her and her bluestocking ways. How any young girl would rather curl up in bed with a good book instead of a young buck was a puzzle to her... but then she never did quite understand why anyone would waste her time learning to read.

A footman opened the door to the library and bowed them inside.

Amy's gaze went first to the fireplace, before which Rupert Effington lounged in a chair, his legs stretched out in front of him, his full, wet lips glistening in the flicker of the flames. Then a movement caught her eye and she turned towards the window wall, where Egan Kimble rested one hip on the edge of a massive desk.

He looked every bit the decadent buck, a debauchee of the first water. He had a slender waist, broad shoulders, and muscular thighs that most certainly needed no sawdust pads to give them shape. Amy glanced at his face but regretted it when his heavy-lidded gaze settled on hers, pinning her like a butterfly to a mat. Amy was forced to look away, despite her determination to make him be the first to back down.

Curiosity piqued Egan's jaded thoughts as he surveyed the girls. Deuced pretty, they were. The twins, though not identical, had a marked similarity to each other. Something in the wide set of their eyes and the dimples at the corners of their mouths. But while Emerald's hair was the rich colour of spring wheat, Amy's, a shade darker, reminded him of warm honey. He wondered if her mouth would call up the same comparison, then chastised himself for thinking in such a way about someone who was little more than a child.

Unlike most other girls who had been shot off into Society that spring, these girls, fresh from the country, had a certain innocence that appealed to him. Moreover, they were a good influence on Lily, for even his somewhat drab sister had a bit of a bloom on her cheeks today. He stole a look at Effington, who had bounded to his feet and executed an acceptable leg.

Egan bowed, then motioned to Lily to take the seat next to Effington. Either out of stupidity or stubbornness, Egan was not sure which, Lily seated herself next to the twins on the settee. The maid, a tasty little morsel with red hair, gave him a look he couldn't mistake before seating herself on a straight-backed chair near the door. He was amused to see that the abigail was careful to hitch her skirt so that a modicum of nicely turned ankle showed below the hem of her grey skirt. He cleared his throat and adjusted his cravat.

By the saints, he was becoming jaded of late if a servant girl could tweak his buttons. It was time for the ballerina to be replaced. She was a nimble one to be sure, but rather common, if truth be told. His gaze moved back to the twins, one of whom had risen to carefully peruse his bookshelf. He immediately discounted her. All the earmarks of a bluestocking, he thought as he turned his ear to the conversation between Effington and the other two girls.

Rupert Effington appeared singularly animated, his moist lips parted as he listened avidly to Amy. She looked quite fetching as she described an ancient horse owned by a local rag-picker. Another few moments and Rupert would be on his knees begging to rescue the hapless nag. Fair enough. Rupert could well afford to stable it, but the attention he paid Miss Thackery was distracting him from Lily. Egan knew he must put an end to it, else Lily would be left in the cold.

"Miss Amy," Egan said sternly, "I hope you have not come here today seeking sanctuary for yet another homeless animal."

She turned to him with the hint of a dimpled smile. "No, my lord. Not today."

"That is most gratifying. The flea-bitten cur you foisted off on Lily has caused quite enough trouble for the entire Season."

"And the dove with the missing foot?"

"It, at least, has remained in the dovecote where it belongs. Both I and the carpets are grateful for that small mercy." He stroked the palm of one hand with the other. "I wonder that you have not entertained the thought of bestowing such creatures on your own family."

"Oh, I have given them a fair share, but with our six cats and five new kittens, not to mention an injured goat that I found in St. James's Park and a fiddler's monkey that was left homeless when his master expired from consumption, we have quite run out of space."

Egan saw that Rupert, quite unconscious of Lily seated directly across from him, was edging towards Amy. Egan frowned and delicately coughed. "Lily, I believe you promised to show his lordship the Chinese gazebo that I had restored in the maze garden."

"No, I . . ."

His scowl stopped her refusal before it was clearly spoken, but Effington, curse his bottomless nature, was not obliged to cooperate. When it appeared he had no intention of leaving the presence of Amy, Egan grasped his arm in a jovial manner and pulled him to his feet. "Don't cry shy now, Effington. I promised you some time alone with Lily and I am a man of my word."

Effington mumbled something that everyone chose to ignore, and backed from the room until he turned at last to follow Lily out the veranda door.

Maggie, blessedly silent in her corner of the room, shot a knowing wink at Amy, who blushed most becomingly, then thrust out her chin and rose, clutching her silk reticule. "I have heard about the magnificent work you've done in re-creating the gazebo, Lord Farrencourt. I should very much like to see it for myself."

Intercepting her passage to the doorway, Egan put his hand on her shoulder. Seeing her shocked expression, he pulled back with undue haste. "My apologies, Miss Thackery. It would be my pleasure to show you the gazebo at another time. As it is, there is something I wish to say to you in private."

"Sir! If you are suggesting that I dismiss my chaperon, be warned that I am under the protection of my stepfather, Lord Kesterson."

Egan Kimble scowled. "By Jupiter! Must you be so skittish? I had no idea to suggest anything improper. Your abigail is quite welcome to attend us. I wish only to request the honour of escorting you to the Drummond musicale next week. Lily will be attending with Effington, and it is her wish that you accompany her in the carriage."

"And...and you find it necessary to invite me so that I shall have an escort for the evening."

"That is correct."

"How kind of you to condescend to invite me, Lord Farrencourt. I'm sure it must be a great sacrifice on your part."

Her icy tone should have warned him, but he was too full of himself to notice. "Think nothing of it, my girl."

"Then the ballet has been cancelled?"

He had the grace to blush. "I have seen the ballet a number of times. It no longer holds my interest. As it happens, I have the evening free."

"Well I do not, my lord. I have already promised to attend the Drummond musicale with someone else."

"Indeed? May I enquire whom?"

"You may."

He waited expectantly, but she kept her own counsel. It was Maggie who broke the silence. "Beggin' your pardon, miss, but 'tis time we must leave. I promised 'er ladyship to 'ave you 'ome within the 'our so that you can dress to receive your callers."

Amy concealed a sigh of relief. "Yes, Maggie. Thank you. The time has got completely away from me." She forced a brilliant smile up at Egan Kimble and bobbed a curtsy. "To your health, my lord. Please extend my regrets to Lily and explain that I have another engagement."

He bowed, not at all pleased with the way the interview had gone. He had almost stuttered in shock over her refusal, but then common sense reigned and he suppressed a smile. Playing the game, she was. He nodded soberly. "I know Lily will be disappointed. Should you change your mind and choose to allow me to escort you, you have only to let me know."

"You are too kind, my lord. Now, you really must excuse me."

It was only when Amy reached the door to the library that she realized they had forgotten Emerald, who, seated in a corner, was completely immersed in a book. Amy managed to get her attention and the three ladies took their departure.

Once in the carriage, Amy yanked at her gloves. "The nerve of the man, offering to take me off the shelf."

Maggie chuckled. "Aye, and did you see the look on 'is face when you turned 'im down? Trip on 'is chin, 'e could." She settled back against the plush cushions and tucked her hands in her sleeves to keep them warm.

Amy looked chagrined. "But I lied, you know. I haven't agreed to attend the dinner party with any man, though several have invited me."

Maggie gave her a significant look. "Lies don't count in the marriage game, but you wasn't too smart to turn 'im down. 'E's a good catch. Sure and you'd 'a' been the talk o' the party."

"What party?" Emerald asked, looking up from the pages of her book.

Amy looked at Maggie, and Maggie rolled her gaze towards the top of the carriage. "Bluestockings!" she said. The word carried all the disdain Maggie could manage.

MAGGIE HAD HIT the mark dead centre when she said that Lady Udora would be displeased by Amy's refusal to attend the Drummond musicale on the arm of Lord Farrencourt.

"Dear child," she said, looking pointedly through her lorgnette. "Do you realize what you have done? Egan Kimble cuts a dash that none can compare to, save for Brummell and a few of the eligible ten of the first consequence. And, if truth be told, I doubt that several of them are on the best list. You could hardly have done better."

"Then I prefer not to *do* at all. Egan Kimble may be rich as a nabob, but he is churlish, loutish and surly."

Emerald closed her book with a snap and faced Amy. "I think not. Churlishness suggests unresponsiveness and ungraciousness, while loutishness implies bodily awkwardness. Lord Farrencourt has none of these qualities. He is, in fact, quite physically attractive," she said, pushing her spectacles back on her nose. "What you intended to convey was boorishness—a certain insensitivity to others' feelings."

Amy raised her gaze to the ceiling. "What I mean to convey is that I have no wish to attend this party or any other with such a conceited oaf. If need be, I would prefer to remain at home.''

Lady Udora shook her abundance of mahogany-red curls, arranged by Maggie in the latest Greek fashion. "Pistachions! That would never do. You cannot fail to put in an appearance at the Drummonds' house. What would people think?''

Amy was spared the task of preparing a reasonable response when her sister burst into the room, followed closely by a winded and red-faced Sally. Sally dropped onto a footstool. "Beg pardon, m'lady. I can't move another step.''

Lady Udora looked over at Topaz, who bubbled with mischief. "All right, miss. Just what have you been up to now? Or dare I ask?''

Topaz moved towards the window, quite unaware that the sun shining through the leaded-pane turned her hair into a silver-gold halo around her head. "It was nothing, Lady Udora. Sally and I simply decided the day was too fine for a ride in Lord Venable's vis-à-vis. Instead we chose a brief stroll down St. James's Street.''

"Stroll, she says. More like a cavalry march 'cross country. My shoes is wore to the ground.''

Udora was appalled. "Surely you don't mean St. James's Street!''

Topaz lifted a shoulder and let it fall.

Udora nearly choked. "Past the men's clubs? No, don't answer. I don't want to hear.''

Topaz clucked her tongue. "Nothing happened, really. Of course dozens of men stared from the windows, but only a few came out to speak to us.''

"Pistachions! We're ruined. You'll be the witches' broth for every tea party from now until the end of the year. What did you say to them? The men, I mean."

Sally was close to tears. "I tried to stop 'er, m'lady, but she was bound to 'ave 'er way."

"Oh, do stop blubbering, Sally," Topaz said. "In fact, nothing happened. At least not much. I did happen to mention to Mr. Brummell that there was a speck of soot on his jacket."

"My poor dear child! What did he say?"

"He was most gratified. He would have escorted us home but apologized, saying that he must immediately return home to change his clothing."

"He would, of course," Udora acknowledged. "What else did he say?"

"Nothing, except that he found me amusing and begged me to save a dance for him at the Drummond party."

Udora sank back in exhaustion. "Then all is not lost. Even though Brummell's popularity has all but faded, to be accepted by him is still tantamount to being accepted by the ton." She straightened once more and pointed a finger at Topaz. "Be warned, young lady, that you cannot flout the strictures of correct conduct and avoid scandal. Now, listen well, the three of you. There are some rules that must be considered unbreakable. Remember, *appearance* is all." Her mouth shaped the word as if it were embossed in gold. "To be seen in the company of libertines is to be considered one of them. To approach a gentlemen's club whether by carriage or on foot is lascivious behaviour. To wear brown shoes is not only *déclassé* but is the badge of a *fille de joie.*'' Her voice droned on and on. The girls' eyes glazed over.

Maggie, sitting across the room, found Udora's entire speech most entertaining. She had been serving her mistress through four of her five marriages. The daughter of an earl, Udora Benson Hendricks Thackery Kinkaid Middlesworth Bently had buried four husbands. Included among them was Harvey Thackery, half-brother to the girls' father, who died along with their mother in a coaching accident. It amused Maggie to hear the gossip that all of Udora's husbands had died with smiles on their faces. She was a woman who all but ignored the rules of proper conduct. And yet no woman had been more envied or more sought after as the perfect dinner guest. She still claimed more than her share of attention, though if truth be told, since having been awarded the guardianship of the Thackery girls just before their sixteenth birthdays, and her subsequent marriage to Aaron Bently, Udora had simmered down some.

Maggie yawned. She hoped Udora's latest marriage wouldn't prove to be too dull. Of course, now that the three girls had made their come out, there were sure to be parties nearly every day. Maggie pushed her mobcap away from her forehead.

If she played her cards right her ladyship might change her mind and let her be chaperon to Miss Topaz. Now there was a girl who knew how to have fun! The twins, Miss Amy and Miss Emmy, though different in their own ways, were both too stiff to suit Maggie's taste. 'Twas Sally, who was afraid of her own shadow, who should be their abigail, not her.

Maggie's musings were cut short by the sound of footsteps in the corridor outside the sitting-room. Lady Udora rose quickly, her face alight with pleasure. "I do believe that is Bently," she said, reverting to his surname, by which she and the girls had come to know him when they lived at the estate adjoining his in Coventry. "I'd know his footsteps anywhere."

He flung open the door and stood there looking windblown and handsome in his nankeens and brown wool coat. "Ladies," he said, inclining his head in greeting, "I have news."

They clamoured round him, Udora being the first to reach his side. "Welcome home, my lord. We have missed you most dreadfully."

He put his arm about her shoulder and kissed her forehead. "It has been only five days since I left for the country."

"Five very long days."

The girls swarmed round him, asking questions about the animals they had left behind at Amberleigh, their home in Coventry, and about the newly hatched birds in the aviary at Partridge Run. He contrived to answer them all until Topaz, standing off a bit to one side, fixed him with her gaze.

"You said you had news, Lord Kesterson. What is it? We're dying to know."

He stroked her silvery-blond hair and planted a kiss on her forehead. "And know you shall. Sit down, all of you."

They scurried to find seats, all except Topaz, who remained standing.

He moved to the centre of the room, spread his legs and locked his hands behind his back. "Now, then.

You have all heard the name of Caulfield, Earl of Sutherland?''

Udora nodded. ''But of course. He owns Diamond Hill, one of the grand country houses in Hampshire. The father of the present earl and my father were acquaintances before they both passed on.''

''Indeed? I hadn't realized it. Then you will be pleased to know that we have been invited to Caulfield's house party in two weeks. We shall be there for three days.''

Udora pressed her hand against her cheek. ''Really, Aaron, it sounds delightful under ordinary circumstances, but I wonder if we can afford to take the time away from London. The Season has just begun, and to be away at this time...''

A playful smile danced across his face. ''My dearest, did you think I wouldn't take that into consideration? I assure you, the guest list is quite extensive. Our girls will have an opportunity to break the hearts of half a dozen eligible young bucks.'' He touched the tips of his fingers. ''Lord Chastain, Lord Everett and Lord Peterbrook will be there, to name a few.''

Amy was amused to see Udora's animation increase with the mention of each gentleman. Of course they would accept. Lady Udora would see to that. But in her own mind, Amy felt strangely disappointed that they would be away from London for three whole days. She had grown used to sharing confidences with Lily Kimble, and she would miss her. It would, however, be a relief not to have Lily's arrogant brother hovering about like a thundercloud.

The house party was still two weeks away. In the meantime there was the Drummond musicale to be concerned with. She had yet to decide on an escort. Prudence as well as good manners dictated that she decide at once. Or else, God forbid, Udora might force her to accept Egan Kimble's presumptuous offer!

CHAPTER TWO

THERE WERE FOUR significant callers at Kesterson House that afternoon. Amy, in a frantic rush to make a decision, finally allowed Richard Cooper, Lord Dunholm, the privilege of escorting her to the Drummond musicale and dinner. After the last guest had taken his departure, Udora gathered her brood together in her chambers.

"Now then, girls, shall we discuss what happened? It pleases me that each of you has secured an acceptable escort for the musical evening." Udora fiddled with the rings on her left hand. "Nevertheless, Topaz, it would have behooved you to accept Lord Croly's bid rather than Lieutenant Bixford's. There is no future there, you see. You must set your sights higher."

All three girls groaned. Emerald squirmed in her chair, trying to find a more comfortable position, then finally extracted the book from the pannier of her velvet skirt. "Oh, please, my lady, you can't foist Lord Croly off on Taz. He reads with his finger."

Topaz shook a lock of silvery-gold hair away from her face. "I would far rather be escorted by a footman than attend the party with Croly. He doesn't know a horse's tail-end from its ears."

Udora gasped. "Topaz Thackery! Apologize this instant. I'll stand for no such vulgarity in this house."

"Yes, my lady. I beg your pardon."

Amy pressed her hands together and leaned forward. "And Lieutenant Bixford is so handsome, Lady Udora." She raised her eyes as if in transports. "And those dark curls. How could one resist a bid from him?"

Udora sighed. "Girls, girls. Have you learned nothing in all the days we've spent discussing this? It's your future that concerns me. You must not be swayed by a good head of curly hair or the way a man sits a horse. You must think of your children and what their stations in life will be."

The girls cast furtive looks at one another, trying without success to hide their smirks. Udora nodded. "Indeed, the idea of children may seem remote to you now, but I venture to say that within two years from now at least one of you will be with child."

Amy clapped her hands. "Oh dear, I hope it will be me. I do so love babies."

Topaz looked at her with ill-concealed pity. "We all hope it will be you, dear sister."

Udora shot her a warning look. "And you, Emerald. Lord Wishram has made his bid to take you to the Drummond party?"

Emerald nodded. "And I have agreed."

"Well and good, but I must warn you of this: Should his suit become serious, you must keep in mind that although he is very wealthy, he is much older than you. Well beyond his active years, I should think."

Topaz settled her gaze on Udora. "Then Em could count on soon becoming a rich widow."

"Really, my dear. One must not speak of such things," Udora admonished her. "Besides, Wishram has a large brood of children. Emerald would stand to gain very little by such an alliance. However, since this engagement is only for a single musical evening . . ." She finished the thought with a wave of her hand.

"And you, my dear child," she said, turning to Amy. "You have done quite well for yourself. Although only a baron, Lord Dunholm has already come into his title. He is young, comely and certainly available. He is in fact one of the most eligible young bucks of the current Season. Tell me, are you developing a *tendre* for him?"

Amy shrugged. "I'm not sure how one knows. I rather enjoy his company, and he is very attentive to my wishes once I make them known. And . . ." She searched wildly for something complimentary to say. "And he doesn't slurp his soup."

Topaz nodded with undue force. "Oh, yes. One must always be aware of soup noises. One could hardly tolerate listening to slurping sounds for the rest of one's life."

Emerald and Amy tittered, but Udora silenced them with a look. "If you refuse to take this seriously then I must insist that you retire to your rooms. Maggie and Sally could use some assistance with mending the lace and ribbons on your bonnets."

THE WEEK PASSED quickly. Too quickly, Amy decided as she stole a look at her escort, who was paying his respects to Lady Udora. It was not that Amy disliked Lord Dunholm. He was most considerate and quite attractive in his dark dress coat and high starcher. His fair hair was a bit too short and he smelled rather strongly of Imperial Water, but the spicy scent was rather pleasant.

Drummond House glittered from top to bottom with flickering torches and candelabra, whose flames were reflected in the many-faceted surfaces of crystal and jewellery. Amy saw that Emerald and her escort had found a quiet sitting area facing the veranda. Lord Wishram looked even more elderly than usual next to Emerald, who appeared exceedingly young and demure in her pale green gown. Was she attracted to him? Amy wondered.

Topaz, on the other hand, looked far from demure. She was nearly as tall as Lieutenant Bixford, who stood close to her, one hand resting against the wall over her head in a gesture of possession. Amy smiled. Udora would not stand for that, once she noticed. But one could hardly blame the young man. Topaz had been besieged by admirers from the moment she arrived.

Amy's gaze was drawn to the entrance, where the butler had just announced the arrival of the Farrencourt party. Lily smiled and waved frantically to her, a fact that did not go unnoticed by Udora. Amy forced herself to return the wave with a discreet nod. But it was Lord Farrencourt who drew her attention. A tremor of something akin to fear shook her for a moment, but she pushed it aside. She had not thought he would be so good-looking dressed in formal attire. He appeared to search the room until his gaze came to rest upon her and her escort. He smiled, and Amy knew instantly that Egan Kimble was not impressed with Lord Dunholm.

Farrencourt said something to Effington, who had apparently asked permission to escort Lily to a chair, but Farrencourt's eyes never once broke contact with Amy's gaze. He'd be damned if he'd be the first to look away. Who did she think she was, anyway? Had it not been for her stubborn refusal to accept his bid to escort her to the party, he would not have arrived alone. Of course, there were any number of débutantes who would have swooned with joy to have accepted his invitation, but somehow he had no interest in any of them.

He swore under his breath. Demme, but Amy was a sweet young thing in her white gown edged with lavender-and-pink flowers at the hem and neckline. But underneath all that sweetness was a granite will demanding to be mastered.

His eyes had begun to burn. The invisible thread that seemed to connect them had become too tangible, too compelling to dismiss. It was an unspoken contest of wills, a challenge he could not deny. Devil take the girl—she refused to look away. He would die before he let her best him. He blinked quickly to moisten his eyes. As he did so, Lady Holland's party passed between him and Amy, breaking the contact. When he looked again, Amy was gone.

Disappointment stabbed at him. He adjusted the tails of his coat and slowly descended the few steps to the main floor, all the while searching the crush of people for a glimpse of her. It came as a surprise to him to discover that his knees were quite unsteady. He stiffened. Amy Thackery had not won! Truth be told, neither had he, he admitted ruefully. But he owed it to himself to even the score. And, by God, he would.

On the other side of the room, Lily found the object of his search. Amy was only too happy to see her, pleased she was alone. Lord Farrencourt had looked so fierce that Amy had been both frightened and thrilled by the intensity of his gaze. She had felt compelled to respond to it, knowing that something profound was happening inside her. Was it truly fear? She had never really been afraid before, except of spiders and noises in the night. The feelings that churned inside her caused her to shiver.

Lily giggled, misunderstanding. "Isn't it all too grand? Come. I must talk to you," she said, pulling Amy into a secluded alcove. "Oh dear. You've gone all white. What is it, Amy? Should I call Lady Udora?"

Amy forced a laugh. "It's nothing. I'm just not used to so many people. You look lovely, Lily. The opal necklace is perfect with your gown."

"It belonged to my mother. Egan says I may keep it if I agree to marry Effington. I won't, of course." She tossed her head. "I know my choices are somewhat limited, but I shan't accept just anyone, no matter how much Egan wants to be rid of me."

Amy opened the fan that dangled from her wrist and passed it quickly in front of her face. "I suppose he wants what's best for you. He knows you want a home and a husband and babies."

Lily snorted in an unladylike fashion. "A home and husband, yes, but I'm not ready to have babies. Eventually I suppose I must, but first I want to do all the things I've never been permitted to do. Egan is so starchy."

"He's only trying to save you from what happened to your sister."

"If he forces me to marry Effington, I shall run off just as she did."

"Oh, but, Lily, she ran off *with* a man, not away from one. It's not the same at all. You couldn't just run off with no one to look after you."

Lily pouted. "Johnny Lapwell could hardly be considered a proper man. He hadn't two coins to rub together when Darlene left, though he was very dashing," she said, a wistful expression clouding her eyes. Her mood changed once again and she lifted her chin. "Besides, if I had to run off alone, I could. But let's not spoil the party." She leaned closer. "And how do you like Lord Dunholm? He is quite the catch this Season."

Amy looked back over her shoulder. "I shouldn't have left him. I know he as well as Lady Udora will wonder where I've got to." Seeing Lily's disappointment, she smiled. "Lord Dunholm is very nice, but alas, I am not attracted to him."

"Then give him to me."

Amy laughed. "All right. Take him, he's yours."

Lily linked her arm in Amy's as they rejoined Lady Udora's party. They were met by a red-faced Effington. "Oh, there you are, Miss Lily. I thought for a moment that you had deserted me. I was about to send for your brother, but then I noticed your abigail standing nearby."

Lily frowned. "Don't presume to monopolize my time, Lord Effington, simply because I agreed to attend the party with you."

He looked apologetic. "I only wished to suggest that we find chairs in the drawing-room before it's too late. You know how crowded it gets once the musicians begin the evening's programme. I thought we might save a place for your brother, since he is alone tonight."

"Egan can find his own place. And I doubt very much that he will be alone for long." She slanted a look at Amy, then fluttered her eyelashes at Effington. "I thought we might join Miss Amy and Lord Dunholm in the drawing-room."

Dunholm, who had been dancing attention upon Lady Udora, apparently overheard the remark and inclined his head. "It would be our pleasure." He said something to Udora and Lord Kesterson before giving Amy his arm, then the group followed the procession moving in the general direction of the drawing-room.

Upon seeing the mass of people crowded onto chairs, stools, sofas and even seated upon the floor, Udora gasped. "Oh, dear, it does seem that Lady Drummond has overextended herself. I doubt that we shall find places next to one another."

"Never fear, my love," Lord Kesterson said. "The girls and their escorts can find places in the back row. We shall be quite comfortable seated along the wall, where we can still keep an eye on them."

"But they are so far from the stage," Udora protested.

His eyes twinkled. "I somehow doubt that the performance is of the utmost importance to them. Come. We had best take our seats while they are still vacant."

Emerald and her escort, along with Topaz and her handsome lieutenant, found chairs near the middle of the row. Amy, in an attempt to oblige Lily, found a seat on a scratchy-looking sofa with wooden arms. Lord Dunholm came next, followed by Lily and Effington. Once they were seated, Lily leaned forward and winked at Amy. At least Lily was happy, for the seating arrangement provided just the opportunity she needed to begin her conquest of Richard Cooper, Lord Dunholm.

Amy raised her fan to cover a smile. Apparently Lily had not been content with the effect the bust improvers had made on her gown and had added even more cotton wool to her bodice, making her appear top-heavy. But one could hardly fault the girl, with only an odious brother to advise her. Amy looked across the room at Udora and silently thanked her for taking the Thackery girls under her wing.

The musicians had no more than begun the overture when a disturbance erupted at the end of the row where Amy was seated. Lord Farrencourt was making his way towards them through a tangle of skirts, trousered legs and closely drawn chairs.

Lily groaned. "I can't believe it. My brother won't even allow me the freedom to enjoy the concert. He is worse than my father ever was."

Effington frowned. "He'll have to sit on the floor, won't he."

Before anyone could agree or disagree, Lord Farrencourt had somehow managed to wedge himself onto the sofa next to Amy. It was obvious to everyone that there was scarcely room enough to seat them all.

His eyes glittered as he smiled and inclined his head. "Good evening, Miss Thackery."

Amy made an effort to squeeze herself into a small space. "Really!" she whispered indignantly. "You might have found another place to sit."

"And where might you suggest?"

"Anywhere but next to me."

"Indeed? Is it your impression, Miss Thackery, that I chose this particular seat just so that I might be near you?"

"*Near* me?" Amy thrust out her chin. "If you were any closer, Lord Farrencourt, you would be on top of me."

No sooner had she said the words than she regretted them. He impaled her with his gaze, and she held her breath awaiting the obvious rejoinder, but either he was too much the gentleman—or too much the coward—to voice it. Instead he motioned with his hand. "I merely chose this seat so that I could watch over my sister."

He was grateful when she lowered her eyelashes and seemed to accept his explanation. It came as a surprise to him that their proximity had robbed him of a certain degree of composure. He shifted, hoping to lessen the pressure of his thigh against hers, but to no avail. The contact made him wish he had thought twice before attempting to even the score with Amy Thackery.

He had thought she would turn pink with embarrassment or become giddy as his sister would have done. Instead, it was he who became red in the face. It was awkward. Demmed awkward. But then nothing had gone right since Amy had refused his invitation to the musicale. He had only invited her for Lily's sake, of course, but it rankled nevertheless.

Farrencourt shifted again and was reprimanded by a glare from Amy. She turned a shoulder to avoid looking at him. Dunholm, seated at Amy's left, was conversing with Lily. Both seemed unaware of the close quarters. Effington, as usual, looked preoccupied with his own thoughts.

For a few minutes Amy's attention was drawn to the arrival of Mrs. Bland on the makeshift stage. The singer dropped a curtsy in response to the enthusiastic applause, then nodded to her accompanist. When they were well into a second ballad, Farrencourt bent to whisper in Amy's ear.

"Mrs. Bland is in fine voice tonight, don't you agree?"

Amy turned to answer him, but when she did so, her face was so close to his that she could feel his breath flutter the fine hair that dusted her forehead. Instinct told her that had they been alone he would have kissed her. She shuddered.

Farrencourt felt her shudder go through him and his voice thickened. "Are you cold, Miss Amy?"

"No, I..." She tried to pull away, but there was nowhere to go. His mouth curved upwards in a knowing smile.

"You are obviously agitated. If there is something I can do to help, all you need do is ask," he whispered.

It took all of her will-power to keep her voice steady. "Then I would ask you to leave."

"Surely you wouldn't want me to leave my seat during the concert. It would be a serious breach of etiquette."

"From what I've heard, sir, you shape etiquette to serve your own purpose." Her voice had risen and he touched his finger to her lips.

"Hush. If you must vent your anger, do so in a whisper."

She pulled back and glared at him. "And furthermore, your word seems to be of little consequence."

"I beg your pardon?"

"I believe you said that all I need do was ask."

"Just so." His face looked frozen. "Never let it be said that I am not a man of my word. If you will excuse me, then?" He pushed himself up and bowed to the rest of the party. Before Amy knew what was happening, Lord Farrencourt had strode the length of the drawing-room and out through the doorway.

Still feeling the pressure of his finger against her lips, she put her hand to her face. *Oh dear. I didn't mean him to leave altogether,* she thought. *What must everyone think?* A quick glance assured her that Lily, still conversing with Lord Dunholm, was quite unaware of what had happened. Lady Udora, however, was not, and gave her a pensive look. She sighed. There would be reprimands before the night was out, and questions, too. What an awful mess she had made of things.

As Fate would have it, Udora was too preoccupied with Topaz's questionable behaviour to remember to chastise Amy that evening. Topaz had somehow slipped away from the party with her young lieutenant in tow. That she admitted only to having satisfied

her curiosity about a certain bay mare owned by Lord
Drummond was of little consequence. Udora deemed
it indecent behaviour and promptly meted out her
punishment. For an entire week Topaz was not to leave
home without being chaperoned by Udora or Lord
Kesterson, and so she missed the events of the following day.

It had become a habit for the girls, along with their
abigails, to stroll in St. James's Park. Amy loved the
swans and the goldfish that swam in the pool at the
base of the fountain. Lily and her abigail, Louella,
often accompanied them, but on this occasion, Emerald and Amethyst went alone, accompanied only by
Maggie and Sally.

They wandered over to the shade of a willow tree,
where Emerald promptly settled onto a bench with her
book.

Amy was vexed. "Em, must you always keep your
nose in your books? I do so want to go over by the
fountain to feed the swans."

Emerald looked owl-eyed through her spectacles.
"Go if you want. I don't wish to."

Maggie plopped down on the bench next to Emerald and looked up with a suspiciously demure expression on her face.

"Go along with you, then. I'll just stay 'ere an' look
after Miss Emmy."

Sally, looking typically uneasy, clasped her hands.
"Will it be all right, do you think? Lady Udora said
as how we should stay together."

"Oh, don't be such a ninnyhammer," Maggie said,
tucking a red curl under her cap. "The park is right

full of people. You'll be safe as a kitten in a feather-bed."

Amy grasped her abigail's hand. "Come, let's hurry, Sally. I'll let you carry the grain for the swans while I take the bread for the goldfish."

Sally was hard put to keep up with Amy, who darted round people strolling in the park or standing in groups and talking. She tugged on Amy's hand. "Do slow down, miss, or 'er ladyship will be after me for lettin' you fergit your manners."

"You would tell her?" Amy asked.

"No, miss, not me. But there's enough ladies 'ere that knows who you are. You can bet your britches you'd be the broth o' the witches' brew at the next tea party."

They had just approached the fountain when a shabbily dressed woman carrying a baby accosted them. She appeared to recognize Amy, and she spoke rapidly.

"Excuse me, miss. You are Miss Amy Thackery, are you not?"

"And wot business is it o' yours?" Sally demanded, showing unusual spirit.

Amy touched Sally's sleeve and turned to the woman. "Do I know you, madam?"

"Unfortunately, no, but I have heard of you and your kindness towards the downtrodden. I wonder, could I beg a few moments of your time?"

"What is it you want? If it's money, I have only a few coins, but if you are in need . . ."

"No, please. It isn't money. I need someone to look after my baby for a few minutes while I repair the damage to my dress. He is asleep and will be no trouble.''

Amy noticed the large stain on the woman's skirt. ''Of course. He is such a pretty baby.''

''Oh, thank you, thank you. I promise I'll return as soon as possible.''

Sally looked dubious. ''You could take 'im with you easy as not.''

''I fear there is no place clean enough to lay him down while I repair the damage. I assure you I wouldn't ask if it weren't absolutely necessary.''

''Don't be ungracious, Sally. Of course we will look after him. I'll take care of him until you return, but I...''

''Thank you, thank you,'' the woman said with a catch in her voice. ''I knew I could trust you.'' She brushed a kiss on the baby's cheek and handed him to Amy.

Sally looked over Amy's shoulder at the sleeping child. ''He's a handsome one, he is, with them big brown eyes.''

''His name is William,'' the woman said, her voice hardly above a whisper.

Amy settled the babe into the crook of her arm, tucking the blanket under his chin with care to avoid waking him. ''Such rosy little cheeks. He is adorable. May I ask how old he is?'' she said, looking up, but there was no answer. The woman had gone.

Sally looked around with surprise. ''Now, if that don't beat all. She just up and disappeared.''

Amy was too enthralled with little William to worry about it. ''Never mind, Sally. I rather imagine she was too embarrassed by the condition of her gown to linger longer than necessary. Let's just sit here on the bench and wait for her to return."

It had all happened so quickly that neither the woman's appearance nor her disappearance created any sort of commotion. The strollers were more interested in being seen in their Spring finery than in paying mind to a colourless woman in an ill-fitting dress. They paid scant attention to Amy seated with the baby on the bench beneath an ancient linden tree. The one matron who did appear to recognize Amy lifted her lorgnette for a closer look before hurrying away to join her party.

Amy cuddled the child closer to her. "Oh, Sally!" she cried. "Isn't it too wonderful? Look, he's yawning. I do hope he wakens before his mother returns."

Sally shifted uneasily. "'Ow long could it take 'er? She musta been gone near on to a quarter-hour."

"I hope it takes her forever!"

"Be careful what you hopes for, miss. You won't be so glad to be 'oldin' 'im once 'e starts to 'owl."

"William is too sweet to cry. Look, he's opened his eyes." A frown creased the baby's forehead as he tried to focus on Amy's face. His chin began to pucker, but Amy spoke to him in a soothing voice and rocked him in her arms until he found his thumb and began to suck noisily.

Nearly an hour passed and still the woman had not returned. Sally knotted her hands. "Mayhap 'tis later than we think. 'Ave you noticed hardly anyone is 'ere?"

Amy looked up in surprise. "It's true, isn't it? Though I hadn't noticed till you mentioned it. I wonder where everyone's gone?"

"Home, most likely. I believe it's going to rain. We'd best find Miss Emerald and Maggie afore it starts to come down."

"But we can't leave until William's mother returns for him."

Sally wrapped her arms around herself. "Somethin's wrong, miss. I kin feel it in me bones. She ain't comin' back. She ain't never comin' back." The wild look in Sally's eyes gave Amy a moment of fright, but she managed to gather her wits about her.

"Don't be ridiculous, Sally. I'm sure she will return any moment."

But it wasn't the mother who approached them a good twenty minutes later. Emerald, her finger still stuck in her book to mark the page, hurried to keep up with Maggie.

Maggie, looking flushed and animated, could scarcely contain her excitement. "Did you see it? It was awful!" She stopped dead. "Now wot's that you've got wrapped up on your lap? Not another cat! 'Er ladyship will skin me alive if I should so much as let you near the front gate wi' another animal."

Emerald came close and lifted the corner of the blanket. "Why, it's a baby. Wherever did you get it, Amy?"

Amy cocked her head to one side. "Isn't he precious? His name is William. I'm taking care of him until his mother returns from repairing her dress."

Sally looked frightened. "She said she'd be gone a few minutes but 'tis over an hour past. I know she ain't comin' back." She moaned. "I read the tea leaves today, and they said as 'ow there was trouble brewing in the 'ouse."

"You can't believe that nonsense, Sally," Amy chided her. "She probably took a wrong turn in the park. I know she will come for him any moment now."

Maggie scowled. "We can't stay 'ere an' wait for 'er. 'Tis startin' to rain."

"I won't go until she returns," Amy said.

"Then I suppose we must find her," Emerald stated sensibly. "You cannot sit holding a baby in a drenching rain. He might catch his death of cold."

Maggie scowled. "And just where do we look? What's 'er name?"

"I . . . I don't know. I never thought to ask," Amy said.

Sally screwed up her face. "I'd say she was ill-dressed. Not the kind one would see takin' the air in St. James's. She 'ad on a grey dress and a blue shawl wi' a fringe at the bottom."

Maggie looked grim. "And did she have on a blue bonnet wot she wore pulled close round her face? And brown hair wot curls like the baby's?"

Amy nodded. "Oh, yes. That sounds like her. You saw her, then. Where is she?"

Maggie sank down on the bench. "Now you've done it. It's trouble that woman's brought. And Lady Udora will 'ave my hide."

"Whatever do you mean, Maggie?" Amy demanded.

"The child's mother is dead, she is. Run down by a carriage at the park's gate."

CHAPTER THREE

MAGGIE SMOOTHED her uniform and tucked a curl beneath the edge of her mob-cap in a determined effort to hide her amusement at Lady Udora's shock. Udora, still wearing her cloak and bonnet, having just returned from the feather merchant's, sank down onto a chair.

"She's brought home what?"

"Aye, 'tis true, m'lady. A baby. I seen it wi' me own eyes."

Udora forced herself to breathe deeply. "What utter nonsense. I know this is one of your little pranks, Maggie, but this time you've gone too far. I demand an explanation at once."

Then she forced a smile. "Oh, I see. A baby, you say. What kind of a baby? A kitten? A puppy? Not another monkey. I detest monkeys."

Maggie giggled. "It weren't none o' them, m'lady. It's a baby boy," she said, twisting a curl round her finger.

Udora fumbled in her reticule for a vinaigrette and inhaled deeply, then spoke in a strangled voice as she waved towards the door. "Go! Bring her to me at once!"

Maggie beat a hasty exit while humming a little tune all the way up the stairs to Amy's room. She found

Amy and Sally tucking the sleeping child into a large drawer that had been removed from the bottom of the armoire.

"She's come 'ome," Maggie said. "An' I told her about the baby."

Amy looked stricken. "Was she very angry?"

Maggie grinned. "Like nothin' I ever seen before. And she wants me fetch you to 'er at once."

"Well, I suppose I must face her sooner or later."

"Sooner would be better, judgin' by the way 'er face turned sorta purple like."

"I imagine she will want to see you, too, Sally," Amy said, turning to her own abigail.

Sally blanched. "Oh, I couldn't face 'er, Miss Amy. Please don't make me do it. Besides, someone has to watch so that the baby don't fall out the drawer and onto the floor. I 'spect 'e's old enough to crawl."

"Maggie can stay with little William."

Maggie snorted. "Not much I won't. I'm not missin' this for anything."

"Oh, very well. Have it your way. Come along with me, then."

Maggie grinned. "Yes, miss. If you insist." She threw a triumphant look over her shoulder at Sally and began humming again.

"Oh, do stop humming," Amy begged. "My nerves are shattered."

During the short drive from the park to Kesterson House, Amy had rehearsed what she was going to say to Lady Udora, and somehow it sounded reasonable. After all, how could one say no to a woman in distress? Hadn't her ladyship been the one to instill in them the value of respect to elders and the need for consideration to those less fortunate? The fact that the baby's mother was only a few years older than Amy was of little consequence.

Thanks to a generous glass of sherry and then a second one for good measure, Udora had managed to get herself under control by the time Amy and Maggie reached the library.

It didn't take Amy long to realize that her justification for bringing the baby home did not sit well with Udora, after all.

"And just where is the child's mother now? Why have you not returned the baby to her?" Udora demanded.

Maggie brushed a bit of lint from her apron. "'Twas me what saw wot 'appened, though truth be told I didn't know it was 'er at the time. I 'eard this crash outside the gate to the park and when I goes to look, there she was, layin' toes-up on the bricks, and lookin' lopsided like a goose what 'ad 'is neck wrung."

Amy's chin trembled. "From Maggie's description of her clothing, I knew at once that she was the same woman. The baby's mother."

"How can you be sure? There must have been dozens of people taking the air in the park. It could have been a mere coincidence."

"I don't think so, m'lady," Maggie answered. "Little William's mother was wearing a very distinctive bonnet. I've never seen one like it."

Udora took a deep breath. "I see. Well, I suppose there's little to be done about it at the present. I shall have to consult Bently and ask him how to go about finding the baby's family."

"Oh, but I thought we could keep him," Amy protested.

Udora gave her an incredulous look. "We are talking about a baby, child. Not a puppy you've found starving in some back-street alleyway. What have you done with him?"

"Sally is looking out for him. He's asleep in my room."

Udora paused, for once at a loss for words. The silence was rent by a yowl that echoed from one end of the house to the other.

Maggie threw up her hands. "Lord a'mighty. Now we're in for hit. 'E's got a voice what would wake the dead."

Udora looked grim. She levelled her gaze at Maggie. "Indeed he has. Now, suppose you run upstairs and look after him, since you are as much to blame as Amy for bringing him into the house."

Maggie's eyebrows shot upward. "Me? I had nothin' to do wi' it."

"You should have been looking after the girls while they were in the park. Correct me if I'm wrong, Maggie, but were you not off flirting with some young groundskeeper when you should have been chaperoning the girls?"

Maggie turned to go, but at the last minute, looked back over her shoulder. "'Twas 'im what was flirting wi' me, if you must know."

Udora rose from her chair and Maggie scurried down the hall.

Amy folded her hands into her sleeves and looked up at Udora with pleading eyes. "I'm so sorry for all the trouble I've caused, Lady Udora. I promise I'll take care of little William all by myself."

"I know your intentions are good, my dear, but this simply cannot be. You have other responsibilities."

Amy looked puzzled. Udora sighed. "Your come out, of course. We are already into the Season and you must take it more seriously. It is a mark against you if you don't find a suitable match before the Season ends. You have no time to waste looking after a baby."

"But someone must."

"Then we shall have to find his family, shan't we?"

"I . . . I suppose so. At least we must try."

AT FARRENCOURT PLACE, Egan Kimble was in high dudgeon. "I'll hear no more of it, Lily. I have already accepted the Richelieus' bid to attend their soirée in Cheshire. Therefore, you shall not be allowed to join Caulfield's house party at Diamond Hill, and this time I will not countenance an argument."

Lily's lower lip protruded in a most unladylike fashion. "But Amy will be there. And Lord Dunholm."

"Dunholm! Do you think for a minute he will have eyes for you when he has already set his cap for Miss Thackery?" He put his hand up to forestall an argument. "No, you have no need to impress me with his brief attention to you at the musicale last week. It was simply because you were seated next to him."

"But Egan, he . . ."

"Granted, my dear sister, he would be a worthy trophy, but you would be far wiser to set your sights on Effington. Need I remind you that he is willing and eager to offer for you?"

"I'd rather join the ranks of ape-leaders than be tied to him for the rest of my life. Besides—" her lips trembled with a sudden vulnerability "—I think I'm falling in love with Lord Dunholm."

"Impossible! I hate to seem unkind, my dear, but it appears to be Miss Thackery who has caught his eye."

Lily laughed. "But Amy has no interest in him, and he will be at Diamond Hill as I shall, no matter what you say."

"So be it, then, but I warn you, your time is running out, Lily. If you don't find a suitable match this Season, then I shall be forced to accept Effington's bid for your hand." His tone softened. "Dear sister, don't look so crestfallen. You know I have only your best interests at heart. I will do everything in my power to wed you to the man of your choice, but be warned: I will not permit you to destroy your life the way your sister ruined hers by running off with some down-at-heel wastrel."

Lily's face brightened. "Then you will permit me to go to Diamond Hill?"

"Reluctantly, yes, my dear. Of course it will mean I must send our regrets to the Richelieus. They will be most put off."

"Perhaps it would be more diplomatic for *you* to attend the Richelieu soirée while I accept the invitation to Diamond Hill."

Farrencourt turned a speculative gaze upon his young sister, who smiled up at him with all the innocence of a dewy-eyed infant. Had she suddenly become devious? Out of habit he was inclined to discount her as being little more than a female child:

sweet in her own way but incapable of intelligent thought, and certainly not capable of using strategy as a means to an end. He patted her head.

"No, Lily. The Richelieus will understand that my responsibility to you must come first. I shall send word round to the Caulfields that we will both accept the invitation to Diamond Hill."

She jumped up from the settee and gave him a most unwelcome kiss on the cheek. "Thank you, Egan. Is there anything else? I must hurry to tell Amy the good news."

Her giddiness irritated him, as did the moisture he wiped from his cheek with a spotless linen handkerchief. Nevertheless he was willing to suffer any discomfort to have her out from underfoot for the rest of the day. It was still early enough that he could spend a few hours with Eva Delight before she must prepare herself for her performance at the ballet. She would of course insist that for once he make an effort to attend. But he would be firm and offer his excuses. He had plans to make.

Diamond Hill was certain to be a bore this time of year, but if his scheme fell into place, Lily would soon no longer be his responsibility and he would be free to concentrate on his own pleasures.

He smiled, knowing that his refusal to attend the ballet would send Eva Delight into a rage. That in turn would give him just the excuse he had been waiting for to terminate their affair. This was, to be sure, an opportune time to start life with a clean slate.

AT KESTERSON HOUSE, all was not well. Bently, with his customary easygoing nature, was not at all disturbed by the presence of a squalling baby in the house. He took Udora's hands and pressed them to his lips.

"I see no need to be so distraught, Udora. I know we agreed we both were beyond the need to have a child of our own, but it's not as if this were permanent. Indeed, if it were, I'm sure I would be as distressed as you are."

"Yes, I know that, Bently. We did agree that having a baby in the house is out of the question."

"Ah, but this is different. In a day or two we shall discover the identity of the baby's family. I've already sent enquiries out to the Charlies and those establishments that border on St. James's Park. We will soon find out where Amy's baby came from."

Udora looked horrified. "Stop! Don't call him that! He isn't Amy's baby and we must never think of him as such. Don't you realize, sir, what an effect such a rumour could have on her reputation?"

Bently drew back. "I...it was just an expression, my dearest. I meant to cast no aspersions on Amy's character."

"Indeed, I'm sure you didn't, but..."

She was interrupted by the appearance of Maggie, who dropped a curtsy and waited until Udora nodded to her.

"Beggin' your pardon, ma'am, but I thought you'd be wantin' to know that we found a wet-nurse for Miss Amy's baby."

Udora threw Bently a look of disgust. "You see, it's as I said. I fear we've taken on something we shall live to regret."

Bently spread his hands in a helpless gesture, and Udora turned back to Maggie. "At least the wet-nurse is a step forward. I assume the woman is in good health."

"I can't speak for wot's covered up, but she looks to be strong as an ox and 'er 'ands and face is clean. Mrs. McMasters found her. She says as how the girl is a cousin of the wife of the third cook at Dobney Square. She got 'erself in trouble wi' the gardener but the babe was born dead."

Udora felt a surge of gratitude towards Mrs. McMasters, Kesterson House's chief servant. "Very well, I'll speak to the wet-nurse later. See that a bed for her is installed in the nursery. I want her to be comfortable."

Maggie started to leave, but a sound from Udora stopped her dead in her tracks. "And one more thing, Maggie McGee. I wish to speak with you and Sally and the girls here in the library within the hour."

Maggie knew better than to argue that she was already busy with three other tasks. She curtsied and carefully closed the door behind her before letting out her breath. "Old biddy! I'd wager a bean to a canary she's goin' to put us all in the suds."

As was to be expected, Amy and Sally were with baby William and the wet-nurse in the nursery, Emerald was reading a book in the window-seat overlooking the garden, and Topaz was finally discovered trying to tame a squirrel near the stone bench. Not one of them looked comfortable about being summoned to Lady Udora's presence. When they arrived in the library, Udora's usually smiling countenance, now grim with determination, only intensified their anxiety.

After her customary reminder that their sole purpose for taking up residence in London was to launch the girls into Society, Udora took up the matter of baby William. Amy, into transports over caring for the child, was unwise enough to open her mouth.

"My lady, I do wish you would come up to the nursery to see him. Liza is a capable wet-nurse, and he is ever so greedy."

Udora gave her a dry look. "The child's appetite is the least of my concerns at the moment. Not once but four times have I heard someone refer to the child as *Amy's baby*. Laugh if you will, but this is more serious than you can imagine. We must put a stop to it at once."

She gathered her skirts round her. "Now then, we must concentrate on our plans for the house party at Diamond Hill. Maggie, you and Sally are to accompany the girls as their abigails. I've seen to it that you have new uniforms as well as an extra gown for special occasions. I know that should please you.

"As for you girls, your new gowns are still at the dressmakers' establishment, but Madame Alexander assures me they will be ready in a day or two."

Amy pressed her palms together beneath her chin. "And what about William's nurse? Will her clothing be suitable?"

Udora looked shocked. "Dear child, surely you don't imagine that the baby and his nurse will accompany us to this fête?"

"But I couldn't leave him behind. I would worry about him. He needs me."

"Should we be so unfortunate as not to have found a home for him, the child will be quite comfortable under the care of our staff. You will do as you are told, Amy. Otherwise the child will be turned over to the parish before the day is out."

"You couldn't do that!" Amy cried. "You can't give him away. I found him and he is mine."

"Don't be absurd, child. He's not a pet animal. We shall do what's best for everyone."

"You wouldn't do this if I were married and had my own home. You'd have no hold over me then."

Udora gave her a telling look. "Marriage, my dear child, is precisely the prize that I am seeking for you."

Topaz leaned her hip against the desk and swung one slippered foot. "Silly goose, Amy. You fell right into that hole without so much as a fare-thee-well. Next thing we know you'll agree to marry the first pudding-headed paper scull you meet, just to keep the baby."

"I would if I had to."

"Stubble it!" Udora said with a less than ladylike demeanour. "When you marry it will be for a far better reason than making a home for a foundling. I have had enough. If I hear one word about the baby spoken outside this house, I shall deem it necessary to punish you. He must be our secret for now, save for Bently's investigation into the child's background. Now, go to your rooms and tend to your needlework. And, Amy, I must forbid you to dawdle in the nursery. The baby needs his sleep."

The five girls were scarcely out of the room when Topaz started laughing. "Secret be switched. One could no more keep this a secret than . . ."

"Than one could hide the truth about Prinny's passion for older women," Maggie finished with a grin.

Emerald pushed her spectacles back into place. "I think perhaps we'd best try. Her ladyship was not amused."

ALTHOUGH AMY SPENT the better part of the week trying to convince Lady Udora to allow the baby to accompany their party to Diamond Hill, her entreaties were to no avail. Udora was adamant that the presence of baby William at Kesterson House be kept secret until such time as Lord Kesterson's solicitor was able to discover the baby's identity. During that week the final preparations for the excursion to Diamond Hill swept through the household like a small whirlwind. Gowns were brought out from the armoires, examined, pressed and carefully packed into trunks. Gifts of silver goblets for the host and hostess were polished to a high sheen and wrapped in tissue paper to protect them. In the stable the horses were groomed and the carriages cleaned and freshly varnished for the drive to Hampshire.

And then the day arrived at last. In truth, Lord Kesterson's party delayed their arrival by a full day thanks to baby William. The wet-nurse could not provide enough milk to satisfy his greedy appetite. His outrage could be heard from the cellar to the attic and Amy refused to leave until the baby was quieted. It was Mrs. McMasters who saved the day from complete disaster by feeding him a bit of warm porridge from a spoon.

Udora had paced the floor in her anxiety to make their departure, knowing that as many as four eligible young noblemen would be attending the party. Unfortunately, twice that many young débutantes would be flaunting themselves in order to gain their approval. A delay in arrival could only serve to reduce the girls' chances to make the first impression. Bently, calm as usual, assured Udora that because of their late arrival they would create a stir none of the other families could hope to equal.

He was right. From the moment their carriage drove up to the *porte-cochère* at Diamond Hill they were surrounded by footmen dressed in white-and-gold livery. Lord and Lady Sutherland greeted them in the grand entrance beneath a sparkling chandelier. Even before the Kesterson party had a chance to be shown to their rooms to refresh themselves other houseguests rushed forward to greet them.

Lily Kimble led the pack. She flung her arms round Amy, who was in so unfortunate a position as to intercept Udora's chilling frown. From the corner of her eye Amy also saw Egan Kimble, Lord Farrencourt, lounging indolently against a statue of a knight in full armour. Her breath constricted. Was she afraid of him, she wondered, or was she attracted to his darkly handsome face? But she couldn't consider for long. Lily, seemingly unconcerned by proper decorum, took Amy's hand and pulled her to one side.

"Where have you been? It's nearly eight days since I have seen you! I thought you were to arrive yesterday."

Amy shifted her reticule to her left hand and returned her friend's kiss on the cheek. "I've missed you, too. There is so much I have to tell you."

Udora moved quickly forward and took Amy's elbow. "Come, child. We must settle in before we cause another commotion. Our late arrival has already upset Lady Sutherland's schedule."

Lily quivered with excitement. "I'll come along. We can talk while you see to the unpacking."

Udora lifted an eyebrow. "That won't be necessary, Miss Kimble. Amy will join you in the garden in a few minutes. Come along, Amethyst, Emerald, Topaz. Let us go to our rooms."

Amy was about to follow the entourage up the winding staircase when she was startled to hear her name.

"Miss Thackery. There you are! I thought you might have changed your mind about coming. I'm so glad you're here."

Amy stopped, one foot on the stairs, her hand resting lightly on the banister. "Lord Dunholm. How nice to see you."

He grasped the front ends of his waistcoat. "I wonder, Miss Thackery, if we might speak for a moment?"

"I'm sorry, we've only just arrived and I promised Lady Udora that I would first go to our rooms."

Udora beamed. "What nonsense. Of course you must speak to Lord Dunholm. Sally will accompany you. You may come upstairs when you've finished."

"But I..."

"Hush. You do not wish to be rude, do you?"

"It's only that I have..." She would have made a further excuse but Lord Farrencourt abruptly left his place by the statue and approached them.

"Aha! There you are, Dunholm. I've been looking everywhere for you. Come, there's something I want to show you."

"Not now, Farrencourt. I'm having a word with Miss Thackery."

"This can't wait, I'm afraid. It's about the grey mare you took such an interest in."

Dunholm hesitated. "Well..."

"A chance of a lifetime, my friend," Farrencourt persisted.

Amy breathed a sigh of relief. "Do not let me detain you, Lord Dunholm. I will be happy to speak with you later on if you arrange it with Lady Udora or leave a message with my abigail."

Smiling smugly, Dunholm leaned forward in an apparent effort to create an air of conspiracy. "Better yet, I'll leave a message for you in the music box on the drum table in the salon."

Farrencourt was delighted by the exchange he had overheard. Now he could put his plan into action. Not only that, but it appeared the little chit would cooperate with him; unknowingly, of course, but one should never look a gift-horse in the mouth, so to speak.

Lily put her hand on his arm and whispered, "I know you did this for me, Egan. Thank you, oh thank you."

Farrencourt looked at his sister with a heavy-lidded gaze. "See that you don't waste this opportunity, miss.

It's costing me a valuable mare that I had set my heart on."

THE GIRLS were barely inside the suite they were to share when Udora stormed into the bedchamber and faced Amy. "Amethyst Thackery, you will be the death of me yet. Of the three of you I thought you would be the most easily moulded into marriageable material, but for every step forward, you take one backward. Lord Dunholm is quite taken with you, and it is only a question of time until he offers for your hand." She shook her head. "And yet you seem to take great pains to avoid his overtures."

Amy fingered the silk fringe on the canopied bed. "I'm sorry, Lady Udora, but I don't *want* him to offer for me."

"Don't be childish. As much as you adore babies, you must surely realize that you can't have children without marriage." She blushed. "Well...can't is putting is rather strongly, but you understand my meaning. Lord Dunholm would make a splendid husband."

"He is very nice, I'm sure, but when he touches me he makes my skin crawl."

Udora snapped to attention. "He's touched you? He had no right! How do you mean, touched you? Amethyst, my dear. If this is true, we can insist that he offer for you."

Amy's face reddened. "I don't mean touched me in *that* way. I only meant when his coat brushes my arm or when he kisses my hand."

Topaz fell across the bed. "Great pistachions! Call out the guards. Amy's been compromised."

Amy hit her with a well-aimed pillow. Udora threw up her hands. "Stop this, stop this nonsense at once! And, Miss Topaz, I've warned you before about using my own personal words. Now listen to me, the three of you. I want you to enjoy your visit to the country, but remember this, we are here for a purpose. You will be allowed a little more freedom here than you would enjoy in London, and it would behoove you to make the most of it."

Topaz sat up. "How do you mean make the most of it? Does that mean we are free to come and go to the stables without benefit of chaperon?"

"It most certainly does not! What I meant was to make the most of your opportunity to find an eligible as well as congenial husband."

"It would be far easier and much more interesting without a chaperon," Topaz said with a devilish glint in her eyes.

Udora smiled in spite of herself. "Now behave, all of you, and take care not to waste your golden opportunities."

Later, Udora's words came back to Amy as she rested in her room. It was true. If she were married, no one could take baby William away from her. She leaned back in a chair and tucked her feet up under her skirt. Dunholm had said he would leave a message in the music box. Diamond Hill was the perfect place for a private assignation. If she saw him alone, perhaps, just perhaps, she could learn to like him.

CHAPTER FOUR

IT WAS NEARLY AN HOUR before Amethyst could slip away undetected to the drawing-room to retrieve Dunholm's message from the music box. She lifted the lid but snapped it shut when the tinkling sound of "Milkmaids in the Meadow" began to play. A quick look about assured her that she was quite alone, and once more she opened the box. A piece of paper was partially hidden beneath the figurine of a sheep.

Amy unfolded it, smoothing it out on the table. The paper was of surprisingly good quality, heavy and creamy in texture. Not at all what she had expected from Dunholm. Nor did the handwriting upon it reflect his usual, spidery scrawl. The words flowed across the paper in a dramatic yet orderly fashion.

My dear girl,
I will be waiting for you at nine beside the Neptune fountain in the hedge maze. For propriety's sake and your own privacy, I suggest that our rendezvous remain a secret.

Your eager and adoring servant

Apparently Dunholm had taken the precaution of leaving the note unsigned. Ah, there was so much to learn about the finer points of assignations. She read the message three more times before folding it and tucking it into the bodice of her blue velvet gown. A secret rendezvous! How thrilling! Omitting, needless to say, the fact that it was Dunholm whom she would be meeting. If they were found out, the scandal would be appalling, and she was already in the soup with Udora because of baby William. And what would this do to Lily? Amy agonized over hurting her friend, but she had little choice. William must come first.

The thought of baby Wills brought a smile to her face. Pressing her hand to her bosom, she was awarded with a satisfying crackle of paper. Yes, Dunholm it must be. Her only hope of keeping the baby was to marry. Dunholm was hardly the knight in shining armour whom she had hoped to wed, but he was the best of the lot. Yes. *Yes.* She would keep their little rendezvous, and if Dame Fortune was with her, it would be possible to manoeuvre him into offering for her before the week was out.

FROM BEHIND a gigantic potted rubber tree, Farrencourt had watched Amy hesitate before concealing the note in her bodice. She was like a butterfly caught up in a web of his making. He smiled in satisfaction. Now all that was left to do was see that Lily received the original note signed by Dunholm.

A thought struck him. But what if Lily, flapjaw that she was, confided her good fortune to Miss Thackery? He clenched his teeth. He wouldn't let it happen, even if he had to lock Lily in her room until it was time for her to meet Dunholm in the gazebo. And, to be sure, it wouldn't hurt if he kept an eye on Amethyst during the remainder of the day. He scowled. There were certainly better ways of spending a holiday at a beautiful country estate, but he was determined to follow this through, no matter what the personal sacrifice. He would see his sister married in spite of the indignities he must endure from Amy Thackery, the devil take her toplofty soul.

As Amy walked down the gallery hall of the main house past the portraits of a score of Caulfields long ago gone to their just reward, a sudden sound caused her to turn sharply. She had thought everyone was involved in a game of tag on the west lawn, but she was not alone.

"Oh, it's you, Lord Farrencourt. I might have known."

He came close to her and stopped. "And what is that supposed to mean?"

"Are you following me?"

"Following you? You flatter yourself, Miss Thackery. Why would I choose to follow you?"

"Your reputation precedes you, sir."

His eyebrows lifted. "And just what reputation of mine could possibly have reached the ears of an innocent young woman like you? One who has spent her entire life in the country?"

"You needn't appear so amused, my lord. You know very well of what I speak. You've courted half the débutantes from the last four Seasons, and I'll warrant you've been escort to more than a dozen of the current crop."

She tilted her head and looked up from beneath lowered lashes. "Then, of course, there is a certain dancer, Miss Eva Delight, whose talents go far beyond those of the ballet, or so I'm told."

He levelled a steely gaze at her. "And what talents are those? If I may be so bold."

Amy couldn't hide her sudden blush. Beast that he was, he would do everything in his power to embarrass her.

"Do go on, Miss Thackery. I'm eager to hear of these hidden talents Miss Delight is supposed to possess."

"Cooking," Amy said decisively. "Yes, that's it. I'm told she is especially known for her *pièce de résistance.*"

Farrencourt tossed his head in a loud guffaw. "Very good. Very good, indeed. I look forward to finding out if what you say is true."

"Of that I have no doubt." But even as she said it, Amy felt a twinge of remorse. What was it some women had that drew men to them like ants to a sugar pot? she wondered.

"It occurs to me, Miss Thackery," Farrencourt said as he leaned towards her in an overly intimate way, "that although what the gossips say about my exploits is grossly exaggerated, I have yet to enjoy the pleasure of *your* company. Perhaps you might consent to join me this evening at half past eight for a stroll in the rose garden, with your chaperon, of course."

Amy was taken aback. "You jest, of course. I could not possibly do so. Besides, I shall be otherwise engaged. Now, if you will be so good as to excuse me, I must go."

Farrencourt bowed. "I assure you, it was not said in jest. But another time, perhaps." Not bothering to reply, she fled from him, and it was all he could do to keep from laughing. She was smart enough to realize that there was little about her to interest him, but he could see that his offer had shaken her.

He stroked his chin. Devil take her, it might be fun at that. The chit was far too sure of herself, he thought as he watched her hurry down the corridor, skirts billowing, hair falling over her shoulders in a honey-gold cascade. And much as he hated to admit it, he enjoyed the challenge of matching wits with her; being with her seemed to rejuvenate him.

He remembered his own first love. Mademoiselle Beaufontaine had taught him French, until the day his father discovered that she was also teaching him a subject more elemental, and far more interesting, than irregular verbs.

A smile widened his mouth and he nodded. It had been his intention all along to divert Miss Thackery's attentions away from Dunholm in order to allow Lily free rein to entice Dunholm into offering for her. And it was only fair. Dunholm had been attracted to Lily before the Thackery Jewels came to Town, and he was too tame for Amethyst by half. Then a new thought struck him. Why not give Miss Thackery a courting she would never forget? It would afford her something to look back on when she was finally offered for by some young buck still wet behind the ears.

"Yes," Farrencourt muttered aloud. "One might even consider it an act of kindness on my part." But first he had to convince her to allow him to see her. And why was that going to be so difficult when with

every other young chit it had proved to be so easy?
Never mind, he decided. He was never one to turn his
back on a challenge.

Amy was nearing the end of the long gallery before
she allowed her shoulders to relax. It was almost as if
Farrencourt were beside her, so strong was his presence. There was no doubt in her mind that he continued to watch her. But it wasn't so much his gaze that
bothered her. It was his intentions. Despite the fact
that she had said he spoke in jest, she knew his invitation was in earnest. He had asked to see her. But
why? Why? Egan Kimble had never been courtly. He
treated her with as much disdain as if she were a
kitchen servant. He was dreadfully outspoken, outrageously condescending and unspeakably overbearing...when he was in a good mood. She had never
seen him in a fit of anger, but she was willing to wager that castle walls would tremble if such were the
case.

Her footsteps slowed as she turned the corner and
passed from his line of vision. She leaned against a
rococo table and allowed her body to wilt. Why must
she always feel so weak after a confrontation with
Egan Kimble? Her heart thudded, her mouth was as
dry as dust, and her knees felt weak. Just what did the
man want from her?

Her thoughts were interrupted when Maggie,
dressed in her new uniform of dove grey with white
tatted collar and cuffs, entered from the veranda. She
closed the French doors behind her. "Oh, there you
are, miss." She stopped short. "Blimey! You look like
you're at sixes and sevens. Wot 'appened?"

"It's nothing. I'm just a little short of breath. That's all."

"Uh-huh. Well, that might do for some, but I'll wager ten against one 'twas a man what was the cause o' it."

Just then Lord Farrencourt came out of the gallery hall and approached. Maggie's eyes widened. "And speakin' o' which, wot's 'appened 'ere? 'Ave you gone and compromised yourself?"

"Don't be a ninnyhammer. We were simply having a discussion."

"Discussion, my foot. You be careful, girl," Maggie whispered. "Lord Farrencourt is too much man for a green girl like you."

"Ladies?" Lord Farrencourt smiled. "Is anything wrong?"

"Not with us, there ain't," Maggie said.

Amy put her hand on Maggie's arm. "We were simply having a...a discussion," Amy finished weakly.

Farrencourt bowed and walked on.

Maggie snorted. "Even I could o' done better than that. And did you see the look on 'is face? 'E's up to somethin', that one. If I was you, I'd make sure I showed him the back o' my 'ead."

Amy gave her a cool look. "Indeed? I don't believe you for a minute. I saw the way you stared at the cut of his inexpressibles when he came walking towards us. You'd tumble for him in a minute if he so much as lifted a brow at you."

Maggie grinned. "Aye, that I might. Then again, I ain't you. What I would do if I was me ain't the same as wot I would do if I was you. There ain't no man alive wot I can't 'andle."

"You may live to rue those words, but since neither of us will have Lord Farrencourt to train to heel, the point is moot."

Maggie sighed. "More's the pity."

A clock struck the hour somewhere deep in the house and Maggie all but jumped. "We best be joinin' the others. Lady Udora's sure to be raising a breeze if I don't return wi' you in tow." She slanted a look at Amy. "And I wouldna' tell 'er I was alone wi' Farrencourt, if I was you. As for me, your secret is safe, but I may want a favour o' me own someday."

"Don't be absurd. I intend to tell her ladyship everything that happened."

"O' course you will." Maggie grinned.

Fortunately for the sake of her conscience, Amy didn't have to come up with a Banbury Tale to explain her absence. Udora had Dunholm by the arm and lost no time in throwing them together. "Amy, my dear. Dunholm has offered to show you the swans down by the river's edge. I'm told they are quite unusual."

Amy took one look at Dunholm, who was practically panting in his eagerness, and forced a smile. "Of course. I'm sure we have much to talk about."

"We do?" Dunholm looked surprised.

Amy moved her shoulders flirtatiously. "Don't pretend with me, Dunholm. I know that daring look in your eye. I doubt that I would be safe without the protection of my abigail. You are so manly and strong." She finished with a flutter of eyelashes and lowered gaze.

Dunholm sputtered, "I assure you, Miss Amethyst, my intentions are quite honourable."

Udora patted his shoulder. "We know you are trustworthy, dear boy."

Maggie burst into a fit of giggles and murmured something about men carrying their brains below their middles as she walked a short distance away.

Udora, who had only faintly heard Maggie's aside to Amy, looked pensive but nevertheless pleased by the way things were progressing. "Perhaps I'd best send Sally instead of Maggie," she mused. "Maggie seems a bit of a bufflehead today."

It took several minutes for Maggie to find Sally and summon her to chaperon Amy and Dunholm on their walk to view the swans. "And would you be after me to go along, too?" Maggie enquired.

Udora gave her a cutting look. "I think we can find another task for you to occupy yourself with." The tone of her voice hinted that it would not be as pleasant as a stroll through the grounds.

Maggie gave Amy a broad wink as she followed Udora's retreating back.

Dunholm wet his lips. "If you would like to take my arm, Miss Thackery? The pathway appears somewhat rough."

"Why, thank you, my lord. How kind of you." She glanced at the surprised expression on Sally's face and shot her a warning look. "Come along, Sally." Sally fell in behind them.

A high canopy of ash trees sheltered the path from the hot sun. In the distance the pond glittered like a burnished mirror broken into a series of shards by the movement of the swans. Farther down, groups of fir trees sheltered tables and benches that were provided for bird-watchers and the occasional picnicker.

Dunholm pressed Amy's arm close to his side. "I must say, Miss Thackery, you do look uncommonly fetching today."

She beamed up at him, practising her worshipful look. "Why, thank you, my lord. I hoped this particular gown would please you." A deft shrug of the shoulders allowed the top of the bodice to slip a bit lower. "I'm afraid it's a bit daring."

He ran his finger along the top of his starched collar. "I confess to finding it quite charming. Ah...quite charming, indeed."

"Just so that it doesn't put ideas into that handsome head of yours." She laughed coyly.

His face flamed. "Did you find my note in the music box?"

"Indeed I did. My, but you are the romantic one."

"And you agree to meet me at nine?"

"Of course. You knew I could not resist, did you not? Does any woman say no to you, my lord?"

His voice cracked. "Only rarely," he lied. "Had I known we would be together, I would have asked you in person."

"But this is much..." She was cut off midsentence when Farrencourt and his sister stepped out from a small clearing.

"What ho? And who have we here?" Farrencourt called. Lily came running towards Amy and gave her a smothering embrace.

"We heard you were coming to view the swans," Lily said. "Egan suggested we join you."

"It was your idea, I think, Lily," Farrencourt corrected her, "but a good one, I am sure. The lawn games have become a bit of a bore."

Dunholm scowled. "Please don't let us detain you. We would not be so rude as to interrupt your stroll."

Farrencourt stepped closer. So close that Amy could see the faint shadow of whiskers beginning to darken the line of his jaw. For some inexplicable reason she wanted to run her fingernails across his chin to hear the sound. He settled his eyes on her as if sensing her thoughts.

"Detain us? My dear Dunholm," he said, never once lifting his gaze from Amy, "what could be more important than spending time with good friends? Please accept my invitation to join Lily and me."

"But you see, old man . . ."

"Nonsense. No apologies. I insist." Finally he looked squarely at Dunholm. "Truth be told, Lily has just been telling me how much she would enjoy showing you a pheasant's nest she discovered yesterday." He slapped his thigh. "Now that I mention it, this is a splendid opportunity."

"But I . . ." Dunholm began.

Before anyone could protest, Farrencourt had relieved Dunholm of Amy's arm and taken possession of it himself. A nod to Lily, and she had captured Dunholm's hand, marching him towards a path that branched off to one side of the trees.

Amy was dumbfounded. She looked at Sally, who looked confused.

Farrencourt laced his fingers with Amy's. "It might be wise to close your mouth, Miss Thackery. The gnats are quite thick near the water's edge."

"Of all the nerve!"

"My apologies. It is quite a lovely mouth, open *or* closed."

"Don't act the fool. You know very well what I mean." She tried to pull away, but he held her arm close against him. "If nothing else, sir, you might at least have regard for your sister's reputation. Letting Lily go off with Dunholm unescorted is scandalous."

"Never fear. Her abigail is waiting just beyond the trees."

"I knew it. You had this all planned in advance."

Sally stepped alongside them, her face a mixture of shyness and determination. "Is everything all right, Miss Amethyst, or best I go for 'elp?"

"No, please don't do that. Lord Farrencourt is about to leave. Is that not so, my lord?"

"Only if you insist."

"I do insist. Just what manner of game are you playing, Farrencourt?"

"The truth?"

"That would be nice for a change."

"Ah...you have a sharp tongue for such an innocent. Very well, the truth." He ran his hand across the faint stubble on his chin. "It's this way. I love my sister very dearly, and I want to protect her. This means finding a suitable match for her. I cannot allow her to ruin her life the way her sister ruined hers."

"But Lily has attracted the eye of more than one eligible bachelor."

"None for whom she can develop a *tendre,* I regret to say. She believes herself to be in love with Dunholm, God help her."

"In love? I knew of her flirtations with him, but..."

"Yes. Unfortunately he is smitten with you, and I felt compelled to afford my sister equal opportunity. However, unless I miss my guess, he will offer for you if he has not already done so." He turned and faced her, holding both her hands in his. His eyes claimed hers, and she was unable to look away. "And what will your answer be, Miss Thackery?"

"I . . . I don't know."

"I don't believe you."

She felt perspiration gather on the bridge of her nose. "I suppose I shall have to say yes."

"Do you love him?"

Anger gave her strength to look away. "That, sir, is none of your business."

"Then why?"

"Because I need a husband, if you must know."

"Need? Isn't that putting it a bit strongly?"

"Let go of me, Farrencourt, or I swear I shall scream."

Before either of them could do or say anything, Sally had approached from behind and kicked Farrencourt soundly on the ankle. He let out a yelp and bent to rub the offended extremity.

"Oh, Miss Amy, wot 'ave I done?" Sally wailed. "And 'im a nob an all."

"You gave him just what he deserved, Sally, and I shall reward you for it."

Farrencourt straightened. He bowed to both women. "I beg your forgiveness, ladies. I admit to being carried away by my desire to help my sister. Nothing more."

"Your apology is accepted, my lord," Amy said stiffly. "Now if you will excuse us?"

He bowed, then watched as they turned away and walked quickly in the direction from which they had come. "Hell and damnation," he muttered aloud. "You certainly handled that with royal aplomb."

He felt a twinge of conscience. Truth be told, he had started this game for Lily's sake, which in turn would free him to follow his own pursuits once she was married. But now the desire to help his sister was beginning to take second place. Amethyst Thackery was proving to be a gem worth testing. Certainly not that he had any aspirations towards marriage. There was still time enough to live the good life before he must be tied and shackled by the bonds of matrimony. And what time he had, he was determined to enjoy to the fullest.

Thinking of his secret rendezvous with Amy brought a smile to his face, and he rubbed his ankle with something akin to pleasure. The look in her eyes when she discovered it was he who kept the tryst instead of Dunholm would be worth all the indignities he had been forced to suffer. How good it would feel to even the score.

A GAME OF HEARTS had been set up in the main floor library for those guests who were uninterested in the drama being staged in the small salon. Amy decided it would be less difficult to disappear from the crowded theatre than from the library, where only a few young people chose to gather.

Emerald gave her an unsettling glance. "I can't believe you want to see another dull performance of *The Quaker*. Why, it was only six weeks ago that you swore you never wanted to see another farce put on by a company of amateurs."

Amy turned away before answering Emerald, who had a devilishly keen eye for a falsehood. "You're right, of course, but they say the stage settings are going to be quite good. Besides, I never could win at cards."

Topaz clipped a burgundy velvet bow to the back of her hair. "And a dark theatre is a much better place to play knees and footsies with a certain Lord Dunholm."

Amy threw her hairbrush, just missing Topaz, who ducked with the natural grace of a horsewoman. The door opened at that moment and the brush caught Udora's skirt.

"And who may I ask is responsible for this little tantrum?"

"Topaz was *responsible*," Amy said, her voice fading, "but I must admit to throwing the brush."

"Both of you should know better. What will the Caulfields think of you, behaving like hoydens in their lovely country home? Now, let me look at the three of you. Um-hm. Yes, I think you will do. Taz, you might have Maggie take a needle to the lace at the back of your dress. Amy, my dear, surely that isn't stuffing I see in your bodice."

"Only a wee bit."

"A wee bit too much, I'd say, for a gel your age. Do remove it. Emerald, you look enchanting. Try not to keep pushing at your spectacles so often. We must try to find some way of making them stay in place."

She lifted the jewelled timepiece adorning her shawl and gasped. "Pistachions! It's nearly half past seven. I promised Lord Bromley and his lady that Bently and I would join them for a game of Hearts." She took a quick look in the mirror, fluffed the red-gold curls around her face, and appeared satisfied. "Now, girls, do enjoy yourselves this evening. Maggie will look after Emerald and Topaz. That leaves Sally to keep watch over you, Amethyst. The two of you do seem to get on rather well."

"Yes, my lady."

"Good. Then you should join the others in the library or the salon as soon as you are ready."

They breathed a combined sigh of relief the moment the door closed behind her. Topaz started to giggle. Emerald looked over at her then dismissed her sister's bout of laughter as just another of Topaz's peculiarities. But Amy was too much on edge to let it pass.

"What's so funny?"

"You are, silly goose. I wonder that her ladyship didn't question you about *your* plans."

"Plans? Whatever are you talking about?"

"Be that way if you want to, but I can recognize that slyboots look in your eyes."

"Stubble it, Topaz," Amy said, and flounced from the room, slamming the door behind her. A breathless Sally caught up with her before she reached the staircase.

The salon was already crowded, but the curtain had not yet risen for the theatre-goers. Amy chose an aisle seat near the back of the room.

Sally was piqued. "Can't we sit near the front, Miss Amethyst? I can't rightly 'ear what they say."

"No, we can't, Sally. And listen, I want you to do just as I say and don't ask any questions. Just be very quiet and follow me when I leave."

"Leave? We just got 'ere. Where're we goin'?"

"I'm going to meet someone, but it must be kept secret."

Sally looked horrified. "'Er ladyship will 'ave your 'ide, and mine, too, more's the pity."

"I promise to take all the blame. It's the only way I can conceive of to keep baby William."

Thirty-five minutes later, during a round of applause for the somewhat overzealous actors, Amy and Sally slipped unnoticed from the room.

Sally's eyes were wide with apprehension as Amy lifted the latch on the French doors and stepped onto the veranda. "Come along, Sally. I'm meeting someone in the hedge maze, but we shall have to be very quiet."

"And who might that be?"

"Shh. Not another word. I want you to stay back out of sight once we approach the fountain."

There was just enough light for them to find their way to the herb garden, then past the espaliered rose garden to the hedge maze. Amy knew the proper twists and turns to take, having strolled through the maze earlier that afternoon. They were just a dozen or so yards from the last turn when Amy stopped.

"There's a stone bench here by the wall. You wait there until I come for you."

"Alone? Not me, miss. It's too dark. I'd be too scared."

Amy was in a quandary. If Sally tagged along, she would ruin everything. What would Udora do? Be firm, of course. She straightened. "I will not permit you to be afraid, Sally. It just isn't done. Now, sit there and don't make a sound until I return for you."

"Yes, miss."

Amy turned away, placing her hand to her breast. Now, that was easy. Why hadn't she thought of trying Udora's methods before?

Finding her way alone was indeed a little more disconcerting than she had expected, but even now she could hear the splash of the Neptune fountain where Dunholm would be waiting. She mentally gathered her courage. This night would change her life forever.

But, dear lord, why did it have to be Dunholm? The thought of his hands touching her most private parts was almost too much to be borne. *Think of the baby,* she chanted silently. *Think of the way his head rests in the palm of your hand and how he smiles up at you when you hold him. This is your only chance to keep him safe from harm. Be brave.*

When she reached the fountain, she looked carefully about her. Nothing moved save for the splash of water falling from the dolphin's mouth. No breath of air stirred the trees, no night birds winged across the faint patch of light from the moon, no gnats braved the fire of a single torchère placed at the far side of the enclosure.

Amy pressed her hands together to keep them from shaking. "Dunholm? Are you there?"

Silence.

Dunholm?

Something touched her shoulder and she spun round, stumbling slightly. And then she felt strong arms closing about her.

CHAPTER FIVE

AMY GASPED. His arms held her so close that there was little chance of escape. She felt a tiny frisson of fear, but there was also an unforeseen surge of pleasure in his touch. She hadn't expected him to be so strong, so compelling.

"Dunholm, please." Her voice quavered. "You are too bold. I only came to speak with you."

"Dunholm be damned," the voice growled.

Before Amy could gather her wits about her, the man had threaded his fingers through her hair, drawn her head back and kissed her firmly on the lips.

She stiffened and pulled back. "Y-you're not Dunholm." Her voice was breathy and thin.

He laughed harshly. "How very perceptive of you."

"Farrencourt! What are you doing here? Let me go!"

"Too late for that, my sweet Pandora." He kissed her again, savouring the freshness of her mouth, the softness of her skin, the faint scent of attar of roses in her hair.

He pulled her closer still, until the heat of his body warmed her. Farrencourt sensed it the moment her resistance vanished. She went limp in his arms, then slowly, reluctantly, as if of their own volition, her hands slid up his arms, onto his shoulders and around his neck. Her lips softened, then responded, timidly at first, then with growing ardour, matched the pressure of his own.

It was her soft whimper that brought him to his senses. Hell and damnation! He hadn't meant it to go this far. He had merely intended to prevent her from seeing Dunholm. Instead, her touch had caused his own heart to pound. Another moment and he would have lost his ability to stop this mad ascent.

"Amethyst. Amethyst, listen to me."

She felt herself drawn unwillingly back to the harsh reality of what had happened, but she was incapable of moving. He held her at arm's length. "I humbly apologize, Miss Thackery, for taking such liberties with your person. Please do forgive me."

She drew a raspy breath, fighting for control. "Forgive you? Why, you insufferable lout! What have you done with Dunholm? How could you behave in such a beastly manner? Lord Kesterson will call you out for such ungentlemanly behaviour."

"He would be a fool to do so. He wouldn't have a chance against me. We both know that," Farrencourt said softly. "I suggest we keep our own counsel about what happened between us. Especially since we were both willing participants."

"Willing participants? I hated every minute of it. It did, in fact, make me quite ill."

He grinned. "You have an odd way of showing it. Admit it, my girl, another few minutes and your innocence would have been but a passing memory."

She drew her hand back to slap him but he caught her wrist. "Again, I offer my most humble regrets. No. I take that back. I don't for one minute regret it.

But I do admit to being ashamed and sorry for having taken advantage of you."

"You are no gentleman, sir, and you shall live to regret it. Mark my words."

"Perhaps. But, ah, my dear girl, the memory of your kiss is well worth whatever price I must be forced to pay."

"Indeed? I warrant you would sing another tune if Lady Udora discovered your attempt to compromise me. You would have no choice but to offer for me."

"Don't place a wager on it, miss. I have no intention of being tethered for at least another five years. Not even to one so delectable as you."

"How fortunate for me. I would not marry you if you were the last man on Earth. Please be so good as to unhand me."

He let her go so abruptly that she nearly lost her balance. He bowed. "Again, may I offer my sincere apologies if I have offended you. If there is anything I can do to make up for it . . ."

"Your apologies are unacceptable," Amy said. It was tempting to even the score by forcing the issue in public, but she knew in her heart that Kesterson would challenge him and come out the loser. And truth be told, a dramatic change had come over her in the last few minutes. For the first time in her life she knew what it was like to feel the heat of womanly desires. And with Egan Kimble, of all people!

She crossed her arms protectively in front of her. "As for your making up for your indiscretion, my lord, be assured that I shall think of some way in which you can absolve yourself."

He smiled. She sensed it more than saw it in the dim light. He chuckled softly. "My person as well as my purse are at your command, Miss Thackery. It is the very least a gentleman can do, and I assure you, I am a gentleman."

"That remains to be seen, doesn't it? Now, if you will excuse me..."

"May I walk you to the house?"

"You've already done quite enough, Lord Farrencourt," she said coldly. "My abigail awaits just around the turn in the hedge."

Farrencourt followed her until she joined Sally, who was waiting on the bench. He pulled his watch from his waistcoat pocket, held it close to the light of the torchère, then swore softly. It had taken longer than he expected. Hell and damnation! What had come over him to kiss her as he had? His carefully laid plans had almost gone down the well. He mentally checked the location of the nearest exit from the maze and took off running in the direction of the gazebo. It was time to put the second half of his plan into action.

There was no difficulty in finding the gazebo in the semi-darkness. The commotion coming from that direction clearly pointed the way.

Farrencourt trotted towards the three men who were scuffling with a fourth man and then pinned him down. "Effington, Skidmore, Radley? What's the fuss all about? Who's that you have there on the ground?"

Effington gave him a broad wink. "Farrencourt, old man. I was about to go looking for you. We caught Dunholm here compromising your sister."

"No! That cannot be. Not Dunholm."

"Farrencourt, get me out of this." Dunholm managed to speak just above a whisper, thanks to the boot at the back of his neck.

Farrencourt spread his feet wide and placed his hands on his hips. "Let him go, lads. Dunholm, is this true? Where is Lily?"

"I'm here, Egan." Lily approached from the far side of the semi-darkened gazebo.

"Thank heaven you are safe. But you appear overset. What did this man do to you?"

Lord Skidmore grinned wickedly. "He took advantage of her without so much as a by-your-leave. Grabbed her and planted one right on the mouth."

"He kissed you, Lily?" Farrencourt sounded appalled.

"Yes, Egan, but I didn't . . ."

"Be still. When I want you to speak, I will tell you. Now then, Dunholm. Is this true?"

"Well, it is, but I thought she was—"

"Really, Dunholm, I would have expected better of you than to compromise an innocent girl. This puts you in a very bad loaf. And in front of witnesses, too."

"How was I to know they were there?"

"Say no more, Dunholm. Suffice it to say that I respect you enough to know that you will do the right thing by Lily."

Dunholm sputtered. "Surely you jest. It was an accident, nothing more. She is none the worse for wear."

Lord Farrencourt scowled. "Careful, my lord, lest I choose to punish you as well as hold you to your obligations. You may be grateful that my three friends were nearby to prevent your passions from going too far. Otherwise I would have had to call you out."

Dunholm brushed himself off. "Forgive me if I fail to appear grateful."

Farrencourt turned to Lily. "And you, miss, come along. I'll see you to your room." He grasped her arm and hustled her towards the house.

Lily, wide-eyed and breathless, stared up at him. "Is it true, Egan? Will you force him to marry me?"

"He will have no choice but to do the right thing. Of that I assure you."

"How delicious! But it's true, you know. He thought I was Amethyst."

"Nonsense. That is merely the rig he used to excuse his unpardonable display of passion for you."

"Yes, you could be right," she said thoughtfully. "You did hand me his note asking me to meet him in the gazebo. I recognized his handwriting, and I kept the note in my reticule. The more I think of it, the more persuaded I am that you are correct." She sighed, a sound of contentment. "How soon do you think we shall marry?"

"Soon, very soon, if I have anything to say about it."

The twinge of conscience he felt at his uncustomary act of deceit vanished when he saw the glow of happiness on his sister's face. He had failed to save Darlene from an ignominious alliance, but at least he was able to protect Lily from a similar fate. She was attracted to Dunholm, and in time, he would learn to care for her. A generous dowry would, of course, serve as encouragement.

AMY WAS STILL TREMBLING when she returned to the salon with Sally. If word got out that Farrencourt had mishandled her, Bently would create a stir that would rock London. Marriage to Farrencourt would solve the problem of how to keep baby Wills, but she could not marry a man who evoked such fear in her. What it was about him that caused such anxiety she wasn't certain, nor did she care to peruse it.

It had not been easy to turn aside Sally's curiosity over the incident in the hedge maze, but a sudden inspiration struck Amy when she saw the minute tear in her shawl. "Oh dear, look what I've done. It must have caught on the hedge."

Sally examined it. "Aye, wot a shame. And 'tis my favourite."

"Then you must keep it," Amy declared. "I know you can mend it so it won't show much."

"Do you mean it, Miss Amethyst?"

"Indeed I do. Take it with my blessing." Sally was in transports, the events of the evening apparently driven from her mind. If Amy felt a shadow of conscience, she reminded herself that it was all for the sake of her baby. She missed him so dreadfully. And worse yet, she had somehow jeopardized her chance to inspire Dunholm to set a wedding date.

The girls had scarcely finished their toilette the next morning when Lily, all a-twitter, arrived at their bedchamber door. "Aren't you ready yet, Amethyst? I've been up ever so long." She plumped herself down on the rumpled bedclothes and swung her legs back and forth. "I've the most wonderful news."

"Tell me."

"Later," she said, savouring the moment. "Egan has promised to take us for a drive through the village. Do say you'll go."

Amy turned away from the dressing-table mirror, the better to study Lily's face. "A drive through the village? Was this Lord Farrencourt's idea or yours?"

"It was Egan's suggestion. He's tired of cards and the lawn games and hopes to look in on a horse the squire has for sale. You can take your abigail, of course, but I've told Louella she can stay here since Egan can look after me." Lily's voice raised in pitch as her eyes took on a sudden glitter. "And Dunholm will accompany us."

"Dunholm? Indeed. I thought Effington was in better favour with Farrencourt these days."

"Not since Egan learned that I have a *tendre* for Dunholm. You did give him to me, didn't you, Amethyst?"

Amethyst slowly turned to face the mirror. "Yes, I suppose I did. But things are different now, Lily. I need to find a husband at once."

"Different? What do you mean, different?" Lily demanded.

"Well, I . . . I just need to find a husband at once." Amy laid the hairbrush next to the gilded hand mirror. Even before Lily said it, Amy knew what her friend was thinking, but there was nothing she could do about it, thanks to Udora's warning not to breathe a word to anyone about baby William.

"Amy, you aren't . . . er . . . you know. This doesn't have anything to do with a baby, does it?"

"No, I am most certainly not in the family way, if that's what you mean, but . . . I suppose it does . . . in . . . in a way have to do with a baby, but I am sworn to secrecy."

"Hell and damnation," Lily said, borrowing her brother's favourite expletive. "It's not Dunholm's, is it?"

"Most certainly not, but that's all I can tell you," Amy said, making a special effort to overlook Lily's profanity. "Well," she added thoughtfully, "truth be told, I can't honestly say, but the chances would be one in a million. I can almost promise you that the child's mother has never met Dunholm."

"Surely you can tell me," Lily said, then, seeing the determination on Amy's face, decided that pressing her would accomplish nothing, at least at the moment. She was dying to know, but she was overcome by her own good news. Still perhaps this was not the best time to tell Amy that Dunholm had compromised her.

"I confess to being relieved—that it wasn't Dunholm, I mean. But should you wish to confide in me, you know that I wouldn't tell a soul...and we *are* best friends." Lily got up and wandered to the window. "Then it is all right if I tell my brother we will accompany him to the village?"

"Yes, I suppose so, providing Lady Udora gives her permission. I shall have to take Sally, of course."

"Then hurry down to have your breakfast. The kippers here at Diamond Hill are the best ever." She went to the door. "I'll just find Egan and enquire what time he will have the carriage brought round."

Amy called Sally to help finish dressing her hair. It was only after Lily had left that she remembered Lily had forgotten to mention her good news. Amy suddenly longed for the comfort of her family, but Emerald had long since gone down to peruse the books in

the library. Topaz, along with Bently, had taken to the
stable to try out a blooded jumper Bently had recently purchased. Udora had said she would have
breakfast in the refectory with some of the ladies who
were also guests at Diamond Hill. Amy hurried down
to join them and gain permission to accompany Lily
and the others.

Once Udora learned that Dunholm would join them
on the drive through the village, she was enthusiastic.
She took Amy aside. "I wouldn't consider it bad form
if you happened to drift away from Farrencourt and
his sister long enough to contrive to get a firm offer for
your hand. But you mustn't be too coming," she cautioned. "I'll tell Sally to be discreet in her watchfulness."

"Yes, my lady."

Udora tapped her fingers against her wrist. "What
is it? You look as if your lower lip could drag the
floor."

"It's nothing. I must change if I am to go riding in
the carriage."

"Yes, my dear. Wear the apricot-sprigged muslin
with the midnight-blue cape. It looks fetching on you,
and it will be a nice change from the white. And take
my apricot parasol if you wish."

Amy's stomach twisted. Udora cherished her sunshade. She never allowed the girls to borrow it. She
must be convinced that this would be the day Amy
would close the trap on Lord Dunholm.

A note from Lily arrived a short time later to inform Amethyst that the carriage would be ready
within the hour. It took both Sally and Maggie to get
her ready in time. Maggie was more vigorous than

might be deemed necessary as she brushed Amy's
honey-coloured hair into a sleek coil down the middle
of her back and fastened her bonnet into place.

"Ouch!" Amy said. "Must you be so hasty?"

"Aye, and I thought you was in an 'urry to meet
your beau."

"Something tells me it's you who's in a rush to get
away." Amy smiled wickedly. "Perhaps I should insist that Lady Udora send *you* to accompany me instead of Sally."

"Do that, miss, and I might have to tell 'er ladyship who it was who was 'avin a tussle in the 'edge
maze last night."

Amy paled. "You wouldn't!" She shot a quick look
at Sally, who had suddenly turned pale. Sally was not
one to keep secrets.

Maggie grinned. "Wouldn't I, now?" She placed
her hands on her hips and leaned back to survey her
handiwork. "Seein' as 'ow a young lady such as you
should be smart enough to keep 'er peace, I might be
counted on to forget certain unladylike be'aviour."

"I suppose that means you plan to keep a secret assignation. And in the middle of the day. Really, Maggie. Who is it this time?"

Maggie looked profoundly pleased with herself. "If
I told you, 'twouldn't be a secret, would it?" She motioned for Amy to stand and then helped her into her
cloak. "Now, then, that should 'old you for a
while... providin' 'is lordship keeps 'is 'ands to 'imself."

"Dunholm is always a true gentleman."

Maggie laughed. "An' who was speakin' o'
Dun'olm?"

"Be still!" Amy cautioned. "Someone will hear you and get the wrong idea. Last night was a mistake."

"Not so much a mistake as Dun'olm would be, 'im with 'is cow's eyes."

"You are incorrigible, Maggie. I wonder why Lady Udora puts up with you." She picked up the parasol and her reticule to the sound of Maggie's laughter.

Lily was waiting in the entrance hall with Dunholm and her brother when Amethyst and Sally descended the staircase. Farrencourt, beaver in hand, legs spread wide to accent, unconsciously or otherwise, the strong curve of his expensively tailored nankeens, fastened his gaze on Amy. His gaze met hers before she looked away.

Lily rushed over to plant the inevitable kiss on Amy's cheek. "Oh, isn't this fun? Egan promised to give us luncheon at the Travellers' Inn in the village. It's all the crack, so I'm told."

Amy looked uncertain. "I didn't think we would be gone that long."

Dunholm ran his tongue across his lips. "I've spoken to Lady Udora. She gave her permission."

Farrencourt nodded to the footman to open the door and motioned for the ladies to precede him. "Should you become bored, Miss Thackery, I'll ask the driver to return to the house, but somehow I think we can keep you entertained."

She turned back to look at him, but his expression was bland. Now, what did he mean by that?

FROM THE MOMENT they entered the open carriage, Amy knew she would not be bored. How it happened she could not decide, but instead of Dunholm, it was

Farrencourt who took the seat next to her. She gave him a surprised look as he settled down beside her, his thigh grazing hers.

He raised his eyebrows, obviously daring her to complain. "Are you quite comfortable, Miss Thackery?"

She gazed at him, eyes like blue flint. "Quite, my lord. I am considered most adaptable. Nothing bothers me."

"I'll make note of that," he said, shifting his weight once again.

Amy gritted her teeth. Try as she might, she could not dispel the image of that brief moment last night by the fountain. Then, too, she had been pressed against him until the blood began to sing in her ears. Nice girls didn't think such thoughts, she reminded herself, at the same time contriving to edge closer to the side of the carriage.

Sally, her hand to her mouth, gave a puzzled look first at Farrencourt, then at Dunholm, then at Amy. She pointed towards Dunholm. "Miss Amethyst, shouldn't 'e . . . ?"

"Be still, Sally," Amy said shortly.

Lily, oblivious to everything but the fact that Dunholm was sitting next to her, was in raptures. "I knew this was going to be a perfect day. Especially after last night," she said, giving Dunholm a gentle nudge in the ribs.

Dunholm grunted.

Farrencourt grinned. "Had I a bottle of spirits, I would offer a toast, dear sister, to a lifetime of perfect days."

"See here, old man," Dunholm interjected. "You can't be serious about..."

"Oh, but I am. Consider it, Dunholm. Have you ever known me to dissemble over something so serious as my sister's reputation?"

Amy felt her heart lurch. "Reputation? What is this? Lily, what have you done?"

Lily started to respond, but a look from Farrencourt stopped her. He slapped his gloves against his knee. "I would have thought by now that Lily would have confided in you, Miss Thackery, but considering the gravity of the incident, I can understand her reticence."

Amy waited but nothing was forthcoming. "Well? Don't keep me in the dark. Tell me." She hesitated. "Or... or is it so unseemly that one cannot discuss it in public? Surely it is not so grave that it can't be rectified?"

"No, it was not at all...." Dunholm began, but Farrencourt held up his hand.

"I fear it is a serious breach of manners, Miss Thackery, but I warrant Dunholm will do the gentlemanly thing. He has, as you might have guessed, compromised my sister."

Amy paled. "He didn't!"

"Oh, but he did!"

"Lily?" Amy questioned in a strangled voice.

Lily giggled. "Egan caught us kissing in the gazebo." She moved nearer to Dunholm, but he cringed closer to the side of the carriage before leaning forward to grasp Amy's hands.

"Miss Thackery, I do beg your forgiveness. It was a mistake."

Sally made a *tsk-tsk* noise and shook her head at Dunholm.

Amy pulled away, inadvertently moving closer to Farrencourt, who took advantage of the moment by easing his arm across the back of the seat behind her.

She clutched her reticule tightly. "Then it's true, Dunholm? You did this?"

"It's not the way it sounds. I never meant, Lily..."

Farrencourt's voice overtook Dunholm like a fox outrunning a rabbit. "There were witnesses, my lord. Three, to be exact."

"And all friends of yours, Farrencourt," Dunholm said drily.

"Granted, but then I call most men my friends. Yourself included, Dunholm. And as your friend I will wait patiently, for a few days, at least, for you to come to your senses and do the right thing by my sister." He leaned back against the squabs and smiled serenely. "Now, then, I see that we are approaching the village. Shall we endeavour to enjoy our little outing?"

A few minutes later he broke the heavy silence by ordering the driver to stop at a park about which were clustered a number of colourful shops, a church and, taking over one full side, the Travellers' Inn with its accompanying outbuildings.

Farrencourt jumped down from the carriage and offered his assistance to Amy. She drew back for an instant, then, realizing how ridiculous it would be to attempt to alight on her own, accepted Farrencourt's hand. His fingers curled around hers, but it was he who drew away before she had a chance to do so—a fact that irritated Amy intensely.

Other guests from the Diamond Hill house party had also elected to spend the day in the village. Amy nodded to the Misses Doolittle, accompanied by Mr. Lance Cloverdale and Lieutenant Higby, along with the Doolittle abigail, a bacon-faced girl of seventeen.

Lady Breckenridge, at long last out of her widow's weeds, strolling with Lady Chillingsworth beneath the shade of a bay laurel tree, inclined her head in greeting when Amy chanced to meet her gaze. Amy turned to speak to Lily when out of the corner of her eye she saw Effington, Skidmore and Radley coming up behind Farrencourt. Dunholm swore softly.

"What's your game, Farrencourt? Have you brought along a trio of chums to follow me?"

Farrencourt looked innocent. "You wound me, Dunholm. I didn't force my friends to follow us. Isn't that right, Effington?"

"Right-o," Effington agreed, pounding Dunholm on the back. "We've come, my good man, to take you and Miss Lily to see an Austrian beer stein the merchant has tucked away in the rear of his establishment. We all know you are a respected collector." He smiled engagingly. "It's to be our gift. One might say it's our way of making up for manhandling you last night."

"Another time, Effington," Dunholm said stiffly.

They took him by the arms, one on either side of him, in a friendly yet determined way. "Oh, come along, old chap. The stein is so unusual you won't be able to resist," Radley said. At the same time he gave possession of Dunholm's arm over to Lily, who was only too willing to oblige.

Amy watched the five of them saunter down the avenue.

Farrencourt felt a surge of triumph. This was going to cost him, but he was determined to make it worthwhile. He had already made arrangements to pay the shopkeeper twice over the asking price just to make sure that Dunholm was satisfied and to make certain that the deal was not completed too quickly. Devil take the man; it was getting more difficult by the day to keep Miss Thackery and Dunholm apart.

At last Amy turned to face him. "Should we not have accompanied them, my lord, inasmuch as Lily is without a chaperon?"

"Have no fear. She is as safe as if she were completely under my thumb."

"Which she is, is she not?" Amy enquired acidly.

Farrencourt smiled. "As she should be. Now, then." He bowed first to Amy and then to Sally. "May I have the pleasure of showing you ladies the splendour of the cemetery gardens? I understand that they are at their best this time of the year."

Amy shrugged. Pouting would bring her little pleasure. Only getting even with Farrencourt might begin to compensate for the way he had destroyed her chances of being wed to Dunholm . . . and of keeping baby William for her own.

CHAPTER SIX

FARRENCOURT HAD SPOKEN the truth when he said that the cemetery gardens were well tended. The headstones were securely anchored, the plots were free of weeds, and the pathways that wound through the graveyard were bordered with flower-beds and shade trees. A bandy-legged man with a hoe and a pair of shears waved a greeting. He appeared frail for a groundskeeper but he obviously loved his work.

He watched them for a few minutes as they wandered among the tombstones, stopping now and then to smell the roses or run their fingers across slowly eroding inscriptions.

At the rear of the cemetery was a walled-in section marked by the statue of an angel cherub and rows of simple wooden crosses. "Oh, look," Amy said with a catch in her voice. "These must be the graves of children."

Sally hitched her shawl closer around her neck. "Orphaned children they be, miss. No flowers 'ere, save for them what's 'alf dead."

Amy knelt to straighten a wooden cross that was softened around the edges by tufts of grey lichen. "Wilda Jane, age seven. Died June 2, 1799. A ward of the Crown." She read the words aloud then looked up at Farrencourt with tears in her eyes. "This might have been me," she murmured, "had circumstances been different. It is a terrible thing to lose both father and mother and be left alone in the world. At least I have my father's name."

Farrencourt felt a stab of sympathy. His own parents were long dead, but it was different for a man. Men weren't shackled by sentiment. He reached down to touch Amy's shoulder. "And you have Lady Udora and Lord Kesterson to look after you, Miss Thackery. Unfortunately for my Lily, she has only me."

Amy rose to a standing position. "Yes, but you love your sister. I can see it in your eyes. I hesitate to admit that it was my mistaken impression that you wished only to be relieved of your responsibility for her." She placed her hand on his coat sleeve. "Your concern comes as a surprise to me, Lord Farrencourt."

He was pleased by the admiration he saw in her eyes. No, "admiration" was incorrect. Respect, perhaps. And wasn't that much better than admiration? The thought warmed him so much that he wanted to prolong the moment. But Dunholm, devil take the man, was coming towards them with Lily clinging to his arm. He was waving a beer stein over his head. The triumph written on Dunholm's face gave Farrencourt a sense of wry satisfaction despite the untimely interruption.

He looked over at Amy. "You and Sally go along with Dunholm to the carriage. I wish to have a word with the groundskeeper."

"Very well," she said, then watched as he strode down the path towards the wiry gardener. Farrencourt reached into his pocket, then handed something to the man. After a short exchange, Farrencourt patted him on the back and walked away.

"I wonder what that was all about," Amy murmured to Sally, not really expecting an answer.

"It wouldn't s'prise me none if Miss Wilda Jane smells flowers on 'er grave tonight."

Amy blinked back unbidden tears. "Oh, do you really think so?"

"Indeed I does, miss. Indeed I does."

After they left the cemetery, they drove down a leafy lane and across a wooden bridge to visit Squire Higgins, a man known for his stable of hunters. He was an affable personage, but the horse, being too broad in the chest, proved to be of little interest to Dunholm. Their departure was followed by a satisfying repast at the inn and a leisurely drive back to Diamond Hill with ample time left to rest and change before the bell rang for tea.

THE EVENING was devoted to music and poetry readings by Miss Margaret Pachurst, pretty young daughter of the Baron Holcbender.

Amy, still mulling over the events of the afternoon, was only vaguely aware when the applause ended and the musicians had begun to play a lively tune. Farrencourt approached her and bowed.

"Our hostess says there is time for a reel or two before our late supper is to be served. May I have the pleasure of this dance, Miss Thackery?"

Lady Udora, who was seated a few chairs away, leaned forward and gave her nod, leaving Amy no chance to refuse. Nor would she have done so, she re-

alized with surprise. Farrencourt held a certain fasci-
nation for her that she could no longer deny.

Dunholm already had Lily in tow, and they had
taken their place at the far end of the line. Farrencourt offered his hand and Amy accepted. His fingers
were strong, and his hands were dry, unlike Dunholm's, which were always a little warm and damp.
Try as she might, Amy could find little fault in Farrencourt. He danced easily, with a manly grace. For
once he was the perfect gentleman—that is, until he
returned her to her chair. Lifting her hand to his lips,
he kissed it with proper deference. Then, rake that he
was, he turned it over and kissed her palm. No one else
was aware of his indiscretion, but Amy was shaken
beyond belief.

"How dare you!" she murmured, but failed to
make her words carry the anger she should have felt.

"I dare because I know it pleases you."

"You are insufferable." A smile escaped unbidden.

"And you are quite beautiful, Miss Thackery." He
bowed with precise formality and walked away.

Amy was left in a daze. There were two other dances
before the bell rang for supper. She couldn't recall who
her partners had been, but she did take note with considerable pleasure that Farrencourt had elected not to
dance with anyone else.

The supper of Westphalian ham, roast pheasant,
Bolognese sausages and cold goose, along with Turk-
ish figs, Jamaican bananas and other assorted delica-
cies, was set out on the sideboard in the great dining
hall.

Amy found herself stealing glances at Lord Farrencourt, as if by looking at him when he was unaware,

she might come to know this unexpected side of a man she had neatly catalogued as a buck of the most arrogant sort. Apparently he was more complex than she had thought. He cared what happened to his sister, cared so much that he was willing to play deep games in order to see that Lily was safely married to the man she loved. One had to admire that in a man.

The roast goose settled like an indigestible lump in the middle of Amy's stomach.

She looked across and down the table at Farrencourt, who was observing her with a keen eye. There was little doubt about his intentions. He had made it all too clear that he preferred the worldly life over the bonds of matrimony. Of course, the time would come when he must choose a wife to continue the line, and it suddenly occurred to Amy that if she chose, she could be the one to bring him to heel. But did she want to? Yes! The thought was unsettling.

Udora leaned forward and caught Amy's attention. "What is it, Amethyst? You look dreadful."

"I . . . I think I'm going to be ill."

"Dear me. Not today of all days. I'll signal our hostess and request that you be excused."

"Thank you. I'm sorry."

"Give me a moment and I'll accompany you."

Topaz hastily put down her fork. "Let me. I'll see that she gets to her room and then I'll fetch Maggie."

"Yes, do that," Udora said after only a brief hesitation. "And if you need me, send someone with a message."

As Amy rose from the table, Farrencourt's questioning gaze claimed hers. It took all of her strength to look away when Topaz took her arm and guided her into the corridor and over to the staircase.

"We're safe now. You can stop pretending."

"Pretending? I don't know what you mean."

Topaz stopped dead in her tracks. "You mean you really are sick?" She snorted. "I should have known you weren't clever enough to dissemble. I thought this was a trick to get away for an assignation with Dunholm. He left the table, too, just moments before you played your little scene."

The mention of Dunholm's name made Amy's stomach churn. She clutched at her middle, causing Topaz to grasp her by the arm and all but drag her upstairs. Once inside their bedroom Topaz took one look at Amy's pallor and stepped away.

"Ugh! Don't cascade all over the carpet. At least wait until I find Maggie to tend to you."

"Hurry!" Amy urged as she sat down at the dressing-table and bent double.

Maggie appeared within minutes. "See 'ere now. Enough o' that, miss. You and your weak stomach. I'll not be 'avin' you mess up your best dress, nor the floor, for that matter. Not when I'm the one what 'as to clean it up."

Topaz slipped a shawl around her shoulders. "Amy has always had a weak stomach. I'm sure she will be all right."

"'Er stomach will. Can't say as 'ow 'er 'ead will start to make sense."

"Then I'll just be off."

"Back to supper are you, Miss Slyboots?" Maggie enquired, a smile flickering across her face before she turned to hand Amy a damp cloth for her forehead.

Topaz stopped abruptly. "Certainly. Where else would I be going?"

"Oh, I dunno. You might be thinkin' o' chattin' up a certain balloon maker what 'appens to be visitin' 'is uncle at 'is nearby country house."

Topaz's face turned pink. "I don't know where you get such outrageous notions, Maggie."

"Aye, it does take some diggin' to come up wi' them, but I 'as me friends, I does."

"You... you won't say anything to Lady Udora, will you?"

"Not if you takes Sally with you, I won't."

"Sally would spoil everything!" Topaz wailed. "Oh, very well. Just don't go telling tales to her lady-ship."

When Topaz had gone Maggie turned back to Amy. "Now, then, miss. 'Ave you decided to 'eave or will you be'ave like a lady? 'Tis all in your 'ead, you know. And most likely it's a man what's put you on bent pins."

"That's ridiculous!" Amy straightened her back and inhaled deeply. "If I broke a fingernail, you'd swear a man was the cause of it."

"Aye, and would be in most cases. Well, who was 'e? Lord Dunholm? I've 'eard 'e went and compromised Miss Lily Kimble." Maggie reached for a comb and began to touch up Amy's mussed curls. "Seems as how that must o' curdled your puddin'...with you countin' on 'im to dance to *your* tune."

Amy sighed. "It's true, I *was* hoping to marry Dunholm. Not that I have a grand passion for him, or anything at all like that."

"An' I should 'ope not!" Maggie let out a whoop. "Kissin' 'im would be like kissin' a wet-nosed cow." She tilted her head back in a coy gesture. "So if it ain't Lord Dunholm, it 'as to be Lord Farrencourt. I seen 'im watchin' you, and take my word for it, miss, 'e 'as more than 'orses and gamin' tables on *his* mind."

"You're wrong this time, Maggie. Farrencourt has no intention of making a permanent alliance with me or anyone else. He told me so just yesterday."

Maggie swore a mild oath. "An' you believed 'im? 'Tis time you learned, Miss Amy, it ain't the man who sets the when and where. 'Tis the woman what decides." She arched her back and fluffed her red curls. "O' course, a smart woman lets 'im think 'e was the one what led the way."

"You make it sound so easy, Maggie. And I do need to find a husband. But I'm not so sure that Farrencourt is the man for me. He frightens me."

Maggie's eyes narrowed. "'E don't seem like the kind o' man what would take a strap to you."

"Heavens, no! It's not that. He just . . . just scares me."

Maggie grinned. "Aye. So that's it, is it? Well, miss, there's scared and there's scared. One way is good, the other's bad."

"I don't know what you mean."

"You know, all right. Young ladies like you 'ave just been brought up to 'ide it. You ain't scared 'e'll beat you. You're scared 'e just might make you feel so good you'll forget 'ow to act like a lady."

Amy blushed. "Be still, Maggie. You shouldn't talk like that. Lady Udora would be outraged."

"You think she don't know about such things? 'Er what's been married five times and still 'avin' a go at it like she was twenty instead o' thirty?"

Amy's voice was frigid. "Some things are just not proper for ladies to talk about."

"Then I thank the Lord I ain't no lady. You just wait. You keep matchin' eyes with Lord Farrencourt, Miss Amethyst, and you won't be talkin'. You'll be doin'! Aye, then see what 'er ladyship 'as to say about that."

Maggie, having bent over to pick up the basin she had placed at Amy's feet, looked up in time to see Amy blush. "Well, miss, seeing as 'ow your colour's come back, you won't be needin' this. I'll just walk you down to the dinin' 'all."

"Thank you, no. Just go along to your friends. I'll stay in my room for a while."

Maggie scrutinized her face. "You wouldn't be running off to meet Lord Dunholm, after all, now would you?"

"Don't be a ninnyhammer. Why would I do that?"

Maggie grinned. "Aye. Now you're beginnin' to talk sense."

Amy threw a pillow that missed Maggie by a hair's breadth before she ducked through the doorway and closed the door behind her.

But Maggie's words stayed with Amy. Why had Dunholm left the dining-room? He hadn't looked ill. To meet Lily? No. Even if he had asked her to, Lily would not dare defy convention by following him. Amy wandered to the window. There was only one likelihood. He had gone to the stable to enquire after his horse, which had thrown a shoe. Nothing, not even a woman, meant more to Dunholm than a good horse. She felt a rush of pity for Lily. How painful it must be to be in love with a man like Dunholm.

Instead of waiting for Sally to return from chaperoning Topaz, Amy undressed herself and went to bed. The time alone would give her the opportunity to think about what she needed to do. It wasn't as if Dunholm and Farrencourt were the only suitable matches. There was Lord Effington, Lord Petrie, Lord Ragsby, and even Lieutenant Davenport, to name a few of the most eligible men. Men who still claimed their own hair and teeth. Even so, she discounted each of them as unappealing for one reason or another.

Of course, there was the the Earl of Pinkham. He was back on the market after the death of his wife nearly two years ago. But his two children would take some getting used to. Lady Udora might approve of him. He had money as well as a title . . . but it was said that he fancied older women.

Amy sighed. It was all so hopeless. If she were to be allowed to keep baby Wills, she might be well advised to accept the first offer that came along. But first she had to make it known that she was not only available, but willing. *Flirt,* she decided. That's what I'll do. By this time tomorrow I'll surely catch the the nod from at least one acceptable man.

MORNING CAME. Farrencourt paced the long veranda that bordered on the acclaimed gardens of Diamond Hill. Dunholm, devil take the man, had as yet refused to make a firm offer for Lily's hand. For some obscure reason, he appeared to still hold out the hope that the Thackery chit would fall under his dubious charms.

And where were they this morning? Were they together? The hour was growing late, even taking into consideration the informality of breakfast at a country house. Emerald and Topaz had long since finished their repast and searched out their friends. Were it not for the fact that he might appear interested in their sister, he would have questioned them as to her whereabouts. Instead, he was left cooling his heels like some jilted lover.

He swore softly and turned towards the French doors just in time to see Amethyst stroll into the breakfast hall on the arm of Lord Effington. She was smiling up into his face like a lap-dog drooling after a bone. And Effington was falling all over himself to please her. Fool! Didn't he know that she would never stoop so low as to accept his bid, even should he be stupid enough to offer for her?

Farrencourt strode through the door and intercepted them as they approached the sideboard. "Rather late, aren't you? You've missed the kippers, I'm afraid. Everyone else finished breakfast hours ago."

Effington grinned. "We went for an early stroll through the grounds. Jolly good it was, too."

Farrencourt regarded Amy with an icy stare. "And did *you* find it jolly good, Miss Thackery?"

"It was…until now, that is." Her voice was as cold as his relentless stare. Then she turned her back on him and began to fill her plate.

Farrencourt forced a smile. "Indeed? I assume you refer to the fact that the breakfast hall is deserted.

Never fear. Although I breakfasted earlier, it will be my pleasure to join the two of you for a cup of chocolate."

"You assume too much, sir!" she said coldly.

Effington looked flustered. "See here, old man, it's good of you, but don't let us detain you."

"Not at all. I would be remiss as a gentleman if I were to walk away now. May I serve the chocolate?"

Amy gave Farrencourt a scathing look and took her modestly filled plate to the table. He seated her and bowed, taking a chair next to her. On the far side of the room Sally was only mildly watchful as she gossiped with a servant girl who was spreading fresh linen on another table. Effington, his plate filled to overflowing, took a chair on Amy's left.

Farrencourt sipped his chocolate. "It's too bad about Lily," he said. "I know you had your heart set on offering for her, Effington."

Effington nearly choked on a boiled potato.

"I'm sure you've heard that my sister is going to marry Lord Dunholm." Once word got round, Dunholm would have to come up to scratch.

Effington let the plum jam drop from his knife onto the tablecloth. "Poor girl. It won't be easy for her, the scandal and all, and then to be shackled to Dunholm. Egads! I say egads!"

Amy looked up at Farrencourt from under lowered lashes. "How true. Only a man of no principles would take advantage of a woman alone."

Farrencourt started to look away, then jerked his head back to study her face. His own face turned faintly pink.

Effington wiped his mouth on his napkin. "Lily was quite taken with me at one time, but I don't have to tell you, Miss Thackery. You are her closest confidante."

Amy sent Farrencourt a swift look, then cooed up at her companion, "To be sure, Lily *was* taken with you, Lord Effington. How could any woman *not* be attracted to you?"

He suddenly stopped chewing and smiled widely, exposing a row of plum-coloured teeth. "Good of you to mention that, dear girl."

Farrencourt's face turned dark red. "You've dropped a bit of jam on your ascot, Effington. I suggest you have it seen to before the stain sets. It would be unfortunate to ruin such an expensive bit of linen."

"Right-o. If you'll excuse me for a minute?" He inclined his head and pushed back from the table.

Farrencourt swivelled to face Amy, hooking one arm over the back of his chair. "Tell me, Miss Thackery. Is Effington to be your next conquest?"

She tossed her head. "If he is it is no concern of yours, my lord. Effington is but one of many close friends. In point of fact, I have consented to go riding in a little while with the Earl of Pinkham. After that I shall join Ragsby in a game of darts on the east lawn."

"Pinkham? Good lord, the man is three times your age! And he has two children who have been sent down from some of the best boarding schools in England. Surely you can't be thinking of him as a suitor."

"He is well respected and quite able to take care of me, if I should decide on him."

Farrencourt regarded her with smouldering eyes. "Take care of you financially, yes, but in other ways? I think not."

Amy blushed. "You know nothing about him. And I would appreciate it if you would keep your opinions to yourself."

"Why this sudden hurry to make an alliance? This is, after all, your first Season. With your obvious and . . . not so obvious advantages, you have no need to fear being left on the shelf." Silent for a minute or two, he stroked his chin. "I cannot believe that you are provoked because Lily has stolen Dunholm from you. You don't love him now, and I can't persuade myself that you ever did have feelings for him."

"How do you know that?"

"I know. Take my word for it. I am not without a modicum of experience where females are concerned. You could not have responded to my kiss with such ardour if you were enamoured of Dunholm."

Amy regarded him with defiance. "For your information, sir, responding to your kiss was simply my way of getting you to unhand me . . . as you did, if you recall."

"Only to avoid losing control." He raised an eyebrow. "My control as well as yours, if you are honest enough to admit it."

"Don't flatter yourself, my lord." Her voice faded with the obvious subterfuge, but she lifted her chin and faced him squarely. "And were you not being overly presumptuous in announcing to Effington that Dunholm and Lily would marry? If he had offered for her, she would have told me so."

Farrencourt's gaze hardened. "If Dunholm knows what's good for him, he'll offer for her." He smiled abruptly, and this time the smile reached his eyes. "I trust, Miss Thackery, that inasmuch as you have no special feeling for Dunholm, you will allow my sister this small triumph."

The truth struck Amy like a sudden blow to the head. "So that's it! I was puzzled over your recent close attention to my social life. You have been afraid that I would succumb to Dunholm's overtures before Lily had a chance to gain his affections. That is why you've managed to confront me round every bush and corner."

He saw anger written on her face, and he hastened to mollify her. "If it seems that way to you, I must offer my apologies. Surely you can understand my need to protect Lily."

"Protect, yes, but you are too condescending towards her. Given a chance, Lily could take care of herself. She is not unattractive." Amy pushed her chair away from the table. "But as far as Dunholm is concerned, I lay no claim to him. Lily is welcome to him."

"Do you mean that?"

"I do. So if you will excuse me, my lord, you no longer have a need to cast yourself in my shadow."

Before Farrencourt could respond, Amy dropped a token curtsy and strode away, her skirts swirling behind her. He stood looking after her for several minutes. Never had he seen her looking so regal. He had won the prize he had worked so hard to gain for Lily's sake, so why did he feel as if he had come up the loser? A sound made him turn quickly. But it was only Sally, wondering how her mistress had contrived to disappear so quickly.

LATER THAT DAY Udora knocked at the door of the suite assigned to the Thackery girls and their abigails. Maggie's eyes flashed.

"You've come just in time, my lady. Another minute and it would 'ave been me what's took French leave."

"What's the trouble? The girls should have been ready to go downstairs for the ball."

"Look at 'er!" Maggie said, pointing the curling tongs at Topaz's hair. "All my work was for nothin', 'er and 'er traipsin' through the woods."

Udora frowned. "It does look a fright, doesn't it? But if anyone can fix it, you can, Maggie. Why else would I have put up with you for all these years?" She gave Maggie a quick hug.

Maggie muttered something unrepeatable but applied the hairbrush and comb with an acceptable measure of enthusiasm. Udora turned to Emerald, who was dressed and waiting. The book she was reading held her complete attention until Udora squeezed her shoulder.

"You look lovely, Em. Didn't I promise that the slippers would be a perfect match for the embroidered ferns at the hem of your gown? But do try to keep your spectacles in place."

Udora then turned to Amy, who sat slouched on a settee. "And why are you looking so Friday-faced, young lady? You are sure to be one of the three prettiest ladies at the ball."

"I miss my baby," Amy said with a pout. "And Dunholm is all but betrothed to my best friend."

Udora looked shocked. "Marry Lily? But I thought he was going to offer for *you*. What a tragedy. I'm so sorry, my dear."

Amy shrugged. "It doesn't matter, really. To be truthful, I can scarcely abide the man. But I do so need to find a father for my baby."

Udora shrieked. "Hush! Not another word. These walls are tissue-thin. If once more I hear you refer to that child as your own, I shall personally see that he is removed from our house immediately."

Her tone softened. "My dear Amy, you are little more than a child yourself. Until you can take care of your own needs you simply cannot afford to think about anyone else." She pressed a kiss against Amy's cheek. "I understand and admire your protective instincts, but you must begin to think more clearly."

Amy pulled away. "I don't think you *can* understand. You never wanted children. You only took us because Mummy and Daddy died and you had no choice."

There was a dead silence in the room. Emerald looked up from her book for the first time and stared with her mouth open. Maggie paused, hairbrush in mid-air. Topaz looked wide-eyed. As for Udora, her face had gone white, and the pain in her eyes was almost tangible.

Amy's hands flew to her mouth. "I...I'm so sorry, my lady. I shouldn't have said that."

Udora drew herself up straight. "If that is what you feel in your heart, my dear, then you have no need to apologize. You have every right to say it." Before anyone could recover, Udora stood and left the room.

"That was unpardonable!" Topaz said, giving Amy her most disgusted look.

Emerald considered the two girls over the top of her spectacles. "And extremely inconsiderate." She closed the book, marking her place with a ribbon. "But it isn't true, you know. Lady Udora may have been reluctant to *become* our guardian, but she has come to love us as much as any mother could do. We all know that."

Maggie snorted. "Aye, and if you don't, then you've got a brain the size of a pea. Look at you. Where would you be now if she 'adn't taken you under 'er wing?"

Amy wailed, "I'm sorry. I know I was wrong. I didn't mean it. Truly, I didn't."

"It ain't us what needs an apology." Maggie's voice was grim. "You'd best go find 'er before she 'as a chance to brood over it."

"Yes, I'll go to her at once." Amy jumped up from the settee, only to stumble over the hem of her gown.

"'Ere now, 'ave a care. I'll not be mendin' your dress this close to time for the ball. And stop that snifflin'. Your eyes look like two red cherries what's been run over by a dogcart," Maggie said, handing her a lace-edged square of linen.

LADY UDORA HAD NOT gone to her room as Amy had suspected. Peggy, her wardrobe servant, had not seen her for more than an hour. That meant that Udora must have gone to search out Bently. She always turned to her husband in times of trouble. Lord Kes-

terson would surely be at the stables making certain
that his horses were bedded down for the night.

Taking care to avoid the other house guests who
were beginning to gather for the evening's entertainment, Amy ran down the veranda steps, through the
herb garden, past the yew hedge, and abruptly collided with a solid body.

"Farrencourt!" she gasped.

He held her at arm's length. "I say now. What's
this? Tears? Has someone made you cry?" The tenderness in his voice was unmistakable. And it was
Amy's complete undoing.

CHAPTER SEVEN

FARRENCOURT PULLED her against his chest and she sobbed until there were no tears left to cry. He spoke soothingly, stroking her hair and kneading the tense muscles in her back. "It's going to be all right, Miss Thackery. Tell me what's wrong so that I can fix it." He was surprised at his own words until he thought about it and realized that it felt wonderful to be taking care of her. She was so small in his arms, so vulnerable. A sudden thought struck him and he felt his gut tighten.

"Has someone hurt you? What has Dunholm done to you?"

"No, no. I haven't seen Dunholm. I did it to myself. I said something awful to Lady Udora, and now I don't know what to do. I can't even find her."

"Then I'll help you look for her. I saw her not five minutes ago at the stables with Lord Kesterson." He continued to hold her in a comforting embrace from which Amy was reluctant to break away. It felt wonderful to be held close in the protection of his arms.

"Th-thank you." She sniffled.

"For what, little one?"

"For not telling me that it was just a silly misunderstanding."

"Is that all?" He laughed, and she felt the laughter rumble through his chest. "My dear girl, words can pierce the heart more easily than a sword. The fact that you have come to realize it simply means that you are growing up."

"I don't think I like it much."

He held her at arm's length. "Nevertheless, it becomes you. The truth is I never quite realized how beautiful you really are. You look radiant in your ball gown."

"Do you truly mean it?"

The look in his eyes soothed the agitation of her nerves. "I truly do." He chuckled. "I have to admit that in the past I have been known to dissemble when complimenting a woman on her appearance, but on my oath, this time every word I speak is the truth."

She sensed that he wanted to kiss her, to hold her close once more, but they had already gone far beyond the bounds of acceptable behaviour. It took all of her will-power to put an end to the moment. "Thank you, Lord Farrencourt, but please, I must find Lady Udora without delay."

He released her and bowed. "To be sure. If I may?" He offered her his arm and directed her towards the stable where he had last seen the Kestersons.

Lady Udora, appearing wan and shaken, turned to look when Farrencourt opened the stable door. "Bently," she whispered, clutching Lord Kesterson's arm.

"Steady on, my dear." He murmured just loud enough that Amy could hear him speak. She was only dimly aware of the rich aroma of fresh straw and the restless movement of sleekly groomed horses bedded down for the night in their separate stalls. Despite the inappropriateness of the setting, Lady Udora looked strangely at home in her gown of Chinese jade silk and her diamond-and-pearl necklace. Amy stopped, unable to speak; then Udora held out her arms and Amy rushed into them.

"I'm so sorry, my lady. I didn't mean what I said. I truly didn't. How can you ever forgive me?"

"Hush. It's all right. I understand perfectly. Let's say no more about it." Udora held Amy and rocked her in her arms. It occurred to Udora that Amy was without chaperon. So unwise, considering Farrencourt's reputation, but one look at his face drove away all her apprehension. Given a second look, one might perceive that he was quite taken with the girl. Odd that a man of his standing would develop a *tendre* for an unsophisticated country girl. And yet when he gazed at Amy, something in his eyes spoke of a gentleness that shook Udora's composure. Could it be possible? she wondered. No. Surely not. Some things were too much to hope for.

Udora straightened the filmy lace that adorned the top of Amy's bodice. "Go back to the house now and splash cold water on your face. You mustn't be late for the ball."

"Aren't you coming, too?"

Bently intervened. "Her ladyship and I will be along in a moment, my dear." He turned towards Farrencourt. "I trust that you will be so good as to see that she returns safely to the house?"

"Of course, Lord Kesterson. You have my word on it."

THEY DIDN'T GO unnoticed. When Amy and Farrencourt entered the ballroom, along with Sally acting as
her chaperon, they triggered comments that swept
around the room like a summer breeze. If Amy's eyes
held a trace of recent tears, it only added to her look
of innocence. Sally had brushed her hair and wound
it into a Grecian knot that ended in a cascade of curls
over her shoulder.

Farrencourt was well aware of the attention they
were receiving. He was used to attention: dowagers
fawning over him, contriving to gain a bid for their
daughters; bolder débutantes flirting outrageously in
the hope that one of them might be chosen to become
the next Viscountess Farrencourt.

But this time it was different. There was a certain
reserve in their demeanour, a watchfulness. It was almost as if they knew he had made a choice. *How pre-
posterous,* he thought. *I have no intention of tying
myself down for another five years at the very least.*
And yet...and yet... He looked down at Amy. There
was something seductive in this girl's innocence. He
vowed to remember to move slowly lest he lose himself completely to this bewitching young woman.

Amy felt a surge of excitement flow through her.
She felt like a queen when she entered the ballroom
with Farrencourt at her side, so tall and handsome in
his knee breeches and white tailcoat. The diamond-
and-ruby stickpin, a gift from Queen Elizabeth to the
first Viscount Farrencourt, sparkled in the reflected
light from the crystal chandeliers.

Her own gown, with its flower-embroidered hem
and bodice, made her look at least two years older, she
decided. Quite old enough to be on the arm of one of

the Season's most eligible bachelors. They paid their respects to their host and hostess, and when the music began again, Farrencourt ushered her onto the dance floor.

The dance was a complicated quadrille, made popular by Lady Jersey, who had discovered the square dance on a visit to France. The Thackery girls had learned the five movements from their dance master when they first arrived at the London house, but now it was all Amy could do to concentrate on the quick changes of tempo. She wasn't fond of switching partners. It was comforting when she once again had Farrencourt's hand in hers. Then the dance was over and Farrencourt returned Amy to Lady Udora's side and made his bow.

"May I pay my respects, my lady, and ask your permission to dance again with Miss Thackery? I see by the dance card that there is to be a waltz later this evening."

Udora looked surprised. "So there is. And you would like Amethyst to reserve the waltz for you?"

"I would be most grateful."

Udora raised an eyebrow at Amy, who turned fetchingly pink. "And do you agree?"

"Yes. I think I would like that."

"Very well. So be it."

Farrencourt inclined his head. "My sincere appreciation, madam."

Amy was disappointed that he did not remain to converse with her, but truth be told, it would have been impossible. She was surrounded by admirers, and in no time her dance card was filled. Once again she noticed that Farrencourt had left the ballroom. She was beginning to feel a sense of smug satisfaction that once again he chose to dance with no one but her. Then suddenly in the middle of a reel, she was handed to him. They linked arms briefly, turning in time to the music.

"Hello again, Miss Thackery," he said, with a self-satisfied grin.

She was too stunned to reply before she was handed off to the next man in line. When they reached their original partners, Amy leaned forward to get a better look.

Penelope Pendergast! She nearly spit out the name aloud. Farrencourt was dancing with *her!* Of all the Season's débutantes, she was the richest and most envied by the other girls. Not for her personality, which, even when being generous, Amy considered poisonous, but for her ability to bewitch men. For around men, Penelope was unfailingly sweet and demure.

And now Miss Pendergast was clutching Farrencourt's arm in a grip that seemed likely to leave a permanent mark. What could he possibly see in her beyond pale green eyes, dimpled cheeks and a Cupid's-bow mouth?

Devil take them both, Amy thought, and promptly stumbled over her elderly partner's foot. "Oh! I'm so sorry, Lord Dumphrey."

"Harrumph. I'm sure it was my fault, my dear. Never was much of a dancer, anyway. Perhaps we might be advised to stroll to the conservatory. I'm told the Sutherlands have a prized collection of ferns."

"If you prefer," Amy said, with some misgivings. Was it better to leave and simply imagine what Farrencourt was doing, or stay and witness his flirtation?

Admittedly, he had been most circumspect in her presence, but he *did* have a reputation. She could not bring herself to watch them.

Amy sighed. "Indeed, I've simply been dying to see their collection of ferns." She nodded to Sally, who joined them as they left the room.

Amy accepted Dumphrey's arm as they strolled the length of the gallery, past gloomy paintings of ancestors long dead and of dark and misty landscapes. A corridor led to the veranda, which extended at one end to encompass a glass-enclosed conservatory. It was lighted now by torches set at wide intervals to enhance the effect of light and shadow.

Sally was enthralled. "Would you look at that, now. Wood violets growing right there in the moss under the fern. And lily-o'-the valley, too, and 'tis nearly summer." She buried her face in the sweet fragrance.

Dumphrey drew Amy towards a miniature grotto carved into the trunk of a dead tree. "I'm told these are some of the Sutherlands' most valued ferns. This one, with the fine spider-web fronds, comes from Peru. And that one with the pale green rib against the bold stripe was brought back from the Indies by the captain of the *Lisa Marie*."

Amy feigned interest, although her thoughts were back in the ballroom. Suddenly their attention was drawn to the top of the glass enclosure. A bird that had been trapped inside when the windows were closed for the night was beating its wings against the glass in a vain effort to escape.

"Oh!" Amy cried. "We must do something. It will surely die of exhaustion."

Dumphrey gave her a dry look. "Well, it's only a bird. Not even big enough to qualify for game, though if truth be told, I've shot many a lark that my cook turned into a succulent feast. Harrumph! Quite good they are with a glass of fine port to wash 'em down."

"Ooh, 'e shouldn'a said that," Sally muttered. "Not to Miss Amy, 'e shouldn't."

Amy glared at him. "A bird is a living creature, sir. We must do our best to see that it is set free."

"Ah, you've a soft heart, Miss Thackery, but like a woman, you've no sense for the practical. Let it be, miss. Suffice it to say, there is nothing we can do without soiling our hands."

The bird, having found a precarious perch, hung nearly upside down on a thin ledge. Amy could sense its terror.

"Come along, then, Miss Thackery. I'll fetch you a glass of syllabub."

Amy muttered a scathing oath which had Udora heard it, would have had her sending Amy to her room. She grabbed her skirt and ran to get a ladder that was propped against a wooden work table. "Help me with this, Sally."

"Yes, miss, but I'll not be climbin' it if that's wot you 'ave in mind. Me, I'm scared o' heights, I am."

"I'll do it myself. Just help me move it into place."

"'Old on. Maybe I'd best call someone."

"There's no time. The bird could be dead by then."

Dumphrey stood by red-faced. "See here now. You can't be serious."

"Oh, but I am." Between them, the two women managed to ease the tall ladder into place.

Sally stood back to look at it. "I dunno, miss. It looks right rickety. See there? It don't even sit straight."

"It will have to do." Amy tucked her skirt between her legs and began to climb upwards when she noticed that Dumphrey had moved to the base of the ladder. She glared at him. "I'll thank you to step away, sir."

He frowned. "Do be careful. I'll never hear the last of this if you should fall."

Sally snorted. "Aye, and it might not be too good for 'er, either."

Amy was at the top of the ladder. The bird was scarcely an inch beyond her fingertips but she could stretch no farther. She reached for the window and tried to push it open, but it was connected to an iron bar of some sort and it refused to budge.

"It's no use, girl. Do come down from there," Dumphrey said in a querulous voice.

At that moment there was a splintering sound. Amy let out a shriek as the rung on which she was standing broke and sent her sliding down to the next rung. Unfortunately, when she slipped, her skirt had ballooned upwards, catching itself on a nail, thereby preventing her from moving either up or down the ladder. Hearing someone enter the conservatory, she turned to look sideways.

"Ladies. Your lordship. May I ask what is going on here?"

Amy looked down to see Lord Farrencourt looking up at her with an amused if puzzled expression. She was furious with him for catching her at a disadvantage. "This doesn't concern you, Lord Farrencourt. Please be good enough to leave us."

"I regret that I cannot do that, Miss Thackery. I have come to remind you of our dance. And—" he made a gesture with his hands "—no gentleman would walk away under these curious circumstances."

Dumphrey was fidgeting. "You must come down, Miss Thackery. I don't wish to be the butt of a scandal at your expense. It would be politically unwise for me at the present time."

"Then do feel free to leave, my lord." Amy's tone was icy. "We have quite finished our dance."

"If you insist."

"I most certainly do."

Sally made a deprecating gesture. "Look at 'im go, would you. Like a fox'ound wi' 'is tail between 'is legs."

Farrencourt stood for a moment, feet spread, then turned and walked towards the far wall of the conservatory.

Amy looked aghast. "Why! The very nerve of him! He's no gentleman, after all." She would have said more but a grating sound caused her to look upward and she was hit in the face by a blast of cold air. With a flutter of wings the bird scrambled through the open window and disappeared into the night sky.

"Now, 'ow did 'e do that?" Sally exclaimed in astonishment.

"It was nothing," Lord Farrencourt said. "There is a rod that controls the lever that opens the high windows for ventilation during the heat of the day. I merely cranked it open." He grinned up at Amy. "You may come down now, Miss Thackery."

"N-not just yet, thank you."

"You're stuck, aren't you?"

"Certainly not. I *like* ladders. I am simply enjoying the view. Do go away."

His grin widened. "Not just yet, thank you," he said, resting his shoe on the bottom rung. "I like ladders. And I enjoy the view from down here."

She sputtered and drew her skirts more closely between her legs. "You are truly despicable, Lord Farrencourt."

"So I've been told. In fact, I do believe it was you who told me. Wasn't it on the occasion of our chance meeting in the maze garden just after nine o'clock?"

"I've no idea what you are talking about."

"Then I'll refresh your memory. You came alone, dressed in a flowing..."

"Oh, do be still. Someone might get the mistaken impression that it was an assignation."

Farrencourt straightened. "Sally, I think it might be wise if you were to lock the door. We wouldn't want someone to wander into the conservatory and start asking questions." He looked up at Amy. "Would you like a glass of punch while you enjoy the view? Or a plate of cheese and fruit?"

"No, thank you." She shifted her weight from one foot to the other. The rungs were narrow and her dancing slippers were of little protection.

Farrencourt adjusted his coat-tails and smoothed his starcher. "I trust that you expect to come down before our dance begins."

"I haven't decided."

"How uncivil of you. I distinctly recall writing my name on your dance card."

"I'm sure Miss Pendergast would be only too pleased to take my place."

"I have no doubt of that."

"Cad. Unspeakable cad!"

"Come now, Miss Thackery. Name-calling doesn't become you." His voice softened. "Whether you admit it or not, we both know that no one could ever take your place."

Amy gasped in surprise, then looked quickly down at him to judge his meaning. At that moment the ladder tilted dangerously. Farrencourt steadied it with his foot.

"Hold on, Miss Thackery. I'm coming up for you."

"Don't you dare. I'll never forgive you."

"You have little choice in the matter, since it appears that you can climb neither up nor down." He hesitated for an instant. "Of course, you could disrobe and leave your gown behind. The ladder is none too strong. Our combined weight might be too great. Perhaps disrobing would be the best solution."

"Don't hold your breath waiting, sir!"

"Then I must come after you." Before she could protest further, he had mounted the ladder. Sally watched, hands pressed tightly against her cheeks.

"Oh, do be careful, my lord. The ladder is rickety, indeed."

"You'll have to turn towards me if you can, Miss Thackery." She did so. The next thing she knew, his hands were around her waist and he was lifting her higher.

"Y-you shouldn't be doing this."

"Be still and unhook your gown from the nail when I lift you high enough."

There was nothing to do but obey him. And then somehow, her skirt was free and her arms had found their way about his neck. It seemed the logical thing to do, for safety's sake, of course.

"There now," he said. "I've got you." He studied her face. "And I agree that the view from up here is excellent. Would you care to remain awhile longer?"

"I've seen quite enough, thank you."

With one arm he held her against him while he negotiated a slow descent, holding on with his free hand. Just before they reached the bottom he called down to Sally. "I think it might be wise if you went in search of a basin of water. Miss Thackery will need to wash her hands before we return to the ballroom."

"Yes, my lord. But I 'spects I'll 'ave to go to the kitchen."

"Yes, I rather imagine so."

"You'll be all right, miss?"

All Amy could do was nod. She knew she was not all right, nor would she ever again be quite the same.

She was still cradled against him when his feet touched the floor. Music from the ballroom drifted faintly through the window high at the top of the conservatory. She was floating. Entranced. It was a moment breathlessly suspended in time. But the moment had to end. She spoke with considerable effort. "You may put me down now, Lord Farrencourt." She was shocked to realize that she really didn't want him to put her down. It was quite pleasant to be held securely in the circle of his arms. To feel the flutter of his breath in her hair, to feel the thud of his heartbeat, fast and solid against her own. He looked down at the same moment she looked up at him, and their gaze met in an exchange of newly discovered passion.

Her arms were still about his neck. "I'm afraid you will have to release me if I'm to put you down, Miss Thackery."

She let go. Then slowly, reluctantly, he allowed her to slide down the length of him until she was standing erect. Her body remembered every inch of him: broad shoulders, hard chest, trim waist, muscled thighs. His voice was husky as his hands brushed down to encircle her waist. "There now. Safe as a kitten on a rug."

The music had ended, marking a period of rest for the musicians. But Amy felt an inner music that seemed to go on and on. "Strange," she murmured. "I don't feel very safe now that I'm standing here." She placed one finger alongside her cheek. "You did that deliberately, didn't you, Lord Farrencourt?"

"May I ask to what you refer?"

Her eyes challenged him. "Why, your sending Sally all the way down to the kitchen, of course. What else could I possibly have meant?"

He swore softly. "Stop looking at me like that or I warrant you'll be left without any doubt of my intentions."

She looked up at him with an expression that belied her innocent tone of voice. "I don't know what you mean, my lord."

"You know, all right. Don't play games with me, little girl."

"And haven't you been playing games with me all along? Among other things, trying to keep me from seeing too much of Lord Dunholm."

"That was different. I had no choice in the matter."

"Ah, yes. You wanted Lily to have him."

He fastened his gaze on hers. "Is that so reprehensible? Lily had no one. You can have anyone you choose."

"Anyone?" Amy's breath caught. "And what if I choose you?"

Beads of sweat broke out on his forehead. "Innocent you may be, my sweet, but I suspect you are far too wise to choose me as a suitor. How many times have you reminded me of my unsavoury reputation?"

"You haven't answered my question, sir."

"Nor do I intend to." He cleared his throat and stepped back. Another moment and he would have been on his knees begging to marry her. "Someone is coming. I think perhaps we should return to the ballroom before the musicians reappear and the waltz begins."

Someone *was* coming, but it was only Sally fetching the wash-basin. Farrencourt strode a discreet distance away while Amy repaired the insignificant damage to her toilette. When she finished she called to him and he offered his arm to escort her back to the ballroom.

From the flurry of whispers that sped across the room as they entered, it appeared that their absence had been duly noted. Udora frowned but appeared to relax when she saw that Sally accompanied them. Amy felt the heat rise in her face. She had done nothing wrong. Perhaps it was only her imagination that people were talking about them. Or perhaps it was her anticipation of the next dance: a waltz.

She wished her heart would stop thudding. This wasn't the first time she had danced the waltz, but a waltz wasn't just any dance. There was touching. An intimacy so great that when at Almack's, permission from a patroness was required before a respectable couple could begin the dance. Farrencourt, despite his penchant for flouting the rules, had asked permission from Lady Udora. Ordinarily Amy would have been comfortable at the thought of dancing with him, but something had changed. It was a heady sensation, one that left her weak-kneed and sent her senses reeling.

"You're trembling, Miss Thackery. Surely you can't be cold. Not with this crush of people."

"It must be your imagination, sir. I was merely waving to Lady Udora. I believe she wishes to speak to me."

He sighed. "Very well, but we must hurry. The musicians are returning to the stand."

She took his arm, and he led her through the crowd to the other side of the room where the Kestersons were seated with Lady Breckenridge. Udora reached for Amy's hand.

"Where were you, my dear? You were gone ever so long. Are you all right? You look a bit flushed."

"We were, er . . . looking at Lord Caulfield's collection of ferns." Seeing Udora's raised eyebrows, Amy hastened to add that Sally had been with them. Before Udora had a chance to question her further, the music began and Farrencourt begged that they be excused.

He swept Amy into his arms and immediately they were caught up in the sensuous flow of music from a dozen violins.

His hand is warm against my waist, she thought. *It's almost as if there is nothing between it and my skin. I wonder what it would be like if...* She looked up into the intensity of his gaze and this time she really did tremble.

He noted with increasing excitement that her eyes had darkened. *I can feel the heat of her body where my hand holds her waist,* he thought. *It's almost as if I'm touching her skin. I wonder what it would be like to...* Realization brought such a sudden rush of passion that he nearly stumbled. *Great heavens! I do believe I've fallen in love with this girl!* In his heart he had known it all along, but had fought against his feelings. Now, all of a sudden, it seemed so right.

He pulled her as close as he dared and whispered, "I can't let you go, Amy. I intend to ask the Kestersons for permission to court you."

She was too stunned to respond. He laughed, and to her it sounded like a chorus of angels. "Well, my girl, haven't you anything to say? I hope the idea is not altogether repugnant to you."

She looked up at him with adoring eyes. "Not altogether, my lord."

"Excellent!" he said, and spun her round in a delirious turn that of necessity brought them closer together. His cheek brushed hers for the briefest instant, and then he settled her back against his arm with acceptable decorum. Her eyes sparkled, causing his stomach to painfully contract. How had he not seen it from the beginning? She was young, yes, but she was also bewitching. She was nearly everything he had been searching for and now...now he wanted her to be his...forever.

The music ended all too soon. He felt more than a little light-headed as he stroked her hand where it rested on his arm. He wanted to dance with her again, but this was no time to create a scandal.

He met her gaze. "Although I would like to take you away from here, I think it would be best if I returned you to the Kestersons. With your permission, I'll speak with his lordship tomorrow."

"Yes. If you wish."

They were proceeding across the dance floor when Penelope Pendergast floated by on the arm of Lord Dumphrey. She winked at Farrencourt. "Ah, there you are at last. Don't forget...the maze garden at nine. That is, if you can avoid falling off a ladder before then." She was gone before her laughter had a chance to fade away.

CHAPTER EIGHT

AMY STARED after Penelope until she was out of sight. When she turned to Farrencourt, her face mirrored her disbelief. "How could you, Farrencourt? Pretending to offer for me when all the time you have been laughing behind my back with Miss Pendergast." Tears spilled down her cheeks. "I can't bear it. I simply cannot," she said as she pushed away from him, then ran across the dance floor to Udora's side.

"I want to go home, my lady. Tonight."

"What? What is this? Only a few moments ago you were in transports and now . . . Are you ill?"

"No. I am simply angry."

Topaz, standing off to one side, came close. "Be careful, Lady Udora. Amy has that look on her face. She could faint at any moment."

"Oh my, do you think so?"

"Don't be ridiculous," Amy said. "I am not going to faint."

Topaz continued as if she hadn't heard. "She does, sometimes. Mummy used to say it was her weak constitution. I always thought she did it to get attention."

"Well, she has mine. Amy, dear, what is it? Has Farrencourt made unwanted advances?"

Amy shook her head. "I just want to go home." Without another word, she ran from the room, barely avoiding a collision with other guests, and dashed up the stairs.

Seeing that Farrencourt was making his way towards her, Udora motioned for Topaz and Sally to go after Amy while she remained behind to question Farrencourt.

He looked unsettled. "I see an explanation is in order, Lady Udora. I don't want you to think that I, in any way, insulted Miss Thackery. It was just a simple misunderstanding. One I sincerely regret." He leaned forward. "I would like to make amends. What did she tell you, if I may be so bold?"

"She said very little, but she was extremely overwrought." Udora snapped her fan shut. "As to your making amends, I am sure you will have an opportunity later, but first I must go to Amy." She rose. "If you will excuse me?"

"I, too, must speak with her as soon as possible. Perhaps I could accompany you to her suite?"

Udora's response was chilly. "I think not, Lord Farrencourt. I will send a maid for you if you are wanted."

He had to be satisfied with that, but he vowed that this was not the end. He had just found Amy and he was not about to let her get away from him.

THEY LEFT DIAMOND HILL early the next day without giving Farrencourt the opportunity to defend himself. Udora, upon considering the three days spent at Diamond Hill, could only conclude that it had been a disappointing holiday. Emerald had spent most of her time perusing the library or talking with Bently and his friends about local and international politics. The men had found it amusing that a young snip of a girl fresh off the farm was able to discuss the latest trade agreements with such understanding. Udora was not amused. Not one of the men was suitable marriage material.

As for Topaz, she, along with Maggie, had disappeared all too frequently for Udora's peace of mind. Of course, they always had an explanation for their absence, but Udora suspected that Topaz was seeing some young man of less than acceptable virtue. It simply could not be tolerated.

As well, Udora worried about Amy's state of mind all during the interminably long drive back to London. It was only as they neared Kesterson House that Amy seemed to come alive. Then the moment the carriage drew to a halt on the cobblestone driveway, Amy jumped down from the carriage without so much as acknowledging the footman who offered to assist her. Racing up the wide entrance steps she nearly collided with the butler.

"Good afternoon, McMasters," she said, handing him her cape and bonnet.

"Welcome home, Miss Thackery. You look a bit out of breath if I may be so bold."

"It's only because I can't wait to see my baby. Where is William? Is he in the nursery?"

"Oh, I'm afraid you're too late, Miss Thackery. The baby's not here."

"You mean he's gone? He's truly not here?"

"That I do, miss." He turned to look at the pedestal clock at the end of the hallway. "She took him away not thirty minutes ago."

Suddenly Amy's head felt as it were floating away from her body.

By this time Udora, Bently and the girls had arrived at the door. Udora took one look at Amy's face and grasped her arm.

"What is it? What's happened, Amy?"

"It's the baby. McMasters says that Wills is gone."

"Gone? Whatever do you mean?"

McMasters looked wary. "It's his nurse, madam. Miss Finkley took the child for a drive in the park. I hope it was not presumptuous of me to permit it."

Amy laughed shakily and Udora patted her back. "No, McMasters. It's quite all right."

Amy let out a long breath of air. "It's just that I've been worried about him. Is he all right?"

"Oh, yes, indeed, miss. He's settled down quite nicely."

Udora brushed Amy's hair away from her face. "You mustn't allow yourself to become so attached to him, Amy. The day will come when you must give him up."

"I won't listen to this!" Amy cried. Before anyone could stop her, she ran up the stairs in the direction of the nursery.

Udora looked stricken. "Oh, my dear. We seem to have a bit of a problem. I quite confess, Bently, I haven't the slightest idea what to do about it."

He put his arm across her shoulder. "Don't fret, my dear. We shall find a solution."

BUT NEARLY A WEEK went by and there was still no word from the authorities or the private detectives Lord Kesterson had engaged concerning either the identity of the baby or the woman who had been fatally struck down at the entrance to the park. Despite the fact that Bently had doubled his efforts to identify the child, no one was able to provide the least clue to the boy's identity.

Of necessity the social routine resumed for the inhabitants of Kesterson House, with their usual Wednesdays at home. As well, a rather significant number of cards continued to accumulate even after their holiday at Diamond Hill. Each one of them required an answer. It was Emerald, with her fine penmanship, who was elected to the task under Udora's guidance.

Lord Farrencourt had called twice a day for a week without having been received by the family. Standing once again before the heavy oak doors, he reflected that no other woman had ever been so bold as to refuse him an audience. As he lifted the heavy brass knocker, he marshalled his determination.

"Good afternoon, my lord," McMasters said with obvious amusement. "I presume you wish to leave another card."

"No, my good man, I do not wish to leave another card. I've come to see Miss Amethyst Thackery and I will not leave until I do so."

"Beg pardon, Lord Farrencourt, but Miss Thackery has asked me to say that she is not receiving today."

"Then may I speak with Lady Udora? It is a matter of some urgency."

"I regret, sir, that her ladyship is at the moment indisposed."

"I am quite willing to wait. All day, in fact, if that should be necessary." Farrencourt pushed his way past the butler and headed towards the drawing-room.

McMasters looked ready to physically remove him, a feat that would have been interesting to watch, allowing for their considerable difference in size, but Lady Udora appeared at the top of the stairs.

"Who is it, McMasters? Oh. It's you, Lord Farrencourt." She dismissed her butler with a motion of her hand. "Won't you join me in the drawing-room, Lord Farrencourt? Or...since you have already made yourself welcome, perhaps the question is pointless."

"I've come to see Amethyst, my lady. I have no wish to be rude, but I'm sure you realize that I have been patient for more than a week."

"Amethyst has made it quite clear that she has no wish to see you. 'Now or ever,' according to her own words."

Farrencourt shuffled his feet and rubbed his hands against each other in an untypical boyish gesture. "I wonder, your ladyship, if I might speak with Lord Kesterson?"

Udora felt as if she had been snubbed. "If it has to do with Miss Amethyst, I can only remind you, sir, that I am her guardian. Anything you have to say to him can be said to me."

Farrencourt swallowed twice before speaking. "Indeed, I suppose that is true. I merely thought..."

Udora was becoming alarmed. "I suggest that you get on with it, Farrencourt, before my imagination leads me to the wrong conclusion. And do sit down," she said, pointing to an uncomfortable-looking straight-back chair. "My neck tires from the necessity of looking up at you."

He did as he was told. "The truth is, Lady Udora, I have come to ask permission to court Miss Amethyst. My intentions are most honourable. If we get on well, I plan to ask for her hand in marriage."

"You..." Udora wished fervently for her vinaigrette. She had always prided herself on her ability to handle any situation, but this was too much to absorb all at one time.

Farrencourt was apparently unaware of her mental state as he continued. "You know, of course, that I can easily provide Amethyst with anything she needs or wants."

Endeavouring to look the part she was expected to play, Udora straightened her back and laced her trembling fingers. "I've no doubt that you can provide for her, Lord Farrencourt. Everyone knows that your holdings are extensive. That is not what concerns me."

"If it is her feelings towards me, I can assure you that she cares for me as much as I care for her." He cleared his throat. "I confess that I made so bold as to tell her that I would request permission to court her."

"Indeed?"

"Unfortunately she overheard a thoughtless remark that led her to doubt my sincerity. If I could speak with her, I'm sure I could convince her that the young woman spoke out of mischief. Not a word of it was true. What Miss Pendergast alluded to was only a figment of her imagination based on stories circulated by Lord Dumphrey, who overheard something I said and took it amiss. Miss Pendergast and I have never been more than friends.''

"I see. Ye-e-es... " Udora drew out the word. "Perhaps it might be best if you first spoke to Lord Kesterson. You will find him at his club. In the meantime, I will talk to Amethyst and see how she feels." She rose, and Farrencourt leapt to his feet.

"Suffice it to say, my lady, that I pray you will be on my side in this matter."

Her eyes twinkled. "Suffice it to say." She extended her hand and he bent to kiss it.

Farrencourt was bursting with excitement when he returned to his carriage. It had all happened so quickly that he was hard put to understand it, but for the first time in his life he was in love. Truly in love. Not just with the exceedingly pleasant thought of taking this girl to bed, but with the knowledge that this beautiful, wonderfully high-spirited, yet at the same time gentle and compassionate woman, was willing to spend the rest of her life with him. For she wouldn't refuse him. She couldn't. He had seen it in her eyes, had sensed it when she returned his kiss.

He had no sooner gone out the door when Udora took a quick glance round, grasped the tail of her skirt and took the stairs two at a time. At the top she placed her hand over her heart, willing it to slow down. *De-meanour, Udora,* she reminded herself. *Remember that you are supposed to set an example. If you let the girl know how thrilled you are, she will surely turn him down without so much as a second thought.*

The three girls were in the nursery. No surprise there. They were often playing with baby William or dressing him in lacy white gowns, more like a doll than a drooling infant.

Udora pretended to be passing by, then stopped and entered the room. "Oh, there you are, Amy. I meant to tell you that you had a caller."

"I don't want to see anyone."

"Of course not. That is why I sent him away."

Topaz started to say something but Udora shot her a quelling look. There was an excruciatingly long silence before Amy placed the baby in the cradle and looked up.

"Who was the caller?"

"Oh...no one of any importance. I sent him away."

"But who was it?"

"If you must know, it was Lord Farrencourt. I rather think he desires to offer for you, but of course we'll refuse, knowing your antipathy towards him."

"I suppose it's for the best."

"Most certainly. He is far too good-looking, much too rich, and such delightful company that one would be hard pressed to keep *that one* close to the home fires." Udora wandered over to the window. "Besides, there are so many eligible men. Lord Dumphrey, to name one, was showing surprising interest in you, as I recall. Granted, he's getting on in years, but that only means he is not inexperienced where women are concerned."

When Amy didn't say anything, Udora walked back to where the girls were seated. It was an effort to keep her voice from shaking. "Of course, there is always Lord Finetree. He would give his right arm to wed you."

All three girls groaned as one.

"Ah, yes, I know," Udora continued. "His personal habits are rather repulsive, but one could be certain that he would willingly accept William as his own child."

Amy, looking thoughtful, pleated the ribbon that decorated her bodice. "I suppose I could at least talk to Farrencourt. He *has* been rather persistent, and he deserves something for that, doesn't he?"

"You mustn't feel obligated just because he's persistent," Udora admonished her.

"Really, I feel I do owe the poor man some small consideration."

"Only if you insist. Shall I send word that you are willing to receive him?"

"Yes. That might be the kindest thing to do."

Udora slowly let out her breath. "How noble of you, Amy. I shall send a messenger along with your card."

Emerald rose and followed Udora into the hallway. "You planned that strategy just as a general would plan a military campaign, didn't you, my lady?"

"I'm sure I don't know what you mean."

Emerald grinned. "Of course you do. I've seen how you work. You rarely do anything without thinking about it first. And you were right, you know. If you had told Amy she must accept Farrencourt's attentions, she would have refused." Emerald pressed one hand to her heart. "But she does love him, even if she is afraid to admit it."

"I hope you are right, Emerald," Udora said, giving her a hug. "And, my dear girl, if you understand me so well, what ever shall I do when it's your turn to be courted?"

Emerald pushed her spectacles into place. "If and when I ever meet a man I can bear to have near me for more than an hour at a time, I'll marry him."

"Indeed? And what if he won't have you?"

"That's when I'll come to you for advice."

"I'm counting on that. The question, Emerald, is whether or not you'll take that advice. How many times have I told you that you must give up this bookishness? Wasn't it Shakespeare who asked, 'How is it possible to expect mankind to take advice when they will not so much as take warning'?"

Emerald tucked the book she was carrying into the pocket of her skirt. "Actually, I believe the quote was from Jonathan Swift. It was Shakespeare who said, 'It is a good divine that follows his own instructions.'"

"Indeed!" Udora looked momentarily put off, but she recovered quickly. "Alas, I've no doubt that you are correct, however, I'll thank you not to be impertinent."

"Yes, my lady." They were both smiling as they went their separate ways.

IT WAS THE NEXT DAY before Farrencourt managed an audience with both Lord Kesterson and Lady Udora. Bently, sober at first over the implications of giving his approval for Farrencourt to attend Amethyst seriously, was quickly won over.

Afterwards, it took the combined opinions of the immediate household to help Amy to decide what to wear for their first meeting. Emerald was surprisingly eager to voice her opinion. "I think it should be something dark and reserved, considering the seriousness of this undertaking." She pushed her spectacles back on her nose. "Maybe the brown linen with the ecru Danish lace collar."

Maggie snorted. "Might just as well put 'er in widow's weeds for all the good that'll do 'er." She ran to the armoire and brought out a red silk gown that was cut low in front. "Now 'ere's a gown wot'll get 'is attention."

Topaz giggled. "It might get more than his attention. Where did you get that dress, Amy? I've never seen it before."

"It was a whim. One that Lady Udora told me I should have ignored. I thought Sally had returned it to the shop."

"Keep it," Topaz ordered. "Then sometime when his lordship refuses to give you what you ask for, you can put it on and I warrant he'll give you anything you want."

"Topaz!" Udora scolded. "Where do you get such ideas?"

"From something you once said, my lady."

Udora coloured. "Well if I did indeed say it, it was said in jest. Now then, enough of this nonsense. I have the perfect suggestion."

When Amy was finally ready to receive her caller, she was wearing a jonquil-yellow morning dress with ruffled lace at the muslin bodice. The long sleeves were slashed and inserted with narrow strips of *capucine* lace. Everyone agreed that it set off the burnt-honey highlights in her hair. Even Maggie admitted that there was something to be said for the demure look.

When McMasters announced that Farrencourt had arrived and was waiting in the salon, Amy took one last look in the mirror and chewed her lips to bring up their colour.

Maggie adjusted the *capucine* velvet bow that held Amy's hair neatly in place. "'Ere now, 'old still. There's no 'arm in keepin' the man waitin'. Only a ninny'ammer lets a swell know she's ready to race 'im to the marriage bed."

Amy scowled. "Don't be vulgar, Maggie. Besides—" she tilted her head and looked down her nose in her best condescending way "—it is only good manners that persuade me to see Farrencourt. Not a great and undying passion."

"Not much, it ain't." Maggie chuckled. "Any fool could read that look in your eyes. It's passion, all right." She patted Amy's hand and her face sobered. "Now, don't you go actin' uppity with 'im, miss. 'E's the best chance you'll 'ave for betterin' your prospects."

Amy gave her a cool look. "I'm not concerned over my prospects, thank you."

"Or keepin' baby William?" Maggie asked slyly.

"Since you put it that way." She couldn't hide her smile. Maggie was too experienced in the ways of love not to know that Amy's friendship for Farrencourt had been, from the start, an *affaire de coeur*. In truth, Amy silently admitted, she had been attracted to him from the first time she saw him. It was only his superior attitude that had reduced her to verbal ridicule.

Had it not been for her friendship with Lily, Farrencourt might never have noticed Amy. Dear, sweet Lily was not always at home to a peg in Society, but she was good-hearted, and it would be nice having her as a sister by marriage, Amy decided.

Udora, looking a little too attractive in a Pomona green muslin gown, breezed into the dressing-room. "You look lovely, Amy. Are you nearly ready? His Lordship has been kept waiting quite long enough."

Amy hesitated overlong, and Udora sensed that something was wrong. "Oh dear. You find my dress unsuitable? A little too revealing, perhaps?"

"It does make you look very young and beautiful. If you weren't married to Bently, I would swear it must be you whom Farrencourt is coming to see."

"You flatter me, child. But yes, I see your point. I am dressed to call upon Lady Oxford, who arrived yesterday from Paris. I was trying to impress her." Udora reached for an ivory shawl, draping it across her shoulders. "There. Is that better? Do I look more the sombre guardian than the giddy matron?"

Amy giggled. "You could never look sombre, my lady. That's one of the reasons we love you."

Udora hugged her. "It's so good to see you smile. I was worried about you for a while." Udora held her at arm's length. "Amy, there's something I must say, though I hesitate to do so. Much as I approve of a possible liaison between you and Lord Farrencourt, I don't want you to feel that you are obliged to marry him, although I certainly believe that Egan loves you. Do you feel that you could care for him?"

"Yes. In truth, I think I love him. Sometimes he makes me angry, but when I look at him he makes my knees tremble and I know it really isn't anger that I feel towards him, but something new to me. Something I've never felt with any other man."

"It's the spice in men that makes us angry, but spice is better than blandness. Don't keep him waiting too long, my dear."

They walked down the stairs together. Amy reached for Udora's hand. "Egan Kimble, Viscount Farrencourt. I love his name."

Udora chuckled. "Amethyst Thackery Kimble, Viscountess Farrencourt, sounds far better, my dear."

FARRENCOURT WAS ADVISED of their approach when he heard their laughter. He rose just as they entered the room, and the sudden rush of pleasure it gave him was just short of amazing. "Ladies. May I say how lovely you both look...like two flowers in a spring meadow."

Udora extended her hand. "Sheer flattery, my lord, but do continue."

"I'm left without adequate words, Lady Udora."

"I trust that won't continue for long, as I am about to take my leave for a previous engagement." She smiled. "Maggie will chaperon you, since Sally is otherwise occupied, but because your intentions have become public knowledge, you will be allowed a bit more leeway. Shall we say thirty minutes instead of ten? I trust you not to take advantage."

"How good of you, my lady. Will you return soon?"

"Most unlikely."

"Then may I have your permission to call again tomorrow?"

"Most certainly. I look forward to seeing you then."

Once Udora had taken her departure, Farrencourt found that he was less relaxed than he had expected to be. *Confound it!* he thought, running his finger between his throat and his neckcloth. *Why am I so ill at ease?*

Amy apparently read his thoughts. "Would you like to sit down, my lord? You look unsettled."

"Er... thank you." He took a seat directly across from her but so close that their knees could have touched, should either one of them have chosen to allow it. "The truth of the matter is, Amethyst, that I do feel strangely unsettled. I lay it in part to our recent misunderstanding, and to the fact that I have never before seriously courted a woman."

"Or could it be that your previous, and dare I say, numerous exploits, are not unknown to me? Miss Pendergast seems to be exceptionally well-informed."

"Miss Pendergast has a vivid imagination and loves to create scandals where none exist. She and Dumphrey make a good pair, for I can only assure you that Miss Pendergast and I were nothing more than friends. Neither did I confide in her at any time. It must have been Dumphrey who spoke to her about the incident on the ladder. As for the maze garden... I can only say that gossip spreads quickly. Perhaps Dumphrey heard me allude to it, or perhaps someone was watching us. However it happened, I hope you can overlook this misunderstanding."

Maggie, sitting off in a corner of the room, cleared her throat and shot a warning look at Amy, who seemed properly chastised. This was hardly the time for recriminations. Farrencourt took courage.

"The past is in the past, Amethyst. Shall we not let it remain there?"

"Do you think that is possible, my lord?"

He smiled, his confidence regained. "Trust me, my dear. If we consider the future, I shall have the pleasure of opening up a whole new world to you."

He warmed to the subject. "There are places I want to take you, things I want to show you. Her ladyship tells me you've never seen the ocean? Or Cornwall? I have a house in Cornwall overlooking the sea. It's not as grand as my other houses, but you will love it."

He watched her carefully. Was he moving too quickly? Strong as she was when she set out to save some starving creature, Amy was still young and vulnerable... and inexperienced, he reminded himself. Still, the look in her eyes gave him courage. He made bold enough to reach for her hands. "Tell me that you approve of our courtship, that our courtship might lead to marriage. For I confess, Amethyst, that I have fallen deeply in love with you."

Her gaze dropped to their hands clasped together on her lap. "I can only speak for myself, my lord."

"And?"

Her face turned a delightful pink. "And I do confess that marriage to you seems rather appealing. I've become very fond of you."

It was less than he had hoped for, but he was aware of her tendency towards caution in expressing her feelings. He was about to say more when McMasters knocked on the door and entered the room.

"Begging your pardon, my lord, but your manservant is here to speak with you on a matter of some importance. I've asked him to wait in the library."

"Thank you, McMasters." He stood and pulled Amy to her feet, still holding both her hands in his warm grasp. "Forgive me, Amethyst. I promise to be only a moment.'' He lifted both her hands to his face and brushed them gently with his lips.

When he had left the room, Maggie jumped up from her chair in the corner and rushed over to Amy. ''Now, that was more like it. Seems to me you 'ave 'im champin' at the bit. Give the man credit. It ain't all of 'em what would take on another man's baby as well as a wife. An' a baby what ain't even 'ers.''

Amy's eyes widened and she looked away.

''Lord-a-mercy! You ain't even told 'im about the baby, now 'ave you?'' Maggie demanded.

Amy shook her head. The expression on Maggie's face only served to increase Amy's growing feeling of apprehension.

CHAPTER NINE

MAGGIE LOOKED APPALLED. "Wot could you be thinkin' of, not tellin' 'im about the baby?"

"It wasn't any of his concern. Not until now, that is." Amethyst lowered her head and knotted her fingers together on her lap. "It's not as if he had anything to do with the baby. I think of William as my very own, even though I can't claim to have given birth to him."

"And we kin thank 'eaven for that!" Maggie said. "Aye, and just when did you plan to tell 'is lordship? When 'e finds the baby in bed wi' 'im on 'is weddin' night?"

"Don't be silly. I will tell Farrencourt when the time is right. It's merely that the subject of children has never been mentioned. We've only just begun courting."

"Sure, and wot difference does another man's child make, eh?"

Even had she been deaf, Amy couldn't have missed the sarcasm. "Oh, do be still. Farrencourt's bound to hear you. I warn you, Maggie, if you breathe one word of this to him, I'll never forgive you."

"Never forgive her for what?" Farrencourt asked as he entered the room.

Amy forced a laugh. "Why, ruining the lace on my gown," Amy said quickly. "Maggie sometimes has a tendency to be heavy-handed." She shot her a quelling look. "To say nothing about being too outspoken."

"As compared to those what 'as a bent to 'old things close to the chest," Maggie murmured.

Farrencourt looked puzzled, then smiled. "Let me say that both of you are charming in your own way."

"I trust the messenger left you with good news?" Amy asked, hoping to change the subject.

"Truth be told, he brought both of us good news."

Amy's attention was drawn to a small parcel wrapped in pale green tissue and tied with a darker green lace ribbon. "For me?" she asked with unconcealed delight.

"Of course it's for you. Who else could it possibly be for?"

The name of Eva Delight crossed Amy's mind, but a sudden fit of coughing on Maggie's part cancelled the thought before Amy could voice it.

"Well, go ahead. Aren't you going to open it?" Farrencourt demanded.

Amy tore away the paper to reveal a square box in tooled silver. When she lifted the lid, she discovered a handsome figure of a dove in flight, carved in some exotic light wood.

"How beautiful!" Amy exclaimed. "I'll love it always. It will remind me of the night you freed the bird I found trapped in the conservatory."

"That is the night I hoped you would remember." His voice was husky with the hidden meaning behind his words. "Lady Udora tells me that you have a collection of porcelain animals."

"Yes, but none as lovely as this carving. Thank you, Lord Farrencourt. I shall cherish it forever."

"The pleasure is mine. May I suggest a walk in the garden?"

"Yes, of course. The roses are nice this time of year. Bently...Lord Kesterson...is particularly skilled in growing them. He raises prized specimens at Partridge Run and Amberleigh."

"Ah, yes. His country home and yours, I believe."

When Amy and Farrencourt reached the garden, Emerald and Topaz were seated on the stone coping of a goldfish pond that was set in the shade of a magnificent beech tree. The filtered sunlight made them look unusually young and pretty, Amy thought. Farrencourt bowed to them.

"I hope we aren't disturbing you."

Emerald tucked the book she had been holding into the pocket of her skirt. "Good afternoon, Lord Farrencourt. How nice to see you."

Topaz jumped up to bob a curtsy. "Nice? It's more like a blessing from heaven. We've been sick with the Lombard Fever." She shrugged. "Well, *I've* been bored silly. Em's never bored when there's a book to stick her nose in."

Farrencourt chuckled. "We can't allow you to be bored, now can we? What would you say to attending a musical presentation this evening? Lady Pendergast has insisted that I be present, and I absolutely refuse to go alone. I know she would be pleased if the three of you would accompany me as my guests."

"Do you mean it?" Topaz demanded.

"Of course I do."

Amy wasn't so sure about it. Lady Pendergast rarely entertained without a purpose, so Lady Udora had told them. There was little doubt that the reason for this party was to bring Penelope and Farrencourt together on her own ground. What a shock it would be when the four of them arrived together.

Amy took Farrencourt's arm in an unconscious gesture of ownership. "Then we shall be happy to attend, assuming we shall have Lady Udora's permission."

Emerald scattered a few breadcrumbs to the waiting fish. "I doubt that her ladyship will object. She's been trying to obtain invitations to the party for well over a week."

Amy gave her a cool look. "There is no need to go into such detail, Emerald. It's enough that we have accepted Lord Farrencourt's invitation."

Farrencourt hid his grin. Emerald looked surprised by the unexpected reprimand from her twin sister, and Amy was immediately contrite. "What I mean to say is, we are delighted that you will escort us, my lord."

Later, after he had taken his departure, Amy was left alone in the garden with baby William, whom the nurse had brought out in his carriage. Thinking back on the events of the afternoon, it occurred to her that for the moment she had been overset when Farrencourt included her sisters in the invitation. She wanted him all to herself. It was that simple.

How had it happened so quickly? she wondered. All she had wanted was a husband so that she could provide a home for the baby. Now, suddenly, she was thinking of Farrencourt not merely as a provider but as a husband in the true sense of the word. In time they would have children of their own. The thought of holding her own son in her arms was too lovely for words. The thought of *making* those babies sent a delicious shiver down her spine.

Admittedly, she was still somewhat afraid of Farrencourt. He was so experienced, so masculine, so much the man about town. Would he be faithful to her or would he miss the charms of Eva Delight? Even now he might be visiting her at the *pied-à-terre* that gossip said he provided for her. The thought caused such pain that she said aloud, "No. He couldn't. He wouldn't do that to me!"

Baby William kicked his legs and grasped her finger in his small fist. Amy reached down to pick him up and held him to her shoulder. "Don't fret, little boy. I'll take care of you. If I have you, I don't need anyone else." She hugged him and he rewarded her with a smile. But in her heart Amy knew that her vow was only a half-truth.

Farrencourt was important to her now. He had been ever since the moment he held her in his arms on the ladder in the conservatory. Important not just to provide a home for the baby, but important in a way she was not yet able to define. She had to find a means to keep both of them, the man as well as the baby boy.

William turned his head and it seemed to fit perfectly against the curve of her throat. She moved her chin back and forth against his silky cap of brown hair. Maggie's warning came back to her. She must tell Farrencourt about the baby. But how, when? Tonight? Yes. It couldn't be put off any longer. She would wear something beautiful. Perhaps Udora would share a bit of her new French perfume. Farrencourt would be so entranced that he would find it impossible to refuse anything she asked of him.

AMY CHOSE a soft muslin gown the colour of fresh tangerines. A good decision, she thought. Penelope Pendergast would no doubt be wearing white. Penelope always wore white. In contrast to the tangerine, the white would fade into the background, and Penelope would fade right along with it. Amy was counting on it. Emerald wore pink and Topaz wore a soft butter-yellow. When the Pendergast butler announced them, along with Lord Farrencourt, Amy knew she had made the right choice. All eyes turned in their direction. A short time later she also realized that it had already become common knowledge that Farrencourt was courting her. A smile curved her mouth. Leave it to Lady Udora to see to that.

Lady Pendergast, her hair hennaed and swept into a dramatically tall cone, pushed her way through the crush of people like a runaway carriage at a country fair. She stopped within inches of Lord Farrencourt and grasped his sleeve with a bejewelled hand. "My deah, deah boy. How sweet of you to honour us with your presence. It is regrettable that Lily is ill and unable to attend."

"It is nothing serious, my lady. Just a mild indisposition."

"Pity." She lifted her lorgnette and looked down her nose at the girls. "And how clever of you to bring not one but three young ladies."

He bowed. "I hoped you would be pleased. I'm sure you've met the Misses Thackery."

"Indeed. How could one avoid it?" She smiled sweetly, no doubt intending to take the bite from her words. "They have been much in the news since their come out as the Thackery Jewels. Rather gauche, wasn't it? But most clever to be sure." She flicked her fan in their direction and snapped it shut. "Well then, shall we circulate? I know Lady Flimsoll and her cousin, Jordice, who is visiting from Sweden, would be pleased to meet the girls. It isn't often that one sees three sisters so close to the same age. Elsie, my deah," she said, turning to a spinsterish woman of forty-odd years, "you know the Flimsolls. Perhaps you would do the honours."

Lady Pendergast gripped Farrencourt's arm and steered him towards her daughter, who was standing at the pianoforte. "And while they are getting acquainted, I know Penelope would like a word of encouragement before she sings for us tonight."

"I can't imagine that your daughter would ever need encouragement," Farrencourt murmured.

"I beg your pardon?" Lady Pendergast shot him a quelling look.

"I only meant that she has, er, such a wealth of talent, madam. It would be hard to find something at which she did not excel."

Lady Pendergast looked mollified. "Well then, here she is."

Penelope smiled, revealing a set of teeth that reminded Farrencourt, much to his discomfort, of the row of keys on the pianoforte. He struggled to suppress his mirth. "My felicitations, Miss Pendergast. You look lovely tonight, as usual. And may I add that the necklace you are wearing is the perfect complement to your eyes."

She batted her lashes as if he had said the magic
word. "Why, thank you, my lord. Since you are such
a darling to notice, I will sing my first song for you
and you alone."

Farrencourt cleared his throat. "That would be a bit
difficult, wouldn't it? Considering the crush of people who have come to hear your lovely voice."

Lady Pendergast stuck her chest out like a pouter
pigeon on parade. "If you wish, I could allow the two
of you a wee bit of time unattended in the library. But
mind you, just a few moments." She waggled her finger playfully.

"You are too kind, Lady Pendergast, but I confess
that I must return to my party. I have left the Thackery girls alone far too long as it is."

She seemed to deflate, as if someone had stuck her
with a very large pin. "Indeed! Well, don't let us detain you, sir."

He bowed, then turned and walked away. *Confound it,* he thought. That was a close one. There was
a time when he had been attracted to Penelope Pendergast, but she was a shallow chit. Nothing behind
those bewitching green eyes that one couldn't uncover in five minutes of boring conversation. And her
mother! A gabster as well as a slyboots, he decided,
and he was fortunate to have escaped their snares.

His party was waiting for him to return before they
took their seats. Amy looked subdued, and he guessed
correctly that she had observed him talking to Penelope. Seeing the hurt in her eyes made him feel contrite, so much so that he wanted nothing more than to

take her in his arms. The thought was tempting. A scandal where females were concerned had never bothered him much in the past, but things were different now. There were appearances to be considered if he hoped to win Amethyst's hand. He bowed to her and offered his arm.

"Forgive me for leaving your side for so long. It was not of my choosing, I assure you."

She visibly brightened. "One could hardly blame you. Miss Pendergast looks quite fetching tonight, you must admit."

"She is but a shadow of your innocent beauty."

Amy laughed. "You are far too extravagant, sir."

Emerald looked pensive. "I wonder, Lord Farrencourt. Is it a woman's beauty or her innocence that a gentleman prizes most?"

He thrust out his chin. "It is hardly a question one would expect from a lady, Miss Thackery. However, since you are known for your inquisitive nature, I will endeavour to answer. It occurs to me that beauty is known to fade." He assumed a thoughtful stance and stroked his chin. "But virtue is like a magnificent shining river that flows on forever."

"How poetic!" Amy beamed.

"How very perceptive." Emerald nodded, peering up at him as if she had just noticed him for the first time.

"How disgustingly predictable," Topaz whispered to Emerald. "Do you suppose he imagines we are unaware of his philanderings with that lightskirt Eva Delight?" She tossed her head. "Or does he imply that virtue in a man counts for nothing?"

"Be still," Emerald cautioned. "We mustn't ruin Amy's chances with careless words."

Apparently Farrencourt had not overheard, because he looked most congenial as he directed the girls to a row of chairs and assisted them to be seated. "Did you enjoy meeting the Flimsoll cousin?" he asked.

All three girls laughed. Then Emerald spoke. "*She* turned out to be a *he*. We thought Jordice was a girl's name."

Topaz leaned forward. "He was quite handsome, too, but he couldn't speak a word of English. Or French! Emmy understood a little of what he said in German."

Emerald reached for her fan, which dangled by a cord from her wrist. "He was not an accomplished linguist, though, at least in the German language. I hadn't thought of learning Swedish. Perhaps I shall."

"And what did *you* think of him, Amethyst?" Farrencourt enquired, almost afraid to ask.

Topaz glanced sideways at her sister. "Amy didn't so much as say hello to him."

"Indeed?" Farrencourt asked, one eyebrow raised.

Topaz grinned impishly, first at Amy and then Farrencourt. "Indeed. She was far too concerned with what was happening where you were, on the other side of the room."

Amy's face flamed. "Oh, do be still, Taz. You're such a noddy, sometimes."

Farrencourt was gratified to learn that Amy had been watching him, and he knew it showed in the huskiness of his voice. "Truth be told, my own thoughts never left *this* side of the room." A quick look at Amy's face told him everything he desired. She wanted, indeed expected, his undivided attention. Anything less would be unacceptable, he thought. It was like an act of providence that he had only a week ago dispensed with Eva Delight's skillful services.

Once they were seated and the signal was given that the music was about to begin, Farrencourt made bold enough to allow his hip to graze Amy's side. If she protested he could always blame it on the closely spaced chairs that left scant room for elbows, not to mention legs.

He felt her stiffen, then slowly relax. He dared a glance at her face. Although she gazed straight ahead, her eyes seemed to have taken on a special gleam. Was it possible that her thoughts were running parallel to his? He fervently hoped so.

Amy was hardly aware that the singer had been announced until she saw Penelope step up to the pianoforte. The melody was unfamiliar to Amy but the lyrics had an annoying way of repeating themselves. Topaz leaned forward.

"I believe she's forgotten the words."

"But she has a lovely voice," Amy said, trying to be generous. The gesture was lost on Topaz who had lifted the edge of her skirt to allow an immodest length of ankle to peep out. It wasn't like Topaz to flirt with men in general as Penelope was wont to do. Amy scanned the audience until she noticed a white-haired man with mutton chop whiskers. Amy sighed. More than likely Topaz had it in her head to tease poor Lord Smitherington. He was fifty if he was a day... and dotty enough to think that all the young girls were setting their caps for him. At present he was all but falling out of his chair to get a better look. Most of the young ladies had used him at one time or another in order to practise flirtation. He rather deserved to be deceived, but Amy felt a twinge of conscience. She was glad it was he, rather than she, who now was suffering Topaz's attention.

The rest of the evening's entertainment was a blur of flautists, clowns and harpists. Although Amy found them entertaining, uppermost in her mind was the need to tell Farrencourt about the baby. Of course Farrencourt would fall under William's spell once he had seen him, so why was she so reluctant to reveal the fact that she had taken Wills under her protection?

The unspoken question caused her to look up at Farrencourt, only to discover that he was looking down at her. The pressure on her hip increased. Good manners decreed that she move farther away but she enjoyed the physical contact. Each time one of them shifted, tremors of warmth pulsated through her body.

Without regard to modest behaviour, her imagination strayed to thoughts of what it would be like to be alone with him. She caught the tip of her tongue between her teeth. He moved again and she looked up at him. His gaze was hooded, intense. It was all she could do to force breath into her lungs. When she did, it made a rasping sound and she turned quickly away.

Farrencourt moved closer, his shoulder behind hers, his arm across the back of her chair. To all appearances he was only making himself comfortable, but Amy knew better. She had seen other men play such games, and she wondered how many times Farrencourt had used similar tactics with the women he had known.

It suddenly occurred to her that he *had* played this game... and with her, only a few short weeks ago at the Drummond musicale. That time she had called his bluff and he had been forced to leave the drawing-room. This time, however, she might just choose to play the game right along with him.

She smiled to herself, anticipating his next move. In a moment now his hand would brush her shoulder. And then the game would be under *her* control. If she scolded him, he would protest that it was merely an accident. If she failed to object, then he would make bold enough to repeat the procedure. Amy held her breath. Any minute now and he would begin. Perhaps after the applause ended for the juggler. She waited. And waited. And waited.

Confound the man! He couldn't be less brazen if he were sitting on his hands. Could it be that his courting was not as serious as she had hoped? If she were Eva Delight, he wouldn't behave so woodenly. His hands would have found any excuse to touch her skin.

But she wasn't Eva Delight, or Penelope Pendergast, or any of the other beautiful women whom Farrencourt had attended. She was just herself. Underneath the pretty gown and the practised manners she was still just a country girl who had only recently come to Town. Had he thought of her as spice to his jaded palate? Someone to savour for a time until he was ready for another change of taste?

Farrencourt was popular among the ton. He was a man who enjoyed being seen with an attractive woman on his arm. What could be more eye-catching than having three young ladies to squire about Town? And it was he who had suggested that her sisters join them.

The more Amy thought about it, the more she was convinced of her own inadequacy. It wasn't fair. *She* wanted him. Emerald and Taz could find their own men. It was *she* who had first met him when she befriended Lily, and it was she who needed him. For Wills, of course. To provide a home and a father for him. But she had to move slowly. Perhaps tonight was not the right time after all to tell him about baby Wills.

AS FATE WOULD HAVE IT, the evening held no opportunity for her to reveal her secret, even had she been so inclined. Emerald and Topaz lingered at her side until she finally bade Farrencourt an acceptable but rather stiff good-night. To her surprise, he bent over her hand and kissed it.

"Thank you for a lovely evening, Amethyst. I look forward to seeing you again tomorrow. Perhaps you would care to visit Vauxhall Gardens." He made a gesture with his hand. "Regretfully it is not what it used to be, but I'm told the fountain will be flowing and there are to be fireworks as well as a magic show."

Topaz let out an unladylike whoop. "How exciting. Will you take us, too? Emerald and me?" Emerald started to demur but Topaz gave her an elbow in the ribs.

Farrencourt hid his grin. "Are you an aficionado of magic, Miss Thackery?"

Emerald gave her stepsister a quelling look. "Topaz is an aficionado of handsome young men. A certain balloonist whom she knows full well has been plying his trade at Vauxhall these past few weeks is her current weakness."

"A balloonist?" Farrencourt laughed. "He is *only* a weakness, I presume. Lord Kesterson could never conceive of such an alliance, not to mention permit it." He turned to Amy. "But you haven't answered my question, Amethyst. Could I persuade you to accompany me?"

"Yes, thank you. I would be pleased."

"And Emerald and me?" Topaz asked with obvious anticipation.

"Oh, very well," Lord Farrencourt agreed. "Might as well make a family day out of it. I'm sure Lily will want to be included."

Late that night as Amy lay abed, she thought about what Farrencourt had said. A family day. What a lovely sound it made when spoken. She would love having Lily...and him...as part of her family. What great fun it would be if she could take Wills along on the outing. She smiled, seeing in her mind's eye the look on Farrencourt's face. Nothing ever seemed to shake his lordship's composure but that most certainly would.

THE EXCURSION to Vauxhall would have been delightful had it not been for the fact that Topaz, along with Sally, disappeared for more than an hour's time. No one seriously questioned where they had got to. They knew. But since Sally was in attendance, Farrencourt reluctantly acknowledged that the proprieties were being observed, if somewhat questionably.

Lily, recovered now from her bout of indigestion, skipped alongside Amy. "I'm so glad to see you. It's been ever so long and I've so much to tell you."

"Is Dunholm dancing attendance upon you as he was at Diamond Hill?" Amy enquired.

Lily made a face and touched her finger to her lips. The gesture did not go unnoticed by her brother.

"Secrets, my dear Lily? Just what is going on between you and Dunholm?"

"Nothing, Egan. Nothing that I care to speak about. I find Dunholm as tedious as yesterday's sour milk."

Farrencourt swore softly. "Well, you had best find a way to sweeten him up, my girl, considering what I've gone through to establish a liaison between the two of you."

Lily lifted her nose in the air. "Oh, bother! If you insist on being so stuffy I'll walk with Emerald and Maggie," she said, turning and dropping back to where they were perusing a torchlight display of Francis Hayman paintings.

Farrencourt offered his arm to Amy and bent down to whisper softly. "Next time we shall leave our sisters at home. I am quite fond of them, my sweet, but I want you all to myself. Do I dare hope that you have similar feelings?"

She bent her head in a sudden attack of shyness. "It would be unladylike of me to express my feelings, Lord Farrencourt, but each day I grow fonder of you."

He sucked in a gulp of air. "God's breath! You give me courage." He glanced quickly at his sister and saw that the three women were engrossed in the antics of a juggler who was entertaining a small group of people. "Forgive me, Amy. I must do this." Before she had a chance to protest he had pulled her into the deepest shadow of the Dark Walk and planted a kiss squarely on her mouth. When she didn't pull away, he repeated his action, this time with considerably more skill.

Amy moaned softly, and he held her to his chest. "I love you, Amy. I want to marry you. If I obtain permission from your guardians, will you consent to be my bride?"

"Yes. Oh yes. That is—" she hesitated "—providing you forgo your relationship with Miss Delight," Amy said, not daring to look at him.

"But I have already done so, my love. Only last week I had her bags packed and ordered her from my house." He drew a deep breath. "I think we might be wise to look for the girls. If we are seen like this, the scandal would be unbearable."

Once they were back on the lighted pathway Amy knotted her fingers together. "You...you just put Miss Delight out onto the street like yesterday's waste?"

"Certainly not. I arranged for her to stay with a gentleman who has been waiting for weeks for me to be done with her."

"How considerate of you," Amy said drily.

"Please, don't be confused. Miss Delight made it clear from the beginning that her dancing always came first. She wanted a man, but only on an ever-changing basis. I hesitate to explain this to you, considering your innocence, but it is best you understand how it was."

"Thank you. I appreciate your frankness."

"And I appreciate your kind spirit."

Their conversation was interrupted for a few minutes when an acquaintance stopped to chat with Farrencourt. Lily and Emerald, having satisfied their curiosity over the paintings, came up to join them and were momentarily distracted by a statue tucked into a niche in the hedge.

Maggie nudged Amy and made a cradle of her arms, at the same time raising her eyebrows in enquiry. Amy shook her head. Maggie looked appalled. "When?" she demanded.

"Tonight," Amy mouthed. "Tonight." She placed her hand over her heart in a silent vow. It was a vow she had intended to keep, but when they arrived home and her sisters, propelled by Maggie, conveniently left Amy and Farrencourt alone in the library for a few minutes of privacy, everything changed.

CHAPTER TEN

FARRENCOURT DREW HER over to the fireplace, where the smouldering embers cast a rosy glow upon the room. "My dear Amy," he whispered. "You are so lovely, so young, so innocent. I count the days until I can legally claim you as my own."

She laughed softly. "How sure of yourself you are, my lord. Did it never occur to you that my guardians might refuse your offer?"

He echoed her laughter. "Do you think they might?" It was a question that hardly merited an answer. Instead, he drew her close to him. Amy thought he might steal another kiss, and she waited with breathless anticipation. Instead, he raised her hand to his lips and kissed her fingers one by one.

His voice was not quite steady. "My love, that was just a sample of the pleasure we shall share in the years to come."

"Are you so very certain that I can please you, Lord Farrencourt?"

"I was never more sure of anything in my entire life." He lifted her chin between his thumb and forefinger. "There is just one small request, however."

"And that is?"

He chuckled. "My house is large, but not nearly as large as your heart. The fishmonger's nag you left in my stable is eating me out of house and home, and my stableman has not forgiven me for handing it over to his care. You must promise me, my dearest, never, ever, to bring home another helpless creature." He smiled. "Well, at any rate, nothing larger than a very small bird."

He kissed the palm of her hand, and Amy was grateful that he wasn't watching her face. Only moments before she had been prepared to tell him about the baby, but that was impossible now. Quite impossible.

When he had finally taken his departure, Amy made her way slowly upstairs to the nursery.

Maggie, her shoe-button eyes shining with barely leashed curiosity, was waiting there beside William's cradle. "Sure and I knew this was the first place you'd come. 'E's fast asleep, an smilin' like 'e was dreamin' of cakes and sugarplums." She stood to make room for Amy. "Well, wot did 'is lordship say? Was 'e in a pet when you told 'im about the baby?"

"I didn't tell him. I couldn't."

Maggie rolled her eyes towards the ceiling. "Merciful 'eaven, you're slidin' into deep water now, miss, and not a pole to grab on to. You'd best tell 'im afore someone else does the deed for you."

"Surely no one from the household would be so cruel. And no one else knows about my baby."

"Your baby, you say!" Maggie looked at her with censure in her gaze. "Don't be actin' like a ninny-hammer. 'E ain't your baby. If 'is mum's dead, 'e still 'as a papa. Some'un's bound to turn up. Or worse. Some'un's bound to find out what you're keepin' up 'ere in the nursery. You better 'ope that some'un ain't Lord Farrencourt ... or Miss Lily, for that matter.''

It took considerable effort, but Amy managed to push Maggie's warning from her mind. The rapid progression of events served to quiet the nagging voice in the back of her head.

FARRENCOURT SPOKE to the Kestersons on the following day. The news of their betrothal spread quickly throughout the Upper Ten Thousand even before it had been puffed off to the *Times* and the *Morning Post*.

Kesterson House swarmed with dressmakers, decorators and cleaning maids hired to prepare for the betrothal party, which was now little more than ten days away. Udora was at her wits' end trying to keep the existence of the baby a secret. More than once she warned Amy about the importance of being honest with Farrencourt, but for Amy the time never seemed to be quite right to tell him.

Lily was also a problem. Now that she had gained Dunholm's attentions and become bored with him, Lily found it convenient to call upon Amy quite frequently. Amy was rocking Wills to sleep when she heard Lily's voice all the way upstairs from the entrance hall.

"No need to announce me, McMasters. I can find my way upstairs.''

Amy took one frightened look at the baby nurse and handed Wills to her. "Pray, don't let him cry,'' Amy whispered as she left the nursery and closed the door behind her.

Lily, dressed in a fussy green-velvet walking ensemble, bounded up the stairs in a most unladylike fashion, her petticoats and ankles plainly visible. Upon seeing Amy, she stopped dead in her tracks. "So there you are. What on earth? Whatever are you doing with that towel over your shoulder? Is this some new fashion you've failed to tell me about?"

"It's... " Amy was at a loss for an explanation, but it didn't matter because Lily wasn't listening.

"The best news!" she said. "Egan has invited me to accompany you and him to the theatre tonight ... that is, if you have no objection." She followed Amy into her tiny sitting-room and flopped onto a settee. "And he says that you may invite your sisters, too."

Amy did object. This was the night she had vowed to tell Farrencourt about Wills, but how could she object without giving away her secret?

"I'd adore having you join us, Lily, but I regret that Emmy and Taz have already consented to attend the Roxwell soirée."

"Oh, pooh. Don't they know that the Roxwells pare their cheeses so thin one could use it for bookmarks? And they hire Grub Street poets and musicians to entertain just for the cost of their dinners. It's too uncivil."

"Everyone knows how clutch-fisted the Roxwells are, but it seems Emerald's escort is related to the Roxwells and he is obliged to attend. Topaz agreed to go only to keep Emerald from telling Lady Udora that Taz was spending so much time talking to the balloonist. You know, the man she met just before the house party at Diamond Hill."

"She isn't carrying on with him, is she?" Lily demanded. Her eager expression gave rise to the feeling that she rather hoped so. It occurred to Amy that gossip was a part of Lily's life-blood.

"Certainly not!" Amy hoped she sounded convincing. Taz wasn't one to share her private escapades, but at all costs she must be protected from gossip.

"Well, he is handsome, so I'm told." Lily rolled her eyes. "But not of our class, unfortunately. Egan would send me into seclusion if I so much as suggested..." She stopped in midsentence. "What was that? It sounded like a baby crying."

"A...a baby?" Amy put her hand to her mouth. "What nonsense. You must be hearing things."

"No. It's you who is going deaf," Lily persisted with some indignation. "Hear? There it is again."

"Oh...yes...I do hear it, but it must be one of Lady Udora's cats. She keeps three of them here in London. The others are kept at Amberleigh."

"It didn't sound like a cat."

"Really, Lily, what an imagination you have." Amy turned to consult the porcelain clock sitting on her desk. "If I am to attend the theatre tonight with you and your brother, then I must find something to wear." She stood. "And I suppose you will want to look your best, too."

"We've no need for such haste. It won't take me very long to dress." Lily turned her head and listened carefully. "There must be something wrong with that cat, if that's what it is. Have you ever heard such a racket?"

Amy, trying to keep from showing how unsettled she was, played her trump card. "I have it on very good authority that Richard Wilkens will be at the theatre tonight. He's said to be an acquaintance of Edmund Kean."

"You don't mean it!"

"I do. What's more, Cook heard the Battendorfs' cook telling the Gronows' butler that Richard Wilkens and Lucy Battendorf have cried off. Apparently Lucy has been casting sheep's eyes at some French caper merchant who's staying at the Nedderhofts' house in Upper Wimpole Street."

"How could she do that to poor dear Richard? He is so sweet and adorable."

"And could perhaps use some comforting?" Amy suggested.

Lily reached for her reticule. "I perceive the hour is rather late after all, and I don't have the least idea what I'm going to wear tonight." She danced towards the door. "Really, Amy. You must do something about that cat."

Amy, having risen to say goodbye to her friend, sank down onto the chair. Lily must have been in a complete bumble bath to believe for one minute that Wills sounded like one of the cats. When, oh when, could she put an end to this deceit? And what was wrong with Wills that was making him cry?

He was hungry, that was all, Nurse Finkley explained when Amy went to look in on him. It was time to increase his solid foods.

UDORA WAS BEGINNING to show the strain of having three girls shot off into London Society all in one

Season. Her temper was short, and her face appeared more flushed than usual. But aside from that, there was something in her eyes that made Amy question her.

"Are you all right, my lady? You sounded so testy when I asked if I could wear the ermine-trimmed cape tonight."

"I'm sorry, my dear. I didn't mean to speak so abruptly. Of course you may wear the ermine cape. And the burgundy velvet, I presume?"

"Yes, with the ostrich-plume bonnet to match."

"You must mind your manners tonight. Maggie will be with Emerald and Topaz. Since Lily will be going to the opera with you and Farrencourt, you will be all right. Just remember your position."

"I don't have to." Amy grimaced. "Farrencourt does it for me."

Udora smiled. "Am I correct in guessing that you would like more passion from his lordship?"

Amy blushed. "Oh, no! Well, yes, I suppose so. He was much more adventurous before our betrothal was announced. Now he behaves as if I'm untouchable."

"I'm gratified to hear that. For a time I was concerned that you were only marrying him to provide a home for Wills."

"It might have been true at one time, but I become fonder of him with each passing day. I can't think of anyone I'd rather marry."

"Then remember that you have a lifetime ahead of you. A true gentleman of quality does not take into wedlock a woman of easy virtue."

"I'll remember."

"I trust you will, my dear," she said, bestowing a kiss on Amy's forehead.

FOR THE FIRST TIME since it had reopened after the fire, the Theatre Royal Drury Lane was filled to overflowing. The performance of Edmund Kean as Richard III was the reason. Despite his unprepossessing appearance off stage, Kean radiated magic when he took on his various roles.

By sheer determination Farrencourt elbowed their way up the double staircase from the crowded vestibule to the comparative comfort of the domed Corinthian rotunda.

"Forgive me. I had no idea there would be such a crush. This is as crowded as Covent Garden."

Amy's eyes glittered. "But isn't it exciting? Look, there is Lady Jersey."

Lily grabbed Farrencourt's free arm. "See that woman over there? The one with all the diamonds? Do you suppose they are real?"

"I rather imagine they are," he said drily, "considering that she is Catherine, the Grand Duchess of Russia, sister to the Tsar." He directed them towards a narrow corridor. "We had best be seated in our box before the curtain rises."

He settled them one on either side of him. Amy was convinced that they must have made a pretty picture; indeed, they had attracted attention. Many faces turned towards them as they took their seats. For once Lily was dressed to her advantage in a rose-coloured gown of velvet and lace. Amy's own gown was trimmed with ermine to match Udora's cape. Farrencourt was dressed in an immaculate coat with an impressive cream-coloured starcher fashioned *en cascade,* centred with a diamond stickpin.

They had no more than seated themselves when a footman entered the box, bowed and presented a tray bearing writing materials to Lord Farrencourt.

"A message for you, my lord. I am instructed to wait for a reply."

Farrencourt frowned as he opened the envelope and hastily read the note. After only a moment's hesitation, he scribbled something and returned the paper to the envelope.

"Thank you, my lord."

"Be so kind as to see that we are not disturbed again."

"Yes, sir. Indeed."

Both Amy and Lily looked to Farrencourt for an explanation, but none was forthcoming and his attention was obviously drawn to the rabble as the mass of people fought to sit down.

Lily was enraptured by the crowd—by the courtesans displaying themselves in private boxes at one side of the stage, by the fruit sellers whose wares became weapons if the performance was disappointing, and by the glitter of jewels displayed by women of wealth and power.

Amy, too, was enthralled by the scene until her gaze landed on one particular woman who was staring at the Farrencourt box with singular concentration. She was a small woman. Elegant in sable and diamonds, she glittered from head to toe with a hundred tiny jewels scattered throughout her sculptured curls.

Whether it was the woman's expression or some inner voice that warned Amy against it, she didn't question Farrencourt as to the woman's identity. Nor could Amy avoid watching her. Moments later a footman handed the woman a note, which she accepted with apparent nonchalance. Then, casually, as if aware of what it contained, she opened the note and read it before touching it to her lips and tucking it into her bodice.

Amy shot a glance at Farrencourt, who also appeared mesmerized by the bejewelled woman's behaviour. Who was she? What had she said to him? For it was plain to see that the note Farrencourt had returned had originated with her.

Amy shivered with apprehension. It was *her*, of course: Eva Delight, the diminutive ballerina whom Farrencourt had been keeping under his protection. Apparently he had been less than truthful when he said it was over between them.

It was Lily who broke the woman's spell over the two of them. She leaned forward and reached across Farrencourt to grasp Amy's hand. "Look, there he is. In the box nearest the orchestra."

Farrencourt glared. "Who? Who is this of whom you speak?"

Lily giggled. "Oh, no one, Egan. I only meant to point out Lord Benchcroft and his beanpole wife."

"Must you gossip even now?"

"It's not gossip, Egan, it's just interest in other people." She stood. "Be good enough to move down. I want to sit by Amy."

Farrencourt grumbled, but to avoid creating a disturbance, finally agreed to change chairs so that Amy was seated between them.

"Did you see him?" Lily whispered. "Richard Wilkens. He's in the box near the orchestra. I've caught his eye! He looked up at me and made an acknowledgement. I just know he's going to speak to me."

"What will your brother say?"

Lily gave her a dry look. "I hope he won't find out. At least for a while."

Farrencourt hushed the girls, and the players took their places as the music faded into the background.

The program opened with a one-act play that was so poorly enacted that the performers were first hissed and booed, then pelted with fruit, rotten vegetables and what appeared to be a dead chicken. When it seemed impossible for them to continue, a pair of stage-hands stretched a banner across the stage that read We Apologize. Ten-Minute Intermission.

Lily stood. "Egan, it will take them some time to clean the stage for the next play. Please, may we walk about?"

"Amethyst?" he questioned, leaning towards her.

A nudge from Lily left Amy no choice. "Yes, of course."

Once outside the box, Farrencourt touched Amy's arm. "I presume you noticed the message I received?" At Amy's nod he continued. "And I presume you noticed that I responded."

"Yes. One could hardly avoid seeing it."

"But you didn't question me."

"I didn't think I had the right to question you. We are not married as yet. But I assure you, my lord, that I shall not be so considerate once we have wed."

He laughed. "Good. I cannot abide docile women."

"And I cannot abide deceitful men."

"Aha. Then you are observant as well as spirited. You saw the woman seated in the box in the auditorium?"

"Your little ballerina friend, Eva Delight, I presume?"

"Indeed. Although, as I have told you, I no longer have any claim on the woman. Do you believe me?"

"She is very beautiful . . . if one likes the short boyish look in a woman."

Farrencourt grinned. "Don't be waspish, my dear. You have no need to be jealous of Eva Delight."

"How can you say that when she has been . . . when she, er . . . knows all about you?" Amy finished lamely.

Farrencourt stroked his chin. "Consider this. Should I then be jealous of the dancing master who taught you everything you know about the minuet and quadrille and the waltz?"

Amy jerked up her head. "But he was only a teacher to me."

Farrencourt nodded. "Just so, my darling. When a man marries, he must know certain things in order to please his bride and to make her comfortable and happy. So he will oft times take on a . . . a mistress to teach him these things." He mopped his face with his sleeve. "God's breath, we shouldn't be speaking like this. Do you understand what I mean, though?"

Amy looked at his face for a long time before she answered. "I think so. And you required *several* teachers over a period of years, I believe?"

"There was, ah . . . more than one, yes."

"And I trust you didn't enjoy them." She shook her head to add emphasis. "The lessons, I mean."

His face turned red, and he suddenly looked as if he were strangling. Amy waited, tapping her foot. Finally she glared at him and spoke. "Well, did you?"

"I ... somehow managed to survive," he said.

"That is not an acceptable answer, sir."

He apparently noticed that they were attracting attention with their heated conversation, and taking her arm, he drew her into a secluded alcove.

"I cannot lie to you, Amy," he said, holding her by the arms. "I learned much about the pleasures of the body during that time. Now I want nothing more than to teach what I've learned to you."

She saw the intensity of his gaze and giggled. "If you had said you had hated it, I would have known you were lying to me."

"Then you baited me, you minx. You set a trap, and to keep from losing you, I very nearly fell into it."

"I couldn't help it. I saw the way she looked at you and I found it hard to accept that it was over between you."

"It's you I want to marry, Amy. Only you." He lowered his face to hers and kissed her with a passion fuelled by her eager response. Amy was the first to pull away. It occurred to her to wonder if a kiss such as she had given him in a moment of weakness could condemn her as a woman of easy virtue. Somehow, at that moment, it didn't really signify.

But the moment was gone. Farrencourt suddenly stiffened. "Great heaven! Lily. I'd forgotten all about her. Come, we'd best find her before she creates a scandal."

"There she is," Amy pointed out, "standing over by the pilaster talking to Lord Franklin and his party."

Farrencourt swore softly and cut a path through the
crowd for Amy and himself. Lily, the centre of attention for one of the few times in her life, seemed to be
enjoying the regard of a half dozen men of varying
ages.

"Gentlemen, if you will pardon me?" Farrencourt
bowed. "I do beg your forgiveness, Lily, for having
deserted you. A...er...matter of some importance
arose and..."

She smiled and placed her hand on his arm. "My
dear brother, as you can see, I am in safe hands. These
kind gentlemen have been most protective when they
observed that I was temporarily without chaperon."

"Then I am in their debt," Farrencourt said, and
once more bowed to include the six of them. "I believe the signal has been given and the play is about to
resume."

Lord Greydon, a hawk-nosed individual with
parched skin, motioned with his forefinger. "Just one
moment, Farrencourt. If I may have a word with you
after the play is over? It's a matter of some importance."

"Yes, I suppose so," Farrencourt said reluctantly.
They paid their respects and each went his own direction. Lily, catching Amy's eye, gave her a broad wink
and preceded her into the box.

Once they were seated, Farrencourt leaned across
Amy to confront Lily. "You shouldn't have run off
like that, Lily. I was worried about you."

"I thought it was you and Amy who had disappeared," she said in an unusual show of spirit.

"Be that as it may, you should have tried to find us." He looked pensive. "Whatever did you say to those gentlemen?"

"As a matter of fact, they spoke mainly of you and your betrothal to Amy."

Amy stiffened. "Indeed? What did they say?"

"Just the usual questions. How long have you known each other? How soon do you plan to marry? And one of the men, Lord Greydon, I believe, asked how *well* you knew her. A bit cheeky, I thought, since it was accompanied by a leer."

Farrencourt's mouth tightened. "Never mind. I'll speak to him and set him straight." He settled back in his chair as the music began again. The curtain had already been raised for the one-act disaster. It was not the custom to lower it between performances. Two orange girls, instead of the usual workmen, who were still busy cleaning up, tripped onto the stage bearing a printed banner: To Welcome Edmund Kean as Richard III.

Farrencourt sighed along with the rest of the audience and folded his hands in contentment. Amy was still aglow with the remembered warmth of his embrace, but Lily's exuberance was not so easily restrained. She put her hand over her mouth and whispered to Amy.

"I did it! He asked to see me!"

"Richard Wilkens? Surely he will call first to ask permission?"

Lily gave Amy a quelling look. "He isn't a sapscull. Egan would destroy him. We are to meet at the museum on Thursday. Will you go with me? I daren't go alone."

"I suppose so. But..."

Farrencourt gave them a look that succeeded in quieting both of the girls. And Amy was truly grateful, because she had never before seen a performance by Edmund Kean, who as Richard III, was in his glory.

The play ended all too soon, although someone said that the time was approaching midnight. Twice during the performance, Amy had felt Farrencourt's knee graze her leg. It did little to help her concentrate on the dialogue, but it occurred to her that she could see a play anytime.

Lily started to rise, but Farrencourt motioned for her to be seated. "If you ladies will excuse me for a moment, I must speak with someone before we leave. You may wait safely here for the few minutes I'll be away."

Lily dropped back into her chair. "Good, I wanted a chance to talk to you alone. I simply must tell you what Richard Wilkens said to me."

But Amy didn't comprehend a word Lily said. She was too busy watching Eva Delight. As Fate would have it, Farrencourt made no attempt even to look at the ballerina. Instead, he approached Lord Greydon, who stood near the orchestra and confronted him rather abruptly. Their conversation appeared to be lively. At one point it seemed as though Farrencourt might be threatening the man, but he apparently controlled himself and walked away.

When he returned to escort them to the carriage, there was a grim set to Farrencourt's mouth. Lily, with her steady stream of chatter, was unaware of his obvious change in mood, but Amy felt as if the sky were about to fall. She sensed it in his cold blue eyes as they regarded her from across the carriage, and she sensed it in the way he held himself stiffly erect as if to avoid contact with anyone. Herself in particular, she decided.

When at long last they reached Kesterson House, he spoke to Lily. "Wait for me in the carriage. I shan't be long."

"Can't I come inside for a minute? It's cold out here."

"Then cover yourself," he said, tossing a rug at her feet.

Amy's voice was strained when she said good-night to Lily. And Lily's response was no less so. In the dim light of the carriage lamps, Amy saw the puzzled look on Lily's face and knew that her expression mirrored her own uneasy feelings. When Farrencourt reached up to hand Amy down from the carriage, her hands were shaking.

Lily leaned towards the open doorway. "Egan, please let me come inside."

He didn't bother to respond but merely closed the door with authority.

McMasters opened the heavy double doors to the house before they had reached the top step. "Good evening, my lord, Miss Amethyst. May I take your coat, sir?"

"No, thank you. I'll not be staying more than a moment. Please see that we are not disturbed."

McMasters looked quickly at Amy, who nodded before handing him her cloak and bonnet. She saw the questioning look in his eyes and worried that he would send for Udora. Lady Udora was the last person Amy wanted to see right now. "It's all right, McMasters. We'll only be a moment or two."

Whatever Farrencourt had to say to her was between the two of them. Udora might not agree but seeing him alone was the right thing to do. She started towards the library without looking back to see if Farrencourt followed. He had. He closed the door after them as if he were already her lord and master.

"Sit down," he ordered.

Amy took a straight-back chair next to the fireplace while Farrencourt continued to pace the room in silence. When she could take no more she stood and confronted him.

"What is it, Egan? Why are you so distressed?"

He stopped directly in front of her and drew a deep breath. His eyes seemed to glow with anger but it could have been a reflection from the burning logs. And still he was silent.

Her stomach constricted. "Please tell me what it is."

He exhaled slowly and put his hands on her shoulders. "Forgive me, but I must ask you this. Is it true that you have a baby?"

"I . . . I . . ."

"By all that's holy, answer me, girl."

But she couldn't. Fear constricted her throat, and it was all she could do to keep from bursting into tears.

CHAPTER ELEVEN

FARRENCOURT WANTED TO shake her but he somehow managed to suppress his anger. He clutched his hands to his sides. "God's breath, Amy. Answer me now before I lose complete control. Is it true? Do you have a baby boy?"

"Wh-who told you?"

"Who told me! Is that what you care about? It doesn't matter who told me, but if you must know, it was Lord Greydon." He waited, seeing the hurt in her eyes. His voice lowered. "Then I take it the gossips are right for once?"

Tears welled up in her eyes and threatened to overflow. "I meant to tell you, my lord, but the time never seemed quite right. William is such a beautiful boy, and he needs us so desperately. You must see him for yourself."

William! Even the name turned his heart to stone. "I have no wish to see this...this proof that you have deceived me. Why on earth didn't you tell me about him before I came to love you?"

"I tried to tell you more than once, but the time never seemed right. And...and I was so afraid of losing you."

He drew back from her despite the temptation to kiss away her tears. "I can forgive many things, Amy.

I cannot, however, countenance deception in the woman I hoped to marry."

"Please, if you would just let me explain. It happened in St. James's Park...."

He raised both hands and turned away. "No, I could not bear to hear how you were seduced. I'll not listen to any of this." He strode from the room without so much as saying good-night. McMasters, apparently noticing his agitation, looked concerned.

"Is everything all right, my lord? May I be of service?"

"I'm afraid there's nothing anyone can do."

"Yes, sir. Have a pleasant evening, Lord Farrencourt."

Farrencourt hesitated for a moment, looked the butler squarely in the face, shook his head and left without pausing for McMasters to open the door for him. He couldn't speak. The ache in his heart was too intense for him to think of anything but his beautiful Amy and how he had lost her.

When he swung himself into his waiting carriage, Lily, unaware of what had happened, complained, "You took so long that I was about to come and fetch you. Did you ask Amy if she would like to go to the Gilmore tea party Tuesday afternoon?"

"No."

"Why not, Egan? You promised you would take both of us. I know that Amy wants to see the Gilmores' new water garden, and so do I."

"For God's sake, be still, Lily. I don't wish to talk to you at the moment."

"You never wish to talk to me when I want to talk to you." She continued her endless chatter, but he contrived not to hear it until she nudged his leg with her foot.

"Why don't you answer me, Egan?"

"Because I'm not listening to you, Lily." He spoke in measured cadence. "You are like a flea burrowing under my skin when I try to think."

"Think about what?"

About what? The pain of loss, he thought. *Of losing the one person he had ever truly loved.* But he couldn't speak of it now. He swore softly, then sighed in resignation. "Tell me, has Amy ever said anything to you about having a baby?"

"Yes, indeed. We often talk about babies. We both want to have dozens of them." She appeared to have seen the expression on his face because she gave an embarrassed little laugh. "Well, she does, anyway. I'd be satisfied with one or two... after I'd been married for ten years or so."

Her chatter fanned his irritation. "No, no! You misunderstand. I mean has she ever said anything..." He paused. "Never mind. I shouldn't have troubled you with such questions." The effort required to explain was just too much, considering his present mood.

Lily was quiet for a moment. When she finally spoke, she seemed rather unsure of herself. "Now that I think of it, there was something Amy said once concerning a baby. I believe it was at Diamond Hill. I can't believe it slipped my mind, because at the time I thought it was quite an *on dit.*"

"Well tell me, girl. What did she say!"

"She made a remark that caused me to wonder, but on thinking it over, I decided it was just idle conver-

sation she thought up to amuse me. We used to do
that, you know, when we first became friends at the
beginning of the Season. I'd tell her about the handsome men I'd met and how they contrived to meet me
in secret, and she . . . well, she talked about things like
naming her children after all the famous kings and
queens or having a country house with a deer park
where no one was allowed to hunt."

"Get to it, for God's sake."

"It seems ridiculous now, but I thought she was
going to tell me that she had a baby, but then she said
Dunholm had nothing to do with it, and then . . . well
he could have been but she didn't know . . . and . . ." Her
voice rattled on and on.

Farrencourt put his hands to his face and swore
softly. Lily leaned forward, eyes bulging. "Are you
saying that there really *is* a baby?"

"It would seem so."

"I don't believe it. Not Amy. She is too . . . pure.
But . . . but a strange thing happened when I called
upon her this afternoon. I thought I heard a baby
crying somewhere upstairs. She said it was one of the
cats, but I wondered. . . . Still, I cannot believe this of
Amy. I would have to hear it from her own lips."

Farrencourt noticed the sudden emptiness in the pit
of his stomach. Pure she might *appear* to be, but when
he had kissed her, he had unleashed an unexpected
passion. Now it would seem that he had not been the
first to discover this hidden well of sensuality. Devil
take the woman! Why did this have to happen now?
Now, when he had already fallen in love with her!

His mouth tightened. "Nor could I believe it on first
hearing, but the gossip is too widespread not to hold

a grain of truth. And . . . she all but admitted it." He paused as if gathering his thoughts while he looked out the carriage window at a brilliant display of torch-lights bordering the drive of an imposing house. "Lily, my dear, I think it best if you refrain from visiting Miss Thackery for the present. From what I gather, she intends to keep the baby. Once the word is out, a scandal is bound to ensue. And I, of course, shall have to put an end to our betrothal."

"But that would ruin her."

"Nevertheless, I cannot bring such a scandal down upon our name."

"But she is my best friend. My only *real* friend, Egan. I cannot desert her when she needs me."

"I'm afraid you must do as I say, Lily. You cannot afford to risk your own reputation. Your eventual marriage, your entire future, depends on a spotless reputation."

"But you were going to marry her. You love her, Egan, I know you do."

"Unfortunately, that is the case, my dear sister, but one cannot allow sentiment to get in the way of marriage."

Lily was about to say something, then stopped abruptly. "Did you hear what you just said, Egan? You sound so cold, so calculating. You might be wise not to act in haste."

"Enough, Lily. I don't wish to discuss this any further," he warned, but he thought about what she had said.

AMY REMAINED ALONE in the library for nearly an hour after Farrencourt had gone. It was Udora who found her there, huddled in the corner of the settee.

"My dear Amy, whatever has happened? Is it Farrencourt? Has he cried off on you?"

Amy nodded. "He . . . he found out about Wills before I had a chance to tell him."

"Surely he couldn't have been angry enough to lose interest in you just because you temporarily gave shelter to a foundling."

"He . . . he thinks Wills is my own. I started to tell him how I was given the baby in St. James's Park but he didn't allow me time to finish the story."

"Men! They can be so volatile. Indeed, if he understood only half the story I don't wonder that he was put off, but all is not lost, my dear. All we need do is tell him the truth and he will come to his senses."

"I don't think so, my lady. He feels that I have deceived him. Omitting the truth is almost as bad as lying. I love Egan, but not enough to give up Wills when he has no one else."

"We are still looking for the boy's father. It is too soon to give up hope."

"But what will I do if I lose Egan? There is no one else for me, either. There never can be."

"Don't say that, child." Udora smiled. "Look at me. Four wonderful husbands gone to their maker, yet number five has made me happier than I'd ever dared dream I could be. One mustn't try to predict the future . . . or to limit one's aspirations." She rearranged the panels of her skirt and crossed her ankles.

"Let me speak with Farrencourt and try to explain how you came to have the baby."

"No! No, you mustn't do that. If he loves me he will give *me* a chance to explain before he makes a public announcement. If he loved me, he would love my baby, too, wouldn't he?"

"Oh, my dear! Another man's child? I don't know, Amy. Men are foolish about such things. Remember how tediously Charles behaved when he found out I'd inherited three girls instead of a collection of jewels? He wasn't pleased."

Amy smiled, recalling the man Udora had been betrothed to before she met Lord Kesterson.

Udora shook her head. "I just can't tell you what Farrencourt might do or how he would behave." She reached for Amy's hand. "But you must go to him and confront him with the truth before he sees fit to revoke his offer for you. You cannot let him continue to believe that William is your own flesh and blood."

"I cannot bear to face him."

"But you must, and the sooner the better. Off to bed now. When morning comes, we'll know what we must do."

THE FOLLOWING MORNING, Udora, looking more distressed than usual, called the girls together in her sitting-room. When they were seated, she rose and walked to the window. "My dears, things have come to an unexpected pass, and I fear we must take steps, else your first Season will surely end in disaster."

Amy pressed her palms together. "I'm so sorry, my lady. I know this is all my fault. If it were not for Wills none of this would have happened, but I can't give him up."

"Oh, don't be a sapscull," Topaz ordered. "None of us wants you to give William over to an orphanage. We've all come to love him. Beside, it matters not a whit either to me or to Emerald if no one invites us to their parties. I prefer to make my own friends."

Emerald nodded. "I am quite content to stay at home, that is, providing I am allowed, on occasion, to go to the lending library."

Udora whirled round. "Listen to you! You have no idea what you are saying. Everything, everything we've done so far was to prepare you for the future. Are you going to tell me it was all for naught?"

Amy shrugged. "What can we do?"

Udora's voice was cold. "You could begin by making it clear to Farrencourt exactly how you came to find this baby. Somehow you have got the idea that stubbornness is a virtue comparable to honesty." Udora stood as stiff as an icicle in December. "I am disappointed in your recent behaviour, Amethyst, and it's time you made amends. Do I make myself understood?"

"Yes, my lady."

"And as for you, Topaz, I am not unaware of your little adventures. I want you to cease your wild ways before you bring down yet another scandal on the House of Kesterson." She crossed her arms in front of her, tucking her hands into the sleeves of her gown. "And you, Emerald, have done little to change your ways. If it is your desire to moulder away like some unused book left too long on the shelf, you are well on your way to doing so. I cannot abide wasted opportunity. It is time that you stopped arguing with men about politics and began matching wits with them on the subject of marriage.'' She turned and started from the room, apparently too overset to wait for a reply.

Maggie rose quickly from her chair and would have followed after her, but Udora waved her back into the room and closed the door behind her. Maggie turned towards the girls, concern written all over her face. ''Now see wot you've done. You've gone an' made 'er browsick. 'Er, what wants nothin' for you but the best o' everything. Be shamed!'' she said, shaking her finger at all three of them.

For the first time it occurred to Amy how drawn Udora had appeared. Although she had put on a bit of weight, the dark circles under her eyes and the uncharacteristic droop to her mouth was clear evidence that she was not herself. Still, Amy felt powerless to do anything about it.

She waited for her sisters to say something, but Emerald was absorbed in contemplating a length of green ribbon she was tying in a bow, and Topaz had gone to the window to look at the sky. No doubt she was wondering if her balloonist friend was drifting by in the clouds, Amy thought. As for herself, her mind kept straying to Wills, but more frequently to Farrencourt.

Maggie snorted impatiently. ''Aye, and you've nothin' to say for yourselves, 'ave you? If I didn't know better, I'd wager you was still the selfish little 'oydens you was when 'er ladyship took you in.''

Maggie's words came so close to the truth that Amy felt the tears well up in her eyes and begin to roll down her cheeks. ''I know I've been thinking only of myself and the baby, but what can I do? How can I make amends?''

"You can start by settin' 'is lordship straight, you
can. You don't even 'ave to see 'im. You can write 'im
a letter and send it round wi' a footman. Mr. Chalker
could get himself there before the ink was dry, 'e being that moonwitted for the Farrencourts' upstairs
maid."

"But I'd be so embarrassed to go begging...."

"Aye, then you'd rather lose 'im than eat a bit o'
crow? Seems to me, miss, that you've put the cart before the 'orse."

Amy pressed her hands to her face. "I know that
what you say is true, but I . . . All right. I'll do it."

Maggie opened the lid of the writing desk and
handed Amy a sheet of foolscap. "There's no better
time than now."

Emerald and Topaz had apparently not missed a
word of the conversation. It took all four of them to
write the letter. An hour later, Mr. Chalker, who seized
the opportunity to change into his most elegant attire, was on his way to the Farrencourt domain.

The girls scurried to find the proper gown for Amy
to wear on the chance that Farrencourt might arrive
that very day to mend their differences.

"Lilac is best for her," Emerald said. "It brings out
the colour in her eyes."

"Ninnyhammer! Lilac is a colour for mourning,"
Topaz insisted, pulling a bishop's blue muslin from the
armoire. "She is too pale. This will brighten her face."

"Aye, an' she's neither dressin' for a wake nor a
ball, now is she?" Maggie put the dress back into the
wardrobe and withdrew a dainty white muslin sprigged
with tiny embroidered butterflies.

"But the white makes her look even more pale," Emerald protested.

Maggie grinned. "And 'is lordship will be the first in line to catch 'er should she just 'appen to 'ave a fit o' the vapours. I'd bet me best bonnet 'e'd want to take 'er 'ome right then and there to look after 'er."

They were still laughing when Sally knocked on the door to say that Farrencourt had asked permission to see Miss Amethyst at once.

Maggie grinned. "You see? I was right. Pity them poor 'orses. Sure and 'e put them in one fine sweat to get 'ere so quick."

Amazingly enough, it took the women only a scant ten minutes to primp, powder and comb Amy into what Maggie said was the innocence of a rosebud. Amy was sure she looked anything but sweet and innocent. It was only the thought of losing Farrencourt that made it possible for her to face him and his justifiable anger. She should have told him about William from the first. But at least now he knew. Her letter had taken care of that. He was here to see her... and she had never been quite so anxious in all her life.

He was waiting in the library, one elbow resting on the mantelpiece as he gazed at an etching by Charles Heathcote Tatham. Her heart skipped a beat or two. He was so handsome in his dark brown waistcoat and superbly tailored fawn trousers. His thick brown hair, usually so well tamed, appeared to have been recently slept in.

He straightened and turned as she entered the room. She dropped a curtsy and inclined her head. "My lord? I had no idea you would respond so quickly."

He bowed then straightened to consider her face. "Quickly? The night seemed like an eternity. I haven't slept or eaten since I left you. Do you see what you have done to me?"

"I...I am so sorry. I missed you so dreadfully, and it broke my heart to know what you must have been thinking about me. I should have told you about William from the first, but I couldn't bear to lose you."

He came towards her and she could see the torment written on his face as he took her in his arms. "My dear, sweet girl. I couldn't bear to let you go no matter what you've done. I love you more than life itself, and I want to marry you."

"And William?" she asked, barely above a whisper. "I love you dearly, my lord, but I could never give up Wills. He needs me, and, strange as it may sound, I think I need him, too."

Farrencourt's eyes darkened. "The gossips be damned. I would never ask you to give up your son."

Amy drew back. "But he isn't... he wasn't *born* to me. Didn't I make that clear in my letter?"

"Letter? What letter?"

"Why, the one I had delivered by messenger just this morning. That's why you're here, isn't it? Because you read my letter in which I explained that a woman in St. James's Park had temporarily entrusted her baby to my care?"

Confusion covered his face. "What's this?"

"Will's mother. Unfortunately, she was killed in a carriage mishap not twenty minutes after she left us."

"I received no such letter. Do you mean to say that this baby is not really yours? By Gad! I can't believe it. What a remarkable turn of events."

His face glowed with happiness, and he took her in his arms and whirled her round.

"Egan," she protested. "You mustn't do this. Someone will see us."

"Let them! I want the whole world to know how happy I am."

When he finally released her, she stepped back to survey his face. "Farrencourt, what are you saying? Is it true that you didn't know? And...and you would have taken me to be your wife, thinking that I had already been...been touched by another man and...and had his child to prove it?"

He nodded and tears filled her eyes. "Oh, Egan. How kind you are. And what a wonderful father you will be."

She threw her arms about him and kissed his cheek. His voice sounded strained when he spoke. "Would you be so kind as to do that again?"

She laughed and leaned towards his cheek. At the crucial moment he turned his head and the kiss landed squarely on his mouth. Amy's gasp of surprise soon turned to a purr of contentment. "You are quite devious, my lord. You shouldn't have done that."

"Indeed? Then I have no choice but to take it back," he said, and proceeded to kiss her long and thoroughly. This time there was a difference in the way he kissed her. His mouth demanded satisfaction and she gave it to him willingly.

WHEN BENTLY AND Lady Udora arrived home just before teatime, Farrencourt made it clear that the differences between him and Amy had been settled before word of their short-lived estrangement could become known.

They were less fortunate in keeping William's presence a secret. The less charitable gossips were convinced that the child belonged to Amy. A few even dared voice the possibility that Farrencourt might be the father, but when Farrencourt confronted the gossip-mongers with the truth, they were forced to retract their stories.

"Curiosity, that's all it is," Udora snapped as the calling cards began to pile up. "It is unheard of to include a baby in family invitations, but look, here's another."

Emerald pushed her spectacles onto her nose and perused the heavily embossed invitation. "From Estelle Lexington, no less. Isn't she related to Jonathan Trent, Marquess of Milford?"

"Um. His aunt, I believe."

"He's said to have the best library of Elizabethan history in all of London."

Udora gave her a droll look. "A good enough reason to send our regrets. You've seen quite enough libraries to last you a lifetime, Miss Bluestocking."

Topaz was sprawled in front of the fireplace. The dying coals were meant only to take the chill from the room and not to provide real heat on such a pleasant day. She stretched like a cat with a full stomach. "Farrencourt has invited us to accompany him and Amy to the soirée at the Beersfords' house tomorrow night. Can William go, too?"

"Absolutely not!" Udora put down the letter opener with undue emphasis. "We have no right to place him on public display... like... like some prize pig at a country fair. The betrothal ball is just a few days away. We might conceivably introduce William to a select group of friends.''

"Are you afraid something might go wrong if too much is said about the baby?" Emerald questioned.

Once again Udora was astounded by her ward's perception. Putting aside the tiny worry that niggled at the back of her head, Udora tried to reassure the girls. "I'll admit that Amy does have a tendency to hitch the cart before the horse, as Maggie's so fond of saying, but this time I think she knows what she wants. I believe she trusts Farrencourt, and the truth is, so do I. So you see, there is very little that could possibly go wrong."

Maggie, coming into the room, heard just the tail-end of the conversation, but it was enough to make her snort. "Now if that ain't just askin' for trouble, I'm the Duchess of Kent."

THE FOURTH VISCOUNT Beersford and his lady lived at Warden House, a magnificent stone and marble structure near Great Stanhope Street. Designed in the popular Palladian style, Warden House had become a gathering place for the younger members of the haut ton. Tonight its wide entrance hall was crowded with guests attempting to gain access to the drawing-room. Lady Beersford considered no party a success unless at least three women had to be revived with a vinai-grette and a cold compress.

Farrencourt was beginning to regret allowing Emerald and Topaz, along with Sally and Maggie and his sister, to accompany Amethyst and him to the party. He was responsible for their safety, yet how could he be accountable for them if they became separated? And they did a mere five minutes after they gained entrance to the salon.

Sally managed to find her way back to them, no doubt painfully aware that word would reach Udora if Amy were left unattended. "Where have the others got to?" he asked.

Sally shrugged. "I can't say, my lord. But Maggie would be knowin'. I 'eard there was a dancin' bear in the garden. Mayhap they went to see it."

"Don't let Amy hear you say that," he cautioned. "She'll want to rescue it." Sally nodded and grinned.

There was food everywhere: large collations of cold meats and cheeses as well as footed servers of candied fruits, brandied figs, and pastries filled with every conceivable kind of sweetmeat. Footmen made their way among the party-goers with fragile goblets containing syllabub and sherry. Live birds, including parrots, macaws and other exotic creatures flew at will beneath the vaulted ceilings or perched at random on branches of specially designed artificial trees.

"Isn't it beautiful?" Amy said when she could tear herself away from the Jenkins sisters, who had questioned her at length about the baby.

"Beautiful is hardly the word for it," Farrencourt replied in a droll voice. "Reminds me of the Prince's party to honour his appointment to the Regency. He ordered his staff to construct a winding stream right down the middle of the dining table and stock it with goldfish." He paused to pluck a parrot feather from the lip of his wineglass. "Unfortunately, most of the fish expired before the night was over."

"I'm glad I wasn't there," Amy said, shuddering.

"I'm also glad you were not there, my sweet. You would have been climbing the table with a net to try and save the fish before they died."

Although his words were stern, Amy heard the tenderness in his voice and she gazed at him with adoration.

The effort to create a tropical wonderland in the Beersford drawing-room proved ultimately to be a disaster. When an Amazon green parrot attempted to perch on a torchère, the fixture tilted, sending flames shooting up the velvet drapery like a Chinese rocket. The fire was extinguished immediately, but not before the hundreds of guests took flight. Farrencourt seized the opportunity to gather the girls together to make their own departure.

The decision proved to be ill-considered because the streets were jammed with vehicles. The Farrencourt carriage had hardly moved more than a few hundred yards before it stopped again. Farrencourt swore softly and opened the window to stick his head outside. The street was blocked by conveyances as far ahead as he could see. He called to the driver.

"Cosgrove, turn left when you reach the next street. If we don't find another way out, we could be here for hours."

"Yes, m'lord, I ken do thet but can't say as I knows my way through the back streets."

"Anything is better than standing still. The wind is starting to blow and it's sure to start raining in a little while."

Lily huddled in a corner against the burgundy plush bolster. "It smells bad on this street. We shall get lost, I know it."

Farrencourt gave her a scathing look. "You should be quite comfortable then, sister dear. It occurs to me that you kept yourself lost all evening. Dunholm was looking for you."

"Precisely why I became lost," she said. "But I did speak to him. It looked as though a pigeon had rested too long on his shoulder. There was a white . . ."

"Enough! And just where *were* you, if I may be so bold?"

"Quite safe, thank you. Lady Hereford decided to protect my reputation and wouldn't let me out of her sight all evening."

"Then I am in her debt."

Lily leaned over to whisper in Amy's ear. "I'm the one who's indebted to her. She introduced me to Lord Mockerby. I think I'm in love!"

Amy smiled and squeezed Lily's hand. Maybe this time Lily's infatuation might last. At least Egan would approve.

The stench had become almost unbearable. Sewage smells mixed with smoke and mist from the heavy fog hung like a curtain all around them. The street they had taken was becoming narrower by the minute until they reached a poor district that was crowded with riff-raff hovering round meagre bonfires to keep warm. Amy leaned forward.

"Look! Did you see those people?" It was a family with three children, one of which was a baby. "We have to go back and help them. They must be cold and hungry with no place to go. We must do something."

Farrencourt pressed her back against the seat. "We can't go back, Amy. There's no way to turn round."

"Then let me out. I have a few coins in my purse."

"A few coins would hardly get them through the night."

"But I have to help them. You said yourself it's going to rain. They may die."

She tried to reach the handle of the door but Farrencourt held her back.

"Stop this, Amy. There's nothing you can do."

"There must be!" she wailed. "How could you be so cruel? I hate you, Farrencourt. I hate everything about you."

"You don't hate me, my love. As you grow older you'll realize you simply cannot save every creature who needs help. But it's your compassion that makes me love you so very deeply." He kissed the top of her head.

She hid her face in the folds of his coat and dissolved into helpless tears.

CHAPTER TWELVE

THE RETURN to Kesterson House that night seemed to take forever. Uppermost in Amy's mind was the picture of the destitute children, who were alarmingly thin and ill-clothed for even a late Spring night. How would they fare when Winter came with its icy winds? Farrencourt had seemed so unaffected by their plight. How could this man she had come to love be so heartless?

At first Topaz and Farrencourt tried to lift the heavy silence by talking about the more bizarre aspects of the Beersford soirée, but the conversation brought no response from the others and it soon died.

Amy tried to avoid Farrencourt's gaze but she was compelled to look at him. He reached out to grasp her hand but she moved away, pretending to adjust the hood of her cloak.

When they finally arrived home, he escorted them to the house, and while Lily waited in the carriage, the others discreetly left Amy alone with him in the forecourt. McMasters came out to assist them but Farrencourt waved him away.

He took her hands in his. "Why are you so cold, my dear?"

She looked away. "The weather is unseasonably cool."

"I wasn't referring to your hands, as you well know. Surely you don't fault me for not stopping to help that poor family." His eyebrows drew together in a frown. "God's breath, Amy, you know there are hundreds of families as desperate as they are. We can't begin to help them all."

Amy's throat constricted. "I know. I... It doesn't matter. It breaks my heart to see them so helpless."

"And I adore you for being so tender-hearted, my love, but don't let this come between us. Must you break *my* heart as well?"

She took his hands and placed them on either side of her face. Then, pulling his face down to hers, she kissed him softly on the mouth. He made a sound deep in his throat that could not mask the pleasure he felt in her touch.

For a moment Amy rejoiced in the power she held over him, but then she drew back. "I must go now or her ladyship will give me a scolding. Will I see you tomorrow?"

"Nothing could keep me away." He kissed her lightly on the mouth before taking his leave.

All that time Amy thought they had been alone, but Maggie popped out from behind the statue of a Greek god. "Aye, now you're beginnin' to get the idea." She took Amy's cloak and hung it on the statue's extended arm for McMasters to deal with. "I had me purse ready to bang you over the 'ead for 'ow you treated 'im in the carriage, but sure an' you pulled the fat out o' the fire."

"Was it necessary to wound me? My ankle is still sore from when you kicked me in the carriage," Amy said. There was laughter in her voice.

"''Twas just a bit of a nudge. 'E's comin' round fine, miss. I'll wager 'e'll make one grand husband."

"And father," Amy added.

"Aye, several times over, unless I miss my bet." They both dissolved in laughter as they climbed the stairs together.

PREPARATIONS WERE well under way for the betrothal ball to be held seven days hence at Kesterson House. Amy was too excited to do much more than stand for fittings and play with William. Farrencourt surprised her one day by suggesting that they take William for a stroll in St. James's Park. Amy was delighted with the chance to show off the baby in public. She had planned to allow only her abigail to accompany them to the park that afternoon but Topaz, who had a sudden and inexplicable desire to get back to nature, prevailed upon Farrencourt to invite her. Emerald declined, having received an invitation through a certain Major Vonnegut, whom she had met at the Beersford soirée, to peruse a private library that was said to have no equal in all of London. Lily had been invited to attend a showing at the Royal Gallery with her latest suitor, Lord Mockerby, much to Farrencourt's delight.

Amy was pleased that Lily was happy for the first time in weeks. Perhaps something would come of this tentative alliance. Lily wouldn't admit to anything, but the gleam in her eyes was unmistakable.

Amy felt a stab of disappointment that Lily had begun to confide less and less in her now that Amy was betrothed to her brother. It occurred to her that growing up meant gaining some advantages while at the same time losing others.

For their sojourn to the park, Amy chose a walking dress of nakara velvet slashed with willow green on the puffed sleeves. An inset of green at the scalloped hem was threaded with pinkish-pearl beadwork, a shade darker than the nakara, sewn in the shape of leaves and flowers. Her straw bonnet was banded with matching beadwork sewn onto the velvet ribbons that surrounded the hat and trailed down her back. Farrencourt's look of admiration made it well worth the high price Lady Udora had paid for the ensemble.

While William's coach was being placed in Farrencourt's carriage, Nurse Finkley brought Wills down from the nursery and handed him to Sally, who was to accompany them. The baby screwed up his face, huge tears pooled in his eyes, and he immediately began to howl. Amy looked distraught.

"I'm so sorry. I can't imagine what's come over him. He is usually so sweet and docile."

"Is he going to be sick?" Farrencourt asked, looking uncomfortable and wary.

"No. He's neither sick nor hungry."

"Mayhap 'tis the new bonnet," the nurse said. "Shall I fetch the old one?"

"Oh, I don't know. It's so dreadfully worn. Well, perhaps he could have it to hold in his hands. It does seem to quiet him."

The nurse dropped a curtsy, then ran to fetch it. Amy took the baby from Sally, but it wasn't until the nurse returned with the blue-and-grey wool bonnet that Wills became content.

Topaz came flying down the stairs, her skirt held so high that Farrencourt was forced to turn away. "I hope I'm not late," she said, pushing her straw bonnet down over her silver-gold hair. "I forgot my parasol."

Farrencourt regarded her as he would a child. "You'd best take a cloak, Miss Topaz. The weather is still cool."

McMasters, having anticipated the order, had already brought her hooded *poussière de Paris* with the ermine trim from the armoire and assisted her into it.

It was still more than an hour before the fashionable hour of five, but the park was already crowded. Topaz was not content to allow them to remain in the landau, insisting instead that they stroll the paths and walkways to take full advantage of the afternoon sunshine. When they reached a grove of beech trees, the reason soon became apparent. She leapt down from the carriage and ran to meet a young man who was manoeuvring aloft a brilliant red kite whose string was anchored to a convenient hitching post.

Farrencourt looked alarmed. "I say, does she know this person?"

Amy sighed. "I'm afraid so. He's Mr. Endicott, her balloonist friend."

"Should we be concerned? Perhaps I should insist she stay with us."

Amy laughed. "When Taz makes up her mind to something there's no stopping her. But for propriety's sake I think it would be best if we didn't stray too far."

Farrencourt agreed, then turned his attention to watching Sally settle Wills into his baby coach. Within moments a crowd of curious passers-by gathered. Here he was at last, the baby everyone was so curious to see.

Today Amy was especially proud of the way William looked in his white silk gown, blue coat and bonnet. Having the old bonnet in his hand seemed to be enough to pacify him. He gurgled and cooed and made baby faces at everyone who spoke to him. But more than that, Amy was delighted with the way Farrencourt enjoyed playing the role into which he had been forced.

One elderly couple who had recently returned from the Indies, mistakenly assumed that Amy and Farrencourt were already wed and that William was their own child.

"Well, I'll be blessed!" the portly gentleman exclaimed. "He's the spittin' image of you, my boy. I used to dandle you on my knee when you were a mere tadpole." He adjusted a monocle to his eye. "Yes sir, looks just like you when you were a lad." He winked at Amy. "You made a good job of it, madam," he said, tipping his top hat in her direction. "Now that this one's up to snuff, it's my guess you'll be starting the next one. Harrumph. Pays to have a spare you know, just to keep the name going."

Farrencourt started to deny being the father, but the woman patted him on the arm. "Don't let Cyrus tease you, my lord. He's been in the Indies for so long that he's forgotten how to be civil."

"Think nothing of it, madam, but I . . . "

Cyrus chucked William under the chin and the baby giggled and threw his arms about so hard that the bonnet he was holding flew from his hands. Farrencourt picked it up and pleated it between his fingers.

Once again he started to explain that the baby was a foundling, but no sooner had he begun than a trio of men in a carriage caught Cyrus's attention and the couple begged to be excused.

Farrencourt blew out his cheeks. "I couldn't get a word in if I'd used a pickaxe."

Amy laughed. "I wonder if you really were that chubby when you were a baby."

Wills looked up at them, and his face spread in a wide grin. He gurgled and waved his fists so that both Amy and Farrencourt laughed. The sound seemed to echo from across the grounds, but when Amy looked in that direction she saw the balloonist and Topaz laughing as he took her hand.

"Farrencourt, I think we ought to speak to Topaz before she gets into trouble."

"You go, my sweet, if you don't object. Topaz doesn't take kindly to my criticism. While you caution her, I'll just take a moment to speak with Sir Archmont, who is motioning to me." He touched her cheek. "I promise not to let you out of my sight."

Amy was relieved. Sally trundled William's coach while Amy went on ahead to speak to Topaz.

Their laughter had ended and they seemed to be involved in a serious conversation, so serious that they were unaware when Amy came up behind them. They were talking about her and Lord Farrencourt . . . and Eva Delight. It was this last name that stirred Amy's apprehensions. Her face sobered.

Topaz looked unsettled when she became aware of Amy's presence. She laughed shakily. "I was afraid our handholding might bring you over to scold me.

Amy, you are so predictable. You are becoming more like Lady Udora every day.''

"Taz, I shouldn't have to remind you...."

"Now, don't chastise me, Amy. Mr. Endicott is just showing me how to hold the kite string." She motioned to the tall youth standing next to her.

"You remember my friend, David Endicott."

He doffed an imaginary cap and bowed. "Miss Thackery. It's a pleasure to see you again. Miss Topaz tells me that you are recently betrothed."

Having spoken to him for only a brief time at Vauxhall Gardens, Amy was once again taken aback by the smoothness of his manners. He didn't seem at all like a wastrel or ne'er-do-well. And he was quite handsome in a boyish way. She smiled and inclined her head. But all three of them were aware that the smile did not reach her eyes.

Topaz caught her lip between her teeth. "You overheard part of our conversation, didn't you?"

Amy shrugged. "I would like to know what it was concerning me that caused such a serious look on your face, Topaz."

Topaz appeared stricken. "It's nothing, really. Just idle gossip."

"I can always tell when you're lying."

Topaz looked up at Mr. Endicott. "We have no choice, David. She has a right to know."

David took a deep breath, wiped his hand against his trouser leg and knotted his fingers behind his back. When he spoke, he appeared to choose his words with care.

"Miss Thackery, I would much prefer not to be the one to repeat the gossip that has been going round, but I agree with Topaz—you do have a right to know...before you make a mistake that is difficult to rectify.''

She sensed his discomfort but she was insistent. "I assume you are speaking of my approaching marriage. Do go on.''

"Just this. It is a well-known fact that Lord Farrencourt keeps a small establishment for his female friends. One friend in particular.''

"Eva Delight?''

"Yes. Topaz said that Farrencourt told you it was over between them, but I don't think he is telling the truth." He hesitated for a moment, then rushed on. "I myself have seen him go there twice a day just in this past week. Unless I miss my guess, he will be there again sometime within the next two hours.''

Amy's heart nearly stopped. "I don't believe it. I'll never believe it unless I see it with my own eyes.''

"I'm sorry to be the one who must destroy your opinion of him, but it is better to know the truth.''

"Just tell me where this place is.''

He gave her an address near the Pulteney Hotel. Amy remembered that was the hotel where Eva Delight was known to have stayed. It was uncomfortably logical that she might seek to remain in the same area.

Topaz looked crushed. "I'm sorry, Amy. I didn't know whether or not to tell you...."

"It's all right. Thank you, Mr. Endicott. I'll warrant the story is nothing but idle gossip, but I prefer to know the truth. Come along, Topaz. I wish to go home. William has had enough air for one day.''

Farrencourt was a little surprised by their sudden departure, but he raised no protest. Everything considered, it had been a perfect afternoon. He allowed his knee to lean against Amy's skirt, where the outline of her hip was clearly defined, but there was no answering movement on her part. One look at her face told him something was wrong. Indeed, she hardly spoke at all until they arrived at the house and he confronted her alone.

"What is it, Amethyst? Are you displeased because I left you to speak with my friends?"

"Certainly not." She looked closely at his face in order to judge his reaction. "I assume you have the rest of the afternoon free. Would you care to stay at the house until Lord Kesterson returns home? I know that Lady Udora would be pleased to have you join us for tea."

"I . . . er, thank you, but I cannot. I fear that I have a previous engagement."

"Indeed?" His words made her wince inwardly. Was this previous engagement, in truth, a rendezvous with Eva Delight? He didn't offer an explanation and it took all of her will-power to keep from questioning him.

He stroked his chin. "But if I may, I would like to see you later this evening."

"Yes, if you wish."

"It's settled then. I shall endeavour to return as quickly as possible," he said, patting his coat. "Ah, yes, William's bonnet. I found it on the ground where we stood before you left to speak to Miss Topaz. I trust it would be a disaster if I neglected to return it."

He held it in both hands, turning it in his fingers as he settled his gaze on Amy. "I can well understand your affection for the boy, my dearest. He is quite bewitching...." He stopped suddenly and gazed at the bonnet. "What's this?" he said, looking more closely. "An embroidered crest. I can just barely see it, it is so faded."

"Let me see." Amy took the bonnet and held it in the light. "Yes. How odd that we never noticed it. It appears to be two lions and a flame."

"Give it to me!" Farrencourt demanded.

Amy was surprised by his abruptness, but she handed the bonnet over to him.

"God's blood! This is impossible!"

"What...what is it, my lord?"

"This is the Farrencourt Crest. See, a tiny *F* is sewn at the base of the flame."

"But...but why would your family crest be embroidered on William's bonnet?"

"Why indeed? Where did this come from?"

"Why...William was wearing it when his mother gave him to me before she disappeared."

"Tell me, what did she look like?"

"It's...it's hard to remember her, but she was a little taller than I, her hair was brown and she had brown eyes. Yes, I remember that. They were quite large...or perhaps they only seemed that way because she was so thin. And she wore a small gold locket in the shape of a leaf. I remember it because Wills kept reaching for it."

Farrencourt sank down onto a chair. His hands went to his face. "Impossible. Yet it must be true. This is my sister's child. I had no idea she had become a mother.''

Amy's face clouded. "But...but you do know that she is dead, my lord. The woman was killed only moments after she left us.''

"Do you think I'm not aware of that? My God! What have I done to her... banishing her from our home? She would still be alive if I hadn't been so harsh with her.''

Amy put her hands on his shoulders. "You can't blame yourself. Lily tells me that your sister was quite strong-willed. I'm sure you did what you thought was right.''

"I do blame myself. But I'll make up for it if it takes all my life.'' He rose abruptly. "She left me the boy. At least I can raise him the way she would have wanted him to be raised.''

"Wh-what do you mean?''

"I'll take him home, of course, and install him in my household. It will be his home as long as he wants to make it so.''

"You can't take him now, today!''

"Is there any reason to delay?''

"Every reason! I can't let him go. I love him.''

"But he will be yours, too, as soon as we are wed.''

"That is over a month away. You can't do this to him, Farrencourt. He has already lost one family. Don't force him into another change. You can't possibly love him the way I do.''

He stroked his chin. "I can see that you might be right. Very well. I shall allow him to remain here while I have the nursery renovated and arrangements made for someone to care for him.''

He pulled his watch from his pocket and lifted the cover. "Egad. I'm late. If I don't leave now..."

"Must you go? Is it so important?"

He bent down and kissed her forehead. "I shall return this evening to see the boy and to discuss this with Lord Kesterson."

Amy saw him to the door and watched him leave. Could she trust him? Not if he had lied to her about Eva Delight. And there was one way to find out. As soon as his carriage was out of sight, she ran upstairs to change into something less noticeable. Sally finally appeared after a long delay. "'Ere now, let me do them hooks."

"Never mind. I'm in a hurry. Run down to the stable and tell McPherson to ready a carriage."

"What? You're going out now? 'Er ladyship said as 'ow I could 'ave a mo' to sit in the kitchen wi' Mr. Brimm and 'ave me a cup o' tea."

"You're staying here this time. Send Maggie to me and be sure to tell the stable-boy to bring round the brougham and not the cabriolet. I want a carriage that's covered."

"Where shall I say you're going, miss?"

"Never mind. I'll give him his instructions later. Now go."

Sally looked puzzled as usual, but at least she must have done as she was told, because a few minutes later Maggie breezed into the bedroom.

"Now wot 'ave you gone an' done?" she asked, more curious than accusatory. "Sally says you're up to no good."

"Get your cloak and bonnet. We're going out."

"And just where are we off to?"

"I'll tell you about it in the carriage."

Maggie grinned. "Aye, so 'tis mischief we're up to, is it now? 'Er ladyship won't be lookin' on *this* with favour."

"There's no reason she should find out, now is there?"

Maggie laughed. "Some things is sure to happen. Aye, there ain't nothin' you can do to stop the snow, nor keep the river from risin'. She knows everything that goes on in this 'ouse."

"Well, see that *you* don't tell her. And hurry. We've no time to lose. Fetch your cloak and I'll join you downstairs."

"Yes, mistress." Maggie made an exaggerated curtsy and left the room.

A few minutes later Amy went quietly down the back stairs and into the front entrance to get her cloak. McMasters was just coming down the main staircase.

"Oh, there you are, miss. Sally says to tell you that Maggie and your carriage are waiting in the drive."

"Th-thank you, McMasters," Amy said, casting a sideways glance at Lady Udora, who, having suddenly appeared in the foyer, was unfortunately not caught napping.

"Carriage? You're going out now?"

"Only for a short time."

"Really! You have that look in your eyes, Amy, as if you're hiding something." She tucked her hands in her sleeves. "You'd best be honest with me, because you can be certain that I'll find out eventually."

Amy burst into tears. It was several minutes before she could manage to tell Udora everything that had transpired.

"So that's who the baby is," Udora said. "No wonder the mother called you by name when she handed the baby over to you. She must have heard of your friendship with Lily and wanted the boy to have part of his rightful heritage."

"But how did she know she would be killed in the carriage accident?"

"She couldn't have, of course. I suspect she found she was unable to care for the baby and decided to run away. But that doesn't answer my question, dear. Where are you going in such a hurry?"

"I mean to follow Farrencourt. I'm told on good authority that he is keeping a mistress, even after he swore to me that he had stopped seeing her."

"Pity. But not unusual, you know. It would be best that you pretend ignorance. You aren't, after all, married as yet. And even then . . ."

"But he swore to me. If I can't trust him, how can I trust him with Wills?"

"At any rate, he's gone. It's too late to follow him."

"I don't need to. I know where he is going."

Udora shook her head. "I strongly advise against confronting him, Amy. You could ruin everything and lose the baby, as well."

"I must know the truth."

Udora sighed. "Then I'll go with you. McMasters, my cloak and bonnet."

THE THREE WOMEN were pensive during the carriage ride until Udora finally broke the silence. "Pistachions! I wish Bently had been home. He would have known what to do about all this. Perhaps we should have waited for him."

Amy sat tight-lipped.

Maggie eyed both of them with heightened curiosity. "I don't know wot all the fuss is about. Tom-cats stray but they always come 'ome. Sure and you can't 'ope to lead the man by the rope until you've at least tied the knot."

Udora gave her a quelling look, and for once Maggie became silent. They had no sooner passed the Pulteney Hotel than, some distance ahead, they saw Farrencourt's carriage pull to a stop in front of a small grey house tucked back under the trees. Farrencourt alighted with a spring in his step and went into the house as if he belonged there.

Amy's voice sounded strange even to her own ears. "Then it's true what Topaz's friend said. Farrencourt is still seeing her."

Udora's face hardened. "Pistachions. I had hoped it was a rumour." She straightened. "Well, my girl, now you know. It's time to go home. And on the way you must tell me about Topaz's friend."

"I'll not go home until I know the truth. I've come this far, and I'm going in there."

Both Maggie and Udora gasped, but Amy was out of the carriage before they could stop her. There was nothing to do but follow.

Amy was trembling so hard that she could scarcely lift the door knocker. A quick look told her that the windows were shuttered. Within, the house was quiet.

Udora touched Amy's arm, causing her to jump. "I'm sorry, my dear, but just what are you going to say to them?"

They heard footsteps before Amy could answer. The door was opened by a plain-looking woman in a grey dress and a blue shawl. The housekeeper, Amy assumed.

"Yes. May I help you?"

"I've come to see Lord Farrencourt," Amy said, pushing her way past the startled woman. Udora and Maggie followed.

The woman looked alarmed. "But...you mustn't... Wait. You can't just..."

Apparently hearing the disturbance, Farrencourt stepped into the hallway to determine the cause. The surprise on his face at seeing Amy mirrored her own shock, because Farrencourt was holding a baby in his arms.

"Dear heaven," she murmured. "Isn't it enough that you're still seeing her? Now you're going to admit to giving her a child?"

Farrencourt handed the infant to the housekeeper. "What nonsense is this, Amy? What are you doing here?" He struck his forehead with the palm of his hand. "God's blood! You followed me? You actually followed me!"

"I didn't need to. Everyone in London is aware of your philandering ways. I came to see the evidence with my own eyes before I believed it, but...but I had no idea it had gone this far." Her voice trembled and broke. "How could you, Farrencourt? How could you do this when I loved you so much?"

A smile crinkled the corners of his eyes. "So that's how it is, eh? Then you might as well meet the rest of the family. Roger, Mary. Come join us, won't you?"

Udora's face had turned a dull red. "Farrencourt, indeed! This is despicable. Surely you are too much the gentleman to flaunt your..."

"My what? My friends?" He turned to the "housekeeper," and putting his arm across her shoulder, drew her towards him. "Lady Udora, Miss Thackery, may I present my new friend and her family, Mrs. Samuel Lockerby and her children."

The woman moved the baby to her shoulder and curtsied awkwardly. Farrencourt grinned. "Mr. Lockerby will be disappointed in having missed you, but he has gone to the market to buy food."

Mrs. Lockerby looked up at Farrencourt. "Is she the one, then, the girl?"

"She's the one. The one with the fire in her eyes."

Mrs. Lockerby looked at Amy with an expression of gratitude. "Then 'tis you I must thank for savin' us, miss. His lordship said 'twas you who saw us sittin' by the fire in the mews and wanted to help us. It was an answer to our prayers that night when he came and brought us here to a warm fire and a clean bed. And 'twas him who gave us food, too, thanks to your kind heart."

Farrencourt met Amy's gaze, and the love that shone from her eyes was so intense that he had, for an instant, to look away. Never before had he been so moved. Never before had he felt such euphoria. Never before had he loved anyone so irrevocably.

"Egan, I'm sorry," she whispered.

"Sorry?"

"For not trusting you. I was so afraid of losing you."

"You could never lose me. And one thing more. I've decided, upon discussing the raising of children with Mrs. Lockerby, to allow you to keep Wills until our marriage, at which time I will bring the two of you home to my house.''

Amy was too overwhelmed to speak, but her happiness showed through her tears.

Maggie, however, was not quite so moved. She gave Udora a knowing look. ''Now, if this ain't somethin'. 'E's gone and caught 'er 'abit of takin' in strays. I hope 'is house is as big as their hearts.''

But neither Amy nor Farrencourt heard, because she had flung herself into his arms and was kissing him in a most unladylike way.

EPILOGUE

THROUGH THE COMBINED resources of the Kestersons and Farrencourts, they were at last able to learn
the fate of Johnny Lapwell, William's father. Johnny
and Darlene had been married at Gretna Green a few
months before the birth of their child. Shortly after
their marriage, Johnny, while working on the docks,
had sacrificed his own life to rescue a fellow worker
who had fallen in the river. Darlene, left to provide for
herself and her new baby, apparently soon discovered
that she could not make sufficient wages and had decided to give up her son so that he might have a decent life.

During the three remaining weeks before his wedding, Egan spent a part of each day with his nephew
and soon came to love him as much as he adored Amy.

Lily, much to her surprise, was being seriously
courted by Lord Mockerby. She appeared to be deliriously happy, and Egan vowed that this time he would
not interfere.

Both Emerald and Topaz were of constant concern
to Lady Udora. The Season was concluding and they
were still not offered for. Topaz showed little interest
in any one man, save her balloonist friend, whom
Udora considered beyond the pale. As for Emerald...bluestocking that she was, only a miracle could

save her from being cast on the shelf before she turned eighteen. But then one day that miracle happened and it rocked all of London to its foundations.

* * * * *

Look for Emerald's story in Book 2 of the Thackery Jewels Trilogy.

EMERALD

EMERALD

CHAPTER ONE

JONATHAN TRENT forced himself to concentrate on what Lady Ethridge was saying. It wasn't easy, considering his present anxiety, and particularly since her face reminded him of the dried up river bed at the family's country home in Cheshire. *His* home now, he reminded himself. He steeled himself to keep from flinching as she placed her liver-spotted hands on his arms and drew him close.

"Now, listen to me, my boy, the torch has been passed to you and you must accept your responsibilities. Roger was a decent young man but far too..." She waggled her fingers in front of his face. "If you know what I mean. Cared more for the lightskirts than he did for the name, don't you know."

Over her shoulder Jonathan saw Fulbright step inside the salon and bow in deference to Jonathan's recently acquired station. "Begging your pardon, my lord, but your solicitor must see you before he leaves. Regarding a most urgent matter, sir."

"Thank you, Fulbright. If you will be so good as to see Lady Ethridge to the door." He bowed to her ladyship. "And I must thank you again, madam, for your condolences as well as your good wishes."

"Indeed. And I assure you, Jonathan, that we are ever here to advise and to comfort you in the loss of your nephew." She pressed a hand to her chest. "Such tragedies you've endured! How many does that make now? Your father, your two brothers and now young Roger. One would hardly have guessed that succession would fall to you."

"That, my lady, is to understate the case. Now, if you will kindly excuse me?" He nodded to Fulbright, who immediately picked up the cue and steered her in the direction of the main entrance.

Jonathan straightened his waistcoat and adjusted his cravat. "Silly old biddy," he muttered. "As if she cared a fig for my family."

"What's that you say, my lord?" Albert Thadeus, Lord Grafton, straightened from a lounging position against a pilaster and stubbed out his cheroot in a large Grecian pot containing a rubber tree.

"Grafton!" Jonathan's voice echoed his surprise. "I wondered where you'd got to." He motioned to his lanky friend. "Come along with me to the study. I could use your corrupting influence just now. I've had my fill of virtue and good wishes. Enough to last a lifetime, I'd say."

"Tired of playing the congenial host and bereaved uncle, eh? Well, get used to it, Milford. Believe me, the worst is yet to be, now that you've become lord of the manor."

Jonathan opened the door to the study, and waving his friend inside, nodded to the solicitor who rose to greet him.

"My lord, forgive me for intruding upon your bereavement, but I must have a word with you before I depart for the country."

"No need to apologize, Mr. Skinner. Lord Grafton, I believe you have met my solicitor, Mr. Harold Skinner?"

They shook hands and murmured pleasantries. Then Skinner, looking absurdly uncomfortable, asked to speak with Jonathan in private.

Jonathan scowled. "There is no need. Grafton is my closest friend and confidant. He knows everything there is to know about me."

For the briefest instant a cunning look flickered across the solicitor's face and he cocked his head to one side. "Not quite everything, my lord." He smiled. "But if you wish him to stay..." He moved to the opposite side of the desk. "May we sit down? This will only take a few minutes."

Jonathan felt his belly tighten as he settled into his chair and waited while the solicitor shuffled through his papers. He hadn't been this helpless since four years ago when his favourite mare had run amok with a rag picker's stallion on St. Swithen's day. Once again things were happening that he couldn't put a stop to. Each time someone addressed him by his newly acquired title he became more deeply conscious of the passage of time as well as the approaching end of his carefree youth. He fidgeted in his chair.

"Do get on with it, man," Jonathan ordered.

"Yes, yes, here it is. I'll just jump to the part that is most vital. The section, ah...concerning your age."

"My age? By the gods above, I've only just turned eight and twenty. It's not as if I'm an old man. The last marquess was but nineteen when he died."

"Ah, just so. And that is the crux of the will, my lord. You see, no one wishes to contest your claim to the title, but there is one small stipulation."

"And what might that be?"

Harold Skinner appeared hard put to conceal a gleeful smile. "Only this, Lord Milford, and I use your title with the certain confidence that you will not turn it down."

Jonathan shot him a warning look, and the solicitor pointed to a passage of text. "Yes, well, the point of the stipulation is that if you wish to assume the title and all that it entails—and I might add that the amount is quite considerable—then you must, because you have passed the age of one and twenty, take a wife within one year of the day you become heir to the title. That would fall upon the first anniversary of young Roger's death three days ago."

Jonathan jumped to his feet and swore competently. "What do you mean, I must marry? What will happen if I don't?"

"Why, you will lose everything, my lord. Everything. It all reverts to the Crown."

Lord Grafton leaned forward and placed his elbows on the desk. "And may I ask, Mr. Skinner, what you might have to gain from this if my friend should fail to take a wife?" he asked, brushing a lock of fine gold hair away from his forehead.

Harold Skinner mouthed the air like a fish out of water. "Why, nothing, nothing at all, my lord. Of course, my firm would be appointed to oversee the transfer of the estate as well as the management of same until..."

"Just as I thought." Grafton leaned back, balancing his chair on its hind legs, and studied the carved plaster ceiling.

"See here, if you mean to imply..."

"I imply nothing, Mr. Skinner. It only appears to me that you are a little too pleased by the prospect that my friend may lose his inheritance."

Jonathan strode back to the desk. "I assume there is no way of getting round this stipulation. Is there anything else that I should know?"

"Er... only that you must remain wed to the same woman for a period of five years before the marriage is considered valid."

"And?"

"That is all, my lord... that is, except for the fact that should you refuse to take a wife, you will lose not only your inheritance but the monthly stipend you've been receiving from the estate since the age of sixteen." He hesitated as if organizing his thoughts. "Of course, you will be granted the title and all its privileges until the time comes for you to forfeit.

"And, er—" he pulled a kerchief from his pocket and mopped his brow "—there is also a clause to prevent your absconding with the funds or selling the property. Not that the thought would enter your mind. It is important that you read the other clauses regarding disbursement of various belongings. And if you have further questions I will be happy to speak with you again." He rose. "If there is nothing else, my lord, I must be on my way."

"Fulbright will see you to the door," Jonathan stated, knowing full well that his butler would doubtless be within earshot just outside the room.

Skinner looked strained. "Good day, Lord Milford, Lord Grafton." He didn't wait for them to answer, but scurried to the door, ducking under Fulbright's arm in his haste to depart.

Jonathan slammed his fist on the desk and looked over at his companion. "Gods above, Grafton. I don't want this."

"What, old man? Don't want your inheritance? There's a thousand men who would kill without blinkin' an eye for what you've come into."

"At the cost of my freedom, I might add."

"Nonsense. Marriage is nothing more than a mere annoyance. Ask any of the young blades we know who got themselves leg shackled to some giddy debutante just to keep the family name alive. Once the deed is accomplished and she takes a son to suckle, you've done your part and you're free to go your own way. As long as you are reasonably discreet," he added with a wink.

Jonathan grinned as he walked round the desk and gave his friend a playful shove. "Grafton, you are a cad."

Grafton, though still seated, made a caricature of a bow, sweeping an imaginary hat from his head. "Then I count myself in good company, sir. I would be the first to admit that we have made a merry time of it ever since that first day at school when we dipped Herr Professor's chair in sheep's piss."

They laughed together recalling their student days, then Grafton folded his arms across his chest and studied Jonathan's face. "Just to make this a bit more interesting, old man, suppose we place a wager on your impending change of fortune."

"What did you have in mind? Surely you can't believe that I'll find it impossible to persuade some female to accept my offer for her hand in marriage?"

"The thought did cross my mind," Grafton said, knowing that Milford was considered exceptionally eligible, in view of his wealth and position, and despite his reputation as a rake. They laughed again, then he continued, "Actually, what I had in mind was a slightly different wager. With just a wee hint of danger involved," he said, placing his thumb and index finger a fraction apart.

"Danger?" Milford asked, eyebrows raised.

"Just enough to add a drop of vinegar to this sweet wager."

"Go on."

Grafton was obviously struggling to keep from laughing. When he was able to control himself he confronted Jonathan with an innocent expression. "Well, old man, since we both know that you currently have no *grande passion* for any single bit of female fluff the ton has to offer..." He drew a deep breath. "I'll wager my collection of porcelain music boxes of which you are so enamoured against your gilded *vis-à-vis* that you will refuse to marry the next woman who comes through this study door."

"No, my friend. There are a half-dozen servant girls scurrying about here doing God knows what. If I must marry to preserve the name, then I'd surely be expected to marry someone of my own class."

"Granted... and point well taken. Suppose we discount servants and anyone of low breeding? And since I'm in a generous mood, we will also discount any woman over the age of thirty."

"Forgive me if I fail to recognize your generosity." Milford thought for a moment and then grinned. "Very well, if you are absolutely sure about this. But be warned. I have a glass-fronted chest designed by Reginald Beech that would be the perfect home for your collection of music boxes."

Grafton stuck out his hand. "Agreed." The lines around his eyes crinkled in amusement. "I wish Percy Martin and the major were here. I'd feel much better if I had a witness to your most recent folly."

"My folly, indeed. Before you leave I intend to order Fulbright to forbid entrance to this room to everyone save those of whom I first give approval. And you can be certain that my choice will be a lady of unusual beauty and obedience."

"Not fair, Milford. You're all but rigging the outcome."

"'Twas you who set the rules, my friend. Henceforth you'll be poorer but wiser in how you stage your bets."

Lord Grafton thrust out his chin. "Don't count your coins before you hear them jingle, Milford. Fate is on my side. Even with all your clever ploys you're sure to be the loser. Shall we seal the wager with a glass of port?" Grafton plopped down onto the chair and stretched out his legs. "On second thought, better make it two. I think you're going to need it."

Jonathan lifted the stopper from the decanter. "Just one thing. Not a word of this to the major or Percy. I'll not have them setting traps for me."

"You have my word on it. At least not until your victim has entered the lair."

"Fair enough," Jonathan said as they clinked glasses in a friendly salute. "And that might be sooner than you think, my friend, because in five minutes' time I'm off to kidnap Lucy Tripton and invite her to a cosy little dinner party." He swung his arms wide to take in the room. "I think this should provide the perfect setting for our dark-haired beauty. And you know I'm partial to dark hair and brown eyes."

Grafton scowled. "Particularly when they come with a fat dowry. I think I've been gulled."

"You brought it on yourself, my friend." Milford stroked his chin. "Yes, indeed. The porcelains will look rather smashing in this room, as I'm sure anyone would agree."

EMERALD THACKERY shook out the folds of her brown-and-grey walking dress to dispose of the wrinkles. "Do try not to be so disagreeable, Maggie. If it were up to me I'd dispense entirely with a chaperon. The major is quite capable of looking after me, and he is certainly no threat to my person."

"And no mistake," Maggie muttered under her breath. "The most excitin' thing wot's ever happened to you was the day you broke a fingernail on yer left 'and."

"Don't be impudent, Maggie. And don't spoil this day for me, please. I've been looking forward to exploring this collection of books since I first heard about it from Major Vonnegut. It's one of the largest private libraries in all of England, and thanks to the major, who is a close friend of the owner, I'll have a chance to see it for myself."

"I'll wager 'er ladyship don't know where you're off to."

"Actually, she does. Oh, don't look so surprised." Emerald made a face. "I promised I'd attend the Mullenford soirée with Lord Cullen if she allowed me this favour." She pushed her glasses onto the bridge of her nose. "But come, we mustn't keep the major waiting."

Major Vonnegut rose and bowed as they entered the salon. He bore himself well, thanks to his military training. If he had thickened a bit around the middle, it could be attributed to age and his penchant for blueberry trifle. His moustache tilted to one side as he smiled down at them. "Ladies, may I say how honoured I am that you have allowed me to be your escort today. It is a pleasure I have looked forward to all week."

Emerald returned his smile with enthusiasm. Here was a man with whom she could be comfortable. His thick head of salt-and-pepper hair gave evidence to his forty-three years, but he was well-preserved for an old man, she decided. Not that she had developed an interest in him, save for his brilliant mind, which she considered his best feature. But she enjoyed his company and she took full advantage of the access he gave her to private libraries, for Major Vonnegut was a welcome guest at many of the homes in the Upper Ten Thousand.

He had brought the landau today. The top had been raised in deference to the evening chill, and the Devonshire brown upholstery was cleaned and brushed and sprinkled with just a hint of bayberry scent to prevent it from smelling musty.

Maggie settled into her corner with a sigh of contentment while Emerald took a seat next to her, back straight, feet and knees together, gloved hands folded demurely in her lap.

"Is it far, Major?"

"No, my dear. Just a mere twenty minutes at a leisurely pace. I doubt that his lordship will be at home, but do not be disturbed by this. His staff is in attendance, and I am as much at home in his house as I am in my own."

"Were it not for your unsullied reputation, her ladyship would never have allowed you to take me there without her in attendance."

"I appreciate her concern, Miss Thackery. You are, after all, a very pretty young lady."

Emerald knew he was only being gallant with his compliments. One could hardly be considered pretty when one was forced to wear spectacles to keep from falling over the furniture. "You are too kind, sir, but it is my twin sister, Amethyst, and my adopted sister, Topaz, who are the pretty ones. I, alas, have been blessed with intelligence. Surely you must know by now that I am considered a bluestocking."

"Only by those who envy your excellent mind, I'm sure. I've never before met a young woman who can converse so comfortably on any subject from history to politics to current social issues. Had I been fortunate enough to have a daughter, I would have wanted her to be just like you."

"Thank you. I consider that high praise."

"I understand that the rest of your family has passed on."

"Yes, everyone save a renegade aunt, my father's sister, who ran off in disgrace to the Colonies several years ago. That is why Lady Udora, my father's sister-in-law, was called upon to become guardian to the three of us. And she is quite wonderful, I must add. She all but saved us from a certain disaster."

"And that is how you came to be known as the Thackery Jewels." He smiled. "And now you hold London Society in the palm of your hand."

"Well, not precisely. Amy, of course, has recently become betrothed. Topaz has had several offers, but she is the rebel among us. I can't begin to imagine what Fate has in store for her."

"And you, my dear?" he asked teasingly. "Are you fighting off the young men at your doorstep?"

She laughed. "You overestimate me, sir. It's true, there have been a number of offers, but none that I would even consider. It is only pressure from her ladyship that makes me even think of finding a husband. I am quite content to be married to my books."

"No, my child. Don't even suggest such a thing. You are far too important to be allowed to sit on the shelf. If I were younger..." He laughed. "But never mind. You will find the right man when the time comes. Or he will find you." He turned his head to view the passing scenery. "You see, I told you it wasn't far. We are just moments away from his lordship's residence."

Emerald's first impression of the house was of restrained grandeur. No pretentious white columns here, none of the lavishly carved curlicues that adorned so many grand residences. Instead, it was of redbrick, solid looking and somewhat austere save for its slate blue shutters and mullioned windows, which must have flooded the house with light, for there were more windows than she could count from the moving carriage.

"It's a house that's been loved, I think," she murmured.

The major chuckled. "Yes. You have guessed correctly. The first marquess had the residence built for his bride over a hundred years ago. It has been kept in remarkable repair, though I daresay it has cried out for a woman's touch these past few years. Hasn't been a woman in residence since the old marchioness died in childbirth. Let's see now . . . that must be about thirty years ago."

He straightened as the carriage came to a halt and the driver got down from his perch to assist them.

Emerald had the strangest feeling as they climbed the few steps to the front entrance and lifted the massive gold ring that served as a knocker. Her stomach fluttered and she found that she was trembling. She laughed. "I can't tell you, Major, how excited I am over this opportunity to peruse the library. Look, my hands are shaking."

He had no chance to respond when the door was unceremoniously flung open. The major looked surprised as they were greeted by a very nervous servant girl.

"Aye, 'tis you, Major Vonnegut. Come in, come in. 'Is lordship is away at the moment, sir, but 'e's expected back in a w'ile, 'e is."

"Fanny, isn't it?" She dropped a hasty curtsy and nodded. The major continued. "I say, is something wrong here? Where's the butler, the footman?"

"In the kitchen, sir. There's been a' accident in the kitchen. Walter, the footman, backed into the stove an 'it 'is elbow on the pot what was full o' stew. It tipped bottom end up an' spilled itself all onto Mrs. Perkins's clean floor."

"Was anyone hurt?"

Fanny's cheeks dimpled. "Just a wee bump on Walter's 'ead where Mrs. Perkins 'it 'im with the iron skillet, but Fulbright says there's no need to worry."

"That's a blessing. I told his lordship that I might bring Miss Thackery round one day to look over the library. Miss Thackery is quite an expert on books."

Fanny, a bright-eyed dumpling of a girl, gave Emerald and then Maggie a cursory inspection that registered simple curiosity without indicating either approval or disapproval. "I guess that should be all right, sir, seein' as 'ow you've been 'ere before." She looked back over her shoulder. "You know where the lib'ary is, Major. If you would be needin' me, just give a tug on the bell rope. I'll be in the kitchen seein' wot needs doin'."

Once the girl was out of earshot, Maggie surveyed the hall and let out a low whistle. "Aye, and 'tis no wonder they couldn't afford to fix up the outside. They spent all their blunt on the inside." She was looking at a tapestry, mounted in a gold frame, that covered an entire wall from floor to ceiling. The scene depicted the changing seasons in what appeared to be a deer park beside a swiftly moving stream. Her eyes widened. "And would you look at that chandelier? The cost of them candles alone would keep a family in food for close to a year."

"Hush, Maggie. One would think this is the first time you've seen such wealth."

Maggie sniffed. "Flush in the pockets they must be, but they sure don't know 'ow to run a 'ouse." She ran her hand across a table that stood along the wall of the corridor leading to the library. "Dust! A month's worth if I 'ad my guess. Lady Udora would be in 'igh dudgeon if we let 'er house go like this."

The major agreed. "You're right, Maggie, though I daresay it would be prudent not to voice your opinion in his lordship's presence. He doesn't take well to criticism. But as I said, the house needs a woman's touch."

They proceeded down the wide corridor, past rooms with closed doors and niches that held glass-enclosed displays of *objets d'art*, until they reached a wide area where two other corridors branched off, forming a sort of reception area containing uncomfortable-looking straight-backed chairs and a table centred on a truly lovely Aubusson rug. The door to the library was situated down the first corridor to the right. The major led them to the door and ushered the women inside.

Emerald caught her breath. It was not a large room, but except for several strategically located windows on one side, the walls were lined from top to bottom with shelves containing leather-bound books. There were stacks of books on the floor and on the tables. Books in crates and barrels. Even the chairs were piled with books.

When the major went to the window to open a drapery, the dust flew off in a musty grey cloud. Emerald coughed.

The major looked embarrassed. "Sorry, Miss Thackery. I had no idea they had let the room fall into disuse. His lordship is not one to spend his free time with a book."

"Somehow I rather guessed that," Emerald said with a rueful smile. "But no matter. Might we at least light a candle or two so that I can see the titles?"

"Certainly. Maggie, if you will tend to the candles, I'll see to the tinder and try to get a fire going. Been a while since I've done it on my own but I hate to bother the staff. They seem to have their hands full."

Maggie grinned. "Judgin' from wot I seen so far, they 'as their 'ands tied behind their backs." She took a gypsy match from the box, ignited it and lit three tapers. "But if 'twas me, I'd be careful o' lightin' a fire."

Emerald shot her a quelling look. "I'm sure we can manage just fine without disturbing the staff. Is there anything I can do?" she asked, going over to stand next to the major where he knelt in front of the hearth. "When my sisters and I lived at Amberleigh, I learned all there is to know about starting fires."

The major leaned forward, peering and prodding with a poker as he attempted with his other hand to ignite an unidentifiable pile of debris. "By George, then you know more about it than I do. I can't seem to get the match to burn."

"Let me see." Emerald bent down in front of him to survey the carelessly arranged logs. As she touched the lighted gypsy match to the kindling, they heard a *poof* and the immediate area was suddenly engulfed in flames and sooty black smoke.

Emerald's hands flew to her face. "Great Heavens! What on earth?"

The major jumped to her side with amazing agility. "I say, are you all right?" They both started coughing. Maggie looked on with obvious amusement.

"Hit's like I thought. The girl's been throwin' 'er furniture-polishin' rags in the fireplace. I smelled 'em the minute I walked in the room."

"Oh, don't act so smug, Maggie. Do something," Emerald said through fits of coughing.

The major took Emerald's arm. "My dear girl, I am so sorry. We'd best move to another room before the smoke strangles you."

"But first we must close the fireplace screen. The books! They'll be ruined."

The major sighed. "Yes, I suppose you're right." He fumbled for the enclosure to contain the smoke.

"That should do for now. Come. Let's get some fresh air." He opened a narrow door that was half-hidden behind a rolling ladder and ushered them into the adjoining room. Emerald's first impression was that it appeared to be an office of some sort. There was a desk centred in the bay formed by three windows. Several comfortable chairs were positioned round it. Some official looking papers rested beneath a crystal paperweight.

Maggie was not looking at her surroundings. Her gaze was fixed on Emerald, who stood nearby, and on the major, who had walked over to the desk. It was apparently all she could do to keep from laughing.

"What is it?" Emerald demanded as she cleaned the soot from her spectacles with a square of linen.

The major gave her a curious look then cleared his throat. "Nothing serious, Miss Thackery. It's just…"

He was about to continue when they heard laughter and conversation from the corridor seconds before the door was flung open.

"Oh, it's you, Major," Jonathan said. "I hear we've had a bit of a commotion below stairs, but it seems to be over. Will you join us for dinner? Grafton and Lady Tripton are with me," he said, moving farther into the room.

Sensing that something wasn't quite right, Jonathan turned abruptly in the direction from which he had entered. There, standing off to one side, were two women. One was obviously an abigail, for she was dressed neatly in the soft grey uniform of a servant. The other woman… He took a second look and nearly lost his footing. The other woman wore a mask. As if that were not enough, the truth of what had just transpired hit him suddenly… like the proverbial bolt of lightning. He looked quickly over at Grafton who was bent nearly double in silent laughter.

CHAPTER TWO

To Emerald, standing with her spectacles still in hand, the man who had just spoken was little more than a hazy blur. It was, however, impossible to miss the sharp edge of surprise in his voice. He was not pleased by their intrusion into his home. Having hastily removed the last trace of soot from the glass, she replaced her spectacles and regarded the new arrivals with considerable curiosity.

Two men and a lady, whom she recognized as Lucy Tripton. The lady's abigail, needless to say, was in attendance. Miss Tripton was attractive enough to catch the eye of most males over the age of thirteen, but too buffleheaded to carry on any conversation that didn't concern her own person.

Lord Grafton she had seen once before at Almack's. He had sandy blond hair, a shade or two lighter than her own, and slippery eyes that refused to meet hers. Of course, one could lay that to the fact that he was bent over with laughter. What he found so humorous could only be imagined.

It was Jonathan Trent, Lord Milford himself, who held her attention. He was taller than she had thought at first glance, and exquisitely groomed. His dark hair waved back from his forehead, giving him an appearance of intelligence and breeding. A square jaw, thrust out now in apparent anger, did little to ease the tension created by his mere presence in the room.

The major stepped forward with a jovial slap to his lordship's shoulder. "I say there, Milford, you're just in time to oversee this mess."

Milford shifted his gaze from the major to Emerald. His voice was as uncompromising as his stance. "It appears that someone must. Just how does it happen that Fulbright allowed you into the study? I gave explicit orders that no one was to be allowed entry."

"See here, dear boy, it was not my intention to start a bumble broth. Fulbright was not about. I've been in this room more times than I can count. I saw no harm in our taking refuge from the smoke."

"Smoke? I fail to comprehend. Has this to do with the accident in the kitchen?"

"Oh, no. You've got it all wrong, dear boy. Miss Thackery and I were attempting to light the tinder in the library fireplace when it attacked us." He stole a glance at Emerald. "I say, do forgive me. I haven't introduced you."

Lord Milford looked white faced and angry, Lucy Tripton snickered, Lord Grafton was grinning like a fox in the henhouse, and even the major seemed to have trouble suppressing a smile. Emerald couldn't for the life of her imagine what was so funny. As soon as the introductions were performed, Maggie whispered something to the major.

He nodded and said something in a low voice. Then Maggie whispered to Emerald, "We'd best excuse ourselves to freshen up, miss."

Emerald started to protest, but Maggie gave her a no-nonsense look that she must have learned from

Lady Udora. Turning to follow Maggie, Emerald caught a glimpse of herself in the mirror. Her face was covered with soot, save for two perfectly round white circles where her spectacles rested over her eyes.

"Oh...oh...oh!" she cried, then grabbed her skirts and fled the room.

When she was safely out of earshot, Grafton burst into laughter, then fell into a chair. "Well, Milford, you've done it this time. I admit that for a while you had me worried, but thanks to our good friend the major, we've added a trump card to our little game."

Lucy Tripton stamped her foot. "Just what is going on? I'll not stand here like an odd guest at a party while the three of you...and...and that *person* treat me as if I were not in the room."

Milford took her hand and kissed it. "Miss Tripton, I do beg your forgiveness. I had anticipated a quiet dinner for just the two of us...and, well, I suppose Grafton might have been here, too, but with all the confusion caused by the commotion in the kitchen, perhaps we should put it off to another night."

"Well, I never..." she began in a huff, but Grafton interrupted.

"With your permission, Miss Tripton, I would be happy to escort you home. Milford seems to have other things to concern himself with at the moment."

She gave her abigail a shove towards the door. "No, thank you, Lord Grafton. I'm sure Lord Milford's driver will see to our safe return. I bid you goodnight."

Milford had sufficient wit to see her to the door and give orders to his driver before he returned to the study, where the major all but pounced on him. "See here, dear boy. Are you going to tell me what this is all about or must I beat it out of you?''

Milford looked first at Grafton, then back at the major, and shook his head. Grafton, mischief written on his face with a broad pen, spoke through his laughter. ''Shall I tell him, Milford? We both know the secret cannot be kept for long.''

Milford looked pained. ''Do as you please. I daresay it's too late now to repair the damage.''

Again Grafton broke into unrestrained laughter. When he finally wiped away his tears with the sleeve of his coat, he lifted an imaginary glass to the room. ''Major Vonnegut, I believe felicitations are in order. Our friend Milford here has just been speaking to his future wife.''

The major's face beamed. ''You don't say! Well, congratulations, my dear boy. You couldn't do much better than Miss Tripton. I'm told she's worth a bloody fortune.''

''No, no, Major. You misunderstand,'' Grafton protested between bouts of laughter. ''It wasn't Miss Tripton to whom I referred. It was the other one, Miss Thackery.''

''Zounds! You don't mean it! She never mentioned a word of it to me. I was so sure that they had never before met.'' He placed his hand over his heart. ''I'm crushed. No. No, I can't believe it, sir. Is this true, Jonathan?''

Milford gave him a scalding look. ''It was a mistake, Major. One that I'm sure Grafton, gentleman that he is, will agree can be quickly and easily rectified.''

Grafton grinned. "Go back on a wager? Not a chance. For once, our friend Milford has done himself in... and I thank the gods that be that I was here to see it."

The major looked uncertain. "Is this some sort of joke? Surely you don't expect to wed that young woman—you have nothing in common. She boasts a dowry, of course, but it's a pit in a peach orchard compared to what the Tripton wench can bring to the purse. And Miss Thackery's a bluestocking. She's far too intelligent for you, Milford, and she would bore you to death."

Milford gave him a cutting look. "I am aware of her limitations, Major, but why do I have the feeling that you are quite taken with her?"

"To be truthful, the girl does appeal to me. For one thing, she plays a good game of chess. But you and I are cut from different cloth, my boy. If I were a few years younger I might seriously consider taking Miss Thackery to wife." He grasped the ends of his waistcoat. "On the other hand, since I lost my lady wife five years ago, I am quite content to play the jovial man about Town, ready to fill in should a hostess need an extra guest."

He would have said more, but at that moment Emerald and Maggie returned to the study. Emerald glanced at the three men, then spoke in a stiff voice. "I must apologize for my previous unseemly appearance. I had no idea that the soot had discoloured my face."

Jonathan's voice was equally stiff, as was his posture. "You've no need to apologize, Miss Thackery.

The vagaries of my fireplace cannot be laid at your feet. Are you quite all right?''

"Yes, thank you, but I worry about the books. A few of them may have been damaged."

He gave her a dry look. "They are only books, Miss Thackery. They can easily be disposed of."

Everyone heard her drawn-out gasp. "Only books! My lord, surely you jest. I consider all books sacred, but some books could never be replaced."

"Who would choose to, for that matter?" Milford asked, more to dilute his own irritation with her pompousness than to mollify her guilt at taking part in their ruin.

Her eyes widened at his icy demeanour and she seemed to be left speechless. Grafton made some comment to which the major responded but Jonathan was not listening. He was watching this owl-eyed, sharp tongued snip of a girl with considerable distaste.

Fate had dealt him a miserable hand. How could he be expected to marry this . . . this bluestocking? Never had he felt so close to disaster. Betting was not a game to him. He played to win. He *had* to win. It wasn't so much losing the gilded coach to Grafton as it was a question of honour.

Seen in retrospect, it had been such a simple wager. A sure win, he had thought, because no one ever came to his house uninvited, save for his close male friends. And they never brought anyone with them . . . until now. Now, when it could easily destroy his life as he had known it. He cursed silently. He would find a way out of this difficulty. He always had in the past. But at the moment he could not bear the sight of any of them, least of all . . . her.

He cleared his throat to gain their attention. "I regret that I must ask you to leave so that I may see to the repair of whatever damage there might be. Gentlemen . . . I trust that both of you will keep our conversation to yourselves. As to you, Miss Thackery, I regret having inconvenienced you. I trust we shall meet again."

"I rather doubt it, sir."

Her response surprised and irritated him. Females were not in the habit of refusing his attentions.

Grafton apparently took notice of the exchange, but the warning look Milford shot at him promptly put an end to his laughter before it could start.

LADY UDORA WAS ALONE in the library when Emerald and Maggie arrived home. She looked much younger than her thirty-odd years. Certainly too young to have been married five times and widowed four, Emerald thought as she took a seat opposite her guardian.

Udora tucked her knitting into a basket and leaned back against the cushions of her chair. "My, but you're home early. Was the library not to your liking?"

"I had little time to enjoy it," Emerald stated, pushing her spectacles further onto her nose. "It seems there was a bundle of rags in amongst the logs of Lord Milford's fireplace, and when the fire was lit, smoke enveloped the room."

Maggie snorted. "'Twasn't the room what was enveloped. Looked to me like it was 'erself what turned black wi' soot.''

Udora looked shocked and Emerald hastened to assure her that it was nothing.

Maggie chuckled. "'Is lordship might say different, though, seein' as 'ow she looked like a raccoon what's been chased up a tree,'' she said, making circles over her eyes with her thumbs and forefingers.

Udora was obviously appalled. "His lordship? That would be Milford, wouldn't it?"

"Aye, and Lord Grafton, too, as well as Miss Nose-in-the-air Tripton,'' Maggie added with considerable glee.

"Pistachions!" Udora frowned. "We can hardly afford another scandal, albeit an innocent one. I refer to your twin sister and her on- and off-again betrothal to Lord Farrencourt,'' Udora pointed out quite unnecessarily.

"Emerald, my dear, how could you have been so thoughtless, And you, Maggie—you're supposed to be looking after her. How could you allow your charge to embarrass herself in such a ridiculous way?"

Emerald raised her hands. "Wait, my lady. You cannot blame Maggie, at least this time, though I daresay she deserves to be chastised, for she is unforgivably outspoken. But it was I who undertook to light the tinder in the fireplace. It was simply an accident. Neither Maggie nor the major were at fault. And . . . I daresay, neither was I.''

"Humph. Behaving like a charwoman, and a dull witted one at that. And what did Lord Milford have to say about all this infantile behaviour?''

Emerald shuddered. "Very little. And we can be grateful for that, I assure you."

"Indeed. May I ask why?"

"Because Lord Milford is probably the most obnoxious man I have ever met. I shall make it a point never to speak to him again."

Udora considered it for a moment and then nodded. "I suppose it's for the best. While it is true that he appears to have come into his title, his reputation as a womanizer and gambler makes him less than desirable as husband material. Particularly for a woman of your needs."

Maggie fluffed her mop of red curls and sighed. "Just where one might find such a one is beyond me, 'ceptin' maybe a man o' the cloth. No *man* I know of would sooner have 'is 'ands on a book 'stead o' a willin' woman." She cocked her head. "Leastways, no man worth 'is salt. As for me, I say 'is lordship is one fine gentleman."

Emerald glared at her. "We know how you feel about men, Maggie, but not everyone judges a man by the way he fills out his breeches."

"Aye, so you noticed him, too." Maggie grinned. "Mayhap there's hope for you yet, Miss Bluestocking."

"All right, ladies. That is quite enough," Udora admonished. "But think about this, Emerald. We are already well into the Season and you have yet to make a single conquest. Granted, you have caught the eye of one or two young men. Unfortunately, you have made it abundantly clear that you wanted to have nothing to do with them."

"But your ladyship, neither has Topaz been willing to accept her offers."

"Your stepsister can take care of herself. She has a bit of a wild streak, what with the way she has pursued this . . . this balloonist fellow, but I promise you that she will keep her feet on the ground when it comes to marriage. For one thing, she knows I won't permit her to wed a commoner."

Maggie chuckled. "As if that would stop her. Miss Topaz is smarter than all of us put together."

Emerald pursed her lips. "How utterly absurd. I love my stepsister, Maggie, but Taz doesn't know a pasquinade from a *pas de deux*."

Maggie shrugged. "Who does? And if they do, it don't matter a whit. Miss Topaz is smart up here," she said tapping her head. "Aye, and it don't come from books, I'd be thinkin', but from how she was born."

"Well, since none of us know how that came about or where she came from, your argument is not valid. Besides, if birth was so important, Amy would be as smart as I am, since we're twins."

"An' who's to say she ain't? Truth is, 'er good sense is all in 'er 'eart, not 'er 'ead. Look 'ow she takes care of baby William what was dropped on 'er lap one day in the park."

Udora stood up. "I think this argument has gone on long enough. Maggie, there surely must be some mending left for you in the box in my sitting-room. And you, Emerald. Suppose you spend some time at the pianoforte. A little practice before you retire might be just what you need to attract some gentleman's eye."

EMERALD WAITED up for her sisters to return home that night. After they told her all about their parties, she recounted her adventure to them, leaving out none of the details about the infamous Lord Milford. The more she thought about him, the more she wanted to even the score.

Topaz, in a typically uninhibited assessment of the situation, had tossed her hair in a silvery gold cascade over her shoulders and dropped the brush on the floor. "The best way to get even is to marry him. Then you can make him pay for the rest of his life."

"Marry him! I can't abide being in the same room with him. Nor he with me, for that matter. He is abrasive and pigheaded and utterly despicable."

"But very nicely turned out," Amethyst added. "I saw him one night at the Huntington soirée. He was with that awful Keplington girl. The one with the high voice."

"I doubt it was her voice he noticed," Topaz said, making two large cups with her hands. All three girls laughed, causing Lady Udora to knock on their door and order them to be silent.

After Amy and Taz had fallen asleep, Emerald lay thinking about what Topaz had said. Marry Lord Milford? What an extraordinary idea! Especially considering that he would probably give her the cut sublime if he chanced to lay eyes upon her again, for it had been plain that he had taken an instant dislike to her. Nasty man. It would serve him right if she were to marry him. She could make his life miserable. It would almost be worth it. A picture flashed through her mind of her leading him about on a gold leash. She fell asleep with a smile on her face.

THERE WERE FLOWERS waiting for Emerald when she went downstairs for a late breakfast the following morning. Her sisters were more excited than she was.

"Hurry, Em, see who they're from," Amy said.

"There is no name on the card," Emerald said, "but I know who they are from. Lord Milford sent them in an attempt to make amends for his odious behaviour." She handed the bouquet to a bandy-legged servant girl who was filling the chocolate pot. "Betty, would you see that Cook gets these? Mc-Masters tells me that she is still not feeling well."

"Yes, miss. I'll see to it right this minute."

Topaz studied Emerald over the rim of her cup. "I say, can it be that his lordship is trying to tell you something? I cannot imagine that he would go to such trouble just to make up for a few careless words said under trying circumstances. Unless..." She waved her fingers in the air as she left the sentence incomplete.

Amy leaned forward, her voice breathless. "Oh, Em. Do you think it's possible? Lady Udora would be so thrilled. A marquess. Just imagine. And she thought you might be left on the shelf!" Suddenly aware of her thoughtlessness, Amy put her hand over her mouth. "Oh! I'm so sorry, I didn't mean..."

Emerald laughed. "It's all right. I know what you mean, but it's not that I haven't had offers, you know."

Topaz giggled. "Don't worry about Amy. She hasn't made good sense since the day baby William was given to her. Now that she's going to marry Lord Farrencourt, she's all but turned bottom-side-up."

Amy made a face at her adopted sister. "And what about you...running off whenever you can to keep a secret rendezvous with your balloonist friend. Her ladyship is bound to find out the truth."

Topaz laughed. "I'll worry about that when it happens."

Maggie, overhearing the last of the conversation as she entered the breakfast room, stopped at the end of the table and put her hands on her hips. "Sure an' what makes sense is the three of you gettin' yourselves upstairs to the sewin' room so you can be fitted for your new gowns." Maggie plucked a thread from the cuff of her uniform and frowned. "There's but three days till the 'opewell party and not one of the dresses is fit to wear. And this is Wednesday. There'll be callers tonight, God willing, and there's 'air to be done and gowns to be laid out. So get on with you before 'er ladyship catches you dawdling."

Topaz muttered. "One of these days you'll go too far, Maggie McGee."

MAGGIE WAS RIGHT to keep after them, Emerald decided that evening as she made last-minute adjustments to her hair before going downstairs to the drawing-room. It had taken all day to get ready for their evening "at home." She looked across at her twin and then over at Topaz. They both looked so beautiful—Amy in lavender and Taz in burnt orange. Her own gown of moss green and gold was quite pretty, but must she be the one to wear spectacles? It ruined everything.

She hated the silliness of having to vie for the affections of a man. She didn't need a man. She could do quite well on her own, with the money her father had left in trust for her dowry. She did, in fact, prefer to be alone.

Lady Udora knocked on the door and entered. "Girls, hurry along. Our guests are arriving. And I daresay we are quite fortunate in the significant attention our little 'at home' is receiving. Quite deserved, of course. I count Major Vonnegut, no surprise there, a knight of the garter, a baronet, two barons, a viscount and a marquess. Of course, Lieutenant Bixford is here sniffing after Topaz, but he does not signify."

The girls tittered as they followed her down the stairway. Topaz had long ago lost interest in the handsome lieutenant, but no one had bothered to inform Udora. One title stuck in Emerald's head. A marquess! Could it be Jonathan Trent, Lord Milford? Her face flamed. To be sure! He was just the kind of man who would do everything in his power to cause her further embarrassment.

Udora took one look at her stormy face and nudged her with an elbow. "For pity's sake, smile, Emerald. Your face is enough to scare off the bravest of the brave."

Emerald steeled herself to smile. She followed behind her sisters as they entered the drawing room, hoping that it would give her time to prepare herself to face the Marquess of Milford.

But she needn't have bothered. The marquess in attendance proved to be none other than Carruthers Delafield, Marquess of Venneton, a meek little man who was hardly a threat to anyone, save perhaps himself. Emerald slowly let out her breath. As her gaze skipped round the room she felt an inexplicable sense of disappointment. She had been so certain that he would put in an appearance, especially after having sent the flowers. Her mouth tightened. Very well, if that was the way he wanted to be, it mattered not one whit to her whether he apologized or not.

The few ladies smiled their greetings, and the gentlemen rose when the girls and Udora began to circulate among them. Udora had hired the services of a harpist to provide a pleasant background for their conversation. McMasters supervised a footman who attended the visitors with a tray of wine and sweetmeats.

The major was his usual cordial self. "Dear girl," he said, taking Emerald's hands in his, "you look ravishing tonight. Green is definitely your colour."

"Thank you, Major, you are too kind. Shall we find a quiet place where we may chat?"

"I'd like nothing better my child, but I fear that her ladyship would much prefer that you not allow me to monopolize your time. I am hardly considered eligible, I fear."

Emerald tilted her head and frowned. "But I find you the most interesting of all the gentlemen in attendance. However, I suppose you are correct in your assessment."

"Shall we join your stepsister and Lord Flemington?"

Emerald was about to agree when McMasters announced another caller: Lord Milford.

"How dare he!" she fumed.

The major looked surprised. "Come now, dear girl. I assured him you would be kind enough to receive him. Surely you can't be holding a grudge for what happened yesterday?"

"Can't I? Just watch. He knows he was in the wrong to make me look so ridiculous. He even sent flowers to apologize," she said as Milford recognized them and nodded a greeting.

"But he didn't..." the major began but was cut off by Emerald's emphatic words.

"And if he thinks I intend to let him off that easily, he is not quite so intelligent as he looks." He was coming towards them, and she braced herself for the scene that was sure to follow.

The major stroked his moustache. "Oh, do be careful, Miss Emerald. One wouldn't want to say something one might come to regret."

She smiled bewitchingly. "Don't worry, Major. I never do."

CHAPTER THREE

JONATHAN ADJUSTED his waistcoat as he started towards them, only to be stopped by various people who wished to be recognized: doting dowagers who hoped to draw attention to their vapid daughters, he acknowledged, and Cyprians who knew he was good for a wager or two.

A wager. Damnation! It had been a wager that led him into this cul-de-sac. His honour as a gentleman rested on the bet he had made with Grafton yesterday in his study. Now he had no choice in the matter but to marry the Thackery girl. No choice at all, he mused ruefully, for unknowingly, he had bargained away the carriage Grafton so eagerly coveted, when, in truth, the carriage did not belong to him. Milford had been unaware, until he read the exact details of the will, that the carriage had been lent to his nephew with the stipulation that, upon his death, it would be returned to the Duke of Wellington. Milford cursed his luck. He knew now, and ignorance did not undo a bargain made in good faith.

He was hardly aware that he had made the correct responses to the lady who clutched his arm. He patted her hand. "If you will excuse me, Lady Hammond, I see my friend waving at me."

He managed to slip away but at the same time wondered if he was jumping from the frying pan into the fire. For it was fire he saw magnified through the windows of Miss Thackery's spectacles. Fate had decreed he face this young harpy and do what he could to salvage his pride. The major, at least, was pleased to see him.

"Milford, my boy. I had almost given up on you. It's good to see you."

Jonathan bowed. "Major, Miss Thackery." He inclined his head and forced a smile. If he must indeed start courting this lemon-faced chit, he had to make at least an effort to be civil. Apparently she felt no similar obligation, because she didn't bother to curtsy. The stubborn twit. To spite her, he reached for her hand and bent over it, barely brushing it with his lips. She all but snatched it away.

At the same time he was quite surprised by the softness of her skin and the faint hint of attar of roses that wafted from her person. He was grateful that she, unlike some of the females he had escorted rather recently, made it a point to bathe on a regular basis. But any leanings he had in her direction were immediately squelched when she spoke.

"Don't expect me to thank you for the lilies, my lord." She smiled as if enjoying herself. "Perhaps my cook might do so, since I gave them to her."

Milford sucked in his breath. *Damnation! He should have thought of sending her flowers. Well, no matter. He had been given the credit for them.* He tilted his head and gave her a practised look that never failed to win a woman's attention.

"Then I can only hope that your cook enjoys the flowers with...er...as much enjoyment as I found in offering them."

Emerald was taken aback. She had expected him to receive the cut the way it was intended. Cold, sharp and to the bone. Instead, he was behaving quite gallantly.

He apparently noticed her discomposure and took advantage of it. "It is my hope, Miss Thackery, that we shall have an opportunity to get to know each other under less awkward circumstances than occurred yesterday. You will be pleased to hear that I'm having the library cleaned and aired so that you may avail yourself of its books whenever you choose."

The major, looking from one of them to the other and then back, beamed like a conductor directing a musical score. "I say now, what a jolly good idea." He nudged Milford's arm. "Jonathan, my boy, doesn't Miss Thackery look fetching in green?"

He hesitated overlong, Emerald thought, but his enquiring gaze left little of her unassessed. She stood stiffly as he scrutinized her like a gentleman farmer appraising a brood mare at a horse fair. If only she could relax in the playful way that Topaz would have done, given the same circumstances.

"Miss Thackery's gown is quite attractive, to be sure," Milford said with the conciliatory tone one might use when speaking to a child.

The gown? Emerald thought. *The gown is attractive!* She would have hit him over the head with a book if she had had one in hand. Instead, she gritted her teeth and gave him a wide smile.

"Why thank you, Lord Milford. Your compliment is far too extravagant."

Whether it was her tone of voice or the stone-cold look in her eyes, Jonathan, despite her smile, realized he had missed the mark. This country girl wasn't going to be as easy as he had thought. He was going to have to exert himself if he expected her to swoon, as most women did, over his meagre attentions.

He gave her a calculated smile. "The flowers were nothing, nothing at all, I assure you, but it would be my pleasure if you would accompany me to the Hopewell party."

Emerald was shocked into silence. Surely he couldn't be serious.

The major, obviously aware of her hesitation, clasped his hands and rubbed them together. "Dear boy! For once you have chosen wisely. Miss Thackery is such delightful company. Of course she will accept."

At that moment Lord Venable approached and broke into the conversation. He was a studious looking man about five years her senior, Emerald decided. The most outstanding feature about him was his hair, which was thick and fair. He wore it parted in the middle with carefully balanced waves on either side that lent a cherubic quality to his face.

He briefly acknowledged the gentlemen and then turned to Emerald. "Ah. Miss Thackery. So this is where you've been hiding. I wanted to ask how you liked the lilies I sent to you this morning. My gardener tells me they are a special species of plant he raised from stock sent to him from Japan."

Emerald looked quickly at Milford and then back at Lord Venable. "Then it was *you* who sent them."

"I should have included my card, but I assumed that you would recall our conversation about the fine Japanese art of horticulture and know that it was I who sent them."

"The lilies are lovely, Lord Venable. You are most considerate. I can't find words to thank you."

He looked at her with an approving gaze. "They cannot begin to compare to your own loveliness, Miss Thackery. I do so hope that I may have the privilege of seeing you again soon."

"But of course. I always enjoy your company, Lord Venable. Perhaps we shall meet again at the Hope-well party."

He looked decidedly uncomfortable. "I know you've already been asked a dozen times, Miss Thackery, but if you haven't accepted an invitation, it would give me extreme pleasure to be considered as an escort."

"While it is true that I have been asked by a few gentlemen, they are of no consequence. No consequence at all. Nothing would please me more, Lord Venable, than to attend the party with you. Shall I expect you at seven?"

"Yes, yes. Seven would be excellent. Forgive me for interrupting your conversation," he said, looking first at Milford and then at the major. "I'll just excuse myself and speak with Lady Udora before I take my departure."

Milford, his face a mixture of red-and-white blotches from anger too-well contained, waited for him to leave before he confronted Emerald. "I was under the impression, Miss Thackery, that you had just agreed to attend the Hopewell party with *me.*" His voice was sufficiently cold to chill the glass of port he had just put down on a nearby table.

Emerald took a sip from her syllabub and peered at him over the rim of her glass. "You assumed incorrectly, Lord Milford. As I recall, you offered to escort me but I did not reply."

"I consider it a breach of good manners to accept another man's offer before—"

"Manners, Lord Milford? This from one who steals credit for another man's gifts?" She tapped her closed fan against his sleeve and shook her head. "I hardly think you have room to criticize, sir, but if you must have an answer to your invitation, then the answer is no. Thank you, but I shall be attending with Lord Venable."

The major laughed and slapped his thigh. "She has you there, Milford. Didn't I tell you Miss Thackery is a one to match wits with? And don't ever debate with her on the subject of the Corn Laws or the Spitalfields riots. She can argue either side and come out the victor."

"Fascinating, I'm sure," Milford commented drily. "I can hardly think of a subject more stimulating than the price of corn."

Emerald pushed her spectacles further onto her nose. "If you gentlemen will excuse me, I must speak with Lady Breckenridge."

Jonathan was beginning to perspire. He had counted on her accepting his bid to escort her to the Hopewell party. Bluestocking she might be, but she was certainly not without prospects. If she married before he had a chance to offer for her, the bet would be lost. If he offered for her now, he was certain that she would laugh in his face, stubborn girl that she was. He stepped forward to prevent her departure.

"Miss Thackery, I understand that Madame Tussaud's travelling museum will still be in Town for another week. If I were to invite you, would you be willing to attend with me?"

"*If* you were to invite me, I would certainly consider your offer very carefully, as I do all my invitations."

Milford's face turned red. "Confound it all, what I meant to say was may I have the honour of escorting you to the wax museum this Friday afternoon?"

Emerald fluttered her fan across her face. "Regretfully, no, your lordship. As it happens, I have already visited the wax museum. While the exhibit is most stimulating, it is not the sort of thing one wishes to see a second time. I do, however, thank you for your kind invitation. Gentlemen," she said, and dropped a brief curtsy before turning and walking away.

Embarrassed, Milford glanced over at the major, whose eyes sparkled with admiration. "Isn't she something! Egad. I wish I were twenty years younger."

Milford flushed indignantly. "What *I* wish for Miss Thackery at the present moment would singe the gates of Hell. If it takes the rest of my life, I will give that young woman the set down she deserves." It occurred to him even as he said it that if he were to save his honour he must indeed spend the rest of his life with her. He paled at the thought.

The major lifted his quizzing glass to his eye, the better to read the expression on his young friend's face. "Milford, dear boy, just what scheme are you concocting? Keep in mind, my good fellow, that Miss Thackery is not one of your lightskirts. Her father was titled. She is the ward of the Kestersons. One must be circumspect in the way one seeks to retaliate."

"Be advised, Major, that where my family honour is concerned, I deem anything short of murder quite acceptable."

The major shook his head, allowing the quizzing glass to fall on its chain. "I hope you won't live to rue the day, my friend. For your own sake as well as that of Miss Thackery."

THE NIGHT OF the Hopewell party finally arrived. It had taken Jonathan's valet four full hours to achieve the look that his master demanded for this evening's venture into Society. Jonathan smiled wickedly as his carriage pulled to a stop in front of Kesterson House. He could hardly wait to see the expression on Miss Thackery's face. He was at his best. The white cutaway coat had arrived only this afternoon from his Bond Street tailors. His dark hair had been washed and brushed in the most becoming style, and his neckcloth was pristine white and folded into the popular *en cascade* fashion.

So why did his uneasy stomach make him feel like an unlicked cub? He had handled the matter of Lord Venable with his usual aplomb. The man was, after all, indebted to him for services rendered when Venable had needed a witness to his presence at a certain levee. It had gone against the grain for Jonathan to lie, so if Venable had been vexed because Jonathan chose to stand in for him as escort to Miss Thackery at the Hopewell party, so much the better.

He smiled once again as he strode up the walk to the door of Kesterson House and lifted the knocker. McMasters answered within seconds.

Jonathan handed him his top hat. "Will you please tell Miss Emerald Thackery that her escort has arrived?"

McMasters looked puzzled, but he apparently decided not to question Jonathan. "If you would wait in the drawing-room, my lord."

"Thank you." He didn't have long to wait. Apparently Miss Thackery, with her country-miss ingenuousness, had not learned the merit of keeping a man waiting. She stopped short when she entered the room and saw Jonathan.

"Wh-why, you're not Lord Venable."

"Indeed, I am not. And for that we can both be thankful." He bowed. "It is my pleasure to be your escort tonight, Miss Thackery. Lord Venable wishes to express his deepest regrets, but at the last minute he found himself unable to attend."

"That's impossible. I don't believe you."

"I thought that might be the case, so I took the precaution of asking his lordship to pen a brief note of explanation." He handed her the letter. As she read, he watched her with considerable interest. Her long hair was pulled back from her face in a fetching though rather severe style that seemed to give her eyes an upward slant at the corners. At the back of her head the curls cascaded downward to her shoulders, which were modestly covered by the high-necked velvet gown of jade green. His mouth tightened. No bare arms or shoulders here to entice a gentleman's eye. She was wrapped to her neck like an Egyptian mummy.

Emerald looked up at him with owlish eyes as she laid the note on the table. "Yes, I admit that I misjudged you when I doubted your word, Lord Milford, but I cannot accept your generosity in offering to stand in for him. Thank you, but I prefer to remain at home this evening."

At that moment Lady Udora entered the drawing-room on a cloud of some spicy floral fragrance. When she greeted Jonathan he bowed and kissed her hand. Before she had a chance to question him about the last-minute substitution, he hastened to explain that Venable had another obligation.

"But how kind of you to stand in for him, Lord Milford. I'm sure that Emerald will be pleased to have you to escort her."

"Oh, no. I couldn't accept such a sacrifice on Lord Milford's part. I think it would be better if I remained at home this evening."

"Nonsense, Emerald. His lordship has already gone to the trouble of putting in an appearance. Of course you will go. Now let's hear no more of this."

Milford was hard put to wipe the smug look from his face before he offered Emerald his arm.

EMERALD WAS SEETHING with anger all during the carriage ride. Milford kept up a seemingly endless conversation about the Hopewells and how they had somehow managed to become the latest example of the blatantly gauche *nouveaux riches*.

"I haven't seen it, of course, but they say the drawing-room is decorated in an outrageous mixture of

Chinese and Egyptian artifacts, not to mention an African mask or two."

She considered him with a disconcerting look. "I wonder, then, why you bother to attend their parties if their manners are so objectionable."

"For the same reason everyone else does. It's the thing to do. Everyone will be there . . . including your sisters, I believe?"

"Yes. Both Amethyst and Topaz will be in attendance. Lord Farrencourt and Lord Huxley arrived before you did. They should already be there."

"You are close to your sisters, are you not?"

"Yes. Very close. Amethyst and I are twins, though we hardly resemble each other. Topaz, whom my parents adopted when she was a baby, is two months older."

"Ah, yes. The Thackery Jewels. How nice it must be to be good friends with your sisters. I myself had two brothers and a sister, but Fate intervened and now I am the sole survivor. That is how I came into the title."

"How fortunate for you," Emerald said with a touch of sarcasm.

"It wasn't something I would have chosen."

Despite herself she was surprised. "I can't believe that you would look askance at all the money and power."

"Money I already had. The power, if indeed there is such an advantage, is permanently tied to responsibility."

"Yes, I can see how responsibility might be a burden for one of your particular sensibilities."

Sally, Emerald's abigail for the evening, gasped aloud.

Milford's voice was harsh. "Just what do you mean by that?"

She smiled and patted his hand. "Why, only that one who is reputedly so self-indulgent might find it difficult to see beyond his own needs to those of an estate."

Even in the darkened carriage she could see that her words had hit their mark. His face flushed. Fortunately they had arrived at their destination and there was no chance for him to respond.

Topaz, Amethyst and their escorts had already blended into the throng of guests who seemed to be occupying every available space in the large drawing-room. It took several minutes for Milford to find them and for him to be introduced to the young ladies. He was already acquainted with Lord Farrencourt, with whom he had attended school, and Huxley, whom he had met at Watier's over a fast-paced game of Macao.

Miss Amethyst Thackery appeared to be a demure bit of fluff, but she was betrothed to and obviously enamoured of Lord Farrencourt. Miss Topaz Thackery, with her mischievous smile and hair the colour of sun-dried wheat, merited more than a cursory glance. Curse his foul luck! Why had she not been the one whom he was being forced to marry? She had adventurous eyes that seemed to memorize him from head to foot before he could so much as acknowledge her curtsy. The lucky man who stole her heart must surely dance to a merry tune. He studied her escort with a casual eye and immediately discounted him. *No*. Huxley would not be the one.

Milford turned to speak to Emerald, but she, with Sally in attendance, had moved away to speak with the Duke of Sussex and two other gentlemen. Augustus, Milford mused, was as dotty about books as was Miss Thackery. He frowned. It was inconceivable that Miss Thackery would choose their companionship over his.

Topaz, apparently seeing the frown on his face, chuckled softly. "It seems that my sister has given you the go-by, Lord Milford."

He pretended to be stretching his neck. "Oh, really? I hadn't noticed. Ah, yes, there she is." The expression on Topaz's face proved he had not fooled her.

"I don't envy you, my lord. Emerald is hardly ever still unless she has a book in her hands. If I may be so bold, how does it happen that you chose her to escort to the party? You don't seem the sort of man who would be interested in a young country girl, not to mention a bluestocking."

He looked at her with mock seriousness. "Are you asking what my intentions are toward your sister, Miss Thackery?"

"I care very much for my sister and don't wish to see her hurt."

"Most admirable, to be sure. I have no wish to hurt your sister. If nothing else, Miss Thackery, I am a gentleman of honour."

"So I've heard. But how does it happen that you have brought her here, when we understood that Lord Venable was to be her escort? I find it hard to believe that Emerald willingly agreed to accompany you."

Milford smiled. "She had little choice in the matter. Lady Udora was most helpful in pleading my case."

Topaz swung her silver-beaded reticule, which hung by a ribbon from her wrist. "I see. Don't underestimate my sister, Lord Milford. She may seem to be distant and reserved but she has a granite determination you might not expect. Perhaps, in the end, it is you who will be the one to be hurt."

"Don't waste your pity on me, young lady. I always manage to get what I want."

"And what *do* you want, if I may enquire?"

He laughed at her audacity, then bowed. "What I want at this moment is to return to the side of my companion for the evening. If you will excuse me?" He left before she had a chance to answer.

Emerald, out of the corner of her eye, saw him approaching. It surprised her that he chose to leave Topaz's company. Few men did. But he was coming toward her now, and the very thought of it gave her a shiver of anticipation. She shifted sideways to make room for him. There was something dangerous about him. She wasn't used to danger.

He greeted the other men, then offered his arm to Emerald. "I believe I have shared you enough for one evening, Miss Thackery. Would you care to stroll in the garden before we are summoned to supper?"

"The garden? Whatever for? It's rather dark, is it not?" Seeing the look on his face, she patted his arm. "Oh, forgive me. Are you a student of horticulture, my lord?"

"Egad, no. I wouldn't know a flower from a weed."

"Then why do you wish to stroll in the garden? The paths are sure to be wet from the brief rainstorm we had this afternoon."

He cast a sidelong glance at her. Could she really be so naive? Any other young chit would drag him down the garden path before he had a chance to finish his wine.

He cleared his throat and lowered his voice to a husky level. "I thought we might find the garden a bit more romantic than standing here with a dozen elbows in our ribs."

"Romantic!" The word was not one that was common in her vocabulary. She repeated it again. "Well, I suppose we could take the air, but I assure you, Lord Milford, romance will not enter the picture. Trust me. I could never think of you in quite that way."

Something in her voice didn't quite ring true, even to her own ears. Milford chose to ignore the statement altogether as he guided her to the terrace door. Sally tagged along close behind them until Milford slipped her a pair of coins and she dropped back an acceptable distance.

A full moon illuminated the flowers and shrubbery with a greenish glow, but thanks to the flaming torchères, the paths looked warmly inviting. The scent of roses and the rich odour of damp moss hung heavily in the air. Nearby, round a bend in the hedge, they could hear the splash of water in the fish pond.

Milford warmed to the task ahead. No woman could resist his charm when it was combined with a setting such as this. "Listen," he said, bending close. "Listen to the nightingale sing."

He heard her breathing stop as she hearkened to the sound. After a moment she filled her lungs with air. "Lovely, isn't it?"

"Lovely, indeed, but not so lovely as the sound of your own voice."

"Surely you jest. When I sing even the dogs run to hide under the table."

"I refer to your speaking voice, Miss Thackery," he said, trying without success to keep the irritation from his own voice, but apparently she was deaf to it, for her thoughts had already raced on ahead.

"How strange you should say that. My tutor, the Reverend Mr. Barker, always said that my voice was far too low for a young girl. I try hard to speak with more of a nasal sound so that I will more closely resemble the other ladies of my age."

He stroked her hand, but she seemed to be in a brown study. Even so, it came as a blow to his charm when she resumed speaking.

"As to the identity of the bird," she said, "I think you'll find it's a warbler, not a nightingale."

He sighed. "Perhaps so. At any rate, it was merely a comment. It was not my intention to conduct a class in, er..."

"Aviculture?" she provided before he could finish. "The study of birds. I assume this is what you meant to say."

They were standing in a pattern of light cast by one of the torchères. The intensity of her concern over a mere word drove him to grasp her shoulders in his hands.

"What I mean to say, Miss Thackery, is that I didn't bring you here to identify bird-calls or discuss the study of their mating habits."

"Just why did you bring me out here, Lord Milford? And for that matter, why did you choose to force your company upon me this evening when you knew very well that it was unwelcome?"

"If you must know, it was for one reason, and one reason only."

"And that is?"

Before she had a chance to protest, he bent down to kiss her. But in his eagerness to win her over, he forgot to close his eyes, and in the flickering shadow of the light from the torchère he caught the reflection of her spectacles. At that single moment of passion, all he could think of was seeing her yesterday in his study, her white eyes set like a mask in her blackened face.

Despite himself, he burst into laughter.

CHAPTER FOUR

EMERALD WAS NOT AMUSED. Milford's laughter echoed through the stillness of the garden until she reached the end of her tolerance. She merely looked at him in the speculative way that she knew to be highly disconcerting. When at last he managed to get his laughter under control, Emerald spoke.

"I'm sure you must find me very amusing, my lord, but I would much prefer to be a bluestocking country girl than a rude, self-important popinjay. If you will kindly unhand me, sir, I would like to return to the house."

He sobered immediately. God's blood! This wasn't going well. He was losing rather than gaining ground as he had hoped to do. Dropping his hands to his sides, he gazed down at her with a newfound feeling of respect.

"I do most humbly apologize, Miss Thackery. Not for thinking of kissing you, but for my most untimely laughter."

"You have never kissed a woman who wore spectacles?" she asked with a faint trace of irony. "Never mind. As it was, I had no desire to be so singularly honoured."

"I'm sure the honour would have been mine," he said, hoping she wouldn't suspect he was boldly facing things out. "But you are most surprisingly considerate of me. Any other woman would have slapped my face."

"The thought did cross my mind."

"It did? Then what held you back?"

"I don't know. I...I suppose I rather liked the sound of your laughter. It comes from deep inside you. Not like the mincing snigger that some dandies affect, nor like the chortle of an old man. It had a hearty, robust sound to it."

Her honesty was appalling. He took her hand between his, rubbing his thumb across the softly defined bones, then placed it against his cheek. "You had every right to strike me, Miss Thackery. I behaved quite unforgivably." When he took his hand away, her hand remained there, feather light, soft as the touch of a butterfly.

"Yes. Do what you will," he said. "Wound me, hurt me, scar me for life. I promise not to flinch."

Emerald stood there for a minute too mesmerized by the warmth of his skin against her hand to know what to do. Her anger had disappeared, washed away by his idiotic suggestions. Now all she felt was ridiculous. She pulled away and rubbed her palm down the length of her hip. When she dared look at him, something in his gaze made her think of an actor rehearsing a role. The nerve of the man! He was play-acting, and none too successfully at that. Her mouth curved up at the corners and she began to giggle as she hadn't done since she and her sisters were six years old. When she managed to control herself she covered her mouth.

"Oh, dear, I shouldn't have done that. I'm so sorry."

Milford's face was grim. He had put into practice one of his most prized moves and what did she do but laugh? Any other woman... Damnation! But never mind. He wasn't ready to be bested. He was, after all, an expert at this game of romance.

He took her hand and kissed it. "Don't apologize, Miss Thackery. Perhaps it is time for us to join the others. I see that your abigail is uneasy with our conversation."

"Yes, I think you are correct. Shall we?" she said, reaching for his arm. One look at his face told her she had scored a point.

Sally looked more than a little relieved when they joined the others. Amethyst was too enamoured of her fiancé to do more than greet them with a smile. Topaz gave Emerald a questioning look, but when Emerald failed to acknowledge it, Topaz raised her gaze to the ceiling and sighed.

"Sister dear, perhaps we should retire to the ladies' convenience room and powder our noses."

"I don't really..."

"Oh, don't be a twit. Come along. I know the gentlemen will excuse us."

"Of course," Milford said.

Lord Huxley inclined his head. "May we fetch some refreshments for you while you are gone?"

Topaz gave her escort a dazzling smile. "A glass of syllabub, perhaps." She took her sister's arm and guided her toward the door with Sally following like a silent ghost. "Now tell me what happened. I saw the two of you go into the garden. Did he kiss you?"

"What a ridiculous question."

"Yes, yes, I suppose it is, considering everything."

"What do you mean by that?" Emerald demanded.

Topaz gave her stepsister a quick hug. "Oh, you know. You've never really been interested in boys. When I was frolicking with the stable-boy up in the hayloft at Amberleigh, you were most likely curled up in a chair with your nose in a book that was bigger than you were."

"I *was* interested in boys, but not the kind of boys—or men—that you seem to attract."

Topaz laughed. "Most men are good to practise on. Then when you meet the one you want to keep, you'll know how to go about getting him."

"You sound like Lady Udora. I thought men were supposed to do the choosing."

"Don't be a bufflehead. We only let them think they do."

A group of elegantly gowned ladies returning from the ladies' convenience room greeted them but continued on without stopping. Topaz remained silent until after the footman closed the door behind them.

The room was well lighted, with half a dozen lavishly appointed dressing-tables and mirrors set up for their use. Only one place was occupied. A spindly matron with thin white hair that barely covered her pink scalp nodded and smiled, then continued to watch them through the mirror.

Topaz took a seat next to Emerald. "You could do worse, you know. Milford may have his faults, but now that he has come into his title he is quite acceptable."

"I don't think I could like him, let alone come to love him. I'm not even sure why he is with me tonight. I rejected his bid to be my escort, but it was he, not Venable, who arrived at the appointed time.''

Topaz looked intrigued. "He must have a reason."

The woman at the next table looked across at them. "Lord Milford, is it? That fellow never does anything without a reason. He's a worldly young man, not to mention handsome. One who usually gets what he wants, I think, but—" she waved a veiny, beringed hand "—if I were twenty years younger, miss, I'd be willing to dance to his tune." She fixed Emerald with her gaze. "Take my advice, my dear, and put him to leash before he has the chance to stray."

The girls laughed at her audacity but Emerald shook her head. "Actually, the man is as deep as a dry river bed. I doubt that he's read a book since he left Eton, if indeed he did then."

The woman snorted. "What has that to do with it? Warm your bed first. Then, if you must, you can teach him to read. From what I hear, my dear, your young man is very good at warming beds."

Sally was looking very uneasy. She whispered to Emerald, "Her ladyship would be most unhappy, miss, hearin' you go on like this. We best get back to the drawin'-room."

Emerald rose. "Yes, we shouldn't keep the men waiting."

Topaz gave her a dry look. "Sister dear, you have a lot to learn about how to entice men."

Emerald looked at her with surprise. "Entice them? But I . . . it never occurred to me that that was what I should be doing."

She said it with such ingenuousness that at first there was silence, and then Topaz and the other woman looked at each other and began laughing. Even sober Sally managed a small titter.

"Stop it, all of you," Emerald said. "This isn't the least bit funny. If you choose to waste your time that way it is no concern of mine but don't expect me to do so."

The older woman winked boldly. "Do not fret, young lady. If you can interest a man like Lord Milford without so much as batting an eyelash, then you have nothing to be concerned about."

IT OCCURRED TO MILFORD as he watched the ladies return, that they had been gone overlong. Lord Huxley had fetched their drinks and placed them on a small table. The major had joined the party, and he spoke in glowing terms as the girls made their way through the throng.

"Beautiful, aren't they?" His face beamed.

Lord Huxley contemplated the older man. "You seem to be such a connoisseur of feminine beauty, Major. How does it happen that you haven't chosen to wed again?"

"My dear young fellow, when one attends a banquet of gastronomic delights, one does not limit oneself to a single dish. If I were in your position and that of Milford, here, who must produce an heir to carry on the title, then I would of course have to change my ways."

Milford laughed and slapped the major on the back. "Well said, Robert." He sighed in mock resignation. "Well, here they are, gentlemen. Duty calls."

Jonathan wondered if he were the only one who noticed how pleased Emerald was that the major had joined them. Egads! The man was three times her age. What could she possibly see in him? Although Major Vonnegut was rich, having made a fortune in shipping, then going on to buy himself a commission in the army, he had no claim to a title. And yet, Jonathan mused, no man was more welcome at a festive gathering than the major.

Topaz and Lord Huxley wandered off to fill their plates at the table, but Emerald had not finished her syllabub. Curiosity drove Jonathan to watch her face as she chatted with the major. The subject was architecture, presumably concerning the recent repairs to Carlton House and a scathing article said to have been written by Gronow, who despised the prince's residence. Jonathan made the appropriate responses, but he was not actually listening.

There was something about this young woman that kept his attention. Was it simply the fact that she had suddenly become an important, if unwelcome, part of his life? No, it was more than that. When she was intrigued by something, she exuded a certain vitality that flowed from her like a current of light. Her voice became animated and she reached out to the person, touching him on the arm or the hand, as if by mere physical contact she could clarify the point she was trying to make. He wished, suddenly, that she were touching him, and then he wondered at his capricious nature. Surely it was merely his concern over paying the wager that was responsible for this sudden attraction.

He put his hand on the major's shoulder and gently eased him back. "Forgive me, Major, but Miss Thackery and I have not dined as yet."

"Oh...dear boy, do forgive me. When Miss Thackery and I get started on the subject of architecture there is no stopping us. I'll just be off. Milford, Miss Thackery, I look forward to seeing you again soon." He made a token bow and waved before melting into the crowd.

Emerald gave Milford a most disconcerting look. "You could have invited the major to join us."

"I suppose I could have."

"May I ask why you did not? It appeared rather rude to exclude him."

"The major will understand that I want you all to myself." Even as he said the words, it occurred to Jonathan that he meant them.

"Whatever for?" she asked.

He levelled his gaze at her. "Do you always ask such pointed questions? I want you alone, of course, so that I may sweep you off your feet and carry you away to my private trysting place."

She looked up at him, eyes enormous behind her spectacles. Then her face creased in a wide smile. "Of course! You were joking. I might have guessed. I had no idea you had such a delightful sense of humour, my lord."

He hadn't meant it to be humorous, but for some strange reason, she was unable or unwilling to take him seriously. Nevertheless he was determined to put her so off balance that she would lose her stiff-necked self-possession.

"And just what would you do, Miss Thackery, if I should whisk you away to some secret hideaway?"

She placed a finger alongside her cheek. "Let me think. Yes, first I would make sure that I had my spectacles with me. I'm quite blind without them, you know, and if your hideaway is anything like your house in Town, then it must have a well-stocked library."

He studied her face for a moment, then wiped his hand across his chin. Damnation! For every step forward he had managed only to fall back two. He took a deep breath. "Perhaps we should see what our host has provided in the way of food."

"But you haven't said what *you* would do."

"I beg your pardon?"

"If we were to go off to your secret hideaway, I mean. I know very little about you. What do you do when you are not in Town? Do you sail, do you shoot animals, do you raise pigs at your country house?"

"I can assure you, I would not be chasing pigs. If we were alone in the quiet seclusion of my country house, I would probably take advantage of you, with your permission, of course. I would begin first by removing your spectacles. Then I would take the pins from that mass of shiny hair and let it fall around your shoulders. After that I would begin to undo the multitude of hooks running down the front of your dress until I..."

"Stop, stop. If you say any more I shall be laughing so hard that I cannot control myself. For the first time I can well understand, my lord, why this Season's debutantes find your company so delightful. You have a truly fine imagination as well as an irrepressible wit."

"Wit? It was not my intention to be witty, Miss Thackery. I meant every word I said."

"Oh. Oh, I see." She averted her gaze. "Then perhaps you are right. Shall we see what our host has to offer?"

Jonathan, placated somewhat by her discomfort, presented his arm and directed them toward the massive array of food set out on tables in the adjoining room.

"I hope you are hungry, Miss Thackery. The Hopewells are known for their culinary staff, the best of whom was a student of Antonin Carême."

Suddenly, the very thought of food made Emerald's stomach lurch. But she could hardly demur. As it happened, the crush of guests was deep enough to prevent easy passage round the buffet table. Furthermore, she and Jonathan, by their mere presence together, had caused enough stir that nearly everyone stopped to chat with them. Even Jonathan was pleased when they had finished off their meagre plates, listened to the musicians, watched the antics of a speckle-faced clown, made the obligatory gestures of thanks and were able to take their departure.

Once inside his carriage, Jonathan moved restlessly under the cool gaze of Emerald and the curious yet passive eyes of her abigail. Damnation! The evening had not gone at all as he had planned. It had been his intention to impress Emerald with his *savoir faire* and then to make the grand gesture of inviting her to take in the theatre or the opera. He had impressed her all right, but not in the way he had expected. She found his overtures laughable.

But he could not let it go at that. There was still the wager to consider. As the carriage jolted along the cobblestone street, Jonathan leaned back against the burgundy squabs and crossed his knees. "I find, Miss Thackery, that I would very much like to know you better." He raised his hands before she could speak. "And please, I beg of you, do not ask me why. I think that should be quite obvious, given the fact that you were launched into Society only a few weeks ago."

Thankfully she remained silent while he continued. "May I request the honour of calling upon you tomorrow afternoon?"

"Well, actually there are several things I must do tomorrow. I rather suspect that it would be in both our best interests if I were to say no."

"At the most I would only stay the acceptable twenty minutes. Please. I won't take no for an answer. Shall we say at two?"

"I don't quite understand your motives, Lord Milford, but if you insist, then I think perhaps three might be better."

"Then three it is." He wondered if she was expecting another caller at two, but he refrained from asking. With her penchant for candour she would no doubt tell him without hesitation. He wasn't sure he wanted to know.

Settling again into a more comfortable position, he slapped his gloves against his bare hand. "As far as my motives are concerned, Miss Thackery, I feel that I must in some way try to make up for the rather uncomfortable evening we spent together. The Hopewell party was not the success I had assumed it would be."

"Through no fault of yours, I assure you. The food looked delicious but it would have been impossible to make our way through the crowd. We were fortunate to get even that very small sample."

"Hmm, yes. At this moment a platter of that Westphalian ham sounds most enticing."

He had not meant to suggest that she invite him in for a late snack, but Heaven smiled upon him and that was precisely what she did. *Egad,* he thought. *If I had suggested it, she probably would have evicted me from my own carriage. Females! How does one come to understand them?*

"Of course I'm not sure what Cook has in the larder," she continued, "but I'm sure Mrs. McMasters can manage a pot of chocolate and some buttered scones."

A short time later they arrived at the house and Emerald sent Sally off to the kitchen with her request for a platter of food. McMasters looked a little surprised to see Emerald with Lord Milford in tow. Emerald enquired about Lady Udora.

McMasters inclined his head. "My lord and lady have taken the opportunity to visit with the Bancrofts on the occasion of the young master's birthday. I expect them to return within the hour."

"Yes, I had forgotten. Topaz and Amethyst?"

"They have not as yet returned from the party, miss. Is there anything else?"

"No, thank you, McMasters. We shall be in the library."

"Yes, miss. There is a small fire in the grate, I believe."

Emerald looked up at Milford and gestured with her hand. "Shall we?" She felt surprisingly comfortable with Milford, due probably to the fact that once again she was on familiar ground. It was only his attitude that made her wonder. She held no fantasies about her own appeal, at least when compared to the other debutantes who were always available to him. So what did he want with her? Perhaps access to Lord Kesterson, who wielded not a small measure of influence among several politicians? No, Milford had no political aspirations. But what, then?

The answer came to her when they reached the library and he immediately wandered over to peruse the handsome leather-bound volumes that graced one shelf. Of course! Her own reputation as a bibliophile was rather well-known. Now that he had inherited the Milford collection, he no doubt wanted to improve his knowledge. Who better to point him in the right direction? She drew a deep sigh of relief. It was good to know where she stood, even though she suffered a considerable blow to her pride. She went over to join him.

"Aren't they wonderful? Just look," she said, running her fingers delicately across the matching leather spines. "The collected works of Sir Walter Scott, the first volume of *The Parliamentary History of England,* by William Cobbett, John Debrett's *Baronetage of England.* One could spend a lifetime reading and rereading these marvelous treasures."

"I'm sure it would take at least that long," Milford said drily.

She looked at him to see if the irony she heard in his voice was imagined. Surely it must be. She smiled. "But then I have no need to tell you. Not when you are in possession of a library a hundred times more valu-

able than this one. What would you say is your favourite book among the thousands you own?"

His hand went to his neckcloth and he ran his finger around the top as if it had suddenly become too
tight. "My favourite? I can't say. How does one
choose when there are so many choices?"

"Yes, yes, I suppose you have a point but..."

He interrupted her before she could ask him to
name two or three choices. "But I suppose you have
no difficulty in naming your favourite book?" he
asked with a smile.

"It would surely be a collection of Elizabethan history. Yes, I understand what you mean. It is very difficult to choose because reading depends so much on
one's mood at that particular time, doesn't it?"

She thought she heard him breathe a sigh of relief
as he moved to the mantel to observe a bronze figure
of a horse. "Now this is something I can really appreciate," he said.

"Yes, it's very pretty."

"Pretty? Egad, woman, it's elegant. Notice the fine
attention to detail, the flared nostrils, the tiny etching
on the hooves, the strong withers. It's a hackney, of
course. Probably a chestnut, considering the tooled
effect. A workhorse to be sure, but a high stepping
one, I'd wager."

"I believe it's a replica of a horse Lord Kesterson
owns at Pheasant Run."

"His country place?"

"Yes, in Coventry. It adjoins Amberleigh, the house
where I was born."

"And does he still have a stable of horses?"

"Of course. It is a working farm." Emerald was fast becoming bored with the conversation. How did he manage to move the conversation from books to horses without so much as a batted eyelash? It just proved what she already knew: they had nothing in common. It was a relief when Sally appeared at the door with a large tray of food and a pot of chocolate.

"Just put it on the table in front of the fireplace, Sally. We can serve ourselves."

"Yes, miss. Cook says as how she can heat some turtle soup if you wants something more."

Emerald lifted the silver dome that covered a portion of the food. "I rather think this will be quite enough, don't you, Lord Milford?"

He moved over beside her and looked at the array of meats and cheeses in the cold collation, and the apricot tarts under a glass lid. "This will do very nicely, thank you."

Sally curtsied, then found an unobtrusive seat in the corner to work on her tatting.

Lord Milford seated Emerald and then moved his own chair closer to the tray. She offered him a plate and he selected a chunk of aromatic bread along with a generous helping of cheese and roast pheasant.

Emerald selected a bunch of grapes and placed some on his plate. "Try these. They are a special early grape that comes from vines imported from France. Kesterson raises them at Pheasant Run." She lifted another small bunch to her mouth and plucked one off with her teeth.

Milford watched the procedure with interest. Was she being deliberately sensuous? First one grape, then another and another; in between she took care to remove the seeds from her mouth. Even such a mundane task was made erotic by the movement of her wrist and fingers.

"You're not eating, Lord Milford. Are you after all not as hungry as you thought? Or does the food not appeal to you?"

He somehow managed to draw his gaze away from her mouth and meet her eyes. "Hungry? I am famished." *In more ways than I care to name,* he thought. "And yes. At this moment, at least, I find it very appealing." He was not referring to the food, but apparently his innuendo passed right over her head, because she reached for his cup.

"Then let me pour the chocolate," she said, obviously pleased. "You'll like it, I think. Cook prepares it with cream and a touch of nutmeg."

She handed him the cup and he took a sip. "Ah, quite good, indeed. My own chef has a recipe for chocolate that you might find interesting. It's a bit different."

"Another ingredient?"

"Yes, though he refuses to tell me what it is. One day you must try it."

She looked at him in surprise and he hastily added, "When you come to use my library, of course."

"Of course."

"Unless, that is, you might allow me the honour of your presence at dinner."

"Oh, I don't know. I am not sure her ladyship would permit it."

"I didn't mean to suggest anything improper. There would be other guests, of course. My great-aunt Cordelia, as well as the major and some other friends. It

would give you an excellent chance to make suggestions about the refurbishment of my library. Such a
waste, you know. All those valuable books gathering
dust . . . and weevils," he added as extra inducement.

"Weevils, too? Oh, dear. How tragic."

He saw by her face that he had finally struck the
right chord. Flirtation be damned. If he ever hoped to
find the high road with this young country miss, it
would not be because of his charm, but through his
private library. What was his life coming to?

She took a healthy sip of chocolate, then put her cup
down on the table. "I'm so pleased to see that you are
beginning to appreciate the great value of the books in
your collection."

Then seeing the intensity of his gaze that was fixed
on her teeth, she asked "What, what is it?"

"It's your lip. You have a moustache of cream on
your upper lip." Before she could say or do anything
he wiped it away with his thumb.

"There. That's better." He touched his thumb to
her lips. "Lick," he ordered.

Her tongue darted out and wiped the pad of his
thumb. "There's more," he said. It was with considerable difficulty that he suppressed a groan. There was
no question in his mind what the silly gesture had done
to him. The question was . . . how had it affected her?

CHAPTER FIVE

HE WAS TREATING HER as he would a child, Emerald thought with no small degree of irritation. A sudden picture of her mother flashed before her mind. They had been on a picnic at Amberleigh. On the way home in the gig her mother took one look at her face and saw the remains of the blueberries they had found near the stream. Her mother had taken a square of linen and told Emerald to stick out her tongue so that she could clean her face. It wasn't a pleasant process.

And yet there was no comparison between then and now. Dampened linen hadn't caused the sensations she felt now when her tongue stroked Milford's thumb. For some inexplicable reason her bones had become warm and rubbery, and had it not been for the fact that she was already sitting down, she might have collapsed. What utter nonsense! It was Amy, not she, who could faint under the least provocation.

Emerald fought to control her sense of imbalance. "Would you care for a spiced pear, Lord Milford?" she enquired a little too brightly.

"I think not," he said tightly. "Truth be told, I've had quite enough for one evening."

"But you've hardly eaten a thing." Seeing the pained expression on his face, she boldly asked, "Have you suddenly taken ill?"

"No, certainly not." But he admitted silently that he wasn't feeling quite himself. This girl didn't have one flirtatious bone in her body. Marry her? Hell and damnation. What would become of him? Flirtation was a way of life, a vastly pleasant way of life.

Appealing though she might be in a fresh and wholesome sort of way, how could a man of the world such as he chain himself for the rest of his life to a bluestocking such as Emerald Thackery?

He rose from his chair and she followed suit. Vexation was clearly written on her face. "Very well, if you wish to go, I will see you to the door." She turned abruptly and strode ahead of him. It occurred to her that his sudden departure meant only one thing. He had a previously planned engagement with another woman. That would account for his eagerness to leave the Hopewell soirée.

She waited while McMasters helped him into his coat and then stepped discreetly aside. Her voice was cool. "I suppose I should thank you for standing in for Lord Venable as my escort tonight, Lord Milford, but I would wager that the choice was not one you were happy to make."

Wager! The very word turned his blood to ice. "Let me make one suggestion, Miss Thackery. Never take on the habit of betting. It can only bring ruin to your life."

"I fail to follow your train of thought, sir, but I only bet when I know I shall win."

"My very own words not twenty four hours ago." He doffed his top hat and inclined his head. "I must say in all honesty that there were one or two brief moments when I enjoyed our evening together. Perhaps next time we will enjoy it even more.''

"Next time? Surely you don't expect ..."

He felt some satisfaction on seeing the surprise in her eyes. "Of course, next time. Didn't I mention that I would like to see you again?''

"But I ..."

He bent over her hand and kissed the air. "Good night, Miss Thackery. Until tomorrow.''

Before she could recover he had gone.

EMERALD WAS STILL attempting to analyse his behaviour when Lady Udora arrived home. After a brief exchange with McMasters in the foyer, she appeared at the library door. "Home so soon, my dear? I rather thought that the Hopewell parties continued long into the night.''

Emerald peered over the top of her spectacles. "I suppose some people fancy such occasions, but I consider it a waste of time.''

"How odd. I spoke with Lord Milford just as he was leaving and he rather seemed to enjoy the evening. In fact, he asked our permission to call again.''

"I can't imagine why. He was less than congenial.''

"And you?''

"Me? I don't know what you mean.''

"My dear girl, you do have a tendency to go about with your nose in the air. Although we mere mortals may not share your penchant for books, you might discover that there are other things we have to offer that are equally enthralling.''

Emerald looked startled. It was unusual for Lady Udora to speak so shortly. Emerald pressed her hands together in front of her. "I know how important it is for me to make a proper alliance, and I'm so sorry if I've displeased you, my lady." She pressed her fingertips together in an unconscious gesture of entreaty. "It is never my intention to pretend to be more than I am, but Lord Milford seems to bring out the worst in me. Actually, I believe it is he who is condescending, and not I, for he treats me as if I were a mindless schoolgirl."

"And yet he wishes to see you again. My dear, that just doesn't make sense, now does it?"

"No sense at all. But you gave him your blessing?"

"Yes. It seemed the right thing to do at the time." She straightened her lace fichu. "Perhaps I should send him a message that I have changed my mind."

"No!" Emerald said a little too quickly. "I couldn't allow you to be embarrassed in such a way." She forced a smile. "And as Topaz is so fond of saying, I shall use him to practise on."

Seeing the faint blush on Emerald's usually pale face, Udora laughed. "I had a feeling that might be your answer. He has my permission to call on you tomorrow afternoon. I trust that meets with your approval?"

Emerald turned away quickly. It wasn't easy to fool her ladyship, especially when she looked straight into your eyes. "I suppose so. After all, one can abide almost anything for a mere twenty minutes." She waited for Udora's response, but her guardian appeared lost in thought.

"What is it, my lady? Is there something else? You've suddenly gone quiet."

"What? Oh. No, nothing." Udora tucked her hands into the long sleeves of her gown. "Well, yes, I suppose there is, though I dare say I'm not sure of anything just now." She took a deep breath. "I think perhaps it would be wise for our little family to have a conference. Would you ask your sisters to join us tomorrow morning at breakfast? There is something we have to say to the three of you."

A chill went down Emerald's spine. "Something to tell us? May I ask what it is about?"

Udora stroked Emerald's hair. "I would rather wait and talk to the three of you at one time. You must excuse me now, my dear. I promised Bently I would be upstairs directly."

She said good-night and kissed Emerald on the cheek. Emerald watched her until she was out of sight in the hallway.

"Well, if that isn't devilish queer," Emerald said to no one in particular. Sally had long since gone upstairs to prepare the bedrooms for the night. "I wonder what she could possibly mean?"

It seemed as if hours had passed before Amethyst and Topaz finally arrived at home. They came to sit together on Emerald's bed. Amethyst was in transports over her impending marriage to Lord Farrencourt. Topaz, suffering from Lombard Fever from having to spend the evening with a man whom she barely tolerated, was only too eager to share the reasons for her boredom with the others.

She pulled the comb from her hair and threaded her fingers through the mass of silvery gold curls. "If I hear one more word about Lord Huxley's sisters and how awful it is to grow up in a household of women, I vow I will cascade all over the carpet.''

Amy tittered. "They spoil him quite outrageously, I'm told. And they used to put him in hoop skirts and a Marie Antoinette wig and take him for a stroll in Green Park when he was five years old. Olivia told me all about him.''

Topaz nodded. "To be truthful, I think he loved it but is ashamed to admit it. That is why he is always complaining.''

Amy kicked off her slipper and sent it sailing across the room. "Then I suppose you have no intention of courting his favours?''

"None at all. He is merely a convenience.''

"You have not told us about your evening, Em,'' Amy said, lying on her stomach and resting her chin on her hand. "Farrencourt and I saw you disappear with Milford into the garden. Was it too, too romantic?''

Taz grinned. "With a man like Milford, how could it not be? Did he steal a kiss, Em?''

"Don't be a noddy. Of course he didn't kiss me. I wouldn't have allowed it.''

"And you call me a noddy!" Taz said, rolling over on her back.

"Taz, if you think he is such a choice morsel, why don't you set your cap for him? I saw you flirting with him whenever I was otherwise occupied. You were practically falling at his feet.''

"Oh, don't be a ninnyhammer. We were simply chatting. He doesn't appeal to me in *that* way.'' She sat up suddenly. "Amy, did you hear that? I think our sister is jealous. Could it be possible that this time our precious bluestocking has found something more interesting than her books?''

Amy smiled. "He is a rather fascinating man. And so handsome. Are you seriously attracted to him, Em?''

Emerald pulled the quilts up to her chin. It wasn't easy to hide things from her sisters, but truth be told, her thoughts returned to Milford more often than she cared to admit. "Just listen to the two of you rattle on. You sound like a pair of old biddies cackling over a cup of scandal broth. But I do have something to tell you,'' she said, then watched with satisfaction as they both leaned closer and seemed to hold their breaths.

"Of course it may mean nothing at all. Then again it could be rather significant. If I knew more about the situation I might be better able to assess the degree of importance.'' She was deliberately drawing it out. And as she guessed, Topaz was the most impatient.

"Oh, do stop chattering to the wind and tell us,'' Topaz demanded.

"Well, it's simply this. Lady Udora asked me to tell the two of you that she and Bently wish to speak to us at breakfast tomorrow . . . or is it today?''

"Go on,'' Amy said. Emerald spread her hands.

Topaz scowled. "That's all? You led us to believe that something momentous was afoot when all it is is a family breakfast? What a thumping exaggeration.''

"But it did sound rather important, and you know how her ladyship has been these past few weeks, as though there was something on her mind.''

Amy looked thoughtful. "Yes, I've noticed that. She hasn't appeared well at all. I even wondered if perhaps she wasn't . . . er, you know.''

Topaz sat up impatiently. "Oh, don't be such a prude. Say it. In the family way."

Emerald pushed herself up in bed. "It couldn't possibly be that. You know how they feel about having children. Neither Bently nor Lady Udora wish to add another member to the family. They are quite happy as they are."

Topaz got up and went over to her own bed. "Sometimes one doesn't have much choice in the matter. But I am certain that is not the problem."

Neither Emerald nor Amy were ready to dispute her word. Topaz had a certain affinity to future events that they had learned not to question. Amy rose and went to look out the window at the darkness beyond.

"But what, then, if it isn't a baby?"

Emerald shook her head. "I haven't the slightest notion, but it can't be good. I suppose we shall discover the answer tomorrow morning when we join them in the breakfast room."

JONATHAN WAS INSPECTING his wardrobe that same night when Lord Grafton arrived unannounced. "Ah, there you are, old man. I saw your coach coming up the street so I thought I'd look in on you. Left the party early, did you?"

Jonathan grunted in reply as Grafton continued. "Looking over the clothes to decide which coat to wear to the wedding? When's it to be, by the way, and will you ask me to stand up for you?"

Jonathan scowled. "I shouldn't even be talking to you after the fix you've got me into."

"Then I take it things have not gone so well? I heard from the major that you were taking our Miss Thackery to the Hopewell soirée tonight. Jumped at your offer, did she?"

Jonathan flushed. "Well, not precisely. I had to finesse Venable into letting me take his place."

"Damned shame. I thought she would be only too thrilled to fall at your feet, considering everything." Despite his effort to be serious Grafton burst into laughter. "A bluestocking! Can anyone imagine a worse fate for a pink of the ton such as you?"

"It could be worse. She has a very acceptable family tree. Granted, her blood seems to run a bit cold, but once we're married and I've sired an heir, I'll be free to do as I please."

"Then she's already agreed to the arrangement?"

"Not yet," Milford said tightly. "But it is only a question of time."

Grafton must have suspected that things were not as they should be, because he leaned against the four-poster and lifted his monocle to his right eye. "I say, old man, is that a new coat *and* a new cravat? It looks to me as if you've had to pull out some fresh ammunition to bag this quarry. Could it be that you're a bit worried about winning the bet?"

"Don't be clearing a space for my carriage until you've won it, Grafton. I've no intention of losing. I stake my reputation as a gentleman upon it. It's just a matter of time until Miss Thackery and I puff our betrothal off to the *Times*."

"Right-o. If you say so." Grafton folded his arms across his chest. "But you don't sound very happy about it, old man. I'm sorry to be the one to put you in bad loaf, Milford. It was meant to be a simple wager."

"Nothing is ever as simple as it sounds. That's one thing I've learned since we became chums."

Grafton laughed. "Well, this does somewhat make up for the time you brought the horse into Mlle. Beaufort's second-floor bedroom and blamed it on me. French class was never the same after that."

Milford grinned, then sobered. "Well, have you come merely to gloat or is it your intention to make sure I don't leave Town?"

"Neither one. I was just passing by and thought I'd stop in to say hello."

"Passing by? What business could you have in this end of Town? The only one we know worth a second glance is Miss Tripton."

Grafton looked properly embarrassed. "To be sure. Since you are out of the running, I thought I might try my luck with her. She's not too bad, you know. Damned pretty, in fact, not to mention a willing spirit and a dowry that could keep a man in style for the rest of his life."

Milford felt a stab of remorse. "You're seeing Lucy?"

"Only since yesterday. You don't mind, do you, old man?"

"Not if she's willing," Milford said, realizing he was shading the truth. Shading it! Damnation, it was a bald-faced lie. Lucy Tripton was his property. She would marry him in a minute if he offered for her. Not that he ever would.

Grafton chuckled. "She's willing, all right. Especially after I told her..."

"You told her about the bet?"

"No. Just that you had developed a sudden *tendre* for Emerald Thackery."

Milford swore softly. Everything was falling apart. His life had become a runaway carriage with no one at the ribbons. And that carriage had just lost a wheel!

DARK CLOUDS LOOMED overhead like a curtain of doom when the girls awoke the following morning. It was not just the early hour that was depressing. Even the house seemed to hold its breath in uneasy anticipation.

Topaz pinned Maggie with her gaze. "Are you absolutely certain you don't know what's going on, Maggie? You're closer than anyone to Lady Udora, save for Lord Kesterson."

"And if I knew, do you think I'd tell the likes o' you three?"

"Yes!" they all chimed in.

Amy shook the wrinkles from her pink morning dress and smiled. "You never could keep a secret from us, Maggie, so we can only surmise that you don't know, either."

Maggie sighed. "Aye, she's been right close-mouthed, she 'as. All I know is that 'er ladyship 'as been after the girls to clean up the yellow suite and 'ave it ready for company."

"Company? Who?" Topaz demanded.

Maggie shrugged. "Could be the Prince 'imself for all I know." She looked at the clock on the table next to Emerald's bed. "Now, get on wi' you or you'll be late for breakfast and it'll be me what gets the blame."

It occurred to Emerald as they went downstairs that even the servants walked and talked more softly this morning, as if sensing that everything was not right. As always, they were sure to be affected by significant changes in the household. It boded ill for all of them.

Bently, Lord Kesterson, rose when they entered the usually cheerful room. Even a blazing fire in the grate did little to lift the all-encompassing gloom. Lady Udora looked up as they entered, motioning them to fill their plates at the sideboard and be seated.

"Good morning, girls," Bently said. "I hope you slept well after your party at the Hopewells."

Topaz regarded him with affection. "My lord, we would have slept better if we had known what is going on. Must we wait until we've eaten for you to talk to us? I, for one, have no appetite."

Bently unbuttoned his morning coat and seated himself. "Yes, I see your point. Very well, sit down and we'll get on with it."

He waited while they took their usual places and then he turned to Lady Udora. "My dear, would you like me to begin?"

She put her hand on his arm. "Would you, my love?"

"Of course." He cleared his throat. "Well, the truth is that we have received a letter from your aunt in the Colonies. Unfortunately the packet was delayed by weather and the message arrived only last week. It seems, however, that your Aunt Prudence has decided to pay you a visit. She will arrive tomorrow."

"Aunt Prudence?" Emerald demanded. "What could she possibly want? She hasn't been part of the family for... it must be eighteen or nineteen years. Before we were born."

Topaz leaned forward, eyes bright. "They say she was sent away in disgrace. That's why Father wanted her to have nothing to do with our upbringing. I wonder what she did?"

Udora gave Topaz a telling look. "What she did to deserve expulsion from the family does not signify. It is why she has decided to come to London at this particular time that concerns me. She is, after all, your only living blood relation."

Amy pressed her hands together in delight. "I, for one, shall be happy to see her. She could have changed, you know. Or maybe she is all alone in the world and simply needs someone to look after her."

Topaz sniffed, Emerald lifted her gaze toward the ceiling, and Udora and Kesterson remained silent. Finally Udora spoke. "Whatever it is she wants from us, we must try to make her comfortable while she is here. It is to be hoped that will only be a matter of a few days. At the same time, we must remember that your father wanted nothing to do with her. He wanted me to respect his wishes with regard to the three of you."

Emerald put her elbows on the table and pinned Udora with her gaze. "Are you afraid that she will try to take away your guardianship of us?"

Udora flushed. "Well, I..."

Bently reached for Udora's hand and tucked it between his. "Girls, you mustn't concern yourself over this. Miss Prudence Thackery has no claim to your guardianship or to Amberleigh, or anything you own. In my opinion we are making a blizzard from a single flake of snow. There is nothing that Miss Thackery could possibly do to upset our plans for you, nothing at all."

"Oh, my dear, I do so hope that you are right," Udora said.

She looked up at him with such adoration that it shook Emerald's composure. For that brief instant she forgot Miss Prudence Thackery and the hidden reason for her untimely visit. All she could think about was what it must be like to love and be loved in the way that Bently and Udora cared for each other. Would she ever feel that way about anyone? Or more importantly, would anyone ever feel that way about her?

She immediately thought of Milford, then mentally chastised herself for thinking like a fool. Why would a man of the world, handsome, wealthy, debonair, give her a second look? But he had. He had! And he was coming to call in less than five hours. Emerald was appalled by her eagerness to see him. He had a certain male magnetism that no woman could resist completely, but was that all there was to him? She was quite convinced she knew the answer, but one couldn't have everything, could one? And despite his shortcomings, Jonathan Trent was the most exciting man she had ever met.

"Emerald Thackery! You haven't heard a word I said," Lady Udora admonished.

"I'm sorry, my lady."

"I asked if you would see to my correspondence. There is so much to be done before Prudence arrives that I really must ask you girls to assist me. Amy and Taz have their share of the tasks."

"Yes, of course. I can see to it this morning since Lord Milford is not expected until this afternoon."

"Ye-e-es." Udora drew out the word. "My dear, has he given any indication of his intentions?"

"None whatsoever. I rather think this is a lark for him. Sometimes I feel that he rather resents me. That is why I refuse to take him seriously."

"My dear, you are not obliged to see him if you don't wish to. I thought I made that clear."

"Yes, my lady."

Udora appeared to consider Emerald's response, then brushed it aside. "Very well, then. We all have our work to do. I suggest you eat well and build up your strength. Heaven knows, I think we shall need it. From what little I've learned about Prudence Thackery, she makes quite an impression."

Later, as they were dressing for the afternoon, Amy helped Topaz fasten the hooks that ran down the back of her gown. "Why do you think she is coming back to England after all these years?"

Topaz stared at her reflection in the mirror and frowned. "It matters not one whit to me. There's nothing she could do to hurt us. Papa saw to that by making certain in his will that Lady Udora was to be our guardian. Now, of course, we have Bently on our side, too. We are quite safe, just as her ladyship told us. What I wonder is why she left in the first place."

Emerald, seated at the dressing-table, swivelled to face them. "I know why she left."

Amy giggled. "No you don't. You're just making it up."

"Very well. If that's the way you feel, I'll keep it to myself."

Topaz, her catches all fastened, plopped down on the bed. "Oh, don't be tiresome, Emmy. If you know anything, tell us."

"Since you insist." Emerald drew a deep breath.
"The truth is, Prudence Thackery was in the family
way with a merry-begotten child."

Amy clasped her hands together. "A love-child!
How romantic. But how do you know this? Did Bently
tell you? After all, he owned the neighbouring estate
in Coventry. The Kestersons were close to our parents. He might know."

"No, it wasn't Bently. I read about it in Papa's
journal. Prudence was *enceinte* when she left for the
Colonies." Emerald glanced over at Topaz, who had
suddenly gone pale. "What is it, Taz? You look awful."

"I thought for a moment that she might have been
my mother."

"No, it's not possible. She was gone before you
were born."

Amy looked stricken. "Then who was the father?
It wasn't Papa, was it? Her own brother?"

"No," Emerald said. "It wasn't Papa. I don't recall the name precisely, but it was some scapegallows
who ran off with her just one step ahead of the con-
stables."

Amy sighed. "Then I can scarcely wait until tomorrow. What a colorful person she must be. And
what a devoted mother she must be to give up her life
just to take care of her child."

Topaz gave her a quelling look. "The next thing we
know you'll be setting the story to music."

Maggie chose that moment to pop her head in the
doorway. "Sure an' I knew if I left you alone you'd be
makin' a mess o' things. Lord Milford's already pacin'
the floor and you with your 'air goin' off in all direc-

tions. Give me the brush, miss, and let me undo what's already done.''

"How long has he been here, Maggie?"

"Long enough to whet 'is interest. Now you be careful, miss, and don't go puttin' 'im off with talk o' history and politics and things what no nice young lady should be thinkin' about."

"Talk about *him*," Topaz said. "That is, if you want to keep his interest."

Emerald sighed. "I'm not looking forward to this."

CHAPTER SIX

MILFORD ACTUALLY WAS PACING the floor when Emerald made her appearance in the drawing-room. He stopped when he saw her with Sally, as always, in discreet attendance. Egad, she wasn't bad, not bad at all. Her muslin gown of pale green embroidered with pink-and-yellow flowers at the high waist and in rows that circled the skirt was quite fetching. But it was her hair that pleased him most. It lay thick and luxuriant, swept like a cluster of silken tassels to the back of her head and tied with a pink ribbon.

He remembered how in a moment of weakness he had told her he would like to take the pins from it and let it flow round her shoulders. Egad, he had been impertinent. But that was his style. Women adored it. This woman could be no different.

"Good afternoon, Lord Milford," Emerald said as she came forward and offered a practised curtsy.

He bowed deeply. "Miss Thackery, you look especially lovely today."

"Thank you. Won't you sit down?"

"After you." He motioned to the settee.

She took a straight-back chair across from the settee. He noted the small defeat and sat down. There was an awkward silence that seemed to go on forever. Then she spoke.

"The weather has been quite wet for this time of year. Will it affect your mare's performance in the races at Newmarket this month?"

"I doubt it very much. Colleen is sure-footed and strong for a filly. She hasn't lost a race since I first entered her in the Cheshire one-miler. Do you enjoy the races?" he asked hopefully.

"Not in the least! I think they are such a dreadful waste of time," she said before she caught Sally's warning glance.

"Indeed." His voice had an ironic edge to it. "Have you ever been to a horse-race?"

"No. I have not."

"Do you ride?"

"Of course. Though I can't say it is a favourite pastime. We do have horses at Amberleigh, though none to be compared to your stock, I'm sure. Lord Kesterson has an excellent stable at Pheasant Run. But then his country house is a showplace in many ways." Her face brightened. "He has a wonderful collection of paintings, one of which he acquired from the private collection of Lord Radstock and which is on display at the Royal Academy. I'm sure you've seen it, though."

"No, I'm afraid I haven't."

"When was the last time you visited a gallery?"

"I can't really say."

"Astonishing! Then galleries do not appeal to you, sir?"

"Tell me, Miss Thackery, why would one want to stare at a painting of the sea when one can view the real thing?" Too late he saw the look in her eyes. It was such good fun toying with her, but this was not the way to win her heart. Damn, but she was difficult! He cleared his throat and leaned forward, allowing the toe of his boot to graze the toe of her slipper. Surprisingly, she didn't pull away. He took courage.

"Perhaps you could teach me."

"Teach you?" Her voice sounded strained.

"About art and books."

"Oh . . . Well, I'm not at all certain that one can acquire a taste. I think one is either born with it or one is not."

He gazed into her eyes with as much enthusiasm as he could muster. "I believe that, given the opportunity, one can acquire a taste for most things."

"I find that very hard to believe."

"Then let's put it to the test. There is to be a race on Saturday at Newmarket. I would like to take you to see it."

"Oh, I think not. Besides, we are expecting a female house guest and I'm sure my presence will be required at home."

"Bring her along, if you wish."

"No, I . . ."

"Afraid you might develop a taste for horse-racing?"

"Not at all. But I . . ."

"No arguments. I'll call for you at three."

"Oh, very well. That is, if the Kestersons will allow it."

"I'll see that they do."

Emerald laughed at his brashness. "Then you must agree to visit the museums with me."

"Rather! I was counting on it."

"Never let it be said that you are unsure of yourself, sir."

He grinned. "No one ever has." He meant it when he said it, but in his heart he knew that things were changing. Especially where Miss Thackery was concerned. With her he never knew from one minute to the next where he stood in her estimation. It was unsettling...perhaps even a bit exciting. Would marriage to her give him the same breathless feeling? As if he were poised on the brink of some strange new adventure? He found the idea remarkably appealing. Today, at least, he had made a small measure of progress.

"May I call this evening and again tomorrow afternoon?"

"Why are you being so persistent, Lord Milford?"

He stroked his chin. This was the moment when he would customarily look deep into a lady's eyes and tell her that without her his life was meaningless. But somehow he knew she would laugh, or worse yet, giggle. Instead, he crossed his arms and rested his chin on his hand.

"You're different, Miss Thackery. Different from any lady I have ever known." He lowered his voice seductively. "But you have not answered my question. May I call on you this evening?"

"No. I'm afraid I have previous plans."

He was more than a little surprised. "Then tomorrow?"

"I'm sorry. My Aunt Prudence is due to arrive, and I'm sure Lady Udora would prefer that it just be the family to welcome her."

"Miss Thackery, are you trying to give me the go-by?"

"No, I..."

"Then I shall see you the day after tomorrow. No excuses."

"All right. If you insist."

"I do, and as I have overstayed the acceptable twenty minutes, I fear I must leave."

This time when he kissed her hand he left no doubt that his lips were warm against her skin. He held it overlong and was gratified by the look of surprise on her face. Another favourable omen!

Later that evening, when the girls were dressing for a family visit to the Harringtons, Topaz reached for a crimson shawl and placed it round Emerald's shoulders.

"There, that's better." She touched her fingertips to her mouth. "It gives you that special *je ne sais quoi*."

"Crimson with tangerine?" Emerald said. "I don't think so. While it might look dashing on you, for me it is a touch too *outré*."

"Still pretending to be the quiet little bookworm?"

"What do you mean, pretending?"

"You know what I mean."

Maggie, standing next to Amethyst, brandished a pair of curling tongs. "Mind your tongue, Miss Topaz. And don't you be spreadin' gossip."

"You mean she doesn't know?"

"Know what?" Emerald demanded.

Before Topaz could answer, Sally, looking flushed and overwrought, stuck her head in the doorway. "'Er ladyship would like to see you in the library, Miss Emerald."

Maggie grinned. "Sure an' I think she's about to find out."

Emerald didn't wait to assess her appearance in the mirror. She hurried downstairs as fast as she dared.

Lord Kesterson rose when she entered the library. Emerald curtsied, then went to sit next to Lady Udora on the settee. What happened next left her head in a turmoil. In her confusion, Emerald hardly heard what they were saying to her.

She clutched her hands in her lap and looked first at Kesterson and then at Lady Udora. "Are you saying that Jonathan Trent, Lord Milford, has asked for my hand in marriage?"

Udora inclined her head. "It does seem that way. We are to assume he has serious intentions. One does not jest about such things."

"But . . . but shouldn't he have mentioned it to me before he asked your permission?"

"It would have been more correct, I think, but Lord Milford is not one to stand on formalities. He is considered quite impetuous by some people, but he is also acknowledged to be quite the catch since he came into his title."

Kesterson linked his hands behind his back. "We have given our permission for him to court you. I doubt that you could make a better connection, my dear, but it must be you who makes the choice in the end."

"You seem more than a little surprised, Emerald," Lady Udora said. "Has there been no indication from him that he wished to take you to wife?"

"He has been most persistent, but it never occurred to me that he had marriage in mind. One could hardly consider me the most desirable among this year's debutantes."

Kesterson patted her on the head. "Don't be too sure about that, my girl. You have many wonderful qualities."

Emerald smiled. If no one else respected her for what she was, she could always rely on the Kestersons. "When...how soon must I give him my answer?" she asked.

Lord Kesterson crossed his arms in front of him. "I believe he wishes to announce the betrothal as soon as possible. This must be your own decision and it is something you should discuss with him."

"Yes, of course."

They talked for a while about the ramifications of being married to a marquess and then Emerald left the library in a state of numbness. Marriage to Lord Milford? What an extraordinary idea! One of the greatest collections of books in all of London would be there at her fingertips to read whenever she so desired.

But there was the other business to contend with. The business that would take place in the privacy of their bedchamber. She felt the heat rise in her face. Had he been thinking about that all this time? Was that why he had been so persistent? Surely not. She was no love goddess like some of the other females he had been known to favour. Nor was her lineage as remarkable as most of the girls who had been launched into Society this year. But still...it was she who would be called upon to bear his children. Why? Why? Surely there was a reason. The unanswered question was an affront to the orderliness of her mind.

When Emerald returned to their bedchamber, Topaz regarded her with obvious satisfaction. "So they told you. I can tell by the look in your eyes that you are not altogether displeased. Ah! My sister, the Marchioness of Milford. Who would have thought it?"

Amy came over and gave her a kiss on the cheek. "I'm so happy for you, Emerald. That makes two of us betrothed. Now we have to find a suitable man for Topaz."

Emerald started to protest that she hadn't yet accepted Milford's proposal, but Topaz threw a pillow at them. "Don't play the matchmaker for me. When I see the man I wish to marry, I'll marry him."

They laughed. Topaz had been saying the same thing since the day she turned five years old.

Somehow Emerald managed to get through the rather dull evening at the home of Mr. and Mrs. Harrington, close friends of Lady Udora. Mrs. Harrington, or, the countess, as she was called, an affectionate title Lady Udora confided to them, was usually quite entertaining, but Emerald could not concentrate on her tales of travel 'round the world.

They were all exhausted by the time they returned home and retired to their rooms. Not one of them chose to admit that their ennui was in part due to their uncertainty about what the morrow would bring, along with the arrival of Prudence Thackery.

"I'll bet she will be beautiful . . . and colourful," Topaz said. "She did, after all, run away with a man to whom she was not wed. And she was with child! I wonder if he ever married her."

"Oh, go to sleep, Topaz," Amy wailed. "We'll know soon enough."

Emerald yawned. "Maybe we'll wish we didn't."

Topaz pulled the covers up around her neck. "Don't be a ninnyhammer. At least she'll be exciting. I feel it in my bones. Imagine. Living in the Colonies!"

THE DAY DAWNED bright and sunny, but by midafternoon the sky turned a dirty blue and mist began to fall in oily grey sheets. "A bad omen," Sally predicted.

In an effort to lift the gloom, Udora ordered baskets of bright yellow daffodils brought into the house from the garden. Prudence was due to arrive at three. By two o'clock everyone was dressed and waiting in varying states of anticipation.

Emerald noticed with considerable interest the differences between Amy, who was so much in love that nothing affected her, and Udora, who was so nervous that she gave the impression of a leashed bolt of lightning.

Promptly at three o'clock they heard the carriage approach on the gravel drive. Moments later the knocker sounded and McMasters admitted Prudence Thackery.

Prudence Thackery wore grey. In fact, everything about her was grey, from the top of her unadorned bonnet to the soles of her plain grey shoes. Her hair had been drawn into a bun at the back of her head in an effort to control the unruly red corkscrew curls that constantly escaped. Her eyes, a pale blue against a complexion dulled by weeks spent on board ship, looked more grey than blue, Emerald decided, and cold! Her impression was not softened when a short time later everyone was seated in the library before a blazing fire.

"May I offer you some sherry, Miss Thackery?" Udora asked.

"Spirits are a tool of the devil, Lady Udora. I do not imbibe."

"Then perhaps some tea?"

"Only with my meals, thank you. I consider it a form of self-discipline not to partake of food between meals."

Bently, Lord Kesterson, tapped his finger against the arm of his chair in an impatient gesture. "We're grateful that you had a safe passage, Miss Thackery. From all reports I understand that the sea was unseasonably rough."

"Not to mention that the captain was incompetent as well as immoral. I cannot describe the things he allowed to take place during the weeks we were at sea."

"What things?" Topaz demanded.

Prudence turned to confront the girls, who were seated in a row on the settee. "Things young girls should not ask about," she said, levelling Topaz with her gaze.

"So these are Quentin Thackery's twin girls. Humph. Out of black gloves already? Seems to me you might have shown more respect for your dear father. Then, I suppose this bold one must be the orphan girl."

"Topaz is not just an orphan girl," Emerald said. "We think of her as our sister. We lost our mother, too, if you will recall, and it has been above a year since our parents passed away."

"Don't be impertinent, young lady. A year is nothing compared to the years they gave to you. When *my* father crossed over I wore the crepe for two full years."

Udora hastened to change the subject. "Do you find that London has changed much since you left to go to the Colonies?"

"Changed? Of course it's changed. The air is dirtier and the streets are crammed with horses and carriages. Nothing at all like it was eighteen years ago. I dare say the manners of the rabble have not improved, either."

Kesterson adjusted his waistcoat and crossed his leg over one knee. "It must have been difficult to leave your home and make the journey back to England. Is it a holiday that brings you here?"

She put her lorgnette to her eyes and fixed her gaze on him. "A holiday? Indeed, what a question. I've come to pack up the girls and take them back with me to Boston. But that is not the only reason for my journey. It will take me the better part of a year to accomplish all that I need to do. I trust that I shall be welcome to remain here, inasmuch as you seem to have ample space for house guests?"

Bently, Lord Kesterson, gave her a sobering look. "You are welcome to remain here for the present. However, I must inform you that under no circumstances will I permit the girls to return to Boston with you. Their parents made strict provisions in their wills, giving sole guardianship of them to Lady Udora."

"Well, we shall see about that, shan't we?" She rose. "Now then, I've had a long, tiresome journey. Perhaps you could have someone show me to my room."

Udora fairly jumped out of her chair. "Of course. If you will come with me." When the footman opened the door, Udora allowed Prudence to precede her. Looking back over her shoulder, she gave Bently a helpless look before following their guest into the hallway.

Once the door was closed Emerald turned to Bently. "Did you notice she never did say what her second reason was for coming here."

Bently stroked his chin. "By George, you're right. I wonder if it was a deliberate omission or merely an oversight."

Topaz, with her penchant for mimicry, placed an imaginary lorgnette against her nose, stiffened her back and intoned, "Well, we shall see about that, shan't we?"

Bently smiled. "Mind your manners, Topaz. You know how we dislike your tendency to imitate people, and always to their disadvantage."

Amy smiled. "I think Topaz is trying to make us forget she said that given her colourful past, Aunt Prudence was sure to be a beautiful and exciting woman."

Emerald grinned. "If one can call a mud fence beautiful and exciting...."

Bently frowned. "Emmy, my dear, you must watch your tendency to stand in judgement." But even he had to join in the laughter, and for a time at least, the tension in the house was eased.

PRUDENCE THACKERY DID NOT settle easily into life at Kesterson House. She was not a woman who enjoyed life. Furthermore, it seemed to them that her primary mission was to bring everyone else down to her level of discontent, and all in the name of piety.

It required only one visit to Lord Kesterson's barristers and a study of the Thackery will to convince Prudence that she had no claim over any of the three girls. Once that fact was firmly established, the family was able to relax and allow some of Prudence's complaints and dire predictions to pass them by.

Amy, with her gentle nature, was determined to bring some happiness into Prudence's bleak life, though Topaz took a less-generous attitude.

Emerald was bothered least of all by the presence of Prudence in the house. Her concerns centred on the decision she must make in regard to Milford's offer of marriage. Her sisters were certain that marriage was the right thing to do, considering her comparatively few chances of finding a reasonably acceptable suitor.

Finally Emerald brought up the subject over the dinner table. "I have come to a decision. It took some time, but I made a list of reasons both for and against accepting Milford's offer of marriage."

Udora rattled the cup against the saucer in her apparent eagerness. "And what have you decided, Emmy, my dear?"

"I've decided he must give me more time to make up my mind."

Prudence sniffed. "The girl's smarter than I gave her credit for. Why should she tie herself to a man? Heaven knows a woman goes from her father's house to her husband's bed with naught to call her own but her good name. Half of that she loses once the knot is tied. 'Tis far better to devote one's life to the Scriptures."

"But what about children?" Amy asked.

"Humph. Do not count on children to comfort you in your old age, missy, for once they're grown they run off and that's the last you see of them."

Topaz stopped buttering a piece of bread and looked at Prudence with genuine interest. "Is that what happened with your child?"

There was a dead silence in the room until Udora spoke. "Really, Topaz, it is ill-mannered to ask such personal questions."

"But I ..."

Prudence stiffened. "Rude, to say the least. However, I suppose you will find out sooner or later. It's true. I have a daughter. Or at least I did have one. She ran off when she was fourteen and I haven't heard directly from her for more than three years."

"I am so sorry, Prudence," Udora said. "Haven't you the least idea where she's got to?"

"She was said to have lived in the Indies for a while." Prudence paused, as if taking into consideration how much she wanted them to know. "I recently learned that she had taken passage on a ship to England."

"Then you've come to find her and make peace with her?" Amy asked.

"Find her? Yes, indeed. But make peace with her? Not very likely. She's a wayward, high-spirited child. Not unlike her father," Prudence added as an afterthought. "Had he lived, they would have been quite a pair." She apparently saw that she had caught their complete attention, because she closed her eyes and appeared to withdraw into herself. "But if you will excuse me, I do not wish to discuss it now." With that, she stood up, dropped a stiff curtsy and walked away. Even the crisp rustle of her grey dress sounded dry and lifeless as she passed by the table and left the room.

Amy looked stricken. "Shouldn't someone go after her?"

Lord Kesterson shook his head. "I believe she needs some time alone, but we must try to be more kind to her."

"Suffice it to say, Bently, I agree with you, but I have no time to cater to her sensibilities. My immediate concern is for Emerald. You know, my dear, you stand the chance of losing Milford if you delay in accepting his offer."

"I know. But if Milford retracts his offer, then I shall not be forced to make a wrong decision, shall I?"

Bently chuckled. "She has us there, Udora. Give Emerald credit. She has a talent for thinking things out. I'm sure she will do the right thing." He reached for Emerald's hand. "I hope you will understand, Emmy, that we have given Lord Milford permission to see you tomorrow afternoon. You must understand his wish to know your answer."

"Yes. Of course I will speak with him."

EMERALD WAS LESS CONFIDENT of her decision than she allowed the others to believe. If truth were told, her knees were not altogether steady when she went downstairs to meet Lord Milford the next afternoon. He was standing beside the pedestal globe that was set in a window alcove. It was not his custom to be still for long, but this time he was lost in thought and had apparently not heard Emerald enter the room. It gave her the opportunity to study him without being subjected to his caustic comments or innuendoes.

He *was* good-looking. Topaz was right about that. His dark, thick hair was just long enough to brush the collar of his coat, and his clean-shaven face was too rugged to be considered pretty. He possessed broad shoulders, trim waist and hips, muscular thighs and legs. He was strong. He could pick her up, if he chose to do so and ... No, she dared not pursue the idle fantasies that had begun to plague her of late.

As if sensing her presence in the room, he turned toward her. If she expected him to greet her with open arms, she was disappointed. Instead, she thought she saw a look of resignation flash across his face. When at length he reached for her hands, he did, at least, manage a warm smile.

"Ah, Emerald. There you are at last. I see they've told you. And you've come prepared to set the date for our wedding?"

"Wedding? My lord, you have yet to say one word to me about a wedding."

"But I ... I thought surely Lord Kesterson would have confided to you that I have asked for your hand in marriage."

"He did, indeed, but it is not he who is proposing marriage."

Milford's face flushed. "Egad, woman. Did you expect me to get down on bended knee and pledge my eternal devotion to you?"

She tilted her head without responding. His face turned white. "Hell and damnation! If that's all you want." He adjusted his coat and sank down on one knee. "Miss Emerald Thackery, may I request the honour of your hand in marriage?"

He looked confused when she didn't respond, but then the light seemed to dawn and he coughed in embarrassment. "I vow to keep you forever as my wife and to care for you and our children with unfailing regard. Will you accept my offer?"

She crossed her arms and rested her chin in her hand. "No. I...think not, Lord Milford, though I thank you with the same sincerity with which the offer was made."

It would have been impossible to miss the sarcasm in her voice. He got up a little more quickly than good manners would dictate. "You can't be serious. Are you actually refusing my offer? I...I don't believe it. You...you cannot do such a thing."

"I believe, sir, that I just have."

"But I..." Anger overcame his good sense and he took her by the shoulders. He should have finished what he had started to do once before when his laughter had broken the spell. Now he bent and kissed her with a sense of frustration that was akin to passion. When it was over he drew back and held her with shaking palms.

"I can't take no for an answer, Emerald. I need to marry you."

"Need to? What an odd thing to say."

"You need me, too, if you are to be honest. I know how it is with young women who've just been launched into Society. It's important for you to make a match the first Season. It is especially important for you, considering your prospects as well as your background. Lady Udora and Lord Kesterson have been good to you, but you can't expect them to look after you forever."

He saw by the expression on her face that he had struck a nerve, but it was momentary.

"No. I'm sorry. I can't."

He swore and dropped his hands to his sides. "Let us come to an understanding on one thing. Once we marry I shall not insist on my husbandly rights except for the purpose of begetting an heir. You will be free to come and go as you please as long as you remain discreet."

He decided that he was making little or no impression. "In addition to the arrangements I have made with your guardian, I will give to you as part of our marriage contract the entire contents of my library. And I will give you three days in which to make up your mind before I withdraw my offer. Agreed?"

"I need at least one month."

"No. A week."

"No. Three weeks."

"Two weeks, my final offer. Now do you agree or shall I leave?"

"Very well," she said with a sigh. "Two weeks it is."

"I trust that during that time you will permit me to act as your escort so that we may get to know each other a little better?"

"Yes, of course."

"Would you care to take the air at Green Park tomorrow afternoon? I regret that I have an engagement at my club this evening."

"Tomorrow will be fine."

"Very well, I shall call for you at four."

He considered kissing her again to seal the bargain, but their first kiss had left him unsettled. Instead, he reached for her hand and shook it. Only later did he wonder what had made her change her mind about considering his proposal. Was it the fact that he had promised her the privacy of her own bed? Or was it the gift of his library? The question, a decided affront to his manhood, continued to bedevil him for days.

CHAPTER SEVEN

HE LEFT SOON AFTER they settled the business of their
impending betrothal. *Business!* Emerald thought
grimly. That's just what it was. A business agreement, cold, all-encompassing and filled with risk. If
that was the way he wanted it, she could be as busi-
nesslike as he.

But something had happened to her when he kissed
her—something that she had made certain he was unaware of. If she had been undecided before, the kiss
had sealed their bargain beyond any doubt. For the
first time in her life Emerald had felt a twinge of the
kind of feelings upon which Amy had waxed so eloquently since the day she first became enamoured of
Farrencourt. If she had hoped to rid herself of the romantic fantasies that had bedevilled her since the day
she met Lord Milford, she was taking the wrong direction. Her mouth still remembered the pressure of
his lips against hers.

A wave of remorse swept through her. If she had finally met a man to whom she could respond, there was
little doubt that her feelings were not returned. Milford had made that all too clear. Once she had given
him an heir, she would be of little consequence to him.
She lifted her chin. No matter. It was apparent to her
that his intelligence left much to be desired. Perhaps

his knowledge of women was as incomplete as his knowledge of the classics. She might be able to teach him a thing or two before he cast her aside like a used brood mare.

MILFORD STOPPED OFF at White's Club before he went home. He needed to be in the company of men. Grafton was not in attendance, so there was no opportunity to gloat over his betrothal. But the major was ensconced in a chair in the club room, a glass of sherry in his hand. He motioned Milford to join him.

"I say, old boy. You look like the cat who drank the cream."

Milford sank down into a chair and motioned for the waiter to bring a drink. "What makes you say that, Major?"

"Why the look in your eye, boy. That gleam of accomplishment. Of battles fought and won, so to speak."

Milford grinned broadly. "Keep this to yourself, Major, until I've had a chance to tell Grafton, but I consider his porcelain music-box collection as having already passed into my possession."

"And a good thing, too," the major said grimly. "I heard that the coach you bargained away did not rightly belong to you."

"True, though I was unaware of the fact until I read my father's will, or else I never would have placed a wager against it. But once the wager was made I had to do the gentlemanly thing, hadn't I?"

"So... Miss Thackery has accepted your offer?"

"Well, not in so many words, but she is considering it, and her guardians have agreed to the contract."

"She's a prize worth winning, my boy."

"So you've told me before. I only wish I could believe it. She's comely enough once one sees beyond her spectacles, but Emerald is *not* what one might consider a warm-blooded female."

"You've known her for less than a week, Milford. Isn't that a little soon to judge her?"

"Take my word, Major, I know women. One look and I could tell that this one is no wanton."

"Aren't you being a little too sure of yourself, Jonathan?"

Milford looked surprised. "Why? Have you heard otherwise about her?"

"Oh, dear me, no. And would I tell you if I had? Far be it from me to carry tales."

"Oh? Then how does it happen that all of our immediate friends seem to have heard of the wager between Grafton and myself?"

The major had the grace to blush. "Gossip, Jonathan. You know how it spreads. Your servants, perhaps?"

Milford grunted. "In a pig's eye. But I forgive you, Major, now that the deed is all but accomplished. Take care not to mention a word to Emerald, though, or I'll have your hide stretched and dried and hanging from my gatepost."

"You can't hope to keep the wager a secret from her for long. She's an exceedingly bright young lady and she's bound to find out."

"I suppose so, but I'm hoping it won't happen until the banns have been published. That way it would be deuced awkward for her to change her mind."

The major grinned. "Something tells me that you don't know Miss Thackery as well as you think. Gossip wouldn't stop her from crying off on you. If you have any hope of taking vows with her, you'd better plan your strategy with great care."

"Thank you. I shall remember that." Jonathan crossed his leg over his knee. "My valet happened to say that the wayward aunt has just returned from the Colonies. Odd that Emerald didn't mention it when I saw her. Have you been introduced to her? Do you know anything about her?"

"I haven't been introduced, though I've called upon the family since she arrived." The major picked up his cheroot and blew a cloud of smoke. "The story is out that she was sent packing a dozen-odd years ago because of some indiscretion. A merry-begotten child, one would presume. It seems odd to me that they've kept her away from the public since she returned."

Jonathan nodded. "If she's as wild as the stories lead me to believe, she may be just the one to spice up a dull Season. The Kestersons can hardly avoid giving a party for her, but I intend to meet the woman before then, perhaps even tomorrow when I take Emerald for a drive."

"What? You're not seeing your beloved tonight at the Marybournes?" the major asked, eyes twinkling.

Milford grinned broadly. "My beloved, eh? No, my friend, tonight I have plans for another young miss. One not quite so acceptable in polite society, I'll warrant, but one whose blood runs hot at the mere mention of my name.''

The major shook his head. ''Not a good idea, my boy. You'll live to regret this last-minute fling. Tonight will be a disaster. I give you my word on it.''

''Rubbish. What my intended doesn't know won't hurt her... or me.'' The waiter brought his port and Jonathan leaned back, sipped it and waited for the warmth to flood his veins.

''Speaking of plans. Are you going to the races at Newmarket on Saturday? My filly is entered in the Rowley Mile. Besides that, I've promised Emerald that her Aunt Prudence could accompany us.''

''By Jove, is that so? Of course I'll be there. I'm looking forward to meeting the woman, and I'm not above taking away a bit of your hard-earned gold.''

''I'd gladly hand it over to you if the day is a success.''

''You're that set on winning, are you?''

''I'm that set on lighting a spark of fire in my intended. I'm counting on her aunt's influence to bring her round.''

JONATHAN RECALLED the conversation later that evening when he was on his way home after spending a very disappointing evening with Miss Rosalina. He had gone to her lodgings with the idea of having a jolly romp in her featherbed, but once he arrived, he felt smothered by the lushness of her figure when she embraced him. The laces, the flounces, the clinging scent of musk, and the fact that he'd had more than a little to drink, had made him long for a breath of pure country air. A vision of Emerald flashed in front of his eyes and he cursed in frustration. Was this what he had come to? Was he a man so entrapped in his own game that he could think of no one but Emerald and her innocently beguiling ways? He was at a loss to explain it to anyone, least of all himself. Rosalina was furious when he told her he was leaving, but a few gold coins pacified her.

He was just a short distance from home when it occurred to him that the major had mentioned the party at the Marybourne house near Hanover Square. Emerald had said she would be there. He hadn't received an invitation, but it would be a rare thing for him not to be welcome, especially in a home where there was a daughter who was grist for the marriage mill. He turned his horse in that direction without a second thought. Strange how invigorated the decision made him feel.

The house was set at the end of the street and was surrounded by a low stone wall. The drive and the adjoining street were occupied by waiting carriages—a small number, Jonathan thought, considering that most parties were counted a success by the crowds of people in attendance. Never mind. Success or no, if Emerald was here, then this is where he must be. He couldn't wait to see the expression on her face when he walked into the room.

The white-haired butler responded immediately to the thud of the brass door knocker. "Good evening, Lord Milford. Is there something I can do for you, m'lord?"

"Parsons, isn't it? I've come to join the party."

"Indeed, sir, but I don't think..."

"If it's my invitation you're concerned about, I seem to have left it at home," Jonathan said as he handed the butler his top hat and cape. "But I'm sure her ladyship will forgive me." He adjusted his neckcloth. "Where will I find them? In the salon?"

"Yes, m'lord, but I don't think..."

"It's all right, Parsons, I know the way."

Before the butler had a chance to protest too strongly, he stepped round him and strode down the wide, ornate hallway to the salon. All the fuss about an invitation had provoked Jonathan, and he was more than ever determined to make his presence known.

Even if he had not remembered which door was the correct one, the chatter of voices would have shown the way. Liveried footman stood at attention alongside the great double doors but made no move to open them.

Jonathan scowled. "Well, are you going to stand there or will you announce me?"

"M-m'lord, are you quite certain you wish to enter?"

"I'm not only certain, I'm damned well determined."

"Very well, my lord." The larger footman nodded to the other and they opened the doors simultaneously. "Jonathan Trent, Lord Milford," he announced in a loud, clear voice.

Jonathan stepped inside and the door closed abruptly behind him. There was a sudden, dead silence. A moment later a titter began at the back of the room and swept through the guests like sunshine moving through the treetops.

Jonathan's gaze scoured the room. Females! All females. Not a single man to be seen. Not even a servant. Lady Marybourne rose from a silken settee and extended her hand. An enormous smile split her face from cheek to cheek.

"Jonathan, what an unexpected pleasure. Do join us for a glass of sherry." She gave him a cool look. "Or have you already had more than your share?"

She was rewarded by a burst of laughter. Someone seated at a far corner spoke in a soothing voice. "Now, Bella, be good to him. P'raps he thinks he's just one of the girls?"

Again the room resounded with laughter. Alicia Fenworth, a diminutive creature with frizzled hair, stood and drew him toward a chair. Jonathan was all but paralysed. Alicia had no sympathy for him. He had danced attention upon her for a few weeks before stalking more interesting quarry, and she had never forgiven him. Now there was a dangerous light in her eyes.

She pushed him down onto the chair. "We all know that Lord Milford is a man who enjoys variety but I had no idea he also demanded quantity. Silly me. I ought to have known."

Jonathan tried unsuccessfully to stem the tide of red that began at his neckcloth and flowed quickly upward to his cheeks. Damnation! He had to get out of there. He tried to stand but another woman pushed him back onto the chair. Adorée Crimpton! Another one of his discarded affairs of the heart.

"Oh, don't go now, Lord Milford. You're just the person we need to display our little treasures. Am I not right, girls?"

There was a chorus of yeses while Alicia and Adorée drew him to his feet. Adorée picked up a bolt of red satin and draped one end over his shoulder. While he tried to untangle himself, Alicia flattened a straw bonnet on his head. A dark-haired woman handed Adorée a cluster of ostrich feathers which she stuck into a fold of the satin.

As he attempted to remove the bonnet, Alicia draped a mink cape around his shoulders. "All right," he said. "You've had your fun. No one told me this was a ladies' evening. I've learned my lesson."

"But we haven't come to the best part," Lady Marybourne said. "A bit later I plan to show the ladies some of the lacy underpinnings I have just brought back from France. One or two of them would fit you perfectly." She put her hand to her cheek in a pensive gesture. "Although it might require a good bit more cotton-wool stuffing than I have on hand."

He was shaking by this time. "Get that thing off me or I swear I won't be responsible," he said through clenched teeth.

No one seemed to care. They were having too much fun. Except for Emerald. When he chanced to meet her gaze across the crowded room, she was not smiling. Her eyes, through the magnification of her glasses, seemed to bore into him. She was seeing him as the fool they had made him out to be, and it was nothing to be proud of. What to do now? Turn tail and run or... He clenched his jaw and slowly unwound himself from the length of satin.

"Ladies, I apologize for arriving uninvited." He strode to the door and turned at the last minute. "While I agree that the merchandise is of the finest

quality, red is definitely *not* my colour. The green, I
think. It happens to be my favourite. And, may I add,
my favourite lady wears green.''

There was a stunned silence in the room. Then, as
he watched, Emerald, dressed in glowing jade velvet,
lifted her hands from her lap and began to applaud.
Seconds later everyone joined in. Jonathan smiled,
made an elaborate bow, and took a hasty departure.
Their laughter followed him all the way to the front
door. Parsons was obviously burning with curiosity as
he handed over the top hat and cloak, but Jonathan
ignored him and left without a word of acknowledgement.

It was only after the door closed behind him that he
was able to breath a sigh of relief. He should have
taken the major's advice and stayed home. A pox on
the major! It was then it occurred to him that the major had known all along that the party was for ladies
only.

EMERALD HAD BEEN fully aware of the looks sent her
way by Amy and Topaz the moment Milford entered
the salon at Marybourne House. They assumed that
Milford had braved the company of women just to see
her. But that couldn't be true, could it? He hadn't
given her more than a fleeting glance. And yet when
he looked again, she had read something in his eyes
that caught her sympathy. A little-boy look that said
''Help me, I didn't mean to do it.'' She had to admire
the way he seemingly recovered his self-possession.

She thought about the incident again the following
afternoon when he arrived to take her for a stroll in

Green Park. As it happened he was the one to bring up the subject.

"I suppose I was the spice for the witches' brew after I left the Marybournes' last night."

"Of course you were. You must admit that you looked rather ridiculous. Nothing else, not even an incredibly beautiful bolt of blue-and-silver lace that Mrs. Harrington brought back from China, could outshine your performance."

"Must you be so insufferably honest? You might at least have allowed me to believe that my appearance there was of little consequence."

Emerald chuckled. "Would you have believed me?"

He matched her smile with his own. "No, I suppose not."

"The truth of the matter is that you made a rather dull occasion into an evening to be remembered."

"One I hope never to repeat again," he assured her, "but I suppose the afterclap will be heard about Town for the next month or two."

He adjusted the sunshade and looked to see if she was protected from the glare. "I was hoping that you might have asked your Aunt Prudence to join us today. She must be eager to see what she can before she returns to the Colonies."

Emerald waved to some ladies strolling by on the other side of the fountain, then tucked her hands in her sleeves. "I don't believe that Prudence has as yet recovered from her journey."

"Indeed. But I trust she will be able to attend the races with us on Saturday. I look forward to meeting such a colourful and adventurous woman."

Emerald shot him a questioning look, but seeing no guile in his expression, smiled and nodded. "I doubt she's quite the sort you think. Prudence is unique in her personality. But if you insist, I shall do my best to persuade her."

"Well, I naturally assumed that she would not be a young woman, considering that she is said to have a child older than you. Nevertheless, I feel that as your fiancé I should do my best to make her feel welcome in Society."

"How generous. But need I remind you that you are not my fiancé as yet, Lord Milford."

He looked apologetic. "Forgive my eagerness." He reached over to touch her hand. "In my mind's eye we are already betrothed. I hope I am not being overconfident. Is it foolish of me to be so hopeful?"

"I…I cannot truly say, my lord. I still need time to make up my mind."

"Of course. I will try not to press you for a response, but I can only remind you that I pray for an answer in my favour."

It was her intention to ask why, but she remembered in time that he was not fond of her inquisitive nature. Still, it puzzled her. Wasn't a man supposed to speak of love when he proposed marriage?

The stroll in Green Park ended before Emerald had time to appreciate the beautiful grounds. Predictably, word had got round about Milford's foray into female territory the night before and everyone they met deemed it necessary to let him know that they had heard about it.

At least three of the evening papers carried cartoons of Jonathan. One of them depicted his lordship dressed in bonnet and shawl and holding a rose in his teeth. Emerald considered it memorable, if unflattering, and she took great care to see that neither of her sisters mentioned it to him when he arrived that Saturday to take her to the races. It never occurred to her to caution Prudence into silence.

Prudence Thackery had protested loudly about going to the races, but Udora insisted politely but firmly that Emerald required a chaperon and no one else was available. When she came downstairs to the library to wait for Jonathan's arrival, Prudence's face was more white than grey.

"This is the devil's work, Udora," she insisted. "I'll not watch for a minute, I assure you. Furthermore, I shall take along my Old Testament to ward off the evil that might come our way."

Amy reached for Prudence's hands and held them between her own palms. "Oh, do try to be happy, Aunt Prudence. I have been to two races with my betrothed, and really, it is quite exciting. The ladies are so pretty in their flowered bonnets and bright parasols and the men look quite dashing in their colourful jackets."

"Humph."

"I know just the thing to make you smile. Lady Udora has a sprigged muslin that will fit you perfectly, and I have a new straw hat you may borrow, and I know that Topaz will let you use her silk parasol."

Emerald noticed that neither Udora nor Topaz had expected to be part of the generous suggestion, but they had the grace not to protest. It wouldn't have mattered. To say that Prudence was affronted would have been a serious understatement. The veins in her neck began to throb and she looked down her nose at Amy with all the disdain of a dowager duchess.

"I consider your offer to be nothing short of an obscenity, Miss Amethyst. Kindly refrain from making my situation more difficult than it already is."

"Oh, I'm so sorry. I didn't mean . . ."

"Of course you did, girl, but I will overlook your behaviour, considering the way you've been brought up. If my black-gloves attire is so repugnant to everyone, then perhaps I should remain at home."

"No! You mustn't do that," Udora protested a bit too quickly. She forced a sickly smile. "That is, I'm sure everyone will understand and sympathize with your bereavement."

What Emerald understood was that Udora was entertaining a group of her lady friends with a lively game of hearts. Udora had made it all too clear to the girls that she did not intend to allow Prudence's long face and dire predictions to spoil the afternoon's fun. Emerald, on the other hand, was not looking forward to the afternoon at the races, so what difference would it make if Prudence was there? Besides, hadn't Milford been rather insistent about meeting Prudence Thackery?

LATER THAT DAY Udora and Emerald greeted Jonathan in the library when he arrived. His face was alight with anticipation. "Are we to have the honour of your presence with us at the races, Lady Udora?"

"Oh, dear me, no, though I'm flattered that you mentioned it. Prudence will accompany you as Emerald's chaperon. She should be downstairs any minute now. Ah, yes, here she is.''

Udora moved toward the door to greet her.

Jonathan took one look at Prudence, then turned his gaze swiftly to Emerald. ''That cannot be your Aunt Prudence—the one from the Colonies,'' he muttered behind his hand.

''Oh, but it is. Is she not quite what you expected, my lord?'' Emerald enquired sweetly.

His jaw dropped as he made a quick assessment of the woman who was attired from head to foot in dark grey and looked somewhat less friendly than a champion fighting cock. Jonathan wet his lips. ''No, I regret to say she is not what I expected. Of course, one cannot judge by appearances. I'm sure she is a dear lady.'' Even he knew that his comment sounded lame, but it was the best he could do, given the circumstances.

Emerald had no chance to respond because Udora had drawn Prudence towards them and had begun the introductions. Jonathan bowed in acknowledgement, but at that moment Prudence stabbed the air with the end of her closed parasol.

''I know that face. I saw your likeness in one of Mr. Smythe's cartoons. You were dressed in women's clothes and wearing a heathenish bonnet on your head.''

She turned to Udora. ''What kind of lady are you to allow your charge to be seen in his company?''

Both Udora and Jonathan blushed, but Udora managed to collect herself and explained that he had been caught unaware by a playful hostess. Prudence set her lips in a thin line.

"Such frivolities are a waste of time." She looked pointedly at Jonathan. "As is spending a day at the races. But I suppose one must endure. Come along, then. Let's go and have done with it." She stuck her nose in the air and swept from the room without a backward glance.

Jonathan looked at Udora, who gave him a helpless smile, then he offered his arm to Emerald, who grinned up at him. "Did I say that I'd find the races boring?"

"I believe you did," he said through tight lips.

"Then I must admit that I have changed my mind. I think the day is going to be quite unusual."

Jonathan groaned. "And unforgettable. I can't wait for the major to meet your aunt."

Emerald chuckled. "If anyone could prove to be her match, it's the major. The major could charm the birds from the trees."

IT OCCURRED TO EMERALD as they took their seats in the adequate, if somewhat spartan, grandstand, that perhaps she had overestimated Major Vonnegut's appeal. One look at his brightly embroidered waistcoat, diamond-and-ruby stickpin and ornately jewelled walking stick sent Prudence's eyebrows shooting upward. She acknowledged the introduction with her usual stiff grimace.

"How'd you do, Major. Emerald omitted to tell me that you were to be one of today's performers."

"Performers?" He shot a quick look at Milford and then at Emerald. "Ah. You refer to my sartorial splendour. I do confess, Miss Thackery, that my valet has a penchant for the colourful. It does so much for one's state of mind, wouldn't you say?''

"Humph. I suppose it depends on one's calling.'' She gestured to a half-dozen men gathered round a woman dressed in purple satin and adorned with a multitude of white ostrich plumes. Emerald recognized Harriette Wilson, the most infamous courtesan in all regards.

Prudence sniffed. ''If one is a clown or a person of ill repute such as she, then such dress might be deemed appropriate.''

Emerald felt compelled to save face for the major. ''Truly, Aunt Prudence, flowered waistcoats have been quite the fashion since the end of the war.''

"Peacocks!'' she sniffed. ''Slaves to one's base instincts.'' She turned her gaze to Milford. ''You, sir, at least have the decency not to flaunt your appetites and imperfections.''

Fortunately for everyone, the conversation was interrupted by the arrival of a scruffy-looking individual who doffed his cap when he saw Lord Milford.

"'Tis bad news I 'ave, m'lord. 'Twern't no one to blame, 'cept maybe Piggy Grodin and his bo-kicker what he bought last week from a coper.''

Milford spread his legs and folded his arms across his chest. ''Well don't stand there, man. What's happened? Is it my filly?''

"That it is, sir. She was struck in the withers when that two-year-old jumped 'er 'obble. Come up lame, she 'as.'' His bushy eyebrows drew together. ''Wot you want me to do, sir?''

"Damnation!'' Milford said, then shot an apologetic look at Aunt Prudence, who gasped audibly and clutched her black leather-bound testament to her breast.

The handler looked hopeful. "It ain't like she's gone completely lame, m'lord. The Rowley Mile would be too 'ard on 'er, but she could be entered in the Ditch Mile."

Milford tapped his forearm with his fingers as he gave the situation some thought. "No. I don't want to ruin her. Have my groom take a look at her and then see that she's sent round to the stable and bedded down."

"Yessir. I'll do that, guvnor." He stood there for a moment, then ducked his head and scurried away.

Major Vonnegut wiped his hand across his moustache. "Dammed shame, that. I'd counted on seeing your three-year-old run today."

Prudence unclasped her hands. "Then I presume we might as well leave?" she said, starting to rise.

Milford touched her arm, then drew back when she flinched away from him. "There is still much to see, Miss Thackery. I wouldn't dream of depriving you and Emerald of such an invigorating experience."

Emerald glanced at Milford and then at Prudence, and shrugged. It would be a waste of time to leave now and have to repeat the dreadful experience another day. She had, after all, made that unfortunate promise to Milford.

The two ladies were left alone for a few minutes while the major and Jonathan went to place wagers on their favourite horses. Prudence moved protectively closer to Emerald, who in turn wondered if it was Prudence who needed the protection.

"Dear child, we were foolish to let that man provoke us into coming here. Look, there are almost no ladies in attendance, save for those few courtesans flaunting themselves." She pointed to two women seated at the far right, who had attracted some male interest.

Emerald followed her line of vision. "I think you'll find, Aunt Prudence, that those are the daughters of a royal duke. Ladies of considerable consequence frequently attend the races."

"Humph. Well I dare say they must have their reasons. Reasons as good as yours, I suppose."

"Mine?"

"Yes, of course. You came to please your betrothed."

"He is not yet my betrothed."

"All the more reason to please him. While I am convinced that marriage is more of a nuisance than a blessing, at your age you need a man to look after you. A woman alone..." Her voice trailed off, then she seemed to collect herself. "Milford is a decent man. He'll make you a good husband, I think. It's plain to see that he has no interest in you... in that way." She wrinkled her nose. "Once you've bred him an heir he'll let you alone."

She drew her skirts around her ankles and seemed to prepare herself for the next indignity. As for Emerald, she was too stunned to answer.

CHAPTER EIGHT

THE MORE SHE THOUGHT about it, the more angry Emerald became. "What do you mean, he hasn't any interest in me?" she demanded with an uncharacteristic burst of temper.

Prudence looked at her in surprise. "You needn't be so testy, miss. It's plain to see, isn't it?" She tapped her head. "You have too much up here for any man to look twice at you."

"Then why would he propose marriage? He could have chosen among a dozen or more young ladies."

"The *why* isn't important. He's made it official. Now it's up to you. Once you've said yes, he daren't go back on his offer. You can ignore him." She looked quickly away. "That is, once you've got through the messy business of giving him a child."

Emerald let her gaze drift across the scarcely filled grandstand to where Milford was deep in conversation with a well-dressed young buck. They both looked her way, and it occurred to her that she was the object of their conversation.

Was it true that Milford had no real interest in her? She had been privy to dozens of conversations between young debutantes who giggled with delight when they recounted their amorous adventures with overeager swains. Not once had Milford made what

might be considered a truly improper advance upon
her person. That could mean only one of two things:
that instead of love, he had an ulterior motive for
proposing marriage, or that he was too shy to make his
needs known. Shy? He wouldn't even comprehend the
meaning of the word. Motive? Yes, there must be one.
And she would learn what it was no matter what the
cost. She looked up to see the major picking his way
among the seats. If anyone knew the answer, the major would.

He seated himself next to Prudence. "Ladies, forgive us for leaving you alone for so long." He leaned
toward Prudence. "Since this is your first horse-race,
I took the liberty of placing a small wager on a nag
running in the first heat."

Prudence snatched her lorgnette from her bosom
and perched it on the end of her nose. "You did what?
You had no right to involve my good name in such an
evil pursuit. I demand that you undo the damage at
once."

The major sighed. "I'm so sorry, madam. I thought
it might help banish the cloud of gloom that seems to
hover over you."

"The cloud of gloom, as you so aptly put it, is due
to nothing more than your presence at my side. If you
will excuse me."

She rose and moved to the seat on the other side of
Emerald. The major grimaced. "It seems I have over-
stepped myself."

Emerald winked at him and patted his hand. "Don't
be dismayed. Aunt Prudence is not yet used to our
ways."

She tilted her head in the direction where Milford was standing and then returned her gaze to the major. "One must give Milford credit. He's been quite attentive these past few days. I wonder how long he thinks he can keep me from knowing."

"Knowing what?" The major looked apprehensive.

Emerald laughed. "Oh, come now, Major. I'm not a child. A secret such as that stays secret for only as long as it takes two people to know it. Especially during the Season, when one never has a single moment to oneself."

He groaned and wiped his moustache. "Oh, my dear girl. You do know, don't you? Who was it who told you about the wager? Was it Grafton hedging his bet?"

"Please, Major. You mustn't ask me to betray a confidence. One breach of good manners is enough. Milford will in time pay for his impertinence."

"Then you will refuse his offer?"

"It would be the sensible thing to do, wouldn't it?"

"Yes, on the surface I suppose it would seem that way. You realize, of course, you were not intended to be the first to enter his study that day. It was to be Lucy Tripton. He had it all planned, but he hadn't counted on the soot from the fireplace and your having to take refuge in the next room. Even Grafton was shocked by his own good fortune at finding you there. He never thought for a moment that Milford would offer for you."

Emerald drew a sharp breath.

The major looked taken aback. "Sorry, my girl. I didn't mean it to sound that way. I've told the boy a dozen times that he's far better off with you than he would have been with the Tripton chit.''

"Is he in love with her, then?"

"Oh dear me, no. Milford is attracted to her because she is . . . er . . ."

"Voluptuous?" Emerald supplied.

"Well, yes, but I was thinking more along the lines of accessible and uncomplicated."

"I see. Yes, I think I understand. Is that the kind of female he prefers?"

"He does seem to lean in that direction. I suppose that now you know the truth, you will cry off?"

"I would prefer to get even. His losing the bet wouldn't be enough." She twisted the cord to her reticule around her finger. "Does he intend to marry me or will he leave me at the altar?" His answer meant more than she had realized, because in that single moment she knew that despite his machinations, the secret to her happiness rested in the hands of Jonathan Trent.

The major looked surprised. "Marry you, of course. His need to marry in order to inherit the title was at the heart of the bet. I thought you knew."

Emerald smiled. "I know now."

To say that the major looked taken aback would have been an understatement.

Emerald was hardly aware of Milford's return and the horses being brought out for the first race. Milford handed her a ticket. "I placed a wager for you on Sentinel, the roan gelding."

Emerald clapped her hands. "Oh, thank you. Does he have a chance?" she asked, beginning to enter into the spirit of the race.

"An excellent one. I put my own bet on him, too."

The major rose and resumed his place next to Prudence, who looked not at all pleased. He leaned forward, resting his gloved hands on the jewelled head of his walking stick. "Milford, old boy, you should have listened to me. Our money's on the Black Vicar. I'll warrant he's fast on dry turf, but seeing Miss Prudence with her book of scriptures proved to be an omen worth putting my money on."

"You are a true gambler, Major."

"Ah, yes. The Vicar's a long shot but I feel lucky."

Prudence paled. "You are too presumptuous, sir. I neither wish to participate nor to be blamed for your losses which are sure to follow, given your blasphemous use of the Scriptures."

The major chuckled. "Dear lady, I give you my word that I shall hold you blameless should our gelding, by some odd quirk of Fate, fail to arrive first at the finish line."

She snorted. "For that matter, just what is a gelding?"

Her voice, more strident than usual, caught the attention of several men seated round them. One dandiprat tapped the major on the shoulder and spoke in a booming voice. "I've wondered the same thing, Major. Tell us, just what is a gelding? Do enlighten us all."

Emerald saw the major blush for perhaps the first time since she had met him. He caught the glint of laughter in her eye and quickly looked away. "A gelding, my dear Miss Thackery, is a male animal who has had surgically removed those portions of his anatomy that would have brought him the greatest pleasure.'' The sudden silence was broken by loud guffaws.

Prudence paled. "You don't mean . . .''

"Yes. That is precisely what I mean.''

"Oh. Oh!'' She fumbled in her reticule for her vinaigrette, and after struggling with the hinged lid, inhaled deeply.

"Are you all right, dear lady?''

"Quite. Yes. Quite all right. Do let's watch the race. I believe it is about to begin.''

Milford was more than a little relieved to have the major attend to Prudence Thackery. He was almost as elated to discover that Emerald was intent upon watching the horses settle into their starting positions.

"Which one is ours?'' she demanded.

"The third horse from the left. The major's horse is on the outside.''

"What a shame that you are not holding the reins. I've heard that you are unequalled as a horseman.''

"An exaggeration, of course. The young man at the ribbons weighs much less than I do. This allows the horse to put his strength into running. I assure you, the boy is an expert. Sentinel is favoured to win.'' A pistol sounded. "They're off!''

Suddenly the grandstand was thrown into an uproar of shouts and curses as the ten horses lunged forward, digging their hooves into the dry turf. They were neck and neck until they approached the first turn, then four of the horses edged ahead of the pack. Sentinel and the Black Vicar were among them. When his horse moved ahead, Milford forgot himself and jumped up, urging the roan to victory. To his surprise, Emerald also sprang to her feet and began cheering. He couldn't have been more pleased.

The Black Vicar had moved to the position closest to the rail. The major grabbed Milford's elbow. "What did I tell you, old boy? The Vicar's out front."

Prudence, apparently having decided to find out what all the excitement was about, nudged the major with her elbow. "Look. The rider on the white horse is striking the Black Vicar with a whip."

"Right-o. He's trying to force him into the rail."

"But he can't do that. We must tell someone and make him stop."

Milford suppressed his laughter, but the major had to cough to cover his own amusement. "I assure you, Miss Prudence," the major finally managed to say, "that such behaviour is not uncommon. Our driver knows how to handle it. See? He's pulling ahead now. By Jove! I do believe he's going to win."

"They've still the last turn to go," Milford said hopefully. But he already knew that Sentinel was going to come in fourth. "Damnation," he muttered. "This is the first time in over a year that I've failed to bet on a winner."

Emerald gave him a quelling look that he could not completely read. Her smile was enigmatic. "Perhaps, my lord, you are being repaid for your most recent misdeeds."

"Misdeeds? I fail to understand your meaning."

She cocked her head and allowed her attention to be drawn to the finish line, where the Black Vicar crossed head and neck in front of the white stallion.

Jonathan also was distracted by the excitement of the race. He slapped the major on the back. "By all that's holy, Vonnegut, I can't believe it."

The major was red faced with triumph. "By Jove! It's her I've got to thank. Miss Prudence. Had it not been for her book of Scriptures I'd have gone for Sentinel, same as you."

Prudence clutched her vinaigrette close to her nose. "Does that mean you have won?"

The major chortled. "Dear lady, it means you have won, too."

"H-how much?"

"Well, I'd guess about seventy-five pounds."

"That much?"

Emerald looked at her with undisguised amusement. "That's quite a lot of money, Aunt Prudence. What are you going to do with it?"

For a moment her face lost its pinched look. "It isn't really mine, of course. The major made the bet with his own money."

"What ho!" the major declared. "I promise you, the money is all yours to use as you please."

"How kind of you. Then I shall give it to charity, I think. Or perhaps I should wager a small portion on the next race with the intention of increasing my donation."

Everyone except Prudence laughed. Milford flexed his gloved hands. "Predictable. As for myself, good fortune seems to have deserted me of late. I believe I shall be content with being an observer until Lady Luck sees fit to show me some mercy."

Emerald's eyes narrowed. Was he thinking of his misfortune in finding her, and not Lucy Tripton, ensconced in his study? She gave him a cold look. "I shall be only too happy to replace the money you wagered in my name."

"Nonsense! It was little more than a flea-bite." At the same time he was touched by her offer. Most females he had known would be begging him to place another bet.

They had resumed their seats and were waiting for the next race when Emerald spoke. "You are quite devoted to Lady Luck, are you not?"

Milford looked down into her upturned face. Her eyes were enormous behind her spectacles. Once again he was impressed by the softly fringed lashes and the deep blue irises that seemed to reflect such intelligence and wit.

"Devoted to Lady Luck?" He took her hand and held it in spite of the look of censure that Prudence sent his way. "I hardly think that properly explains my feelings. To put it more correctly, one might say that I am a slave to my intuition."

"And what does your intuition tell you about my answer to your proposal?"

He threaded his fingers between hers and stroked her hand with his thumb. "That is a territory where my intuition is not brave enough to venture."

She was intensely aware of the way their hands fit together. Aware of the pulse that throbbed in his neck. "It was my understanding, my lord, that you were afraid of nothing and no one."

"No man is that brave. If you should refuse me, I would be devastated beyond belief." He could not bring himself to speak words of love. He had said the words because he knew she wanted to hear them. But even as he did so, the thought crossed his mind that it was true. Her refusal would come as a disappointment. A wrenching disappointment, to be precise.

He pressed her hand against his thigh. Surprisingly, she returned the pressure. "Never let it be said, my lord, that I have caused anyone to feel such devastation. I have decided to accept your offer."

He looked at her more closely. "Did you say what I think you said?"

She nodded.

"By all that is holy... are you sure?"

"Yes. If that is what you want." She waited for something but wasn't quite sure what it was. Instead, Milford turned to the major and told him the news.

The major looked surprised. "By Jove, old boy. I didn't think you could pull it off. That is... ahem, congratulations, Milford. You're a lucky devil, you are."

Prudence nodded her approval. "A wise decision. But you might have chosen a more fitting place to seal your fate."

Emerald shivered. Seal her fate! She hadn't planned to say yes to his offer of marriage. At least not yet, though she'd known she would have to accept him in the end. He had behaved abominably, but when he held her hand in his own and she felt the warmth of him seep into her veins, she was compelled to bring him closer still.

After that, Emerald paid scant attention to the races. What had she done? The enormity of her impetuous decision sent shivers of apprehension coursing through her body, and she longed to go home to the safety of her family.

UDORA AND BENTLY were thrilled and delighted by
Emerald's decision. Amy and Topaz were happy for
her. It was Maggie who brought her back to earth.
They were alone in the bedroom where Maggie was
helping her dress for tea.

"So you've gone an' done it, 'av you?" She gave
Emerald a searching look. "And now you're thinkin'
'ow's it come that you got yerself into such a foin ket-
tle o' fish."

"How did you know? And if you say intuition, I'll
gladly break that vase over your head."

Maggie grinned. "Common sense is wot it is. A man
like 'im would scare the wits out of most young girls,
not to mention one wot's innocent as you. But 'e's a
catch, 'e is, even if 'e ain't all 'e claims to be."

Emerald heard the careful tone in Maggie's voice
and she grasped her wrist. "You know, don't you?
About the wager, I mean."

"I 'eard rumours. Just today it was. But it don't
matter none. Once 'e's yours hit's up to you to keep
'im. That is, if you want 'im."

"You don't think he loves me, do you?"

Maggie shrugged. "Sometimes when 'e looks at you
in a certain way, I think 'e loves you. But there's not
many 'igh-class marriages wot starts out wi' love. And
there's nought what says you can't make 'im fall in
love wi' you."

Emerald tied the ribbon on her dress and surveyed
herself in the mirror. "Yes. I think that might be possible. I must search for a book on the subject."

Maggie snorted. "Sure an' if that don't make less
sense than stealin' bones from a dog. It ain't books
wot you need. 'Tis books wot got you into all this

trouble. Wot you need is 'im alone with you in the moonlight. An' maybe two or three glasses of sherry wouldn't 'urt.''

"He doesn't like sherry."

Maggie gave her a quelling look. "I was thinkin' o' you."

"Oh. I see."

THE FOLLOWING DAY Milford paid his compliments to the Kestersons and the formalities were concluded by setting the date to officially announce their engagement with a party at Kesterson House.

When Jonathan met with Grafton and the major at their club the next morning, Grafton regarded Jonathan with undisguised curiosity. "Then you've actually gone and done it? God as my witness, I never thought you'd go through with it, Milford. I can't imagine you tied to a bluestocking for the rest of your life."

"Surprised myself, I guess."

Grafton stabbed his cheroot into a bowl and leaned his elbows on the table. "It ain't too late, old man. You could still step away from it. I'll even cancel our wager if that would help."

The major looked from one to the other. "Damned generous, I'd say. You ought to think about it, Milford."

Jonathan stretched his legs out and sipped his port. "I appreciate your gesture, Grafton, but I can't go back on my word. As for you, Major, I thought you were convinced our little Miss Thackery was a treasure beyond price."

"Indeed, I am, my boy. On the other hand, I'm not so sure she will be getting a prize of equal value."

Grafton laughed. Jonathan frowned, his voice tightly controlled. "Your loyalty is overwhelming, sir."

"I was afraid you'd see it that way. The truth is, my loyalties are divided. I have a great affection and admiration for the girl. Conversely, I know that you are neither the rake nor the thatch-gallows you pretend to be. All the same, marriage should be based on more than a simple wager."

Grafton sniggered. "It is, Major Vonnegut. It's based on the inheritance. Milford needs to marry and beget an heir or the family will lose the title."

Milford took a deep draught of his port and set the empty glass down with a thud, at the same time signalling the waiter for a refill. "What's done is done. I'll have a son on the way before the year's out or kill myself trying."

He laughed, knowing it was the wine talking. "But she's not all that bad, you know. The fact is, she's quite a beauty. If I can keep her hands away from the books for an hour at a time, I might even make her fall in love with me."

Grafton shook his head. "There's nothing she likes better than her books. Better men than you have tried to coax a little warmth to her veins, old boy."

The major nodded in agreement. "She hasn't lacked for attention, Milford, but having seen a man once or twice, she's finished with him."

"She continues to see *you*, Major. And don't give me that Canterbury tale about you being too old for her."

"We have never been romantically involved, Milford. I have never approached her as more than a friend."

Milford stabbed the air with his finger. "Aha! Perhaps she is drawn to you because you appear uninterested. I believe you have given me the answer."

SALLY WAS HELPING Topaz into her riding costume when Emerald staggered into the bedroom, her arms loaded with books. She dropped them into a chair when she saw Topaz.

"Need I ask whom you will be seeing this afternoon?"

Topaz pulled the snug-fitting jacket across her chest and closed the buttons. "You needn't, but since I know you will, I'm merely taking the air with Sally." Her eyes danced. "And of course if a certain young man happens to be in a nearby field assembling his newest balloon project, then all the better."

"This is becoming far too serious, Topaz."

Amethyst came into the room in time to hear what Emerald had said. "What's far too serious?"

"All the attention Topaz is paying to her balloonist friend."

"He has a name, Emmy. Besides, David and I are just friends. I'd like it to be more, but he is completely devoted to his work."

"Then why waste your time on him?"

Topaz shot Em a quelling look. "How can you ask me a question like that when Milford can't see you for the gaming tables?"

"But he asked me to marry him."

"And where was he when he sent the major to escort you to the Flemington tea?"

"He . . . he said he had business to attend to."

"Monkey business, I'll venture. Has he said that he loves you?"

"Well not in so many words."

"Stop that, Topaz," Amy interjected. "Can't you see that Emmy cares for him? You're hurting her."

"I'm sorry, Emzy dear," Topaz said.

"You haven't called me that since we were children."

Topaz gave her sister a hug. "I didn't mean to hurt your feelings. I was mean and spiteful." She waved Sally away and sat down on the bed. "I love you and Amy and I try not to be cruel. It's just that sometimes, the two of you being twins makes me feel like the odd shoe."

"It's because you haven't found a fiancé," Amy said. "When you do, everything will seem different."

"No, it's not that. But forget about me. We must do something for Emmy."

"For me?"

"Yes. We need to teach you about men, I think."

Emmy blushed. "I'm not quite the bumblehead you seem to suggest. I know how babies are made and I know about kissing and all that. I even started reading *Emmeline* and some other romance novels, and I find that I like them."

"And you think you can learn how to please a man from reading a book?" Both Amy and Sally giggled. Topaz shook her head. "Sit down, Emzy. I think we need to have a long talk."

The three girls piled onto the bed in much the same way they had when they were children at Amberleigh.

"First of all," Topaz said, sprawling on her stomach, "you have to hold a man's attention by flirting with him. It's the eyes that are most important of all. You need to keep yours focussed on him."

Amy carefully removed her slippers before sitting cross-legged next to Topaz. "It's like Taz says, but you also have to use your eyes properly. You can give him a shy look by looking down and then up and then down again very quickly."

Topaz nodded. "That's right, but tip your head to one shoulder for the helpless look. Then you can invite him to come closer by fluttering your eyelashes. And don't forget the wide-eyed look that tells him you're listening to every word he says."

Amy giggled. "Farrencourt loves it when I peek at him over the top of my fan. He says I have laughing eyes." For an instant she smiled as if recalling a precious moment, then she brought herself back to the present. "But one must be careful with fans or one can send the wrong message."

Sally uncharacteristically burst into the conversation. "Aye, miss. If you want to learn to flirt, ask Maggie. She knows 'ow to pucker 'er mouth in a way no man can resist."

Amy, looking endearingly innocent, stuck out her lower lip. "She's right, you know. The French call it a moue—a pout."

Emerald swung her feet to the floor. "Enough. I think I can remember everything."

"But wait. We've only just begun," Topaz said, then pushed Emerald back to the pillows. "We haven't even mentioned your hands."

Amy leaned back against the footboard. "Let me see. Yes, I have it. You could fold your hands demurely in your lap as we've always been taught, but men find it so much more bewitching when you take a long curl and pull it across your chin as if you were in deep thought. Or brush a curl away from your face with a practiced flick of the wrist. Of course, you can touch your fingers to his cheek. But I think you'd best leave his cheek until you've had a bit more practice or he might think you were going to strike him."

"Don't be silly. I don't look that awkward."

Topaz regarded her with an expression of sudden inspiration. "I know just the thing. You have such slim ankles. Men do so love ankles. When you're sitting with him in the salon or in the garden, cross your leg over your knee and let your slipper dangle ever so slightly. It will draw attention to your ankles."

"But my feet are so big. Won't he notice?"

"Not if you show enough leg."

"And you can wear smaller slippers," Amy added. "I'll let you borrow mine."

"The jade ones?"

"I'll give them to you. They're a perfect match for your jade velvet. But I still think you ought to practice before you try these things."

"Nonsense. And do stop treating me like a ninny-hammer. I promise you I shall make quite an impression."

She stood and walked to the door. At the last minute she turned, looked over one shoulder and stuck the

tip of her finger in her mouth. She batted her eyelashes at them. "Fank you vewy much," she lisped,
and swung her *derrière* in an exaggerated circle.

Topaz groaned. "I wonder if we did the right
thing."

Amy looked apprehensive. "I'm truly beginning to
doubt it."

CHAPTER NINE

IT HAD BEEN DECIDED by the Kestersons, Milford and his only surviving relative, his aunt, Lady Wingate, that Emerald must be formally introduced to that lady before the betrothal ball on the seventeenth.

To that end, Lady Wingate invited Emerald, along with her sisters and the Kestersons, to a small dinner party at her elegant if small Town house near Hyde Park Corner. As the Kesterson carriage approached the house, Emerald knotted her gloved hands.

"I wonder if she will like me."

Udora leaned forward and patted her knee. "What a foolish conjecture. Everyone likes you, my dear."

Topaz giggled. "Well, not everyone. I can think of a few people who don't. Lord Northrup, for example."

Emerald snapped, "Shut up, Topaz. Everyone knows it was an accident when I spilled that plate of food in his lap."

"A convenient accident, to be sure. Though I did believe him when he said he hadn't meant to paw you. He was just brushing a bit of food from your gown." Topaz fanned herself with her hand. "And let's not forget Lord Chalker. Was it an accident when you set the dog after his horse, and him still astride it?"

"Oh, hush! How was I to know the horse would make for the barn door. Or that the door was six inches too low for both horse and rider. Besides, he shouldn't have said what he did. It was disgusting."

"Both of you be still," Udora ordered. "It's important that we make a good impression on Lady Wingate."

"I should have worn my own shoes," Emerald complained. "These are so tight I'm not sure I can stand in them."

"It's too late now," Udora said. "Besides, we'll be seated most of the time." She closed her reticule and adjusted her Indian silk shawl that emphasized the bronze highlights in her hair. "Look, there's the house now. And isn't it lovely?"

Lord Kesterson parted the carriage window curtain in order to get a better view. "Hmm, rather impressive for a Town house. In the classical tradition of Henry Holland, I believe."

The great brass-plated door opened as the carriage drew to a stop, and four footmen in purple-and-gold livery scurried to assist them.

Once they were inside the house, a stoney-faced butler took their cloaks, then guided them to the salon, where he announced them. Milford, appearing somewhat tense, came forward to take Emerald's arm. "You look even more lovely than usual, Emerald," he said.

It sounded like a prepared and oft-used greeting. She managed only a tight smile, due to her aching feet, but did take note of his elegantly formal attire, his trim figure and the way his hair brushed the collar of his coat in a most appealing way. After that she was hardly aware of her surroundings or what was being said, so intent was she upon watching Lady Wingate.

She was *old*. Ancient, to be precise. Much older than any of their intimate friends. Her face was wrinkled, and her deep-set eyes were faded to an icy blue. Only her hair seemed to have survived the rigours of time. It lay richly coiled like a thick white serpent around her head. Near the front it was studded with two large rubies that glittered like the eyes of a malevolent snake.

Lady Wingate raised her lorgnette and inspected Emerald. "So this is the gel you told me about, is it, Jonathan? The twin?"

"Yes, Aunt Cordelia. My fiancée, Miss Emerald Thackery."

"Take your spectacles off, girl."

Emerald did so reluctantly. Although she was now unable to clearly distinguish Lady Wingate's face, she was aware that her ladyship was walking round her while at the same time muttering under her breath. It took all of Emerald's determination not to squirm. Her feet hurt. Moreover, she detested being put under such minute scrutiny. Her discomfort was beginning to dissolve into anger.

"Umm-huh... Nice eyes. Clear, well spaced, steady. The spectacles are necessary, I suppose." Lady Wingate linked her hands together as if she were holding a prayer book, causing three many-faceted finger rings to dance in the candlelight. A rehearsed gesture, Emerald decided grimly. Cordelia did not appear to be a person who would leave anything to chance.

"Tell me, girl, why do you want to marry my nephew?"

Shaking with subdued anger, Emerald put her spectacles back on, jamming them against her nose. "I'm not altogether sure that I *do* want to marry your nephew, your ladyship. He has quite a number of flaws." She hesitated. "But, given time, I think he will mature rather well."

Milford's mouth set in a grim line. Udora failed to suppress a gasp. Topaz tittered behind her hand. Lady Wingate let out a boisterous guffaw and patted Emerald on the arm. "Well put, my dear. Spirit. I like that. So! So you think you're woman enough to handle him, eh?"

Emerald, fretting now with feet too painful to bear, sighed. "Well, we shall find out, shan't we?"

"Indeed?" Lady Wingate's eyebrows shot upward.

A shocked look from Udora reminded Emerald that she had gone too far. Udora took Emerald's arm. "Please forgive my ward's forwardness, my lady. She suffers under the strain of events that have taken place more quickly than she could have anticipated. I fear she was not emotionally prepared for them."

"Oh, fustian! Stop apologizing for her. I like to see a gel with spirit. None of those white-faced, simpering, faint-hearted maidens for me. Too much of that these days." She patted Milford on the arm. "She'll do, my boy. I didn't know you had it in you."

He sputtered and started to speak but she shushed him, then all but dragged him to a chair. "Well, sit down, sit down, everyone. We'll have a bit of sherry before Cedric announces dinner."

Emerald saw Lady Udora quickly survey the room. The salon glittered from the light of a hundred candles reflected against walls of teal blue, embellished with scrollwork of leaves, tassels and thistle flowers swathed in burnished gold leaf. The chairs were covered in teal-and-ivory-striped damask, stiff and formal. It was far more elegant than the Kesterson house, and it was noticeably devoid of the inviting warmth and comfort that Lady Udora always managed to achieve.

But what her home lacked in warmth, Lady Wingate made up for with her straightforward personality. She carefully drew each of them into the conversation, finding topics of mutual interest to discuss. It didn't take Emerald long to realize that Jonathan adored his feisty aunt and that his affection was returned in kind.

Jonathan listened with divided attention to the lively conversations that criss-crossed the room. He couldn't begin to imagine how on earth Emerald had managed to mesmerize Aunt Cordelia. She was a crusty old bird, widowed now for over fifteen years, rich as Croesus and as set in her ways as a donkey galloping toward home. But she apparently approved of Emerald. Not only approved, but was taken with her.

He turned his attention to Emerald, who was talking about a painting she had seen at some obscure gallery. Maybe it was Emerald's gown. Aunt Cordelia loved green, and Emerald was wearing a bottle green dress embroidered with moss green and ivory roses. He had caught a glimpse or two of matching green slippers that were surprisingly tiny for a girl who was tall enough to reach his shoulder.

Woman, not girl, he reminded himself. A woman who would soon become his wife whether he wanted her or not. To be truthful, he had to admit he admired the way she stood up to his aunt. And he *did* want her, he realized, more than he had wanted any woman—with the possible exception of his dancing teacher, Mlle. Fontaine, whom he had known at boarding school. But once the mademoiselle had proved to be available he found her less attractive, a fact due in part to her profound lack of personal cleanliness.

There was no such worry where Emerald was concerned. He had stood close enough to her to know that she smelled as clean as a dewdrop on a Spring morning.

Damnation, if only Emerald could put as much fervour into her attention to him as that she gave to his aunt. His imagination took them to the bedroom, where he would lift her in his arms and carry her to the massive four-poster bed. He would proceed slowly with her, beginning with her slippers. Then, continuing on, he would divest her of each single garment until all that was left to cover her nakedness was a silken veil of hair. So aroused was he by the pictures he conjured in his mind's eye, that it was all he could do to keep his outward composure.

Unaware of his discomfort, Emerald relaxed now that they were seated. She looked over at him and blinked her eyes. Then she looked up at him, appearing to stare for a moment before looking down. Her head leaned toward one shoulder and once again she began blinking.

Jonathan bent close to her and whispered, "Are you all right, Emerald? Have you got something in your eye?"

Her reply was less than cordial. "I am quite well, thank you."

He was puzzled by her abruptness but shrugged it off. Would he ever come to understand this creature? He had said it before. She was like no other female he had ever known. She made him feel like a green boy starting to learn the secrets of attracting the opposite sex.

It came as a relief when dinner was announced, and they trooped into the dining hall, laid out today in all its finery.

Emerald thought she would faint from pain as she walked the short distance from the salon to the formal refectory. Only her sisters were aware of the agony caused by the simple act of cramming her feet into Amy's jade slippers. Topaz leaned over and whispered, "Don't worry, you can take them off once we sit down. The table is so long that no one will notice."

She was right. No sooner were they seated than Emerald kicked them off one at a time, letting the exquisite coldness of the marble floor soothe the ache in her feet. There was nothing more she wanted at that moment than to revel in its comfort. She even forgave Milford for being so dense that he didn't know a flirtation from a bit of dirt caught in her eyes. Never mind. There was still more ammunition in her storehouse of knowledge, thanks to her dear sisters.

They were watching her now from down the length of the polished table. Feeling more herself, she gave them a sly wink, and they had to struggle to contain their giggles.

A footman stood behind each chair to serve them. Emerald had eaten little during the day, due to her apprehension over meeting Milford's Aunt Cordelia. Now her stomach growled with hunger. Milford heard it and smiled but was kind enough not to remark on it. Emerald chalked it up as a minor irritation but certainly one more mark against her. She had never gone to the trouble to impress anyone before. Now, when it suddenly mattered how she appeared, everything was going wrong.

The menu, extravagant for a small gathering, began with green turtle soup and continued on through courses of venison, potted quail, fish in a disgusting white sauce, crusty potatoes and pickled vegetables, all interspersed with wines and sweet drinks as well as cheeses and bits of sweetmeats on the side.

Was it possible that Lady Wingate was also concerned about putting her best foot forward? The thought gave Emerald a small measure of confidence.

Milford was somewhat withdrawn during the meal in spite of every attempt Emerald made to flirt with him. For each degree of acceptance she accomplished with Lady Wingate, she seemed to lose two degrees with her betrothed. This business of flirting was much harder than she had anticipated. Perhaps her sisters had been correct when they said that she needed to practise before experimenting on her own.

The meal drew to a close with an offering of berry-flavoured ice served in tissue-thin stemmed dishes. Lady Wingate addressed them from the head of the table. "When we've finished here I suggest that we all retire to the salon. The gentlemen may join us." She adjusted her lorgnette. "I detest the tradition of allowing the gentlemen time alone with their port to gossip about their misdeeds and wrongdoings while we ladies twiddle our thumbs and wait for them."

Emerald agreed, though kept silent about it. Men were so much more interesting than women, who prattled on about babies and servants and what gown to wear to what event.

She felt around the floor for her slippers, then stretched her foot a bit farther. Nothing. They were nowhere to be found. She leaned back in her chair and dared a closer inspection into the darkness below, but there was naught to be seen but a bouquet of colourful gowns interspersed with the dark stems of male trousers.

Milford gave her an enquiring look, but she simply forced a smile and nibbled at her ice. When he chanced to look away she dared another survey of the floor round her feet. So intent was she on her quest that his voice startled her.

"Emerald? Is anything wrong?" Milford enquired softly.

"I...er...I do seem to have misplaced my slippers." She waited for the inevitable laughter, but he had the grace not to embarrass her. Instead, he signalled to a footman, to whom he spoke discreetly.

There was the unavoidable moment of confusion while the footman got down on all fours between chairs and began his search.

"Jonathan, my dear," Lady Wingate demanded, "is there something that I should know?"

"Not a thing, madam."

"Very well, then. Lord Kesterson, I believe we were discussing the possible destruction of the Henington estate on Drewsbury Road. Was the land not subject to entailment?''

Milford directed his concentration to the conversation, adding a few words now and then to attest to his attentiveness. Lady Udora shot furtive looks at Emerald while at the same time endeavouring to appear unconcerned. Amy and Topaz were clearly curious. As for Emerald, the search seemed to last an eternity. When it was over, the footman rose and disappeared in the direction of the butler's pantry. Emerald followed him with her gaze, then looked quickly down at the floor. The slippers were nowhere in sight. Had he been unable to find them? She had visions of being forced to go home in her stockinged feet.

"I beg pardon, miss. May I serve you?'' the butler said without so much as a crack in his stony facade. He presented her with a silver-domed serving platter. When he lifted the lid, there in the centre rested her jade slippers.

"I shall be happy to assist you, miss.''

Milford turned in his chair. "That won't be necessary, Cedric. I'll do the honours.'' He took the slippers from the platter and motioned to Emerald to lift her foot. "May I have the pleasure?''

She felt the heat rise from the base of her neck to the top of her skull but there was little she could do, save snatch them away and run from the room. And she'd be damned if she'd run away. Instead, she turned to face him, lifted the hem of her skirt and placed her foot in his lap.

She dared not look at his face. If he was laughing at her, she'd be tempted to stab him with a table fork.

All conversation had ceased. No one could keep up the pretence now, considering all that was happening. But for Milford, it seemed that he was alone in the room with the woman he had come to love and admire.

Her foot was warm against his inner thigh. The heat of it fused with the heat of his body and suddenly he was struck with a barely controlled desire for her. He shifted uncomfortably, regretting the snug fit of his best skin-tights. Her foot was larger than he had thought but smooth and well-formed, as were her ankle and calf. He had to swallow twice to moisten his dry mouth.

The shoe did not go on easily, but determination brought success. He was grateful that he was forced to concentrate. It took his thoughts away from the more dangerous territory that lay concealed just above the hem of her skirt. Finally he finished the second shoe and lifted her foot to the floor.

"Thank you, my lord," she whispered. The feverish look in her eyes did little to cool his blood.

He was too tense to speak but forced a smile and inclined his head, while at the same time noting that her rapid breathing seemed to keep pace with his.

A cumulative sigh echoed round the room. Lady Wingate pushed her chair away from the table with the aid of a footman who snapped to attention. "Now then," she said, "shall we retire to the salon?"

After that, everything was anticlimactic. No one mentioned the incident until the family left the house and was in the carriage on the return drive to Kesterson House. Topaz, as always irrepressible, was the first to bring up the subject.

Emerald looked at her and scowled. "Don't talk to me. I may never speak to anyone ever again."

IT WAS THE MAJOR who was able to lift the cloud of gloom from about Emerald's shoulders the following afternoon. "By Jove, I think you've done it, my girl. I shared a bottle with Milford at my club last night after you left his aunt's house. You made a remarkably good impression on the old Ace of Spades."

Prudence, who was seated with her knitting in a comfortable chair several feet away, sniffed loudly.

The major grinned. "Oh, come now, Miss Prudence. I meant no disrespect. It was only a friendly term we use for a widow lady. Lady Wingate is a respected and proper lady." He turned to Emerald and whispered, "Most of the time, at least."

Prudence tapped her knitting needle against the arm of her chair. "Then you would do well to mind your tongue, sir. And if you say things not intended for my ears, be good enough to save them for a time when I am not present."

The major apologized and looked sheepish. "I only wish, dear lady, that I might give you a better impression—the sort Emerald seems to have made on Lady Wingate."

"A waste of time and effort, I assure you. I have not the least interest in your impressions, good or bad."

Emerald sighed. "It wasn't just Lady Wingate I was hoping to impress. I'm not at all sure of Jonathan's feelings toward me, especially considering the circumstances under which he was forced to offer his hand in marriage."

The major shifted uncomfortably. "Well, I'm certain he has grown very fond of you. Marriage could only enhance those feelings."

"Or destroy them. I wonder if I did the right thing by accepting his hand."

Prudence snapped, "Of course you did."

"But how can I make him fall in love with me? I don't want to be just another wife who bears children and then is left to moulder away alone and lonely."

The major was silent for a moment. "I think you must become less rigid, my dear. Have you noticed how you stand off from people? As though you were afraid they might brush against your person. You affect too serious a demeanour, when in the contest between men and women, your nature should be more playful. Flirtation is always the prelude to proper lovemaking, I believe."

"Flirtation! If I hear that word again I may scream. Let me tell you what happened at dinner last night."

She proceeded to recount the advice given to her by her sisters and finished with the disastrous results.

The major's jaw dropped. "Is that what you were doing? Milford mentioned the incident to me. Thought you might have been a bit foxed, he did."

"Damn him, anyway! Jonathan Trent is beyond the pale."

Prudence stood up quickly. "There will be no more of that, miss, or I'll ask the major to leave."

Emerald apologized and the major gave her a sympathetic look. "The truth is, Emerald, that flirtation is an individual achievement. Perhaps you would be better off to find your own style."

"What other style is there?"

The major looked nonplussed. "Well..." He paused. "It has been my experience that some girls, er...stay close to their beau, er, physically close, I mean. Then other girls prefer to use provocative language."

"Such as?"

His face coloured. "Dear girl, I couldn't possibly use such words in front of—" he glanced over at Prudence, who speared him with an eagle's gaze "—in front of ladies," he finished lamely.

Emerald chewed her lip. "Oh, I see. I'm not altogether sure that I would know how to use those words, anyway. 'Hell' and 'damnation' are the only foul words I'm familiar with, and they don't seem to serve the purpose. I wonder that no one has written a book on the subject."

Prudence rose. "Enough. I believe you have overstayed your welcome, sir. Please be good enough to leave before I am forced to summon his lordship."

The major rose. Emerald followed suit. "I'm sorry, Major. I would like to have discussed this with you at greater length."

He ran his finger around his neckcloth. "In truth, Emerald, I doubt that it would help."

"Perhaps not. I think you are right. I must find my own style." She followed him into the grand entrance hall with Prudence trailing along as a ghost in grey, for once blessedly silent.

At the door Emerald took the major's arm. "Milford has promised to escort me to the Royal Academy tomorrow. It is not his cup of tea, but since I attended the races with him, he is obliged to take me to the gallery." She smiled. "I am sure he will be bored

beyond belief and would enjoy your company. Why
don't you join us?" She winked. "Aunt Prudence will
also be in attendance."

He made a droll gesture that only Emerald could
see. "How can I refuse such a compelling offer? Yes,
I would be delighted to join the three of you. I'll be
seeing Milford later and will make the arrangements."

THE REST OF THE DAY was spent in making hurried
preparations for the betrothal ball. Invitations had
been sent by special messenger only the day before, but
acceptances were already overflowing the silver bowl
placed in the entrance hall to receive them.

Seeing that the entire idea of a public announcement, not to mention a ball, held little interest for
Emerald, Udora had called upon Mrs. Harrington and
Lady Berringer to assist in the preparations. But there
was one thing she insisted that Emerald take upon
herself. The matter of her trousseau.

She would need carriage dresses, court dresses and
full evening attire, not to mention riding and walking
dresses, as well as a Hungarian wrap for the cool
nights and a Zephyr cloak to cover her wedding gown.

But when it came to nightrails for her trousseau,
Emerald was obstinate. "What difference does it
make? Milford will no doubt spend the night at his
club, drinking, gambling and Heaven only knows
what."

Udora looked sad. "All right, dear girl. We'll let it
go for now, but the collection must be started soon.
I'm sure that Milford will want to announce the date
of your forthcoming marriage at the betrothal party.

He has pointed out that he must marry soon in order to protect his entitlement.''

"Then why has he never mentioned setting a wedding date to me? Sometimes I think our betrothal is merely a gesture, and that he never, ever intended the wedding to take place at all.''

"What nonsense. Don't try to analyse things to death, Emerald. That's one of the disadvantages of having a quick mind. Let's not borrow trouble. Shall we talk about your gown for the ball? I have some lovely drawings I've selected from colour plates in the *Ladies' Magazine*,'' she said, opening it to the place she had marked with a velvet ribbon.

"It is rather pretty, isn't it?'' Emerald agreed. "I suppose I might fancy it in a delicate shade of willow green, or even nakara with an overskirt of Clarence blue.''

"My thoughts exactly. Since you seem to have so little regard for choosing your own wardrobe, would you be willing to leave the choices to me?''

"I'd be delighted to.''

"Good. With one stipulation, Emerald, that you make use of the time by spending it with Milford and getting to know him better. I would so hate to have you trapped in a loveless marriage, or worse yet, become a spinster like your Aunt Prudence.''

Emerald agreed. No one would want to be another Prudence Thackery.

DURING THE NEXT TWO WEEKS Emerald made herself available to Milford as often as possible, taking into consideration all the fittings and shopping she had to do to prepare herself for the "great occasion," as the girls came to describe it.

"One of three," Emerald hastened to remind them. No one could forget that Amy's wedding was set for early fall, and that with any luck, there would be three Thackery weddings before the end of the year. Topaz merely giggled. She was having too much fun to even think of marriage, though the idea of becoming bride to a certain balloonist was rather intriguing. Lady Udora would have her head if she even mentioned it, still... there was that interesting possibility.

On the afternoon of the sixteenth, Emerald finally prevailed upon Milford to fulfil his promise by accompanying her to the Royal Academy to look at a new exhibit.

For some reason Udora's words returned to haunt her. If Milford cried off on her, what would she do? She didn't want to become another Prudence—bitter, unloving and unloved. And so it was with a singular determination that she prepared for their expedition to the Royal Academy. Perhaps she might be able to subtly instruct Milford in acquiring a taste for the better things in life: art and music to replace horse-races and gambling. A wife instead of a harem, she added as an afterthought, then quickly discarded it. The easy things first.

She spent a good two hours selecting the proper gown to wear that afternoon. It was a blush-coloured, high-waisted sprigged muslin accented with tiny splashes of purple-and-lilac flowers. The bodice was embroidered with pink flowers and green leaves, among which were sewn strings of tiny purple beads.

Prudence insisted upon wearing her plain cotton dress of drab grey, along with matching slippers, shawl and bonnet. Nothing Udora or the girls said could convince her to brighten her wardrobe.

Milford arrived promptly at the appointed time, and along with the major, came to the door to fetch them. The major took one look at Prudence and raised his quizzing glass.

"Well, what is it?" Prudence demanded.

"Nothing. Nothing at all."

"Don't be a ninnyhammer. Of course it is something. I can tell by that amused look in your eyes."

"Been studying me quite a bit, have you? I take that as a compliment, Prudence."

"Do not be flattered, sir."

"Since you insist, yes. I was thinking about you. I was wondering why you were still wearing your hair-shirt."

"A hair-shirt? I fail to comprehend."

"It's just that a woman as young and attractive as yourself should be wearing colour. Red, I think."

"Red! How dare you. Red is a colour for light-skirts and women of ill repute."

"Now there I must correct you, dear lady. Red is the colour of life, the bloom of good health, and the passion to sample all that life has to offer." He looked at her with grave concern. "You must stop punishing yourself, my dear Prudence, and allow yourself to be happy."

Milford took the opportunity to end their argument by announcing that the carriage was awaiting them.

The carriage ride to the Royal Academy was punctuated by stony silence, an awkwardness relieved somewhat by the conversation between Emerald and Milford. He said more than once how much he admired her appearance. Emerald was amazed and perhaps a bit frightened to realize how much his approval mattered to her.

"I have been selecting gowns for my new wardrobe," she said. "Do you have a favourite colour?"

"Green, I think, but not that shade of pea green that became so popular a few years ago. I prefer moss green or the deeper bottle green such as you wore to my aunt's dinner party."

Emerald nodded. "I shall have to soon begin planning for my wedding gown. It takes weeks for the modiste to complete such a large task. I suppose we must think about setting a date for the wedding," she said, cautiously.

He trust his chin forward. "Yes, I suppose we must."

He seemed about to continue, but Prudence chose that unfortunate moment to make a caustic comment about the turn that fashions had taken since she had left to go to the Colonies. Emerald could easily have strangled her.

The major was apparently not dismayed by Prudence's sour disposition. He patted her hand. "Dear lady, I for one adore the new fashions and I should think you would, too. A lovely creature such as yourself has no need for corsets and hoops to hide her admirable figure."

Prudence blanched, then colour flooded her face. She sputtered before she could manage to get the words out. "Really, Major, I must insist that you refrain from personal comments . . . even when they are well-intentioned."

He inclined his head, but whether in agreement or disagreement, one could only guess.

The Royal Academy was all that Emerald hoped it would be. She wandered from room to room admiring the outstanding works of students as well as famous artists, at the same time trying to instruct Milford in the finer points of art appreciation. He seemed quite receptive, but at one point he excused himself to speak to another visitor.

While Prudence was also otherwise occupied, Emerald took the opportunity to thank the major for his kindness to her aunt.

He brushed it aside. "Dear girl, there is no thanks necessary. I find her quite amusing as well as a considerable challenge. She is rather fine looking, you know, and quite intelligent, were it not for the cage of guilt she has built around herself."

"Only a man of your sweet nature would see her in that light," Emerald said. "And I love you for being so kind to her." Feeling a sudden rush of tenderness, Emerald kissed the major on the cheek.

The timing was unfortunate. At that precise moment, and unbeknownst to them, Milford appeared in the doorway.

CHAPTER TEN

JONATHAN WAS LIVID. Anger surged through every pore of his body like some virulent fever that crackled and burned out of control. Hell and damnation! Was this why Emerald treated him with such a cavalier attitude? Was she in love with the major? It wouldn't be surprising. Vonnegut had often mentioned that he had a special fondness for her. And he had a way of charming women that few men could equal.

No! Devil take him, no! She was too good for him. Too young, too innocent, and far too sweet for a man whose appetites sometimes ran to the unusual. Of course, if one were to be honest, Emerald herself was a trifle unusual, but it was this very difference that he had come to love and respect in her.

Prudence, thoroughly engrossed in a painting depicting a bucolic scene, was oblivious to what had happened. Milford glanced at an ormolu mirror and noted with surprise the tightness of his mouth, the knotted cords in his neck above his neckcloth. It suddenly occurred to him that he was no longer thinking about losing his inheritance. He was worried about losing Emerald.

His mind made up, he took Prudence by the arm. "I believe it is time we joined Emerald and the major. I wouldn't want her to think I am neglecting her."

The major turned as they approached. "Ah, there you are, my boy. We wondered where you had got to."

"Yes, Major, I noticed how concerned you were." His voice had a hard edge. "I also noticed that the two of you seem to have found ways to occupy your time."

The major's face turned bright red, but he attempted a feeble laugh. "So you've caught us in the act, have you?"

"You made no effort to conceal it."

Emerald's eyes opened wide and she would have said something scathing, but the major stayed her remark with a hand on her sleeve. "See here, my good man, if you're implying that Miss Thackery's innocent peck on the cheek was anything more than a gesture of friendship, then you are either foxed or you have far too much imagination." The major patted him on the back. "My dear boy, I do believe you're jealous."

"How utterly absurd. And don't try to shift the guilt to my shoulders, sir! I'm only concerned about appearances. I've vowed to protect Emerald, and I will not allow you to damage her reputation by making it appear that you are carrying on behind my back."

Emerald pulled at her gloves. "Oh, do be civil, Jonathan. If anyone is hiding things it is certainly not I. Perhaps you should look to your own charade."

"Just what do you mean by that?"

She put the back of her hand to her forehead in a deliberately dramatic gesture. "Oh dear, just where shall we begin? I think the infamous wager between you and Grafton might be appropriate.''

Jonathan was temporarily taken aback, but a timely interruption by Prudence commanded all their attention. She had let out a scream and collapsed in a dead faint. Fortunately the major had turned in time to catch her before she hit the floor.

"What's wrong with her, Emerald? Is she ill?" the major asked as he fanned Prudence with her reticule, still looped over her shoulder by a thin chain.

"I have no idea what happened to her. She seemed healthy as a horse." Emerald knelt beside Prudence and held a vinaigrette to her nose as a small crowd gathered round them.

At that moment Prudence sputtered, then opened her eyes. The major and Emerald helped her to sit up. "What is it, Aunt Prudence? Are you ill?"

"Don't be absurd. I am never ill. It's that! That atrocity," Prudence said, pointing to a marble statue of a surprisingly well-endowed young Greek, sans clothing. "Take me away from this evil place at once."

Milford looked grim. "A splendid suggestion. I couldn't agree more."

As they were about to leave the gallery, a grey-haired gentleman in a striped waistcoat approached them. "Ah, there you are, Lord Milford. Gravers said you were here. I regret that the latest paintings you commissioned for your collection have yet to be framed, but I promise to have them delivered within the week."

"That's quite all right. It was not my intention to hurry you. If you will excuse us . . ."

"Certainly . . . I didn't mean to . . ."

Milford brushed past him with an uncustomary show of rudeness. Emerald was tempted to set him down properly. Here was yet another evidence of his penchant to dissemble, at least where she was concerned, for it was plain to see that he often frequented the gallery. But despite her anger at him for acting the prude over a simple kiss, and for encouraging her to think that he was an uncultured boor, something told her this was not the time to provoke him. It was fortunate that Prudence required all their attention.

THINKING BACK on the incident when he was finally alone in his study, Jonathan realized he had made much of nothing. The major was more like a father to Emerald than a suitor. But the thought of her kissing another man was far too maddening.

He shifted uneasily in his chair and stabbed out his cheroot. He hadn't smoked since boarding-school. What was this female doing to him? And worse yet, what had he done to her?

Seeing it from her side, he could scarcely blame her. Finding out about the wager must have been a ghastly blow to her pride. He would venture ten to one it was the major who had told her.

He placed his head in his hands and ran his fingers through his hair. This was a serious breach between the two of them. She hadn't uttered one word to him after they left the Academy, save to say goodbye to him at the door of her house. Nor did she mention the ball on the following evening. Any other time she would have invited him to come in for a few moments of pleasant conversation and a glass of wine.

He chewed his upper lip. And there was that business of the director of the Academy addressing him on his way out. Had she suddenly realized that he knew more about art than he had pretended? Damnation. It was an interesting game he had played at her expense, but it was beginning to backfire. Now he could only hope that she would be so pleased by their interests in common that she would forgive his childish pursuits. First, however, he would have to see her. He had thought that they would spend the evening together playing hazard as they often did with Udora and Kesterson, but Emerald had just looked at him and turned away, giving him no opportunity to say a word in his defence.

The question was, how to begin rebuilding broken fences? His face hardened. The major could fix things. And he'd jolly well better, Jonathan decided grimly, or he'd have the man's hide for a throw rug.

EMERALD COULD NOT WAIT to get to her room to change clothing. Maggie was in the girls' sitting-room mending a hem in Topaz's white muslin frock. "Sure an' you've come 'ome so soon? I thought 'is lordship might keep you 'til teatime."

"Don't speak to me about him. He's deceitful and proud and I hope I never see him again. Besides, he accused me of... of making up to the major."

Maggie dropped her needlework. "Now that's good news, it is."

"Good news?"

"Aye. It means 'e's jealous."

"One would think so, but he left no doubt that he was simply concerned by what the gossips might say."

Emerald turned while Maggie helped with the fasteners down the back of her gown. "I am at my wits' end trying to find a way to make this man see me for more than a simple convenience. Can you believe that he has yet to suggest a date for our wedding?"

Maggie's hands paused over the last hook. "It could be that 'e needs a proper encouragement." She smiled broadly. "Or maybe not so proper."

Emerald turned to face her. "What? What do you mean?"

"Oh, I was just thinkin' that if the man was in 'is cups and you was to maybe tear your dress a bit and muss your 'air, 'e might think as how he took advantage of you."

"What a dreadful idea."

"Yes, ain't it, though?" Maggie grinned. "It worked for my sister. O' course she 'as the fine big bosom to go wi' it. I can't say as 'ow it would work for you."

Emerald looked down at her own gentle curves and sighed. "There has already been enough deceit between us. All this time Milford has been pretending to be uncultured and boorish. And that's not mentioning the fact that our betrothal was based on a wager. He's made a fool of me. I simply cannot bear it."

"Then 'e deserves to be paid in kind, I'd say."

"No, I could never do such a thing. I'd rather be left on the shelf."

Maggie shrugged. "Aye. The way I see it is if 'e ain't worth the bother then you might as well take the easy way of it and cry off on 'im."

"It's not that he isn't worth it. I love him. But I want him to love me, too."

"An' 'ow do you know 'e don't?"

"He hasn't done...made...you know...any advances."

"Then it's up to you to see that 'e does, would be my guess."

Emerald thought about what Maggie had said. The idea was, of course, quite without merit.

THE NEXT EVENING the three girls were getting dressed for Emerald's ball when Sally finished adjusting her skirt. "There now, miss. It fits right fine, I'd say."

Emerald turned to the mirror and wrinkled her nose. "All except for the top. It's too flat."

Amy, looking younger than ever in a pale lavender gown overlaid with a silver net skirt, shook her head. "It's perfect, Em. Just enough curve to make you look sweet."

Topaz swirled round in her gown of bishop's blue and cocked her head. "It's true. You are rather flat, but we can fix that with some bust improvers."

"The wax kind?"

"No. Cotton wool is much better."

Emerald was uncertain, but she sent Sally scurrying to fetch it. The results proved to be quite remarkable.

"Look," Emerald said, "they also make my waist appear smaller. And...and they even feel like the real thing."

Topaz laughed. "I'm sure Milford will appreciate that."

Emerald turned pink. "I didn't mean that he would..."

"We know what you mean, Em," Amy said. "Hurry up, goose. It's nearly time for you to make your grand entrance. I'll tell Lady Udora you will be down soon."

Emerald was grateful that they gave her a few minutes alone. She hadn't spoken to Milford since the affair at the Royal Academy. What if he decided not to put in an appearance? No. He would not be so thoughtless. He was, after all, a gentleman. He had his own reputation to uphold. Taking one last look at herself in the mirror, she was more than a little pleased.

Lord Kesterson had ordered an especially fine pair of spectacles for her. They were made of thin gold wire with tiny diamonds set into the hinges.

Her gown was exquisite. She must see that a pair of specially made bust improvers were ordered as soon as possible. Never had she felt so feminine. At the last minute she stuffed yet another roll of cotton wool into her bodice and surveyed the results. Astonishing. Surely this would get Milford's attention. Maybe for once he would keep his eyes on her and her alone.

Maggie came rushing into the room. "Do come along now. Everyone's waiting."

Emerald searched her face. "Is . . . is he here?"

"Lord Milford? Sure an' it wouldn't be much of a betrothal ball without the betrothed, now would it? 'E's standin' there at the foot of the stairs waitin' for you to make yer grand entrance."

"Thank you." And thank you, Lord, she breathed silently, then picked up her jewelled fan from the dressing-table and turned to go downstairs.

"'Old on now. What's this?" Maggie demanded, at the same time making two cups of her hands.

"I added a wee bit to my bust improvers. Don't say a word. I think they make me look beautiful."

"Top-heavy's more like it."

"Oh, do be still. When I want your advice I'll ask for it."

"Yes indaid, Miss Thackery. Whatever you say."

Maggie curtsied in mock obedience, though Emerald wondered if Maggie even knew the meaning of the word. But nothing, not even Maggie's caustic wit, could spoil this night now that Milford was here.

He was indeed waiting at the bottom of the stairs. When he saw her he apparently gave a signal that was passed on to the orchestra because they burst into a fanfare. As one, all the guests turned to watch her descend to greet them. She felt like a queen.

Jonathan was more handsome than ever in his white waistcoat and snug knee-breeches. He waited expectantly, hands linked behind him, feet spread wide. But there was something about the way he looked at her that Emerald was unable to comprehend. Had he spoken to Udora and Bently about the wedding date? If so, then she could breathe more easily.

JONATHAN HEARD THE SIGH of approval from the assembled guests as Emerald floated down the stairway to meet him. She was indeed more lovely than he had ever seen her, but there was something different. Had she blossomed into a full-blown woman overnight? Impossible. It was the dress, he decided. She was wearing bust improvers. The idea amused him even though he preferred her own lovely soft curves. He smiled.

She hesitated for the briefest moment at the foot of the stairs as the butler announced their names. Then the orchestra began to play a waltz and Jonathan reached for her hand and pulled her into the curve of his arm, being careful to maintain a respectable distance between them. The guests cleared a space for them to dance.

Emerald looked up into his face and he saw innocence mixed with uncertainty. He could hardly blame her. He had conducted himself like a cad. But that would all change. He would be a different man, beginning tonight. Most of the women he knew liked to be treated with a rough hand, but this creature was a lady: beautiful, intelligent, and so innocent that the thought of it gave him pleasure akin to pain. He had begun to think some time ago that he was in love with her, but tonight it became a certainty.

When the dance was over the guests burst into applause. Emerald, still with her hand on his sleeve, remembered how Farrencourt had kissed Amy at the end of their betrothal dance. It was a tender moment that had brought tears to many eyes. Now she lifted her own face to Milford in anticipation but he bowed and relinquished his hold on her. She automatically dropped a curtsy, but the pain in her heart, not joy, was the source of tears that suddenly burned at the back of her eyes.

In the confusion of greetings from close friends and other guests there was no time to dwell on it. She blinked away the tears, but not before Udora saw them.

"Emerald, my dear child. I'm so proud of you. You've never looked so lovely or presented yourself with such charm. I know it is a strain. Are you all right?"

"Quite, Lady Udora. But rather excited, I must admit. I . . . I just wondered. Has Milford approached you about setting the wedding date?"

"Well, not as yet, my dear, but there is plenty of time for that. We did, after all, extract his promise that he would not force it too quickly. Surely you aren't concerned?"

"No, not really. If there was doubt in his mind he wouldn't have come tonight."

"And is there a doubt in your mind about marrying him?"

Emerald reached for Udora's hands. "None. None whatsoever. I do love him more than I can say."

"I thank heaven for that!"

"Please, may I have your permission to see him alone in the library after the ball?"

"Ten minutes would be appropriate, but really, my dear, any longer and I shall have to ask Maggie to chaperon."

"Yes, yes of course. I'm willing to have Maggie in attendance."

"Just what is the reason for . . . ?"

Emerald blushed. "Jonathan and I have had little time alone to talk. I was hoping . . ."

"Yes, of course. I understand."

Emerald was quite sure she didn't understand, but Maggie would. After all, it was her idea. Now it was up to Emerald to pull it off. If she could.

She had little time to think about it or to plan. After that first dance with Milford, it seemed that every man in the room wanted to take his turn with her on the dance floor. She wondered why that was. She had read that the bloom of young love makes a woman doubly desirable. But common sense told her that it was the bust improvers that had attracted their attention.

It was nearly thirty minutes later before Milford again had the chance to dance with her. She had been looking for him, but he was nowhere in evidence.

"So here you are at last, Jonathan. Where have you been?"

"Trying to keep myself occupied while you were being courted by every eligible male in the room, not to mention a good many who are already married. Must you flirt with anyone wearing trousers?"

"Flirt?" She laughed. "Is that what I've been doing? And all this time I've been told I haven't the least idea how to flirt."

He guided her to a small alcove that was hidden from the public view. Suddenly he stopped dancing and looked down at her as if lost for words.

"What is it? What are you going to do?" she asked.

"I...er. Forgive me for being uncivil, Emerald, but you seem to have lost your..."

"My what? My combs?" she asked touching her hair.

"Your...ah...stuffing. I'm afraid that during the vigour of the last reel you have become a bit lopsided."

"Damnation," she said as her face turned red. Then without further ado, she reached into the left side of her dress and extracted the extra roll of cotton she had added at the last minute. Heaven only knew where the right side had gone to. "There. Does the left side match the right?"

He grinned. "I do believe it does. And quite handsomely, I might add, though your lovely figure needs no embellishment."

She looked up at him in surprise. "Thank you."

"The pleasure is mine." He cleared his throat. "There is something important I must tell you."

"Yes?"

"Not now. May I remain behind after the guests have departed?"

"Yes, of course. I was about to suggest the same thing. We can use the library."

"It's settled, then. Now I suppose we must join the festivities."

"Yes, I suppose we must." The look that passed between them spoke more eloquently than their words ever had. Emerald was grateful that her bust improvers were made of cotton wool and not wax, for surely the heat his eyes had generated in her blood would have melted them in a minute.

The major was waiting for her when they returned to the dance floor. "Ah, there you are, Emerald. I was beginning to think you were avoiding a dance with me." He stood waiting until Milford made a token bow and walked away.

She smiled and offered the major her hand. "I would never avoid you, Major. The truth is, you're just the man I wanted to see."

"I'm flattered."

"Don't be." She smiled. "What I wanted was your opinion as a man of the world."

"Ask me anything," he said as they waited for the music to begin again.

"What would you do, as a gentleman, if it appeared you had compromised a lady? That is, assuming you were so far into your cups that you couldn't recall a thing?"

"Why, I'd do the right thing by her, as any gentleman would, but I assure you my dear that I would never... Oh, I see. You're thinking about yourself... and Milford, one would hope."

"You know me too well, sir. Tonight, win or lose, I plan to force him to set the date for our wedding. Even if he's too foxed to know that nothing happened."

"That's utterly diabolical, Emerald. Surely you wouldn't attempt to deceive him in that way."

"I would and I will. After all, he is the true master of deceit. Let him have a taste of his own pudding." She saw the shocked expression on the major's face. "And don't you go telling him a word of this," she cautioned, "or I'll never forgive you."

"Who, me? Not a word, my dear. Not a word." He looked more than a little grateful when the musicians struck the first chord and the next set began.

When it was over, Emerald was immediately besieged by young rakes who wanted to dance with her, but she pleaded fatigue and went in search of Maggie.

It was Maggie who actually was fatigued, having worked hard from sun-up until well after dark. "You've decided to do wot?" she enquired wearily.

"I'm going to do what you said. Get him foxed and let him think he compromised me. Tonight in the library," she added.

"Oh, miss, it was just my foolishness talkin'. I don't think..."

"It's too late now. All I want you to do is to sit in the corner and pretend to be a witness."

"Not me, miss. I refuse to be a part of this. 'Er ladyship would chop me up and feed me to the dogs, she would."

"She won't find out. But if you don't help me, she just might happen to learn about you and a certain footman who's supposed to be engaged to the Fordham housekeeper."

"You wouldn't tell on me." Maggie sighed. "Then again, I guess you would."

"Indeed. Now, first of all, you must ask McMasters to make certain the wine cabinet is well stocked. I'll take care of the rest."

"You'll make a mess of it, mark my words."

"Oh, do stop treating me like a child. I've made up my mind and I know exactly what to do."

"And where 'ave I 'eard that before?" Maggie grumbled. "Seems to me you were better off wi' your nose stuck in a book. You'll make a mess o' this. 'Pon my word you will."

CHAPTER ELEVEN

WHEN EMERALD RETURNED to the ballroom she
searched for a moment until she discovered Jonathan
and the major deep in conversation at the far end of
the room. Making her way toward them, she had to
fend off a number of persistent males, included among
whom was Lord Grafton.

"Miss Thackery," he said, bowing over her hand,
"I've been remiss in not yet offering you my best
wishes on the occasion of your betrothal to Lord Milford. He is a very lucky man."

"So I've heard," she mused. "Lucky enough to win
your valuable music-box collection. I shall look forward to giving it a place of honour in our home."

He chewed his lower lip. "So you know about that,
do you?"

"Of course. But don't concern yourself about it. I
find the entire episode quite amusing."

"That's jolly decent of you."

"It is, isn't it? But be warned, Grafton, next time
the two of you won't get off so easily. I happen to
know about a certain bit of fluff you've kept secret for
some time now. You wouldn't want word of that to get
round, would you?"

His face blanched. "But how could you...?" He
grasped the ends of his waistcoat. "I, er... appreciate

your silence, Miss Thackery, and I swear I'll be more circumspect where Milford is concerned."

"I'll remember that, Lord Grafton." She patted his hand. "Thank you." With that she turned and walked away just in time to keep from collapsing with laughter. It had been a lucky guess. She had had no idea that Grafton had a secret mistress, but he seemed the type. Of course she would never mention it to anyone, but revenge gave her a feeling of satisfaction. One day soon she would tell him the truth. That would afford her even greater satisfaction. Emerald was reminded of the games she and her sisters used to play when they lived at Amberleigh. What good fun they had planning tricks to play on one another.

It was very late by the time the last guests paid their respects and departed. Maggie, having a well-deserved fit of the sulks from being overworked, was already in the library when Milford and Emerald arrived.

Emerald took a closer look. There was something about Maggie that didn't seem quite right. It didn't take much to convince Emerald that her abigail had been sampling at the wine. Maggie positioned a tray of food and wine on a low table next to a settee in front of the fireplace. Then, giving Emerald a look that dared her to respond, said, "Will there be anything else, miss?"

"Not at the moment, Maggie." Emerald gestured toward a chair at the far side of the room. Maggie, for once, offered no argument.

Milford waited while Emerald seated herself in a straight-back chair, then he found his own comfortable place on the settee across from her.

"It was a perfect party, Emerald, but I'm glad that we have this chance to be alone. I've been wanting to talk to you."

"And I want to talk to you, Jonathan, but first, let's enjoy the wine and sweetmeats Cook has prepared."

Jonathan smiled. "If you wish."

"Port wine is your favourite, is it not?"

"Yes." He took a sip. "And this is very good. Deep and rich, and at room temperature, just as I like it. McMasters must have been keeping it in the wine cellar for a special occasion."

"A very special occasion."

Milford looked over his shoulder. "Is the fire dying or is it my imagination?"

"It looks fine to me, but I'll stir it with the poker." When she returned she noticed that he had already finished his drink. "May I fill your glass?"

"Please do. I saw you speaking with Grafton tonight. Was he quite civil?"

"Quite. I doubt that he will be making any spontaneous wagers for a while, though."

"You're right. He hated losing his favourite collection."

Emerald smiled. They chatted on and on, with occasional interruptions of one kind or another, when Milford had some minor request. Emerald took each opportunity to refill his wineglass until they had emptied two full bottles. She had been able to give the appearance of matching him glass for glass while at the same time limiting herself to only a few sips.

By the time she was about to open a third, she noticed that he had slumped into a reclining position.

"Jonathan? Are you asleep?" She approached the settee and looked down at him. His eyes were closed and he was breathing deeply, completely relaxed.

She gave a satisfied chuckle. "This will be easier than I thought, my darling," she said softly. But now that the plan had progressed, she wasn't quite sure what her next move should be. One day she must write a book of instructions to aid the would-be bride. It was all so confusing.

He snored suddenly and shifted his position, thereby allowing her the necessary room to sit next to him. She gently edged herself down beside him, being careful not to touch his body.

And it was such a handsome body, she noted. Dark lashes dusted his cheeks, drawing her gaze to the fainter shadow that was starting to show on his usually clean-shaven face. She brushed her knuckles against it, enjoying the rasp of smooth skin against rough stubble. She remembered how, when she was a little girl, her father used to "whisker" her face, making her giggle in delight at his attention.

On impulse, Emerald leaned over Jonathan and pressed her cheek against his. He was so far into his cups that he didn't move, save for a faint quiver. Finding her experiment most enjoyable, she brushed her lips across his mouth. He didn't respond, of course, she hadn't expected him to, but the distinctly male scent of him wafted up to her and she shivered despite the warmth that had generated inside her.

She pressed the palm of her hand to his chest and was surprised by the strength of his heartbeat. The corded muscles of his arms and chest were rigid beneath her fingers, and for one giddy moment her hand drifted lower. His belly tightened spasmodically and she drew back. The situation was getting out of control. And she had forgotten to undo the hooks on her gown. Should she tear it to make the scene more believable? She was about to do so when Milford moaned softly and moved more closely against her, and she was all but enclosed in the circle of his body. He flung his arm across her lap, anchoring his fingers in the fabric of her gown.

Emerald's heart thudded against her ribs. Blood raced through her veins like a river at flood-tide. She was caught up in an emotional flow that threatened to sweep her away to oblivion, and yet a part of her wanted to ride this maelstrom of desire. But a wiser voice cautioned her to wait.

She moistened her dry lips and called out softly. "Maggie. Maggie! What do I do now?" There was no answer. A series of snores from across the room provided the reason. Devil take the girl. Maggie was asleep at her post.

Emerald gazed down at the man who might soon become her husband. This was probably the moment when she should scream and bring the servants running so that she would have witnesses to the fact that she had been compromised. But right now, witnesses didn't matter one whit. All she wanted was for him to take her in his arms and make love to her. It couldn't be wrong, could it? They were, after all, officially betrothed.

She heard a clock ticking nearby. It seemed to grow louder, tick even faster. Or was it her heartbeat? She bent and kissed him again. He moved and opened his eyes.

She gasped and drew back. Did he know what she had just done? How long had he been awake? Suddenly the enormity of it all hit her full in the face like a gust of icy wind. She jumped up at the same time that he started to rise.

Moving away from him toward the fireplace, she watched him stand somewhat unsteadily. "Emerald, I...I'm so sorry. I...I didn't plan to let it go this far."

"Wh-what do you mean?"

"I...I'm sorry. I must go now. If I stay a minute longer I can't be responsible for my actions."

Before she had a chance to respond he had left the room and disappeared from sight. She heard his rapid footsteps grow fainter, in rhythm with the ticking clock.

Ticking clock. Ticking clock? There was no clock in this room. Udora had sent it to be repaired. But it was ticking now, albeit more slowly than ever before. Her eyes followed the source of the sound and she moved toward it until she stopped at the foot of the settee where a potted ivy floated in a saucer of liquid. The overflow fell on the carpet below in pale red droplets.

"Wine!" Emerald all but shouted.

Maggie jumped up. "Wh-what's going on 'ere? You take yer 'ands off 'er or I'll..."

"Stubble it, Maggie!" Emerald said in a dry voice. "He's gone. He walked out on me."

Maggie's jaw dropped. "'E didn't!"

"Do you see him here...hiding behind the potted plants?" Emerald asked bitterly. "You and your advice! Get him foxed, you said. But how was I to know he had emptied his wine onto the ivy?"

Maggie flipped her hair over her shoulder. "Sure an' I'll not be takin' the blame for it when I told you you wasn't right for the part."

"Oh, go to bed. I'm not blaming you. It's me. He just isn't drawn to me in that way. I'm just a convenience where he's concerned."

"I wouldn't be too sure, miss," Maggie said gently. "My old mum used to say that lightnin' strikes in unexpected places."

"Well, it might have struck but it didn't start a fire."

"But the spark is there, miss, I kin feel it in my bones. Sometimes it just takes time for the embers to catch."

JONATHAN WAS keenly aware of the heat as he so hurriedly took his departure from Kesterson House that night. Had he stayed a moment longer he would have shattered the trust placed in him by Lady Udora and Lord Kesterson. He had promised that Emerald would remain intact until she and he exchanged their marriage vows.

Tonight, for the first time, he realized that Emerald was in love with him. He had felt the heat of her passion merge with his as he leaned into her on the settee. Egad. What an incredible discovery. To know that her own blood burned as hotly as his. He had won! Won! Not only the wager, but he had won the heart of the only woman he had ever truly loved. He laughed at the irony of it. In conquering he had also been conquered. And, hell and damnation, it felt good.

He owed the major a debt of gratitude for warning him about Emerald's little plot. But now he wondered how he could get through the hours until the following evening when he would again be able to see her. His body ached to be with her now. Just to see her and talk to her would be enough if he held himself in check. And then it occurred to him that in all the excitement he had forgotten his real reason for asking to speak to her in the library. Only tonight had he and the Kestersons talked about a date for the wedding. It was to take place within two months. They agreed that it was only fitting that he be the one to discuss the arrangements with Emerald. Two months! He wondered if he could wait that long.

IT WAS NEARLY TEN by the time Emerald rose the next morning. When she went downstairs she was already dressed to go out. Breakfast had been cleared away, but McMasters sent down to the kitchen for a pot of chocolate and freshly baked bread. When he brought it to her from the lift in the butler's pantry, the fragrance preceded him. But even the chunk of butter with its droplets of water fresh from the cold cellar couldn't tempt her appetite. She was beyond the comfort of food.

What had she done wrong last night that would make Jonathan walk out on her without so much as a tender word of goodbye? Was it the positioning of her body? Was it the shape of her mouth on his? She had heard stories that some people kissed in the French style, with their mouths open, but she had not done so. Nor could she imagine doing such a thing. Was that her mistake? For obviously he had been awake all the time she was touching him. Acting the fool, she mentally corrected herself.

Well it would not happen again. She had always put her trust in books. There must be a book of instructions on the subject of how to please a man. And if there was, she would find it.

Udora, coming in from the garden, greeted her with a wide smile. "So there you are at last, my lie-abed girl. Are you quite rested from your party?"

"Quite."

"Well, if I may say so, my dear, you don't look that well. Truth be told, you look like you've got a case of the megrims. I hope that Milford said nothing to unsettle you."

"I'm just tired. I thought I might take Sally and spend some time at the lending library. It's been ages since I've had a chance to peruse the new books."

"Well, I suppose it's all right, but there is so little time before..." She was interrupted by one of the servant girls who was in tears over a below stairs disagreement.

Udora stood. "You'll have to excuse me, Emerald, but when you return from your outing we must have a chat. There is so much we have to discuss in regard to your wedding."

"I know. But so far Jonathan hasn't—" Her words were interrupted by a the sound of splintering glass and an outburst of temper from the region of the kitchen.

Udora looked distraught. "Oh, dear. It's the new girl, I'm afraid. I must go before Cook does her a mischief."

THE LENDING LIBRARY was surprisingly busy for this time of day. Sally elected to sit in a corner with a book of water-colour sketches of flowers and birds while Emerald searched the shelves for the kind of book that might help her. She had thumbed through over twenty books and was becoming increasingly irritated by such euphemisms as ''the union of two souls'' and ''the crashing of waves upon the shore.'' Suddenly her attention was drawn to two women who were laughing merrily over something in a book they had found on the bottom shelf. Emerald gave them a casual glance, then looked again. The one woman, with her bright auburn curls and voluptuous bosom, was easily recognizable, though no lady of gentle upbringing would admit to knowing her. She was Harriette Wilson, the infamous courtesan. Emerald was unsure of the identity of the younger woman, but she knew one thing: it could not be Harriette's younger sister, because the two demi-reps were known to be bitter enemies.

What Harriette Wilson lacked in innocence, she made up for in dignity and pride in her appearance. And why not, Emerald thought drily; she has been pursued by noblemen of the highest rank. And it was said that she was most often the one to decide when an affair was over. What was it about her and her sister that drew men to them like the proverbial moths to a flame?

Emerald's gaze turned toward the younger woman who, though probably not a day over seventeen, had already lost the sweetness of youth. Was she a protégée of Harriette Wilson? They seemed too close to be mistress and servant. Emerald edged closer in order to overhear their conversation.

"There, what does that line say under the drawing of Benjamin Franklin, Miss Wilson?" the girl asked breathlessly.

Harriette pulled the book closer and appeared to be squinting at the fine print. "It's a quote from one of Mr. Franklin's speeches. 'If a man empties his purse into his head, no one can take it away from him. An investment in knowledge always pays the best interest.' He's right, you know. The smartest thing I ever did was to learn how to read and write." She gave an exaggerated wink. "Well, the second best, but we didn't learn that from books, now did we, Annabelle?"

Annabelle looked wistful. "I'd give anything to learn to read."

"I'd teach you, girl, but I wouldn't know how to begin. You need someone whose mind is as young and agile as yours." She lifted a heavy tome. "I keep the books mostly for appearance' sake, for there is precious little time to read."

Emerald moved close enough to attract their attention. "I . . . I could teach you to read. Actually, I'm quite good at teaching."

Harriette studied Emerald from head to toe, then bristled. "See here, we don't need any of your impertinence. You keep to your side of the street and we'll keep to ours."

No one had ever spoken to Emerald with such venom and for a moment she was speechless. Then breeding and desperation won out and she faced the two women with a dignity she didn't quite feel. "It was not my intention to be impertinent nor to intrude on your privacy. I merely overheard your conversation.

As it happens, I often acted as tutor to other students when I was attending school, so I consider myself well qualified to teach reading."

The younger woman's eyes lit up with undisguised interest. Then a shadow passed over her face. "But how much would it cost? I don't have very much money, and I'm saving to take care of my young brother."

Emerald looked quickly across at Sally, who was so immersed in looking at the pictures that she had missed what was happening. Deliberately lowering her voice, Emerald drew the two women a few steps closer. "I have a bargain I'd like to make with you. I would like to make use of your services, and, in exchange, I will teach you to read."

"See here—" Harriette Wilson all but exploded in Emerald's face "—one might call me a *fille de joie*, and Annabelle might have come from a School of Venus, but we draw the line at *that* kind of misbehaviour."

"I beg your pardon?" Emerald asked, then put her hand over her mouth. "Oh, I see. No, please, you misunderstand. The service I need is one of instruction only. You see," she spoke more softly, "I am betrothed to a man for whom I care deeply, but he is not in love with me. He thinks of me merely as a convenience. If truth be told, I was part of a wager...."

Harriette's face turned red. "Won you in a poker game, did he? Cads, they're all the same, aren't they? They dance to the tune but they won't pay the piper."

"Well, something of that sort," Emerald said a little vaguely. "You see, I have . . . er, very little knowledge of what it takes to please a man. Nothing I do seems to work. I thought perhaps, with your experience, you could tell me a thing or two that would..."

"Tell you a thing or two! My dear, with your sweet young face and firm figgah, we could teach you to become..." She drew a deep breath. "Well, I suppose that wasn't quite what you had in mind. But yes, I suppose we could teach you how to get your man's attention. What do you think, Annabelle?"

"Easy as breathin', I'd say. And I'd give up my soul to learn how to read."

"Good. It's settled, then," Emerald said. "When shall I come to your house?"

Harriette laughed too loudly and too long. "My dear child. You couldn't possibly come to my house. Not if you want to keep your good name. Suppose you take a room at a hotel tomorrow. Annabelle could meet you there for as many days as it would require."

Emerald considered for a moment, then nodded. "Grillon's Hotel on Albemarle Street?"

"Too proper. The Pulteney Hotel in Piccadilly would be acceptable. They, er... know us there." She smiled as if laughing at her own joke. "I'll give you my calling-card. Should you wish to change your mind you can send a messenger to inform me."

Emerald handed over her own card. "Then am I to assume that you will not be present?"

Harriette smiled. "My activities keep me rather well occupied, but I assure you, my little Annabelle can teach you everything you wish to know, and probably more," she added with another lusty burst of laughter.

At that precise moment Sally looked up from her book and proceeded to drop it on the floor in her haste to reach Emerald's side. Placing herself between Emerald and Harriette, she planted her hands firmly on her hips and confronted Harriette Wilson.

"See 'ere now. What's going on? You take yourself off and be quick about it, and don't be botherin' decent people."

Emerald grasped Sally's elbow. "It's all right, Sally. Miss Wilson and I are friends."

Sally's jaw dropped.

Harriette Wilson beamed. "So we are, my dear. Now isn't that enough to grow hair on the head of a bald man."

"You won't forget, will you, Annabelle?" Emerald pleaded.

"No, miss. You may be sure of that. And you promise you won't change your mind? About teaching me to read, I mean?"

"I promise. No matter what else happens, you can count on that."

They had begun to attract attention. Harriette Wilson scowled at one particularly long-nosed woman who had the grace to turn away, then with a nod to Emerald, Miss Wilson took Annabelle's arm and directed her toward the door.

Sally looked properly pleased with herself for having routed the infamous courtesan and her young friend. She turned to Emerald and frowned. "'Er ladyship won't be pleased to 'ere that you've been 'aving words with the likes o'er."

"Then we won't tell her, will we, Sally?"

"Not me, but it don't matter none. She'll find out. She always does."

Emerald hardly heard what Sally was saying because she had become engrossed in selecting books she
could use to teach Annabelle the fundamentals of
reading. It was nearly two hours later when Sally
shook her sleeve.

"It must be gettin' on to time for the fitting for your
new riding costume. And you 'aven't forgot that 'is
lordship is to come for tea."

Emerald looked at the clock that hung over the
clerk's desk. "Oh, dear. I had no idea. Come along,
then. I think I have what I need."

JONATHAN WAS PACING the floor by the time Emerald
finally came down to join him. He heard her speaking to a footman before he actually saw her, and the
few moments it took gave him time to think about
their last meeting. Egad, what a surprise it had been
to discover that she might indeed be a woman of passion. But he must be careful to control himself.

At that moment she appeared in the doorway, hesitated a moment and then came toward him. She was
wearing a pale blue lace pelisse, fastened down the
front and ending a good six inches above the hem of a
sprigged muslin gown in shades of blue, pink and yellow. She was elegant as always, but this time there was
a difference he found impossible to define.

"Good afternoon, Lord Milford." She gave him her
hand then retrieved it more quickly than he might have
wished. "Won't you sit down?"

He waited for her to be seated, then pulled a footstool close to her knees and sat down. The flicker of
surprise in her eyes gave him confidence.

"I... er... find that I must offer my apologies for last night. In my haste to leave, I doubt that I made my feelings quite clear."

"Not at all, Jonathan. I understood very well that you had emptied your bag of tricks for one evening and without them you were at a loss."

"Tricks? I don't understand."

"Oh, please. Don't try to pretend that you were actually so far under the influence of the wine that you were unaware of what took place. And don't lie. The ivy plant is quite dead. Drowned, I suspect."

"Or pickled," he added, grinning, then was immediately embarrassed by his own levity.

"Play the clown if you wish, sir, but you'll find your humour is wasted on me."

He doubted it. She had a fine sense of humour, but it would take time to dilute the anger she apparently felt over his sudden departure. He hastened to change the subject.

"We have been invited to tea tomorrow afternoon at Lady Halpern's Town house. She is a very close friend of my aunt and she's expressed a desire to meet you."

"Thank you, I will be otherwise occupied. Perhaps another time."

"Then we could go the following afternoon? They say she has a marvellous collection of paintings by Sir Thomas Lawrence."

The mention of paintings had been a mistake, he realized too late, for her face took on a frozen look, as if she were remembering how he had deceived her into thinking he was little more than an ignorant rakehell. He reached for her hand and held it between his own.

"My dear Emerald, forgive me. I should have realized that you would be consumed with preparations, considering that our wedding is less than two months away."

She pulled back quickly. "What is it you're saying?"

He was momentarily confused. "Our wedding. Surely Lady Udora has spoken to you about it. She, Lord Kesterson and I settled the arrangements only last night."

"And why was I not consulted? I am not a child, Jonathan, yet you continue to treat me as one."

"I had thought to tell you last night, but then when you..."

"Please, let us not speak of that again."

"Not speak of it? I will treasure that night for the rest of my life."

"Indeed. And that is why you left so abruptly."

"I was only hoping to protect you, Emerald. As to setting the date for the wedding, her ladyship did, in fact, insist that the arrangements must be approved by you, but she foresaw no reason for you to object."

He was beginning to sweat. His clothing had stuck to the centre of his back and he could feel the heat rise in his face. "Please don't allow these small misunderstandings to come between us, Emerald. I'm sure that with the passage of time I shall discover what it takes to please you." He leaned forward and placed both hands on the arms of her chair, effectively preventing her from rising. "I must know today if you will agree to the plans we have made."

She faced him squarely, and there was no hint of fear in her lovely blue eyes. "I don't trust you one bit,

Lord Milford, but I trust my guardians to make the right decision for me. Yes, I will agree to the terms, but you must also agree to put an end to your little games. I detest deception.''

Relief flooded his face.''You have my word on it. My dear Emerald, I can only tell you that I look forward to our wedding with more than a little anticipation. The next two months are sure to pass slowly.''

She was beyond the ability to hide her feelings from him. He saw the yearning in her eyes, heard her unsteady intake of breath, felt her sway toward him, her hands on his arms.

How easy it would be now to whisk her into his carriage and take her home with him. Somehow he knew that she wouldn't object, but he was a gentleman above all, and there was his promise to the Kestersons that he would not touch her until she became his bride.

He reached for her hands and pressed them to his lips. Damnation! It was not enough. The mere scent of her catapulted him into thinking the unthinkable. God knows, he had denied himself far too long.

He let her hands go and threaded his fingers through her hair on either side of her head. Cupping it thus, he tilted her face upward and bent to kiss her. The softness of her lips did little to cool his heated blood as his body cried out for more.

CHAPTER TWELVE

EMERALD WOUND HER ARMS around him to pull him closer still. His warm breath fanned the hair at the back of her neck as his mouth pressed tender kisses on the spot just below her right ear. She moaned softly. It felt so right to be here in his arms. How could she ever have doubted his love for her?

The door opened suddenly and Prudence came into the library. She stopped as if instantly frozen in place. "Sir! Unhand my niece this minute! How dare you take such liberties with her person? It is plain to see that you are holding her against her will!"

Jonathan started to speak but Emerald touched her fingers to his lips and stepped away from him. Without saying a word she went to Aunt Prudence, wrapped her arms round her and kissed her sweetly on the cheek.

Aunt Prudence looked appalled. "Well, I never!" she sputtered.

"Maybe not, Aunt Prudence, but I hope someday you will."

Prudence was too shocked not to return the hug. "I...I came to tell you that you have been summoned to tea. Do come along," she said, then turned abruptly and left them alone.

Jonathan's face split into a wide grin. "I rather think you took her by surprise."

Emerald looked up at him with all the adoration of a woman who loves and is loved in return. "This is a day for surprises, Jonathan. I...I never truly believed that you loved me until today. I thought you saw me as...as an inconvenience, after the way you discovered me standing in your study that terrible afternoon."

He put his hands on her shoulders. "Forgive me if I admit that I was at first unsettled. But you must believe me when I say that in no time I came to realize that you were someone special. And before I knew what was happening I found that I wanted to be with you forever, for as long as I live."

She looked down to avoid meeting his gaze, then smoothed her hand across his chest. "But I thought that when a man wanted a woman he would show it in little ways, like...like kissing and hugging and holding hands."

"Yes, but wanting is one thing, Emerald, loving is another. There were times when if I so much as touched you I would not be able to control myself. I love you, Emerald. It was easier to keep my distance until I had the right to claim you for my own."

"Oh, there is so much I have to learn, Jonathan."

"And so much I want to teach you."

Emerald lifted her face to his. His eyes held hers in a gaze so compelling that it seemed as if she had become anchored in him; heart of his heart, soul of his soul, their desire lit by a single fuse. Had not Udora opened the door at that very moment, Emerald might have given in to the need that threatened to consume her.

Udora looked at them for an instant, then pressed her hands together beneath her chin. "My dears, I really do think it would be best if you joined us in the dining-room now."

It was all Emerald could do to nod.

LATE THAT SAME EVENING Jonathan stretched his long legs out in front of him as he contemplated the major, who was seated across the table from him at the club. Watier's was noted for its fine food, having been started by the Regent's own chef, but Jonathan wasn't hungry. The major, on the other hand, was merrily eating a third apricot tart after having consumed a rich and flaky pigeon pie.

"I give you credit, Major. You were right when you said that Emerald was a treasure beyond price."

The major took a swallow of wine. "You know, of course, that I adore the girl. If you mistreat her in any way, Milford, I shall be forced to call you out."

Jonathan smiled. "And you know, of course, that I can outshoot you and best you with the sword with one hand tied behind my back. You wouldn't stand a chance."

"I know, old boy. But you would have the blood of a friend on your hands. You couldn't stomach that."

Jonathan nodded. "You have nothing to worry about, my friend. I shall cherish Emerald and protect her for as long as I live."

He raised his arms and linked his hands behind his head. "And what about you, Major? Are you going to remain a bachelor for the rest of your life?"

The major patted his stomach and leaned back in his chair. "Now what female in her right mind would have an old man like me?" He reached for his wineglass and studied Jonathan's face over the rim.

Jonathan responded without guile. "Any number of lucky young chits, I would guess. How about Prudence Thackery?"

The major choked, spraying wine from his mouth onto the table. "Prudence Thackery? You can't be serious, old boy. She's so cold she'd cause a man's member to drop off from frostbite."

Jonathan laughed. "I don't think so. From the way she looks at you I'd venture to say that you've already laid the groundwork for a serious courtship."

"Don't bet your money on it, my boy. If I were interested in tying the knot I'd be more likely to consider Lady Halpern."

"Lydia Gatley? You can't be serious. She's too..."

"Flamboyant? That she is, Jonathan, but she's damned entertaining. It was you who introduced us. A friend of your aunt, I believe you said."

"Yes, and speaking of Lady Halpern, I was supposed to take Emerald there tomorrow to introduce them, but Emerald begged off. It seems she has an appointment. And for the next day, too. Curious, though. Lady Udora was unaware of anyone with whom Emerald was supposed to meet."

"Curious, indeed. Why don't you ask the girl who she has tucked away?"

"I tried hinting around at it but she seemed rather secretive."

The major grinned. "Probably a last-minute rendezvous with one of her recent admirers. She has any number of them, you know, since she began wearing bust improvers in her gowns."

Jonathan scowled. "Guard your tongue, sir."

"Sorry, I didn't realize you'd become so protective."

Neither had Jonathan guessed until that moment how much he wanted to shield Emerald from the baser aspects of the social world. But he suddenly knew that he would find no peace until he learned the truth about whom Emerald planned to see. His mind was made up. He would follow her.

EMERALD KNEW she must dress carefully for her afternoon session with Miss Annabelle. She had almost changed her mind about keeping the appointment, since Jonathan had made it clear yesterday that he loved her. But she had given her word to Miss Annabelle and she could not go back on it.

Emerald lifted a nondescript Devonshire brown dress from the closet. Perfect. It wouldn't do to create a stir or in any way draw attention to herself when she entered the hotel.

But leave it to Topaz to become inquisitive. She came into the bedroom and plopped down on Emerald's bed. "Sally said you were going out. May I go with you, or is Milford taking you some place special?"

"No to both questions. Why do you want to go? You have never wanted to tag along before."

"Lady Udora says I must work on my tapestry if I stay home. If you aren't seeing Milford, who are you seeing?"

"No one you know."

"A man?" Topaz, ever eager for a bit of gossip, watched her with sparkling eyes.

"Don't be absurd. If you must know, I'm going to help a young woman learn to read."

"The devil you say."

"'Don't be crude, Topaz. I'm beginning to think that David is having a bad influence on you."

"Miss Uppity! You sound like her ladyship. If I tell you something, will you keep it a secret?"

"Of course." Emerald gave Topaz her full attention. "You know I'd never tell."

"David is taking me to see his home. So far I've only been to the barn where he works on his balloons."

Emerald regarded her sister with concern. "Do be careful, Taz. You'll take Maggie with you, of course?"

"Perhaps. Or perhaps not. I've grown quite fond of him. It might be interesting to see what would happen if I were to venture out without a proper chaperon."

"You wouldn't!"

"No. I suppose not. He wouldn't touch me, anyway, more's the pity. But it would be more exciting than working at needlepoint all afternoon. Are you sure I cannot come with you?"

"I'm certain of it." She turned as Sally came into the room, dressed in her uniform and summer cape, to tell her that the carriage was waiting at the back door.

"The back door?" Topaz looked up in surprise. "This does sound like an assignation."

"You have too much imagination, Taz." Emerald left quickly to avoid further questions.

If Emerald was nervous over the impending interview with Miss Annabelle, Sally was close to losing her mind by the time they secured a room at the Pulteney Hotel.

"Blimey. I know she'll find out. There ain't nothin' what goes on that 'er ladyship don't know about," Sally said as she paced the floor of the clean, if small hotel room.

"By then it will be too late. I shall already have learned what I need to know."

"Not for me it won't. She can still 'ave my 'ide for this, or worse yet, send me packin'."

"If that happens, you may come to work for me at my new home. Listen, I think I hear someone."

They both became silent at the sound of approaching footsteps outside the hotel room door. Emerald drew a deep breath. "I think she has arrived. Now do try to be civil to Miss Annabelle, Sally. She's just a poor young girl trying to earn money to care for her little brother."

Emerald opened the door a crack, then seeing that it was Annabelle, invited her to come in. As it happened, Harriette Wilson followed behind.

"Well, don't look so surprised. Did you think I would allow one of my best friends to come here alone? I had to make sure that you weren't setting her up to be a cat's paw. After all, it isn't every day that we're approached by a person of the female sex."

"I understand," Emerald said. "Please, do sit down. Now where shall we begin?"

Harriette swirled her ostrich feathers from around her neck and tossed them onto the bed. "You first, and the books second. Now what do you need to know?"

Emerald sank into a chair next to the bed. "Everything. I know so little about what men want or like."

Harriette looked at Annabelle and grinned. Then she turned to Emerald and took her hands in hers. "Lovey, what you have right now is exactly what men like most of all!"

Apparently seeing the look of puzzlement on Emerald's face, she continued. "Why, it's innocence, dear girl. Sweet, untouched innocence. But they also like mystery. Of course I work by myself, except for an occasional protégée, but in the best houses the girls are never allowed to greet a man in the altogether. They dress themselves in silks and laces, yes, and even lacy black pantalettes and tiny corselettes with cups that hold one's bosoms high and round. Then the gentleman has the pleasure of uncovering her treasures one by one."

Annabelle nodded in agreement. "Simone, a dancing girl I know, has a tiny girdle made of rubies and diamonds. She dances most seductively, and I've heard tell that men stuff gold coins into her girdle."

"But I can't dance."

"Neither can I, but I can tell at a glance what a man likes ... whether he wants to lead or he wants to follow. A following man is the hardest."

Harriette guffawed and slapped her on the back. Annabelle's face turned pink. "What I meant was, it isn't always easy to get a man started who wants to follow. The best way is to doff your clothes, slowly as possible, and then when you're all the way bare, start undressin' him, real slowly. By the time you're down to 'is boots, you can bet 'e will be ready to do his business." She sighed.

"But most men want to lead. Then all you have to do is make 'im think you're enjoying it. Moans help, and sometimes screams. It's as easy as falling into bed." She grinned up at Harriette, who nodded in agreement.

"But how can I tell if he wants to lead?"

The two prostitutes regarded each other with blank stares. Annabelle shrugged. "I dunno. You just do. After a while, though, when you've known 'im for a long time, 'e might want you to lead. Just for variety, you know. It keeps 'em from wandering."

She was about to say more when they heard footsteps outside the door. A knock sounded.

Harriette's face turned hard. "If this is a trick, I'll see that you live to regret it."

Emerald felt her stomach turn over. "I swear, I have no idea who it is."

The knocking turned more violent. "Emerald. Open this door. I know you have someone inside there with you."

Sally looked terrified. Emerald's hands flew to her face. "Milford!" she whispered. "What should I do?"

Harriette looked scornful. "Answer the door. It appears you have little choice. Since we are on the second floor, we are hardly prepared to leave through the window."

"Now we're for it," Sally cried. "I told you we shouldn't 'ave come 'ere."

"Stop snivelling," Emerald ordered. She handed Annabelle an open book. "Now sit down again, everyone. I am going to let him in." Despite her attempt at bravery, Emerald was trembling so much that she was afraid her teeth might chatter.

Taking a deep breath, she pasted a smile on her face and opened the door. "Jonathan. What a pleasant surprise. Do come in."

His fist paused in mid-air. "It's about time. I was prepared to break down the door. What is going on here, Emerald?" He stepped into the room. "My God! Harriette Wilson! What the devil are you doing here?"

Emerald stayed his advance with a hand on his sleeve. "Miss Wilson has brought her young friend here for a lesson in reading. I'm quite a good teacher and I have promised to instruct her in how to begin." She smiled up at him with the most innocent expression she could muster.

He hesitated for a minute, then scowled at Sally. "Is it true what she said?"

Sally paused a moment too long. "Well...er, yes, Your Lordship. It's, er...true."

He swore softly. "Get out of here, all of you, except Miss Thackery."

Harriette's eyes narrowed but she didn't move; Sally spread her hands and stood her ground; tears gathered in Annabelle's eyes.

Emerald felt stronger, more alive than she had ever felt in her entire life. "They are not leaving, Jonathan, until I make arrangements to meet with Annabelle again. I have vowed to teach her to read."

"From an upside-down book, I believe," he said with considerable disdain. "Hell and damnation. I'll see that she has a tutor. The best that money can buy."

"Is that a promise?"

"You have my word on it."

Emerald sighed. "Very well." She met Annabelle's gaze. "I'll send a message for you to Miss Wilson about when your lessons are to begin. Will next Thursday be satisfactory?"

Annabelle wiped her eyes. "Yes, miss. And thank you, my lord. I can't tell you how grateful I am, Miss Thackery." She paused. "Will you be all right if we leave you alone with him?"

"Perfect, thanks to you and Miss Wilson." She winked. "He likes to lead, I think. Am I right?"

Both demi-reps beamed their agreement, then excused themselves from the room.

"You, too, Sally," Jonathan ordered.

"Me? Not likely, sir."

Emerald gave her a little shove. "Do as he says, Sally. He won't hurt me."

"Then I'll be right outside the door should you need me. I can scream for 'elp, I can, loud enough to wake the dead."

Emerald closed the door behind her and turned, leaning against the closed door to face Jonathan.

"You followed me, didn't you?" she demanded, knowing instinctively that an attack was her best defence.

"And a good thing, too. Do you have any idea what kind of scandal you may have created? You and the most infamous of prostitutes in all of London?"

"I found her to be very understanding," Emerald said as she walked away from him in order to break his compelling gaze.

"Aha, it's as I guessed. There was more to this than a simple boon for the illiterate mudlark."

"She isn't a mudlark. She's a very sweet young woman who has more than her share of trouble. And how can you say that, Jonathan? You saw the books. I did, in fact, promise to teach her to read."

"Don't take me for a fool, Emerald. And don't let us begin this marriage with another wall of deceit between us. We have both learned the hard way that it does not pay to dissemble or play games with the truth with the one you love."

He came toward her, forcing her to retreat until the backs of her knees were against the bed. Then, putting his hands on her shoulders, he once again pinned her with his gaze. "Tell me the truth, Emerald, before a lie becomes a barrier between us."

"I...I can't, Jonathan. It's far too embarrassing." She sank down on the bed, at the same time lowering her gaze. But not before he saw the traces of tears beginning to fill her eyes.

He knelt down in front of her and lifted her chin with his forefinger.

"In two months' time you are going to become my wife, my darling girl. Don't you know yet that you can tell me anything?"

Her tongue darted out to moisten her lips, in a gesture so endearing that Jonathan had to grit his teeth. Her voice quavered when she spoke. "It is only that I . . . I wanted so much to please you, Jonathan. They tell me I have an excellent mind. That I can discuss politics and history with the most knowledgeable. That I can give the title and name of the artist of almost every well-known painting created during the last half century.

"But I . . . I don't know how to please a man. I cannot pretend to be an ignorant, docile woman, good for nothing but breeding and baking. Not when my mind cries out for knowledge. And yet I want those things, too. I want children, lots of them. And I want to fetch my husband's slippers and sit with him by the fireside, to share with him the joys of domesticity."

Jonathan's heart wrenched. "And you shall have all those things, Emerald. Nothing would please me more than to give them to you. Especially the children," he said, chuckling. "But tell me, my darling. What were you doing with Harriette Wilson, of all people, in your room? And how did you come to know her?"

"I met her at the lending library yesterday, and it occurred to me that she would know, more than anyone, just what it takes to make a man happy. When I learned that her protégée, Miss Annabelle, needed a tutor, we agreed to exchange knowledge.''

Jonathan rocked back on his heels. "Incredible.''

"Of course, after last night I came to realize that you really did care for me and there was perhaps no need for those special instructions, but I had given my word to teach Annabelle to read, so there was little I could do save keep the appointment.''

He laughed aloud. "No one is going to believe this.''

"Then we had better hope that word of it doesn't get out.''

Jonathan rose from his crouch and seated himself next to her on the bed. "Not much chance of that. You rented the room under your own name, and Harriette Wilson is known to every man in London." He stroked his chin as if in deep thought. "Perhaps the sanest idea is to tell everyone that you met with Annabelle in order to sponsor a school for illiterate young ladies. I'm sure she will know other girls who might be eager to learn.''

"But the cost…to pay a tutor and provide space for classes.''

He snapped his fingers. "It means nothing. I have come into a fortune, you know. There is more money than we can ever spend, particularly since I have decided to give up gambling.''

A slow smile spread across Emerald's face. "Learned your lesson, did you? When I walked into that room instead of Lucy Tripton?''

A smile quirked the corner of his mouth. "Let's say that I found something more exciting than a turn of the card to fill the vacant hours. You have opened up a whole new world for me, Emerald."

"A world we can explore together, I think." She reached up and toyed with the hooks on his coat.

"What are you doing?" he asked in alarm as one gave way, and the next, and the next, and the next.

"Just practising what I learned today," she said, running her hand beneath his coat to explore the hard contours of his chest.

He swore softly and pushed her back on the bed, half covering her with his body. "Don't even think of it. Since I met you my self-control has already reached its limit more times than I can say."

"Then one more time won't hurt, will it?"

"I'm not made of iron, girl. I can only take so much." He groaned and covered her mouth with his. He kissed her long and deeply, stroking the inside of her mouth, tasting the sweetness within.

It occurred to Emerald that she had just learned another lesson. She wasn't often wrong, but before, when she had decided that kissing in the French style was too awful to consider, she couldn't have been further from the truth. The tender invasion had caused a tremor in the pit of her stomach that refused to go away. And one other thing. The books had described lovers uniting as a volcanic eruption, as stars bursting in the heavens, as the crashing of waves upon the shore. Perhaps it wasn't just the romantic drivel she had thought it to be. Perhaps, when he actually made love to her, she would know what it meant to "scale the summit and plunge into an abyss of pleasure beyond compare."

His mouth was once again on hers, his breath harsh between kisses. She turned toward him, and as she did so, there was a loud crash. At first they thought it was someone at the door, but a sense of suddenly being off balance made them realize that the foot of the bed had collapsed.

Jonathan lifted her to her feet just at the same moment Sally burst in the door. She looked ready to call for help, but Emerald reassured her that everything was all right.

Sally looked at their state of *déshabillé*. "Seems to me, miss, that it's time we went 'ome."

"I'm afraid you're right, Sally," Jonathan said through gritted teeth. "May I escort you in my carriage?"

"Indeed not, sir," Sally insisted. "We have our own carriage waiting on the street."

Emerald regarded Sally with a dreamy look. "Send our carriage along home, Sally. We shall ride with Lord Milford."

Jonathan put his arm round her waist. "I was hoping you'd say that. We have some unfinished business to take care of."

Emerald's eyes lit up. She chuckled. "I knew from the start that this marriage was going to be a business arrangement, but if what just happened is a sample of unfinished business, I'm quite pleased to become a partner."

DURING THE DAYS that followed, everything began to fall into place for Emerald and the rest of the Kesterson household. Prudence mellowed with time, thanks to the major, who seemed fascinated by her independent attitude and her colourful past. The search for her daughter continued with his help.

All of London was impressed by Jonathan's generosity in establishing the Lady Milford Foundation for Literacy, but he made sure that all the credit went to Emerald.

Amethyst and Emerald were in transports over their pending marriages, but both agreed that there was a piece missing to the Thackery Jewels story. Topaz and her search for romance.

Look for her story and learn about her mysterious birthright in Book Three of The Thackery Jewels Trilogy.

TOPAZ

CHAPTER ONE

TOPAZ THACKERY CAST a hasty glance behind her as she stole quietly down the back stairs of her guardian's palatial London house. If Lady Udora had known of this little escapade she would have been more than a little unsettled. Perhaps furious would be a more appropriate word. Neither Lord Kesterson nor Lady Udora approved of David Endicott, who had not the title nor the blunt to qualify as husband material. Never mind that he was clever, exciting and adventurous. Udora insisted that Topaz must, in this her first Season, ally herself with a man who was more than a mere adventurer.

Ever cautious, Bently, Lord Kesterson, often reminded Topaz that she must learn to control her own flamboyant spirit. Since childhood she had vowed to marry a man who could race with the wind. And David had managed to do just that, for he was an aeronaut, a balloonist of no small renown.

Topaz smiled to herself as she closed the door and scurried to the comparative safety of the rose garden. If truth were told, marriage was the furthest thing from her mind at that moment. David had promised to take her for a ride in his balloon. Not simply a chance to go aloft while remaining tethered to the ground, as she had done a number of times before, but a chance to float, unfettered, above the trees and over the rooftops and spires of London Town as free and unfettered as the birds.

Sally, her abigail, popped out from behind a rose trellis, a frown creasing her young forehead. "You've come early, miss. I told Toby not to bring the carriage round till ten past."

"Then we'll just have to wait, won't we?" Topaz said as she pushed her bonnet aside, allowing it to dangle by its string down her back.

"Oh I wouldna' be doin' that if I was you, miss." Sally's gaze travelled over Topaz's luxuriously thick hair, the colour of moonlight. "We don't want you to be recognized, now, do we? There ain't many young ladies with hair like yours, and if word gets back to 'er ladyship that you're seeing that young rogue again, she'll 'ave my 'ide."

"Oh, very well. You can be such a bore, Sally. I should have brought Maggie along instead of you. Maggie isn't afraid of her own shadow."

"Aye, and that would have pleased me no end," Sally said as she bent to unhook her skirt from a thorn.

A short time later the carriage arrived and Toby jumped down to help them get in. "Sally says you'll be wanting to go to Green Park, Miss Thackery."

"Yes, indeed, Toby, but do let's be quiet. I don't want to disturb Lady Udora and Lord Kesterson."

He doffed his cap and moments later they passed quietly down the mews. The journey should have required only a short time to accomplish, but their arrival at the field was delayed when the road was blocked by an overturned vehicle. Topaz fretted aloud, then cursed silently until the offending landau was finally moved far enough to the side of the street to permit their safe passage.

When they arrived at the park it was plain to see that David's preparations had already attracted a noisy crowd. All along the side of the field that bordered one end of the park, carriages stood at odd angles, as if their passengers had abandoned them in their haste to witness this extraordinary event. Several yards away a hundred or so people pushed against a rope that had been prudently erected to prevent the overeager from moving too close. There were additional precautions in the form of four burly men who did not hesitate to seize the unruly by their coats and escort them some distance away.

Topaz leaned her head through the window to get a better view as Toby attempted to control the horses, while at the same time searching for a safe place to await his mistress's return. He found an open spot beneath the shade of an oak tree, to which he tethered the horses.

Topaz jumped from the carriage without waiting for his assistance. "Oh, do come along," she said, grasping Sally by the arm. "Just look, isn't it magnificent?"

"Nothin' but a big bag o' wind, far as I can see," Sally complained.

"But the colours. Red, blue and yellow. David says it's the varnish that makes the silk glow."

"What's that thing with the ropes 'angin from it?"

"It's called the car, or the basket. David says it's copied from the one which the Montgolfier brothers designed." She gave Sally's cloak an impatient tug. "Can you not walk any faster?"

"Oh, my. 'Tis big, ain't it?"

"It has to be, to carry three people."

The balloon seemed to have a life of its own as it inhaled, expanded, and began to push at its moorings. David was nowhere to be seen.

Topaz took hold of the rope that restrained the crowd and motioned to Sally. "Follow me and be careful of the tethers. They'll soon become taut as the balloon is more completely inflated." She lifted the thick hemp and, gathering her skirts in her free hand, ducked under the barricade. Sally followed her example, albeit with considerably less enthusiasm.

Unfortunately, her hesitation caught the eye of a watchman.

"See 'ere now, girl. Get back there where ye belong," he bellowed, rushing toward her. Sally, caught half inside and half out, didn't know which way to turn. She was close to tears.

Topaz turned just in time to intercept the bully before he could reach Sally's side. "Don't you dare touch her."

"What the . . . ? Where in the name o' Ned did you come from?" A second look at Topaz must have warned him that she was Quality, for he doffed his cap. "Beggin' your pardon, miss, but nobody's allowed this side o' the lines."

"It's quite all right. Mr. Endicott is expecting me, and this woman is my maid and will be accompanying us on our journey."

Sally grasped Topaz's arm. "Journey? And what do you mean by that?"

Topaz gave a delicate shrug. "I didn't want you to become unduly overset. The truth is that this time David has promised to do more than simply take me aloft." Her eyes sparkled with excitement. "This time we are going to drift wherever the wind wants to carry us."

"Not me, it won't. I'll not set one foot on that devil machine."

"Of course you will. It would be impossible for me to go without a chaperon." She was about to say more when David appeared from the other side of the balloon.

His face lit up when he saw her. "So there you are. I knew that if I heard a commotion of some sort it would mean that you had finally arrived. You always cause a stir." Then his expression of admiration gave way to one of annoyance. "You're late. You could have jeopardized our flight."

"I know. I'm sorry. It was early when we left home but a street mishap caused our delay." She smiled at the smudges on his face and the less than immaculate trousers and coat which he wore. Only David could feel completely at ease in such a state of disarray. Even dressed as he was, he was still a handsome young man.

He jerked his head in the direction of the craft. "Well, come along then. The Gypsy is nearly inflated, and if we are to leave the field, we must take advantage of the wind currents."

Topaz followed without hesitation. It was only when David was waiting to lift her into the car that she turned her head to look for Sally. Sally stood frozen in place.

"Oh, do let's get on with it," Topaz called out to her.

"Nothin' can make me put foot in that contraption."

"Don't be silly. You've seen me each time I've ascended in a tethered balloon and you've seen balloons in flight at Vauxhall gardens." The moment she said it Topaz knew she had said too much, because Sally seemed to wilt.

"Aye, the one what caught fire and fell to the ground."

"Well, yes, but that was an accident. Come along now, and as a reward for your courage, I'll give you my red velvet cloak."

Sally wavered for a moment, then shook her head. "I can't do it, miss. I just can't move me legs."

Topaz laughed. "We can fix that, can't we?" She motioned to the more handsome of the four watchmen. "Good sir, would you be kind enough to assist my abigail into the car?"

He grinned, and before Sally knew what was happening, she was thrown over his shoulder and hoisted into the balloon's basket. The crowd applauded.

Topaz held Sally's arm to steady her. "See? There's nothing to it. There's even a place to sit down and a small table for a picnic if we should so choose." Both women fell silent at a soft shooshing sound.

"It's nothing," David said. "Just the hot air filling the last folds in the balloon. We shall soon be ready to ascend." He studied Topaz's face. "It's not too late to change your mind."

Topaz shot him a dazzling smile. "It was too late the day I was born."

He grinned. "Good girl. Remember, though. This isn't just a pleasure excursion. I'll need you to feed straw into the fire."

"I can do it. But I must return here before three o'clock so that I can reach home before Lady Udora discovers where I have been."

"Don't worry. I've done this dozens of times. You shall be back within the hour."

Topaz clasped her hands. "Then let's go!"

He gave her shoulder a quick squeeze and was rewarded with a smile. It occurred to Topaz that for David, this was an eloquent demonstration of his affection.

"All right," he said. "I'll signal the men to release the tethers."

Topaz looked over at Sally, who was gripping the ropes as if they were her only hold on life. Her face was the colour of dried plaster. Topaz felt a flash of irritation with Sally for her reluctance to rise above her menial station and live life to its fullest. But the irritation was mixed with pity for the girl's obvious discomfort. Still, if Sally had refused to go along with them, Topaz would have had, for propriety's sake, to forgo the trip herself.

When all but two of the tethers had been released, the balloon seemed to stretch like an animal awakening from a long sleep. It pulled at the lines, causing them to creak and groan, as eager as Topaz was to leave the confines of the earth. It teetered against its moorings as one side of the car began to lift.

"Drop the ballast," David ordered, and Topaz bent to hoist a sandbag and throw it over the side as David had taught her to do.

"More," he yelled.

"Help us, Sally," Topaz called.

There was a murmured response. A shout went up from the crowd. When Topaz dared stop to take a look, she saw Sally, skirts hiked up to her knees, poised on the ledge of the car. Before Topaz could call out, Sally threw herself over the side of the vehicle, landing squarely in the arms of the watchman.

"Wait, David. We must stop," Topaz shouted.

He apparently hadn't heard, because the balloon had already lifted from the ground.

Topaz was stunned. This was one time she couldn't look to her twin sisters for protection. Emerald and Amethyst had always tried to shield her from scandal, but without a chaperon along to prove that her good name had not been compromised, this time there would be little they could do.

"Throw more ballast!" David commanded. "Anything. We need altitude."

Seeing a small anchor attached to a rope, she picked it up and would have heaved it over the side, but David chanced to look at her over the bale of straw he was tossing onto the fire.

"No! Not that, Topaz. That's our drag line. We'll need it when we land. The table. Throw the table."

There was no time to enjoy the sense of being lifted into the sky. Perspiration had begun to run down her face and she wiped it away with her sleeve. Concern over her impending disgrace also took second place to the task at hand.

Then, a few minutes later, David gave her permission to rest. For the first time since they were adrift, she looked down and saw the ground give way to treetops and the roofs of buildings. Directly below them the crowd cheered and waved shawls and caps to wish them well. Sally, leaning against her newfound protector, pressed her hands to her cheeks with a look of utter dismay.

"Wait for me there, Sally," Topaz called, cupping her hands to her mouth.

"She can't hear you," David said. "Here, try the voice trumpet," he said, handing her a large cone-shaped device.

Topaz placed her mouth near the small end and called again. This time Sally stopped weeping long enough to give an affirmative wave of both arms.

"There, I've done it, haven't I?" Topaz said as David moved to stand next to her while at the same time being cautious not to change the pitch of the balloon. "I've really dumped the pot out with the porridge. When, Lady Udora hears about this, she'll certainly send me off to live in a convent."

David steadied himself on the suspension cords, then rested one foot on the rail next to the crow's-foot where a toggle connected the cords to the car.

"If it's true what they say about Lady Udora, she is hardly in a position to fault you for kicking over the traces once in a while." He leaned his forearm on his bent knee. "After all is said and done, Topaz, one could hardly consider her the perfect lady. Not after having been wed five times."

Topaz whirled on him. "You don't know anything about her. If anyone is perfect, she is. She has become like a mother to the three of us since my father's will made her our guardian."

"Hold on. Don't get all prickly with me, girl."

"Then don't speak unkindly of Lady Udora. I hate to think what would have happened to the three of us after our father and mother were killed. If it weren't for her and Lord Kesterson..."

David held up his hands. "Stop! All right, I withdraw my comment. I vow not to say another word against her. Besides, it was said in jest."

"Do you mean that? Then I'm sorry. I shouldn't have lost my temper." She smiled and touched his sleeve. "Particularly when I know that you don't have an unkind bone in your body. Besides, I couldn't stay angry with you. Not when you've given me all this," she said, gesturing at the panorama of cleanly drawn streets and houses punctuated now and then by ornately carved Gothic spires.

The bustle of horses and carriages and the cry of street vendors was reduced to a whisper from this height.

David put his hand on her shoulder. "Look, there's the cross and dome of St. Paul's Cathedral, and yonder is the bridge. It looks like a painting by Canaletto."

A gust of wind caught the balloon and they began to drift in a new direction. David reached for an oar-like device and attached it to a clamp on the car.

"What are you doing?" Topaz asked.

"Trying to correct our direction. I prefer not to go near the river because the wind currents can change abruptly over water." He checked his instruments. "We're not rising. We need more hot air."

She lifted a bundle of straw and wool onto the fire and stirred it.

"More, Topaz, hurry."

She bent to fork up another bundle, then repeated the procedure. By now she was perspiring freely. It hadn't occurred to her that being an aeronaut would be such hard work. She stopped for a minute or two to wipe the sweat from her eyes.

"More straw, Topaz. Let's go high enough to touch the clouds."

Once again she dug into the pile of fuel and fed some into the greedy mouth of flame. As she worked, her bonnet string kept cutting into her neck. In her haste she tried to untie it but the ribbon broke, and, with an expression of disgust, she took off her bonnet and flung it to the floor of the conveyance.

"All right," David finally said. "You can rest now. We're at a good altitude and the wind has changed in our favour."

She breathed a sigh of relief and straightened, at the same time wiping her forehead and pushing her hair away from her face. David came round to stand beside her.

He laughed. "Ah, you're a sight now, aren't you? If I didn't know better, I'd say you were a char girl all dressed up in her mistress's gown."

Topaz shot him a quelling look. She was about to protest that he had assigned himself the easy job while leaving the dirty work to her, but at that moment she was stopped by the sound of popping and crackling coming from the base of the balloon. She stared up toward the envelope.

"What is it, David? Is it a tear in the silk?"

"I doubt it. Hold on. I'll have a look."

A short time later he put his hands on his hips. "I don't think there's anything to be worried about.

We've broken a pair of suspension lines, but there are still enough to hold us steady and keep the car from tilting. The netting looks to be in good repair and the envelope is fully inflated.''

Topaz frowned. "It's not the same shape."

"I know, but it's perfectly normal for the silk to become elongated as the balloon ascends, and to become round again as we descend."

She leaned over the side and looked down below. Rooftops had given way to countryside; a patchwork of farms neatly divided into rectangles, some very large and some quite small, in varying shades of green and brown. Here and there she could see sheep grazing in the pastures. Occasionally she caught glimpses of farmers in their fields and children running beneath the balloon as it drifted across the landscape.

"It looks so clean," she said. "So perfect."

He was about to respond when all of a sudden they were engulfed in a low-hanging cloud. The balloon shuddered at the sudden temperature change.

"David!" Topaz called in alarm.

"It's all right. We shall be out of it in a moment."

Topaz wrapped her arms around herself. "I feel as if I'm caught up in a bundle of cotton wool. And it's turned quite windy." She laughed and lifted her arms to the sky. "I've never felt so free."

David glanced over at her. "I can't believe you are so courageous."

"You've always known I'm not like most girls. Like no other girl you've ever met, you often remind me."

"True. If you were any different, I'd never have let you chase after me."

"Chase after you! Are you trying to tell me I have been trying to trap you into offering for me?"

He grinned. "Well, haven't you?"

"What is this, David, an inquisition? Oh, I see. You're trying to take my mind away from our imminent danger. But please do not concern yourself. I have no intention of dying." She tried to keep her voice light. "As to the other, I'm not in love with you, David, much as I enjoy your company. Besides, my guardians would never permit me to marry a penniless balloonist."

"Well, not quite penniless, but certainly not rich. If I were, I'd have a better grade of silk in my balloon."

"The wind has turned cold."

"The weather seems to be changing. I'm going to try to land on the green just beyond that row of trees you can see in the distance," he said, then moved round to the other side of the fuel pile, where he pulled a rope that opened a small vent near the top of the balloon. They began to descend immediately, and as quickly, they moved out of the cloud and into filtered sunshine.

Down below, a small copse of beech trees sprang into view, followed by a tapestry of fields and gently rolling hills and then another wooded area. In the distance, just barely visible through the treetops, Topaz caught a glimpse of grey turrets topped with circular teal blue roofs that reminded her of a French château. It looked terribly romantic nestled in amongst the trees.

She leaned further forward to get a better look. At that moment a horseman appeared as if out of nowhere. He was dressed in black and mounted on a huge black stallion. Its neck arched as they galloped across the hill, and from the distance, its tail and flowing mane seemed to float like ebony silk in the wind.

But it was the rider who caused her breath to catch in her throat. He rode straight and strong, his legs moulded to the horse as if rider and steed were one. Sleek animals, both of them, exuding an aura of excitement and danger that by turns called to her and sent a chill of fear coursing through her veins.

All of a sudden, a strong gust of wind caused the balloon to tilt sharply. At the same instant, they heard the crack of another cord and the car began to list to one side.

"David! What's happened? Are we going to fall?"

"Not likely! Another line broke, though. I'm trying to land on the lawn near the house."

"But the trees. Can we fly over them?"

"Just barely. Keep the fire going. The wind gusts..." The rest was unintelligible, but she had no time to worry about it.

She heard the oar rattling against its mount as she tried to concentrate on feeding the fire, but some of the straw had got wet and it wasn't burning well. The tilt was becoming alarming.

She heard a sudden pop and looked up to see a tiny flame burning a hole in the silk just below the netting. Fear began to coagulate like cold porridge in the pit of her stomach. There was no time to alert David. Grasping the sponge that was kept in a pail of water for just such an emergency, she forced it onto the end of a pole, then swabbed the darkening area until the flames were extinguished. A quick glance told her that David had succeeded in skirting the trees.

She breathed a sigh of relief, but in that single moment a warning shout came from below. A second later a blast of wind slammed into them, causing the silk to catch on the limb of a tree. They hung there for what seemed like an age until David managed to break them loose and once again they were adrift. They were within a few feet of the ground now, but the speed of their movement was far too great for them to stop. David was trying desperately to release more air.

"The anchor, Topaz. Throw the anchor," he shouted.

She saw it immediately, lying atop a coil of rope. It was heavier than she remembered, but at last she was able to dump it overboard and the rope quickly uncoiled, burning her hands until she let go.

They were within inches of the ground, but their parallel movement was too fast for them to disembark. David was venting the balloon as quickly as possible, but there was still enough silk for the gusting wind to blow them rapidly over the ground, bumping along on the side where the lines had snapped. So far the anchor had not found purchase.

Topaz searched the ground. There were several outcroppings of rock but the anchor had somehow avoided them. Movement drew her gaze to the left. The horse and rider appeared again, flying more than galloping down from the dark woods and into the green meadow where the sun cast spears of light through soot-grey clouds.

She suddenly remembered a quote from a novel she had read a year ago. "And death came on his dark horse, stealing silently like the night. And when he was gone, she wakened no more.''

Topaz shuddered, tearing her gaze from him. She turned to David. ''There's a man on horseback down there.''

''I didn't see him.''

''We're awfully close to the trees, David,'' Topaz said.

''Never fear. We shall pass right by them. It's the ledge I'm worried about. There's a thirty-foot drop just over the next rise and below that a large pond. If the anchor doesn't hold...''

He didn't bother to finish the sentence. Topaz, with her wild imagination, was already far ahead of him. She had a vision of the car going into the water and the balloon collapsing on top of them. If she were killed, how would she ever explain all this to Lady Udora? She laughed shakily when she realized how ridiculous that sounded.

David looked over the side of the car and studied the ground. His voice was husky when he spoke. ''I do think it would be wise if you were to sit down and find something to hold on to. It does seem that we will experience a rather difficult landing.''

''And the cliff?''

''Still a good distance away. If the anchor doesn't catch, then I shall be forced to cut the envelope and release the air all at once.''

''And destroy the balloon?''

He forced a grin. ''Better it than us.''

She moved closer to him and grasped his arm. ''Wait until the very last moment. I'm not afraid. Truly I'm not.''

He was still working frantically to expel the remaining hot air. His words were broken from exertion. "I...I should have...known better than to...bring you...along. Sorry."

"It's not your fault."

Suddenly the forward edge of the car tilted sharply, bit into a rock formation and flipped over on its side.

Topaz was vaguely aware that she was flying through the air on her own. *This is it,* she thought. *I'm surely going to die.*

SHE HAD NO IDEA how long she lay there, but the pain in her shoulder was most certainly proof that she was not yet dead. "David," she called, but there was no answer. The wind, blowing steadily now, caused the balloon to flap with such vigour that the noise blotted out everything but her pain. She called again, but to no avail. She tried to stand, but her legs were trapped between the car and a cushion of thick grass.

The pain in her shoulder was excruciating. "David," she called again. *Dear Lord, please don't let him be hurt,* she prayed silently. And then, like a miracle, he was standing over her.

She smiled and said, "The answer to my prayer." But then she looked again through the haze of her pain and she could discern that it was not David who was standing over her. It was the horseman. It occurred to her an instant before she fainted that Death had no right to be so handsome.

CHAPTER TWO

WHEN TOPAZ AWOKE she was lying on a bed canopied with ivory lace. Her bodice had been partially undone and her shoes had been removed. *This must be a dream,* she thought, pushing aside the silk coverlet and attempting to rise. The pain in her shoulder made her wince and drop back to the pillow, once again closing her eyes.

It was not so much a sound as an awareness of a presence in the room that dragged her back to consciousness. The horseman, now divested of his cloak, was once again looking down at her.

She moistened her lips with her tongue. "Are you real? Or am I dreaming? I can't be dead. I feel such pain in my arm."

"You're quite alive. I believe you have dislocated your shoulder. I didn't want to do anything until you awakened."

"David. The man I was with in the balloon. Did you find him? Is he all right? I called out to him but he didn't answer."

"David is quite well. He was just knocked unconscious for a few minutes. He enquired after you, of course, but I insisted that he lie down. I assure you, miss, that he only agreed after I gave him my word that I would look after you."

"Thank you. I owe you more than I can say."

His face grew sober. "You may not feel so indebted when I am through with you."

She felt a chill of apprehension. "Wh-what do you mean?"

"We must do something about your shoulder before it becomes inflamed and the condition becomes serious. It will hurt."

"I must go home. My guardian is responsible for my care."

"The decision is yours, of course, but I doubt that you will feel inclined to travel."

"Then shouldn't we send for a doctor? If it's a question of money..."

"Hardly that. But we are not in Town. It would take rather a long time to summon a physician, if indeed he was not off tending to one of the locals. If you are willing to trust me..."

Topaz drew a shaky breath. "Do you know what to do?"

"Yes. I've done much the same a number of times for my valet, who has a recurring problem with his shoulder."

"Then I suppose we had best get on with it."

"Can you sit up?"

"Of course. I... " She let out an uncontrollable gasp.

He nodded. "It's as I thought. Here. Let me help you."

He moved to the side of the bed and placed his hand behind her good shoulder. "Ready now. I'm going to raise you to a sitting position."

"I'm ready." The pain was excruciating but she was determined not to cry out.

"Good girl. Now I'm going to give your arm a quick pull. It should cause your shoulder to snap back into place. Are you quite prepared?"

"Quite," she said with more determination than she felt.

"Try to think about something else."

She wrinkled her nose. "Nothing comes to mind but the pain."

"Think of the Prince Regent or the latest scandals."

Topaz looked at her benefactor. The prince was the furthest thing from her mind. Scandal was more appropriate, she thought as she clutched her open bodice, which, in her seated position, revealed more of her bosom than any man had ever had the good fortune to view. Was it he who had undone the hooks on her gown and then taken off her shoes? Somehow, her state of undress vanished from her mind when he leaned over her.

He wore no cravat and his silk shirt was open nearly to his waist. He seemed completely unaware that the hair on his chest was close to her face, or that the scent of him wafted toward her, creating a heady aura of male sensuality.

He hesitated. "You've gone quite pale. Is it the pain? Are you all right?"

"I think so." She gritted her teeth. She had forgotten about the pain. What she was experiencing for the first time in her life was a different kind of pain: a sudden and nearly indefinable heat in the pit of her stomach. The thought that she might be losing control of the situation angered her.

"Oh, do let's get on with it! If you are determined to maim me for life, then do it."

He gave her a quelling look, at the same time holding her left arm in both hands. "I'll try not to hurt you any more than I have to."

"Do it!" she commanded.

Almost before the words were out of her mouth Topaz felt an excruciating stab of pain rocket through her back and shoulder. The last thing she remembered was a high, keening shriek. She was dimly aware that it had come from her own throat before she fainted.

He laid her gently back down on the pillow and tucked the coverlet under her chin. "Double damnation! I hope I haven't done her damage." He studied the rise and fall of her exquisitely shaped bosom. She was a beauty, there was no doubt of that, but the fact came as no surprise. Even to a recluse such as he, the word had got round about the Thackery Jewels: Amethyst, Emerald and Topaz. In this, their year of introduction into Society, they had taken London by its dreary collar and shaken it into new life.

And this must be Topaz, the one with the silvery hair and blue-green eyes that were said to cause mischief to men's hearts.

Her breathing was regular now and her face had regained most of its colour. He lifted the silk coverlet and drew it across her and up to her chin. She stirred, then opened her eyes.

"I'm sorry. I must have fainted again. Please, just do what you must do and get it over with."

He felt a sudden surge of pleasure. "It's done. I rather imagine your shoulder will be uncomfortable for a while, but I doubt that you will be troubled with it again."

She pushed herself to a sitting position. "Yes, yes! It's ever so much better. There is hardly any pain at all." Flinging back the covers, she swung her feet over the side of the bed and stood next to him. Before he could say a word she had reached for his face with both hands, pulled him down to her level, and kissed him soundly on the cheek.

"Thank you again. And I'm sorry to have been such a pin-wit about it. It's not like me to succumb to the vapours."

He put his hand to his cheek, where the imprint of her kiss must surely have left its mark. He started to speak but his voice deserted him. No matter. She was already asking to see David.

Somehow he managed to get control of himself. He had partaken of his share of females in his day, but this was the first time a lady had initiated an encounter. He was touched. *Girl*, he mentally corrected himself. She was still a girl. Younger even than David. And a person of Quality. Considering her youth, she might be forgiven this untoward breach of etiquette. As for himself, he was quite pleased that she had chosen to do so.

He motioned toward the open doorway. "I believe that David is still resting, but if you will come with me, I shall be glad to show you the way."

She looked down at her feet, then lifted her skirt to reveal a nicely turned ankle. "My slippers, sir. I wonder if . . ."

"But of course. I had forgotten." Retracing his footsteps, he went to the foot of the bed and bent to retrieve her shoes. "May I?" he asked.

"Y—yes, if you please." She sat down and extended her foot. "Was it you who removed them? And . . . and also undid the catches on my dress?"

He felt his face grow warm. "Yes, I'm afraid so. My staff is very small. My housekeeper was visiting a neighbouring farm, and it seemed more appropriate that I, rather than a menial, should attend you. I assure you, I meant no indelicacy or disrespect."

She smiled and her eyes and mouth came alive. "There is no offence taken, sir. But now that we are on such intimate terms, should we not at least know each other's names?" She extended her hand. "I am Topaz Thackery, the ward of Lady Udora Bently, who is married to Lord Kesterson."

"I know. I have heard of you."

"Indeed?"

"Yes. And your sisters, Amethyst and Emerald. It is easy to understand why you have become known as the Thackery Jewels. . . . That is, if your sisters are as beautiful as you are."

Topaz's laughter charmed him. She tilted her head to one side. "You are too kind, sir. I hardly know what to say. I am always at a disadvantage without my shoes."

"Oh, yes." Double damnation! He felt like a blushing schoolboy. Worse yet, he was acting like one. Kneeling down before her, he reached for her foot. "It's cold! Like ice," he said.

"I know. It was very cold in the balloon and I fear I still have not recovered from the chill."

"We can easily fix that. Allow me to warm some bricks in the fireplace."

"Oh, no, thank you. I really mustn't stay that long."

"Then let me massage your feet to start the blood circulating."

"Well, I..." She started to protest, but he had already knelt and pressed his thumbs into the ball of one foot and begun a slow, rhythmic massage. Glancing up at her face, he was reminded of a cat basking in the affection of a loving master.

"That feels marvellous," she murmured. It sounded to him like a purr. And then, to his undoing, she placed her other foot on his knee. Her toes curled against him, kneading the fabric of his trousers and stirring the embers of his heat into sudden flame.

He choked back a groan. He needed desperately to stand, for of a sudden his trousers had become uncomfortably tight.

"I, er...I think I hear David moving about. Perhaps we should see if he is all right." Without waiting for her to respond, he slipped her shoes on her feet and offered her his hand.

Topaz was bewildered. She hadn't heard a thing. If truth were told, she had been lulled into a state of euphoria by his gentle ministrations. The world could have ended and she would have chosen not to move.

She tried valiantly to gather her wits about her. Allowing this man to touch her was of course a dreadful breach of propriety, even given the circumstances. And now that she thought about it, he hadn't so much as told her his name, despite the fact that she had given him the perfect opportunity. Was he in fact trying to keep his identity a secret? Well, he wouldn't get away with it.

When they reached the corridor just outside the bedchamber, she stopped and turned to him. "I don't recall your having offered your name, sir."

"Forgive me. I am Peter, Lord Colby. This is Ridgeview, our home." He motioned once again for her to follow him.

Our home! But of course! Why had it not occurred to her that he would have a wife? And children! Damnation! Why did it feel as if the wind had been driven from her lungs when she could still feel the strength of his fingers curled around her foot? She managed a smile.

"It was good of you and your wife to offer David and me your hospitality."

"Wife?" He smiled. "No, you misunderstand...." He paused as they stopped at a door on the wide landing that led to a handsome staircase. At that moment the door was flung open and David appeared, smiling at them.

"Aha, there you are, Taz, and looking far too beautiful to have just crashed in a balloon. I see you have met my brother."

"Brother? But I didn't realize you were brothers."

Colby nodded. "It was David to whom I referred when I said this is *our* home. I admit that David chooses to spend most of the week at his flat near Green Park, but this is his home nevertheless."

The thought flashed through Topaz's mind that she should have suspected that David was not a commoner, considering the way he spoke.

"I never dreamed . . . David never talks about himself."

"Nor, I'm led to assume, his family."

Topaz shook her head. "He rarely speaks about anything but the science of aeronautics."

David laughed. "There isn't anything else, is there? And speaking of flying, I must get back to my balloon to see how badly the envelope is damaged."

Topaz pressed her hands together in front of her. "I'm so sorry about the accident, David, but I really must go home immediately. Will it be impossible for us to return to London in the balloon or must we find another way to travel?"

Lord Colby gave her a surprised look. "Do you mean to say you would be willing to risk another voyage in that infernal contraption?"

"Of course. Our accident was just an unfortunate occurence."

David stroked his chin. "And a serious one, I'm afraid. It will be some time before I can make repairs and attempt another flight." He took a step closer to his brother.

"I say, Peter, would you do me the great favour of escorting Topaz home? I know you are not otherwise occupied at the moment and I must do what I can to save the balloon."

Lord Colby's face sobered, leading Topaz to think that he was not altogether happy to do as David had asked.

"David, I think it would be more prudent for you to see Miss Thackery home and make the proper apologies to her guardians, would it not?"

David grinned. "Topaz understands that I have to rescue the *Gypsy*. If the silk is left to lie overnight in the rain, there could be even more damage."

David's reasoning obviously did not sit well with Lord Colby, but he asked politely, "Would you care to stay for dinner, Miss Thackery?"

"I cannot, though I thank you for your kindness. Lady Udora is sure to be alarmed when my abigail returns without me, as I've no doubt she will already have done, considering that more than four hours have passed since we left her at Green Park."

"Then, if you wish, we shall leave without further delay. I'll just give you a moment to freshen up whilst I have the carriage brought round." He squared his shoulders, locked his hands behind his back, and looked over to David. "If you will show Miss Thackery to her room?"

"Of course. The French suite?"

"Yes." He nodded to David, then bowed to Topaz and left abruptly.

Once he was gone, Topaz felt as if the corridor where they stood at the top of the stairs had suddenly grown larger. She expelled her breath. "He wasn't at all pleased to have been stuck with me, David. I felt a decided chill in the room when you asked him to escort me back to London."

"Nonsense. Peter is a tad stiff, but he is a good sort. You look a bit pale. Are you sure you are all right?"

"Of course, but I wish you were returning with me."

He brushed his knuckles beneath her chin. "You know I have to look after the *Gypsy*. There's a good girl now. Go comb your hair and be ready when Peter brings the carriage round. He doesn't like to be kept waiting.''

David closed the door after himself, and Topaz wandered over to the dressing-table and sat down. Comb her hair, indeed. If Maggie could see it now, she would be appalled. One of her combs, the silver one with the turquoise-and-ruby butterfly attached to the top, was nowhere to be found.

She sighed. It was a special ornament that Lord Kesterson had given to her on her fifteenth birthday. Well, it was gone now. Much as she loved it, there were more important things to worry about. Once again she turned to the mirror and began the chore of creating order out of chaos.

Arranging her hair into a decent cluster of curls atop her head was much easier than arranging her unruly thoughts. She was certain to find herself in trouble; she had already accepted that fact. But to arrive without benefit of chaperon in a stranger's carriage would be too much for anyone to forgive. The Kestersons were certain to punish her this time, and it would not be a simple matter such as a restriction of privileges or a slap on the knuckles.

Then, too, she wasn't altogether confident that she would be safe in the hands of Lord Colby. Of course, he was David's brother, but save for their thick black hair, there was little resemblance between the two men. Where David's boyish face was pretty enough that any woman would have been pleased to claim it, Peter's strong but finely chiselled features were masculinity itself. The drive back to London would take much longer than the journey in the balloon. Even in the largest carriage there was an undeniable sense of intimacy... a sense of isolation from the rest of the civilized world.

Already she had experienced strange feelings of yearning toward this man. Did he feel the same? Would he attempt to compromise her. And what would she do if he did? A smile spread across her face and she put her hand over the mirror to cover it. Lord Colby was a very presentable and exciting male, but she was an expert at discouraging overeager suitors... if indeed she *wished* to discourage him. Her musings were interrupted by a tap on the door, followed by a male voice.

"Lord Colby wishes me to tell you that the carriage is waiting at the front door, Miss Thackery."

"Thank you. I'll be downstairs directly."

Once in the hallway she noticed the butler, who had apparently delivered the message. She approached him.

"Could you tell me if Mr. David Endicott is still in the house? I should like to bid him goodbye."

The butler bowed. "I'm sorry, miss, but I believe he has already gone out to attend to the wreckage."

"I see. Thank you." She was disappointed. Not so much by not being able to say goodbye, but by the evidence that he cared more for this flying contraption than he cared for her. She hesitated once more before she reached the stairway. "Then please tell him when he returns that I enquired after him."

"I will be sure to do so, Miss Thackery."

For the first time Topaz had a chance to consider her surroundings. The wine, gold and turquoise-coloured rug stretched the entire length of the wide staircase, which led down to the entrance hall on the main floor. The wall along one side of the gently curving staircase was hung with paintings of ships and sailing vessels of various sizes, some of which were certainly quite valuable.

She had almost reached the bottom step when the massive front door was opened and Lord Colby entered the foyer. He stood looking up at her, his dark cloak thrown back over one shoulder, his gloves clutched in one hand.

"Ah, there you are, Miss Thackery. The carriage is waiting."

"Thank you, my lord." There was something in the tone of his voice that set her nerves on edge. She sensed danger—a danger that was too tenuous to name, but danger nevertheless.

He offered his arm and she accompanied him to the carriage. The step was already in place, and when she lowered her head to accommodate the narrow doorway, she realized that they were not alone. An attractive woman some ten years older than Topaz was seated in the corner.

"Good day, Miss Thackery. I am Regina Smythe."

"How do you do," Topaz said, sitting down at the other end of the seat.

The carriage swayed for a moment as Lord Colby added his weight and took a seat across from the ladies. "I see you have introduced yourselves." He leaned toward Topaz. "For propriety's sake I took the liberty of asking my housekeeper to accompany us, since she returned in time to make the journey. From what I understand from David, it will be difficult enough to explain your presence in the balloon without having to deal with another incident, however innocent."

"How kind of you," Topaz said drily. She resented his subtle criticism of her behaviour. "Did David also explain that my abigail jumped from the car as it left the ground? That I had no opportunity to follow her without risk to life and limb?"

Lord Colby lifted an eyebrow. "And would you have chosen to stay behind, given a safe opportunity?"

Topaz knew by the look on his face that he expected her to defend herself. She lifted her chin. "Stay behind? Not for anything in this world. It was a glorious experience. But surely you know that. You must have been aloft on many occasions."

Colby was about to speak when his housekeeper interrupted. "Lord Colby is too intelligent to waste his time on such amusements." Mrs. Smythe untied the ribbons on her bonnet and laid it on the seat next to her. "Young Mr. Endicott is a dear boy, but he has yet to mature."

Topaz tensed. "Indeed? I was of the opinion that David is quite intelligent."

"Ah...but then you are even younger than he, *n'est-ce pas?*"

Topaz felt the heat rise in her face. What right did this woman have to speak in such a manner? She was a servant, yet she acted as if she were the mistress of the house. Turning to face Lord Colby, she contrived to exclude Regina Smythe from the conversation. She gave him an engaging smile.

"Just as I was leaving I noticed a number of exquisite paintings of ships. Have you a fondness for the sea, Lord Colby?"

"Not so much for the sea as for the ships that sail on it. I am intrigued by the effects of wind on sail and the buoyancy of various kinds of wood."

He was about to continue when Mrs. Smythe interrupted. "Lord Colby knows more about the building of ships than most men in England."

"That's nonsense, of course, but the subject does interest me. I spend much of my time drawing designs for small sailing craft."

Topaz was struck by the subtle camaraderie that seemed to exist between master and servant. Was this woman more to him than a housekeeper? It would not be the first time a servant had been seduced by her master... or perhaps it was the other way round. Judging by first impressions, her guess would be that the bold Mrs. Smythe would have been the aggressor.

Topaz tried to ignore her, but the woman was not to be excluded. For a while the conversation flowed so easily between the housekeeper and Lord Colby that Topaz felt like a child whose presence was tolerated only because there was no choice in the matter. Try as she might, Topaz could introduce no subject on which Mrs. Smythe was unable or unwilling to voice an opinion.

She attempted a further effort. "I was quite impressed by the magnificent stallion you were riding just before the balloon crashed into the trees. Do you have an extensive stable, Lord Colby?"

"Rather, though I cannot take credit for it. Mrs. Smythe's father has been the stablemaster at Ridgeview Manor since before I was born. After my father died, some five years ago, I was only too pleased to keep Mr. Smythe in my employ. He knows everything there is to know about breeding horses."

"And your mother? Is she still alive?"

The housekeeper laughed. "Very much so. Her ladyship was swept off her feet by a Swedish nobleman, and they married three years ago."

"How lovely for her," Topaz murmured.

"I suppose it depends on how one views it," the other woman said. There was a touch of ice in her voice. "As for myself, I cannot imagine how she could have left her boys...and Ridgeview as well."

"It is lovely, isn't it?" Topaz pointedly ignored Mrs. Smythe. "The boys? But I assumed that you and David were the only children. Do you have younger brothers?" Topaz tilted her head toward Lord Colby.

Regina Smythe laughed, a silvery sound in the close confines of the carriage. "Forgive me, I do still tend to think of Peter and David as 'the boys.'"

"No, Miss Thackery, there were but the two of us," Lord Colby said, at last contriving to enter the conversation. He turned to his housekeeper. "Regina, you must allow me to speak for myself." There was a note of censure in his voice, a note that Topaz silently applauded. But her victory turned sour when Colby added with a fond glance at the housekeeper. "David and I are brothers, of course, but this hellion grew up with us. It was to be expected, seeing that her mother was our housekeeper and her father, as I mentioned, is our stablemaster. Regina is almost like a sister to David and me."

"Almost, but not quite!" Regina added in a soft voice.

Topaz wondered if the woman was trying to underline the fact that she lacked a noble birthright, or whether she was warning Topaz to keep her distance from the Colby boys. *Men, not boys,* she silently corrected herself, more irritated than she cared to admit.

Apparently Regina took his words seriously, because she was mute unless spoken to for the next twenty minutes. Topaz, however, was exquisitely aware that the atmosphere in the carriage had become strained. She caught Regina Smythe watching her every movement as if memorizing it for later use.

But why? David had obviously mentioned her name, but there was nothing between him and Topaz, save the joy of soaring. Or had he indicated otherwise? Not likely. It was plain to see that David had no time for romance.

And Lord Colby? They had met for the first time only a few hours ago, and he had been less than cordial. She leaned back against the blue squabs and closed her eyes. But, in truth, Peter Endicott, Lord Colby, was a very appealing man, even if he did seem a trifle stiff. She knew, even with her eyes closed, that Colby was watching her now. The knowledge brought warmth to her face, and she closed her eyes more tightly and soon drifted off to sleep.

Colby had been aware of the faint flush in her cheeks, and he wondered what she was dreaming. As for himself, he tried not to think about her, knowing that she was drawn to David and he to her. Nevertheless, his gaze kept returning to Topaz, noticing the way her lashes lay like silvery brown feathers against her cheeks. Her hair, loosely arranged now, for lack of a proper abigail, drifted against the blue upholstery like spindrift touched by the moon.

Once again the stirring in his groin surprised him. It had been a long time since he had really been attracted to a woman. True, there was Camille, but she was only a convenience, a habit. And he had visited her establishment only two or three times in the past two months.

Of course there had been Alicia when he was seventeen, but she had died suddenly of an unexplained fever. And then there was Catherine when he was twenty-two. But she was betrothed to and eventually married a baronet. He expelled his breath. It seemed to be his destiny to desire the unattainable. But not this time! Not again. He would keep his distance from this young creature, who obviously adored his brother.

"Colby." He hardly heard Regina's voice, but he looked over at her. Her eyes were bright and filled with laughter.

"Stop it," she ordered. "You are salivating."

"What utter nonsense," he said, then wiped his face with his hands. "Double damnation! Why don't you take a nap?"

"I forbid you to speak to me that way."

"My apologies. We have known each other far too long, Regina. I have allowed you certain privileges because of our close friendship, but I warn you not to take advantage of your position."

"I would never do that. You know I only want what's best for you, and for Ridgeview Manor. I've always protected you from outsiders. Please, don't ask me to turn away from you now after all these years."

Despite the waning sunlight, he could detect the darkening in her eyes that increased whenever she was threatened with change. Regina didn't like changes. Admittedly, neither did he.

He looked again at the innocently sleeping figure of the girl. Then, suddenly, as if a bolt of lightning had streaked across the sky, he knew that changes were inevitable. And sooner than he could possibly have imagined.

NOTHING MORE WAS SAID until they reached Kesterson House and Colby leaned forward to touch Topaz's arm. "Wake up, Miss Thackery. You have arrived home."

She awoke, instantly alert. "Thank you." She stretched and yawned as innocently as a child, then as quickly, regained her composure. "Forgive me. I would invite you to come in, but I fear there may be a rather uncomfortable scene. I don't wish to cause you embarrassment."

She made a vain attempt to straighten her gown. "Lord Colby, once again I wish to express my appreciation for your kindness toward me. You have gone beyond the dictates of hospitality, and I know that my guardian will eventually wish to express her appreciation."

"That is all well and good, Miss Thackery, but I have no intention of allowing you to face your guardian alone." He opened the carriage door and stepped down to the ground. "If you will?"

He reached for her hand, but as he did so, Topaz misjudged the distance to the step and all but fell into his arms. He caught her against his chest and, for the briefest moment, held her so close that the sudden pounding of his heart became one with hers. The sly look on Regina's face put an end to it.

"Are you all right?" he asked.

She looked startled. Her tongue darted out to moisten her lips. "Quite. I...I, er...I'm so dreadfully sorry," she said. "I am not usually so clumsy."

"No harm done." But even as the words left his mouth he knew it was a lie. For as he had turned to prevent her from falling, his gaze chanced to sweep the front of the house. A curtain moved, then moved again. Someone had seen them.

Topaz trembled as he released her. "I think I had better go inside. Please, I am quite able to speak with my guardian alone."

"I won't hear of it."

Topaz drew a deep breath. "Very well, if you insist." She gave a brief nod to Regina. "Thank you for your services, Mrs. Smythe."

The housekeeper had started to get out of the carriage but Colby spoke over his shoulder. "You may remain in the carriage, Regina. I won't be long."

Topaz flashed him a grateful smile. It would have been unbearable to have Regina Smythe smirking in the background while Lady Udora took her to task.

The wide double doors to Kesterson House were flung open even before Topaz and Lord Colby reached the step. Lady Udora, with Lord Kesterson a few steps behind her, stood like a dragon at the gate.

Topaz greeted Udora and Bently, Lord Kesterson, as they stepped aside to allow her to enter. She was about to perform the introductions when her mind suddenly went blank. "I . . . I'm sorry, my lord. I cannot remember your name."

Udora made a sound that reflected her displeasure, but Colby hastened to intervene. "If I may . . . I am Peter Endicott, Lord Colby. At your service, my lord, my lady."

Bently nodded and introduced himself and his lady. "I thought I recognized you from Parliament. Something about waterway rights and restrictions, wasn't it?"

Udora inclined her head. "Do come into the library. I believe that we are due some explanation concerning my ward's disappearance."

"It was hardly a disappearance," Topaz said. "I was gone less than five hours, and Sally knew I was with David."

"David? But I thought you said your name was Peter," Udora said, fixing Lord Colby with a penetrating gaze.

"And so it is, my lady. If you will but give us a moment, I am certain we can explain everything."

Udora motioned them to be seated when they reached the comfortably warm library. "And what, may I ask, has happened to Sally?"

Topaz sank down into a chair. "Oh, dear. Then she hasn't come home?"

"She has not."

Topaz blew air through her lips. "That idiot girl. I told her to wait for me to return. Apparently she took me at my word."

Lord Kesterson leaned an elbow on the mantelpiece, his eyebrows drawn together in a frown. "You
have a great deal to answer for, my girl. Perhaps you
had better tell us exactly what happened."

CHAPTER THREE

IT SEEMED TO TOPAZ that the inquisition was destined to go on forever. She had gone through quite enough for one day, though, and now that she was quite safe, she could look back on the balloon ride and the ensuing complications with some pleasure.

She watched as Lady Udora queried Lord Colby closely. He was holding up very well under the Kestersons' scrutiny, but enough was enough. Besides, Topaz knew that any punishment meted out by her guardian was sure to be more threat than substance. Lady Udora adored the three girls and could not bear to see them unhappy.

She rose from her seat near the fireplace and confronted the Kestersons. "Please, we have told you every possible detail." *Except for the part where he all but undressed me.* "Lord Colby has a long journey to return home, and his housekeeper is waiting in the carriage. Could we not allow him to take his departure?"

Bently clasped his hands behind his back. "Hmm. Yes, I suppose you are right. May we offer you a small repast before you leave, my lord?"

Colby stood and made a token bow. "Thank you, but I think not. If there is nothing else, I will bid you good-night."

Topaz started to accompany him to the door, but Udora shot her a quelling glance. "We have not finished with you, Topaz. Kindly return to your chair."

Topaz inhaled sharply. This was a bad sign. An ominous cloud had begun to take shape in the room. For the first time she realized that for once Udora was not to be so easily mollified. Nevertheless, she could not allow Colby to leave without properly thanking him for his kindness. She went to him and extended her hand.

"Lord Colby, my guardian would be the first to remind me that I was remiss in my manners if I failed to thank you for your kindness. I regret any discomfort that I have caused you and your housekeeper. I am truly grateful that you came to my rescue."

She was rewarded by a look of surprise on his face. He took her hand, but although he remained silent, something passed between them. What it was, Topaz was not certain, nor did she quite dare to explore the reason behind the sudden weakness in her limbs. She moistened her lips. "Would you please tell David . . ."

Udora stepped between them. "You may tell your young brother that Topaz will not be seeing him again."

Colby inclined his head. "I quite understand, my lady. Again, I bid you good-night."

Topaz was too stunned to do anything but sit down as Udora had ordered her. Not see David? It was unthinkable! But of course she would find a means to overcome this latest edict. Nothing ever stood in her way once her mind was made up.

Udora watched for a moment as the butler directed Lord Colby to the front entrance, then she closed the door behind them. Turning, she began to pace the floor, both hands pressed to her face. Topaz had never seen Udora in such distress.

Bently had taken a seat opposite Topaz next to the fireplace. "Do come sit down, my dear," he said to Udora. "Both Topaz and Lord Colby have assured us that nothing untoward has happened. We can sort all this out later, now that we know our worst fears were for naught."

"Nothing has happened! Do you realize what you are saying, Bently? My charge has risked her life by flying off in a balloon without our permission *and* without benefit of chaperon. She appears to have complete disregard for convention, or how her misconduct might affect her family name as well as her own tenuous prospects. Moreover, Sally was left to wait in the cold and dark without the slightest concern for her discomfort. I simply cannot, and will not, countenance such misbehaviour."

Topaz was about to apologize once more but Udora's hand stayed her. There was silence in the room, save for the soft swish of Udora's petticoats as she paced the floor. Then, even that comforting noise ceased when Udora turned her back to them, placed both hands on the mantel just above her head, and stared down at the dying embers.

Topaz looked to Bently with a questioning gaze but he simply shook his head. Bently had always been on her side. After her parents were killed in the coaching accident it was their neighbor, Bently, who took the Thackery girls under his wing. With no one who could control them, the twins and Topaz, who were within a few months of the same age, had run wild for nearly a year. It was Lady Udora who came to them at Amberleigh, their home in Coventry, and gave them loving discipline. At first they had rebelled against her guardianship but they soon came to love her. Now, Bently and Udora were married and it was just a question of weeks until Amethyst and Emerald would also be wed.

The sadness in Bently's eyes spoke loudly enough. He was disappointed in her. What's more, she knew without even asking, that this time even he was powerless to save her from Udora's wrath.

At last Udora turned. She seemed to have aged months in the past ten minutes. Topaz wanted to reach out to her and comfort her but she was powerless to move. Udora tucked her hands into the full sleeves of her wine-coloured velvet gown.

"I am afraid, my dear Topaz, that this time you have gone too far. I've given you more freedom than your sisters could ever have dreamed of, and you chose to take advantage of it."

"But I did nothing so terribly wrong, my lady."

"You see? You don't even recognize the fact that you flouted the rules of decency. Oh, yes, you escaped comparatively unscathed this time. But what about the next, and the next? You are a wealthy and attractive young woman. If you have not the maturity to protect yourself from harm, then I must do it for you."

"My lady..."

"No. I wish to hear no more from you. The matter is, in fact, already settled. I have dispatched a message to the Throckmortons that you will accept their son's bid for your hand in marriage. You will wed Arthur Ringwald, and that's the end of it.''

"Never! I would rather die than marry Arthur Ringwald.''

"Give me one good reason. He is good-looking, he already has a title, and when his father passes on, Arthur will succeed him.''

"But I don't love him.''

"Pistachions! Marriage has little to do with love. Especially a first marriage. In time you will come to love him.''

"I could never love him. I can hardly tolerate touching his hand.''

"Then your only other choice is to take yourself off to St. Brigit's and live a life of seclusion. I can no longer trust you to obey me.'' She came over to stand behind Topaz, placed her hands on the girl's shoulders, and bent to kiss the top of her head.

"Dear girl, it is not my wish to punish you. You must know that I have come to love you as if you were my own child. But you must trust me in my decision. I know I am doing the right thing for you by agreeing to this alliance.''

"You cannot possibly know.''

"Then all I can do is offer my best judgement. As for now, I suggest that you retire to your room for contemplation. And to repair the damage to your person,'' she said as an afterthought. "Your gown looks as though you have been sleeping in the stable.''

Topaz didn't wait for another reprimand. She dropped a curtsy and rushed to the stairs as quickly as possible.

LORD COLBY'S EMOTIONS were mixed when he climbed into the carriage after having left the Kestersons. On one hand he was relieved to have survived Lady Udora's ire, but on the other hand he was troubled by the need to leave Topaz Thackery to endure the confrontation alone. True, she was a spirited young creature and could probably stand up to them without his help, but he could not erase the vision of her . . . nor the effect she had had on him when he carried her into his house. Had he been a less honourable man, he might have been tempted to take advantage of her defencelessness.

His thoughts naturally turned toward his brother. Had David also been tempted? The girl, enamoured as she was of David, must have given him ample opportunity to take advantage of her innocence.

"Double damnation!" He knocked on the carriage roof with the end of his cane, and the driver, recognizing the signal, urged the horses to greater speed.

Regina, curled up in the corner of the carriage, had been silent when Lord Colby returned. He saw the speculative smile on her face and frowned. "Well, say it. You know you will sooner or later."

"It's nothing. I just wondered what they said to you that's put you in such a blue study."

"They were quite civil, to me at least, though Heaven only knows what they will do to the girl."

"She is far too forward for her age, and too adventurous. It seems to me that they've waited much too long to discipline her. But I suppose there is the danger that they could claim that David compromised her, thereby forcing him into marriage."

"Never. I would not permit it. They are not suited to each other."

Regina raised an eyebrow. "Really! I had no idea you were so protective of David. Or is it the delectable Miss Thackery about whom you are so concerned?"

"Stop talking drivel. Miss Thackery is David's friend, not mine."

"One wouldn't have thought so, considering the way you were looking at her. You couldn't keep your eyes from undressing her."

Colby felt the heat rise in his face, and he wanted to strike out at something. He regarded his housekeeper with tight-lipped fury. "I warn you, Regina, I have nearly reached my limits with your impertinence. It is only out of my regard for your father that I allow you to remain in my household."

The look of shock on her face gave him some small satisfaction. He settled back against the squabs and tried to calm his thoughts about a girl with eyes that could change from the greenish blue of the sky to the deepest ocean blue... and hair that had floated over his arm like silver foam on the crest of a breaking wave.

THE TWINS WERE WAITING for Topaz in her room, which adjoined theirs. Amy, with her usual bent toward rescuing the downtrodden, gave Topaz a quick hug. "Was it too, too awful? I wanted to be there to take your side, but Udora forbade it."

Emerald looked up from the book she had been reading and gazed at them over the top of her spectacles. "It wouldn't have done the least bit of good. Her ladyship was in tears over your disappearance. I am sure that her fear must have degenerated into anger once she found what you were about. It wasn't as if she hadn't warned you about seeing David."

"Oh, don't be so stiff-rumped, Emerald," Amethyst said. "It's not as if you've never done anything wrong. I refer to a recent incident that involved you and the infamous Harriette Wilson." Emerald stuck out her tongue at Amy, who picked up the lace that she had been tatting and turned her gaze back to Topaz.

"Have they told you yet what your punishment is to be? Surely they won't let you off so easily this time. Why, they might even refuse to let you attend the Taggarts' party in Brighton next month."

Topaz flung herself down on the bed. "That would be a pleasure, not a punishment, for I have no wish to attend a dreary house party. The truth is, I am to become betrothed to Arthur Ringwald. Lady Udora has already sent the papers along to the Throckmortons."

Amy jumped up and clapped her hands. "Betrothed! How incredibly delicious. Now the three of us..."

Emerald raised her eyebrows in surprise. "I never thought for a moment that you would choose Arthur. He is quite intelligent, you know. I was speaking with him only three days ago about the new designs for Apsley House. Arthur is a friend of Benjamin Wyatt, who is designing the improvements. I enquired of Arthur concerning the interior decor and he actually understood..."

Topaz gave her a scornful look. "Choose him? How can you be so pin-witted? Being with Arthur Ringwald is as exciting as watching the lake dry up in summer. Oh, do go away and let me suffer in peace!" Topaz wailed. "I don't want to talk about it."

Amy's face crumpled. "Oh, my dear sister. I'm so sorry. You are not at all pleased, are you?"

Topaz sat up. "Pleased? How could I be pleased? Arthur Ringwald may be a lord, but to me he's a chitty-faced, cow-handed cock of the game, and I want nothing to do with him."

Emerald carefully laid her book on the table. "Surely you can't hope to marry David? He has no prospects, none at all."

Topaz flung back her hair, which by now had completely lost its combs. "That's all you know, Miss Bluestocking! I learned only today that David is the young brother of Peter Endicott, the Marquess of Colby."

"No!" Amy said, throwing down her tatting and jumping up. "I've heard of Lord Colby. He is held to be very handsome in a rugged sort of way."

Emerald nodded her head. "Colby... Colby. Yes, the major has mentioned him a number of times. He's devilish queer, they say. I believe he owns a place outside of London called Ridgegate or Ridgehaven or something."

"Ridgeview. I was there today," Topaz said with a touch of smugness in her voice.

"You were?" Amy said. "I don't believe you for a minute."

"I was. The balloon crashed on the Ridgeview lands near the house and Colby had to rescue us."

"What happened then?" the twins demanded in unison.

Topaz began by telling them about Sally's last-minute escape and then went into detail about the exquisite sensation of leaving the earth behind and flying through the clouds.

Amy wriggled impatiently. "Yes, yes, but get to the good part. The part where Lord Colby rescues you."

"Oh, Amy, you're such a romantic," Emerald protested. "You were in his house, then? Did you chance to see his library? Does he have a good collection of books?"

"I have no idea. I spent the time in his bedroom," she added, glancing quickly at her sisters to see if she had properly shocked them.

"In his *bedroom?* Lady Udora must have had a chicken fit."

Topaz threw a quick glance over her shoulder. "Hush, do keep your voice down. It wasn't exactly his bedroom, but it *was* he who carried me into the house, undid my dress and took off my slippers . . . all while I was quite unconscious, if you please." She dropped her voice. "And don't you dare breathe a word of this to Lady Udora. Nothing significant happened, but she would never believe that!"

Emerald took off her spectacles and rubbed the glass with a square of linen. "No wonder they decided to affiance you to Arthur Ringwald. In one afternoon you've single-handedly created a cause for scandal that could bring down the entire House of Kesterson."

"Oh, don't be so dramatic. It can only become a scandal if someone decides to make a fuss about it in public. As Amy pointed out, this is not the first time our family has been forced to stand up under a scandal.''

Emerald lifted her nose in the air. "Nor the second, if I may remind my dear twin about a certain baby boy who just happened to come into her possession.''

Amy paled. "Oh, do let's not be uncivil to one another.'' She made a steeple of her fingers and placed them under her chin. "But what will you do now, Taz? About Arthur, I mean.''

Topaz sighed. "We shall just have to see, won't we? One thing is certain—I intend to make sure he doesn't want to marry me.''

"Not likely," Emerald scoffed. "Arthur is quite enamoured of you, so I'm told.''

"The feelings are not mutual, I assure you, though I do admit that the thought of him in my bed is considerably less repulsive than some of the other young bucks who are available.''

THE FOLLOWING AFTERNOON a message was received from Lord and Lady Throckmorton in which they resoundingly agreed to affiance Arthur and Topaz. Arthur left his calling-card with the promise to pay his respects that same evening.

It was the traditional evening "at home" for the Kestersons, with the usual bustle of friends arriving for a brief visit before moving on to the next "at home." The difference between this and other evenings was that there were fewer eligible bachelors in attendance, now that both Amethyst and Emerald had announced their betrothals. Of course their fiancés were present, both dancing attendance upon their brides-to-be.

Topaz noted with dread that Prudence Thackery, their spinster aunt who had only recently arrived from the Colonies, had already come downstairs to "help entertain" as she preferred to express it. Topaz sincerely doubted that anyone could be entertained by this dour-faced woman who refused to wear anything but black or grey. And appropriately so, Topaz admitted, because such colours defined Prudence's outlook on life, which she saw as something to be endured, not enjoyed.

She looked down her nose in disapproval at Topaz's *décolletage*. "In my day we didn't find it necessary to advertise our wares to attract the attention of a man. Indeed, it seems to me that his lordship would be quite appalled to see his betrothed presenting her bosom for one and all to view."

"I assure you, Prudence," Topaz said with a touch of smugness, "Arthur is quite happy with the way I dress. It's quite *haut ton,* according to the latest pictures in *Le Beau Monde.* And need I mention that Lady Udora chose the style as the one best suited to me?"

Topaz was tempted to point out that Prudence herself had not been successful in leading a man to the altar, but had, in fact, given birth to a merry-begotten child and been banished to the Colonies for her sins. But Topaz managed to control her tongue. Prudence was pathetic enough, having come to London to search without success for her runaway daughter, who by now must be eighteen years old.

Prudence sniffed. "Udora Bently is hardly in a position to dictate morals, considering her colourful past, but to her credit, she has managed to find you a husband. And a titled one at that."

Topaz stiffened. "It would seem so, wouldn't it? In fact, I do believe he has arrived. If you will excuse me."

She left before Prudence could accompany her. Arthur looked for all the world like the typical Bond Street Lounger that he contrived to be. Wispy blond hair falling over his high forehead, skin-tight inexpressibles topped with a white shirt and a starcher so high that he had difficulty turning his head.

"Ah, there you are, princess." He raised a bejewelled hand and waggled his fingers as he negotiated his way between groups of people to reach her side.

Princess? Topaz wondered whether he had forgotten her name or if now that they were officially betrothed, he hoped to elevate her station in life. It didn't matter. She would never marry him. But to keep the peace until she could plan her next move, she must make every effort to cooperate in this ridiculous charade. To that end she forced a smile.

"Yes, Arthur. Here I am."

"Jolly good. I couldn't wait to see you now that we are to be married."

"Is that so? Then why, if you were so eager to see me, did you arrive late?"

"Missed me already, did you?" he said with a grin of self-satisfaction. "The truth is, I stopped off on St. James's Street to say hello to some of my chums. They're having a rousting party tonight. Nothing better to do, don't you know."

"No, I don't. I've never been to a rousting party."

"Well of course you haven't, love. They're not for the fair sex or for the faint of heart."

"Tell me about them," she said, hoping to appear interested in what he had to say.

"Well...I...I find it very difficult to describe. One has to be there to understand the excitement." He smacked his fist into his palm. "I know. After I've said hello to the Kestersons I'll ask his lordship's permission to take you for a drive. You can't get out of the carriage, of course, being a lady, but you can catch the spirit of it all from a distance."

Topaz shrugged. "All right. But I must take my abigail with us."

"Only if you must." He leered at her suggestively. "But I will count the days when we can lock your abigail and the rest of the world out of our house. Then, princess, I shall have you all to myself."

"What a frightful thought," she murmured.

He gave her a sharp look. "What did you say?"

"Er...what a delightful thought," she said, hating herself for her own weakness.

"Isn't it just? I promise you, Topaz, you'll not be wanting another man once we've...well, good manners prevent me from saying more, but my reputation speaks for me."

"What reputation is that?" she enquired sweetly.

"Why..." He blustered in confusion, giving Topaz the satisfaction she had been looking for. "My reputation as a lover," he said in a lowered voice.

"Ah, yes. I've heard about your kept women. But aren't they *paid* to...to—to...make you feel like a man?"

"Bloody nonsense. Now hush, princess. You've no idea what you're saying. You are too innocent to know about such things."

Topaz was tempted to prove he was wrong, but someone tapped her on the shoulder and she turned round to face Major Vonnegut.

"Good evening, Miss Thackery. Emerald has just told me that there is a pending announcement of your betrothal."

Arthur's shining face reminded Topaz of an apple-cheeked boy who had just been offered a sweet. He slapped the major on the back. "Good news, eh what, Major? The Kestersons have said they will send the announcement off to the papers in the morning."

"Congratulations, my boy. You're a lucky fellow, to be sure. And my best wishes to you, Miss Thackery. I hope that you will be very happy." He clicked his heels and bowed just as Aunt Prudence approached from behind him.

Topaz sighed. "Here comes trouble."

Major Vonnegut turned. "Indeed. But what-ho. The old gel just needs someone to sweeten her up."

"And you think you can do that, Major Vonnegut?" Topaz asked, shaking her head. "I know you are renowned for your charm, but I don't think even you are that winning."

He had no time to respond because Prudence was upon them. "Oh, there you are, Major. I've been searching for you in the garden." She lifted a lorgnette that hung from a ribbon round her neck and stared at his green-and-gold embroidered waistcoat. "I see that you have yet another coat that is fit to be worn only by a peacock."

"And you, my dear Prudence, are as usual hiding your beauty under a gown that must have been designed for deep mourning. But never mind. I am quite capable of seeing through your disguise. And, I might add, I am quite flattered that you have seen fit to pursue me." He offered her his arm. "Shall we find some place where we may speak in private?"

No one could overlook the sparkle of mischief in his eyes, nor the reflection of outrage in hers. She sputtered, "I have no intention of going anywhere with you, least of all a place where we are alone. The butler has asked me to relay a message from your driver. There seems to be something amiss with your horses."

"Thank you. I suppose I must attend to it. But mark my words, dear lady, next time I shan't let you off so easily."

Her response was an unladylike snort.

Arthur spoke. "May I be of some assistance, Major?"

"Not necessary, thank you, my boy. If you will excuse me."

"Beastly man," Prudence said as he walked away. "And unbelievably irritating." She forced a smile. "But don't let me keep you. I can see that you were greeting the latecomers."

"As a matter of fact, Arthur has asked me to go for a drive as soon as I speak to her ladyship and find Sally," Topaz said, then regretted it instantly.

"Udora is on the far side of the room. As for Sally, I have no idea where she might be. Lazy girl. Never there when you want her." Prudence cocked her head. "But if you wish, I shall be happy to serve as your chaperon."

Topaz patted Prudence's arm. "You are too kind, but I did promise Sally that I would ask her to go with me if I went out this evening."

"Oh. Very well, then. Have a pleasant drive." She waved her fan and inclined her head in dismissal.

Arthur gave Topaz a curious look. "You're the sly one, aren't you now? I heard that you loved to keep people on their toes, and if that wasn't a bald-faced lie, then I'm a three-headed toad."

"Oh, don't be silly. My abigail is always eager to accompany me."

"Not what I heard, princess. And if you're clever, you will employ an abigail whose favourite pastime is something other than gossip. You know, don't you, that nice young ladies don't go driving down St. James's Street at this time of night?"

"Hush. Here comes Lady Udora."

Thanks to her preoccupation with other matters, Udora paid scant attention to Topaz's request beyond noting that Arthur would escort her and that Sally would accompany them in the carriage as chaperon. She even smiled when she gave them her permission to leave.

Topaz slowly let out her breath as she followed her abigail up the step and into the carriage, then grinned when Arthur settled onto the green plush seat across from her. "That was easy, wasn't it? If it weren't for you, Arthur, I would have been confined to my room for at least a week."

He seemed to glow with pride. "You see? I told you months ago that you and I were meant for each other."

"Well, I wouldn't go that far."

"At least you accepted my proposal."

"Arthur, you must know that it wasn't by choice that I agreed to it. I am not ready to marry."

He reached across and seized her hand. "You only think you aren't. Give me two weeks and I'll have you begging to marry me."

She laughed in spite of herself. "You don't lack for confidence, do you?"

"Not where females are concerned. But look, we are almost there. Unless I miss my guess, we'll see a dozen or more roustings before it's time to take you home."

Sally made a sound and Topaz looked over at her. "What is it? Are you all right?"

"Blimey! It ain't me, it's them. The rousters. If 'twas me I'd send 'em all to the 'angman."

Arthur threw his head back and laughed. "What nonsense. It's all in fun, Sally. Just good clean fun. No one ever gets hurt. Well, at least not seriously."

The sounds of shouting drew their gaze to the windows of the carriage, and the driver automatically slowed down.

"Look," Arthur said, drawing Topaz's attention to a group of six smartly dressed young rakes who were standing outside the men's club. "They're waiting. Look, here comes a pair. Now watch."

"You mean those two young men who look as if they are into their cups?"

"Yes, now watch." He called to the driver. "Pull over to the side, Joseph, and stop."

The carriage had just come to a stop when the group of dandies linked their arms and blocked the sidewalk, thereby forcing the two young men to take to the street. Not content with forcing them off the walk, they crowded them even further until they were endangered by a passing carriage.

"Dirty bastards," Sally muttered.

Topaz looked in disbelief at Arthur, who seemed to be thoroughly enjoying himself.

"Look," he said. "Here comes another one."

CHAPTER FOUR

THIS TIME IT WAS an old man laden with several bundles. The young bucks spotted him almost immediately and took up their positions against the wall.

He apparently sensed that something was amiss, because he halted for a moment, adjusting his load to the other shoulder and leaning his weight on his walking-stick. Then, when the rousters didn't move, he proceeded toward them.

Just as he approached, the group, as if on a given signal, strolled casually over to surround him. One of them jabbed him from behind with a cane while another grabbed a package from the man's hand.

Arthur chuckled. "That should teach him not to be about at night."

"I've seen enough, Arthur. We must help him."

"What? You can't be serious. Why would we want to do that?"

"If you have to ask..."

The man was struggling now, but ineffectually, against his opponents. Topaz was livid. Half standing, she reached over and opened the carriage door. Arthur tried to grasp her but she pushed him aside. "Let me go, I've got to do something. Give me your walking-stick."

"Not likely. It's my ruby-and-diamond stick."

She ignored him, and before he could stop her, Topaz had leaped from the carriage and was running full tilt into the fray. "Get away from him! Leave him alone, you cowards," she shouted, all the while brandishing Arthur's walking-stick over her head.

"Hold on, lads, it looks like a lady. By jove! Miss Thackery, is that you?" someone called in disbelief.

"Yes, it's me. And who the devil are you?" She was all but surrounded by them. Arthur had, at least, followed after her, with Sally only a short distance behind him.

"You, Lord Paxton, and you, Clifford Brimmley, and you, Lord Chafford, and the rest of you. Is this the kind of thing you do to make yourselves feel like men? Six of you against one old man? How disgusting! How utterly obscene. Go on now. Get back into the club or go home. If you don't I shall tell your mothers what you're doing."

It did not seem to occur to anyone that they were all at least a good five years older than she. They grumbled a little, then turned and walked away.

Arthur took her arm. "Do come along. You've made enough of a fool of yourself for one night. They meant no harm to the old man. It was all in good fun. They never really do anything wrong." He was clearly displeased.

"Is that so, Arthur? Then what, may I ask, has happened to your walking-stick? Someone pulled it from my hand and now it's gone."

"The devil you say! They actually stole it!"

"Ridiculous. 'They never do anything wrong,'" Topaz said. She turned to pick up the bundles that had fallen into the gutter and handed them to the old man.

"Are you all right, sir? Have they injured you?"

"I'm quite all right, miss. A bit shaky, p'rhaps, but none the worse for wear, thanks to you." He scratched his beard. "Topaz Thackery, is it? I'll remember your name, miss, for the jewel that ye are. Thank you for helping an old man."

"May we drive you to your destination?"

"No. That won't be necessary. I have just a little way to go now," he said, doffing his cap. Arthur handed the man his cane and he walked away.

Then Arthur turned to Topaz and laughed uneasily. "Well, princess, the evening hasn't turned out quite the way I anticipated, but it was a good one. Rousted the rousters, we did. What a coup. But you know you're going to be fodder for scandal if word gets out."

"I doubt that any one of them will find it necessary to brag about the evening's events." Topaz looked at Arthur's face, knowing his penchant for gossip. "And if you breathe a word of this to anyone, especially my guardian, I shall see that you walk with a limp from now on. The same goes for you, Sally."

Arthur threw his head back and laughed.

Sally's face was pale. "I wouldn'a laugh if I was you, m'lord. She means what she says."

"Hell-fires and hornets! I love a woman with spirit," Arthur said as he helped them into the carriage. Topaz was appalled when he gave her an almost-imperceptible pat on the behind. But then it could have been her imagination, she decided, and chose to say nothing. Quite possibly her behaviour had triggered his less-than-proper gesture.

THE FOLLOWING AFTERNOON Udora and the girls were seated in the drawing-room discussing plans for the three impending weddings. Udora dropped the magazine she was reading on a low table. "I simply haven't seen a single design for a wedding gown that would be suitable for any one of you." She sighed. "Much as I am looking forward to the events, I somehow do not have the stamina I once had."

Emerald tilted her head. "It is not as if you were still a young girl, my lady. You did, after all, turn thirty this year."

Udora shot her a quelling glance. "I am hardly in my dotage, Miss Bluestocking. I'll have you know that I am quite equal to any situation that might arise."

The words were hardly out of her mouth when the new girl, Betty, knocked on the door, entered and curtsied.

"Yes, what is it, Betty?" Udora asked.

"Beggin' your pardon, mum, but McMasters says as 'ow I should tell you there's a nob what wants to speak wi' Miss Topaz about the man whose life she saved last night."

"*She what?*"

"About the man whose . . ."

"Oh, be still, Betty." Udora swung round to face Topaz, who somehow managed not to shrink down into her chair. "What have you done now, child? I thought you went for a short drive in Arthur's carriage last night."

"And so we did. I can't imagine what this person is talking about. I assure you, all that happened was that we chanced to see a small commotion where some young rakes were annoying an old man and we asked them to leave him alone.''

A deep voice interrupted from the doorway. ''That isn't quite the way it was told to me, Miss Thackery.''

As one, the four women turned toward the door to see Lord Colby standing there, legs spread, both hands resting on the curved handle of his walking-stick. ''Forgive me for intruding. I was afraid that you would refuse to see me after our unfortunate meeting two days ago.''

Lady Udora rose. ''You assumed correctly, Lord Colby. I rather thought we had seen the last of your family. May I ask the purpose of your unannounced call?'' No one could miss the irritation in her voice. ''And what nonsense is this about Topaz having saved a man's life?''

''If I may enter?''

''It seems you have already done so,'' she said coldly. ''But yes, do come in and be seated.'' She motioned to an uncomfortable-looking chair set some distance away from their little gathering, waited for him to sit, then took her own seat.

Colby stiffened his face to keep from smiling. He liked Udora Bently despite her icy demeanour toward him. Behind that cold exterior he sensed a woman of humour and vitality. It was no wonder she had attracted five husbands and lived to bury them all, save the one to whom she was currently married.

''Do speak up, Lord Colby. I can hardly wait to hear this latest on dit.''

''It is much more than gossip, my lady, or I vow I would not be here to speak of it.'' He looked over at Topaz, who returned his look with such blazing anger that he had to catch his breath. He blinked. Why was she so distressed? Had she not told her guardian of her most recent adventure? Of course she had not!

Now he had done it. He had come with the intention of giving praise where praise was due and he was about to cause a confrontation. He stood abruptly. "Now that I think on it, my lady, it seems I must have confused Miss Topaz with someone else. If you will be so good as to excuse me, I'll take my leave."

"Sit down, Colby!"

He did so before her words died in the air. The three girls gasped, but Udora paid them no mind. "Now then, Lord Colby. Would you be so good as to continue with what you were saying?" She put it in such a way that no one could have possibly considered it anything but an order.

Colby blew air through his mouth, looked apologetically at Topaz, and adjusted his cravat. "If you insist, Lady Udora."

"I do. Please get on with it."

"Yes, madam. It was this way. My man, Walter Soames, had gone down to St. James's Street to pick up some things I had delivered to the club. Soames was on his way back to the flat where I was visiting friends when he was accosted by a group of young rousters."

No one spoke as he recounted the story, leaving out not one small detail of Topaz's assault on the old man's persecutors. He dared not look at Topaz. Even without seeing her expression, he could sense the anger radiating from her person. It excited him. His own life was so routine that he could hardly remember the last time he had felt so completely alive. But from the moment he first saw her drifting by in David's balloon, Colby had sensed that something inside him had changed. Now, simply being in her presence caused a heady rush of energy. Somehow he managed to drag his thoughts back to Lady Udora, who peered at him with considerable scepticism.

"I cannot believe that Arthur would allow Topaz to involve herself in such a mélée."

Colby spoke sharply. "And I cannot believe that Arthur Ringwald did nothing to assist her."

Udora gave him a measured look. "As I suppose you would have done, sir?"

Colby inclined his head. "We shall never know, shall we, madam?"

Lady Udora appeared taken aback for an instant, but she regained her composure and responded, "One would hope not, though I dare say, with a charge as impulsive and inconsiderate as mine—" she nodded toward Topaz "—one can hardly promise anything."

Topaz started to speak, but Udora silenced her with a look. Lord Colby hastened to fill the brief silence.

"Impulsive it might have been, Lady Udora, but had it not been for Miss Thackery's immediate compassion for an old man, Mr. Soames might well have died last night. And he would not have been the first one to fall victim to what started out as entertainment for a group of young rowdies."

"Thank you so much for letting us know of this untoward incident, my lord. I am grateful that your servant was unharmed, but at the same time, one can hardly condone my charge's behaviour.

"You have done me a favour, sir. I prefer to hear these things in private, rather than have them revealed to me by some harpy who can't wait to embarrass the family in public." She arranged her shawl and collected her skirts. "If there is nothing else, Lord Colby, then I will bid you good-day."

She rose and he followed suit. He stood uncertainly for a moment, then looked over at Topaz and back again to Lady Udora.

"I was hoping, your ladyship, that I might speak with Miss Thackery before I go."

"I don't think that is wise, sir, under the circumstances. You may not have yet heard that my ward has only last night become betrothed to Arthur Ringwald."

Colby's gaze flew across the room to collide with Topaz's wide eyes. The look hung in the air, for so intense was the moment that not one person dared breathe.

Colby's face turned ashen. When he spoke, his voice was soft and measured. "And when is the wedding to be, if I may enquire?"

Udora, sounding uncharacteristically subdued, pressed her palms together. "Soon, I hope. As yet no date has been set, but I rather imagine it will be sometime in the Autumn. During the Little Season, perhaps. September."

"I see. May I offer my best wishes, Miss Thackery, and once again give you my thanks. Now, if you will excuse me, I shall be on my way. No need to see me to the door."

He was gone before anyone could comment.

The room was silent until they heard the murmur of McMasters's voice and the sound of the front door being closed. Then Udora turned toward Topaz and was about to speak when Topaz rose, grasped the side of her skirt in one hand and fled from the room.

Amethyst jumped up. "Did you see? Taz was weeping! She never cries, not even when she cuts her hand. We must go to her."

Udora stopped her with a look. "Not now, my dear. Later we must try to console her, but for now she needs to be alone."

"*I* would want someone to talk to. *I* would want to be comforted."

Emerald considered her twin sister over the top of her spectacles. "You always do, Amy. Taz is different. We all know that." She turned her attention to Udora with a curious look. "Are you going to punish her for this latest escapade?"

Udora threw up her hands. "At this point I have not the least idea what to do with the girl. I've run out of ways to punish her. Nothing seems to work."

Emerald nodded. "Because there's nothing my sister really wants except her freedom. Betrothing her to Arthur was the worst punishment you could devise."

Udora looked genuinely surprised. "Oh, surely not. You don't really mean that, Emerald. Topaz doesn't dislike Arthur, she's admitted as much, and in time, I'm sure she will come to love him."

Amy cocked her head as if pondering the solution. "Maybe not until he gives her a son. After that she cannot help but fall in love with Arthur."

Emerald rolled her eyes to the ceiling. "Must everything revolve around babies, Amy? There are times when I doubt that we are even related, not to mention twins."

Udora stood. "Enough of this. We have much to do. There is the Kennilworth party in a few days, and of course your trousseaus to consider. I told Bently that we would visit the feather merchants today to look for trims for your new bonnets." She sighed. "So much to do and so little time."

UPSTAIRS IN HER BEDROOM, Topaz slammed her fist into the feather pillow. What was happening to her? She never cried—not even when the twins used to tease her unmercifully about who her parents might be. She was determined not to let them know how much she cared.

But now she had done it. And what was worse, she did not even know why the tears had sprung so quickly and uncontrollably to her eyes.

Devil take Colby for interfering. He must have known that she didn't want him there, for at one point he had started to leave, but Udora had stopped him. It would have been far better if he had never come.

What was it about him that stirred her senses until her brain was a jumble of passions she was ill-equipped to understand? For it was true: Peter Endicott, Lord Colby, unsettled her as no one had ever done.

Topaz sat up and dried her tears. The realization came as a surprise to her. Arthur, although he was essentially likeable, had never wreaked such havoc on her emotions. Being with him was like being softly smothered in a feather bed. He enveloped her in a feeling of blandness, of knowing that if she did his bidding she would be protected from the harsh realities of life and every day would be much like the day before. The thought of spending the rest of her life with him was inconceivable. But it was too late now, wasn't it? Soon everyone would know of their betrothal.

Perhaps Udora was right. In time she might come to love him. In time, she might find peace, and a respite from her turbulent longings. A welcome peace, she decided, for the emptiness inside her was far too complicated for her to begin to understand...or to endure for very much longer.

A little while later she heard the twins talking in Emerald's room. Topaz washed her face and opened the door that connected their suites. Amy looked up from the dressing-table, a worried expression on her face.

"Are you all right, Taz? Her ladyship wouldn't let us disturb you."

"I'm quite all right, thank you."

"But you were crying. You never cry."

Topaz forced a grin. "I had to do something, didn't I? Lady Udora was about to send me off to a nunnery."

Amy looked dumbfounded. "Then this was just a charade? Your tears, everything?"

"Of course, silly. Did you for a moment believe otherwise?"

"I...I thought that perhaps you were thinking about David and how much you love him...and how her ladyship was forcing you to marry Arthur."

"I'm not in love with David. I love the excitement of being with him and flying in his balloon," Topaz said thoughtfully, "but David is like a brother to me."

"Then what made you cry?"

"I already told you, did I not? Now stop being such a ninnyhammer and help me decide what to wear this afternoon. Lady Udora says I must accompany her to the modiste to select trimmings for the gown I'll be wearing to the Kennilworth ball."

Amy immediately started discussing the merits of various gowns, but Emerald, who had been changing her slippers, gave Topaz a knowing look. Topaz sighed. One could rarely deceive Emerald.

LORD COLBY WAS SO LOST in thought that he was hardly aware that his carriage had arrived at Ridgeview Manor until it came to a halt at the front entrance. Once inside he gave his cloak over to Rengsdorf, his butler, and started toward the library.

Rengsdorf, having followed him, waited until he was seated at his desk, then enquired, "May I bring you something to eat, my lord, or have you already dined?"

"What? Oh, no, thank you. Nothing. I'm not hungry."

"Yes, sir. Then if there's nothing else, I'll attend to my duties."

"Just...just a moment, Rengsdorf. My mail. Where is it?"

"Right there, my lord. Next to the model of the barquentine."

"No, not my business mail. I mean the other."

"If you mean the invitations, sir—" Rengsdorf looked properly surprised "—I boxed them with the others until you are ready to dispose of them. Would you like me to fetch the lot for you, my lord?"

"Yes, do that, if you would."

Rengsdorf went to the closet and took a box from the shelf. It was a small box, Colby noted, but that made sense. Since he never bothered to attend any of the multitude of parties that took place during the Season, and in fact rarely bothered to respond to the invitations he received, Society had all but given up on him. And he had been content with its decision.

Until now. He thumbed through the neatly filed envelopes of heavy linen paper until he saw the one he was looking for.

"Aha! I'm in luck," he said as he unfolded the single, gold-embossed sheet and quickly scanned the page.

"Sir?"

"Come back in about ten minutes, Rengsdorf. I'd like you to dispatch a messenger with my reply."

"You're not planning to attend, are you, Lord Colby?"

"Yes, I believe I am."

Rengsdorf smiled. "I'm glad to hear that, sir. Very glad. It will do you good to join in the festivities for a change."

"Well, we shall see about that, now, shan't we?" Colby stretched his legs into a more comfortable position and began to make plans.

THAT NIGHT AT DINNER, Colby looked at his brother who was seated across from him in the spacious dining-room, and had second thoughts about having accepted the invitation to the Kennilworth party. He was never one to act on impulse. But now it was too late to back down. *Damned awkward,* he thought. To be fair, it should be David who would be the guest. But then he had an inspiration.

"David," he said, laying his spoon down on the plate next to the bowl of green turtle soup. "How would you like to attend a party on Friday at the Kennilworth House in Grosvenor Square?"

David laughed. "I'd far rather face a hangman at dawn."

"I remember your mentioning to me that the Thackery girls will be attending."

"Of course. That would be the one good thing about it. All three of the girls are quite charming. Even Emerald, who is rather bookish for my taste, though she managed to bag herself a marquess." He grinned. "My thanks, brother, but I prefer to spend my time mending the tears in my silk."

Colby coiled his hand round a goblet half filled with water. "Has it ever occurred to you, David, that if you curried favour with some of the moneyed nobles, you could generate enough interest in your work that you might eventually find someone to sponsor your flights? Then you could have done with the inferior materials you've been forced to use."

"It is something to consider. But the price! It's devilish boring sipping stale sherry with the ton and listening to their stories of running to hounds, or losing a fortune at the turn of a card."

"It can't be all that dull, not with Topaz and the other debutantes dancing attendance on you."

David grinned. "Nothing is ever dull when Topaz is there."

Colby's fingers tightened on the stem of the goblet he was holding. "You love her, don't you?"

"Love her? Of course I do. Everyone does." David leaned his head back and gazed at the ornate ceiling. "She's like a vial of mercury, fluid of motion, with that silvery hair of hers. I've never met another female like her."

"Nor I," Colby murmured. In that instant the stem of the goblet snapped and a shard of glass pierced his hand. "Double damnation. I've broken it."

"Devil take the goblet. It's just a piece of glass. You have cut your hand. It's bleeding."

"The cut is nothing. But the goblet was priceless. One of a dozen given to the family by the fifth duke of Devonshire. The set is a part of our family inheritance."

David speared a kipper from a serving bowl. "Forgive me if I'm not impressed. If it were mine, I'd sell the set and a few other choice pieces and begin construction on a gondola, like the one the Montgolfier brothers used when they flew their balloon over the Channel."

Colby shook his head. "God forbid that you should ever inherit the title. You'd put the house up for sale in two days' time."

"I just might at that. I have never kept it a secret that possessions and creature comforts mean little to me. If I were you, brother mine, I would make damn certain I spawned a son if I wanted to protect the family holdings from someone like me." He smiled when he said it, then lit his cheroot from the candelabrum at the end of the table and leaned back in his chair. Through the puff of grey smoke Colby saw the look in David's eyes. There was no laughter to echo the smile on his face. David had meant what he said.

Colby tightened the handkerchief he had wrapped round his hand. "Thank you for the warning, David. I shall do my best to use it to my advantage. Now, about the Kennilworth party. I have already sent our acceptance."

"Presumptuous of you. You don't give up easily, do you?" He leaned forward and stabbed out his cheroot in a Dresden cup. "Very well, since you've committed us to attending... But I warn you, don't expect to change me. I'll not become a house pet for anyone's sake, not even yours, Peter."

Colby slowly let out his breath. It was too late. It was done. He had set the cart in motion. Only the gods in their wisdom could predict what the outcome would be. For the briefest moment he regretted that he had made the choice. Regretted that he must face the inevitability of seeing David and Topaz laughing together as he held her in his arms for the dance. Unbidden, a vision of Topaz lying on the bed upstairs drifted through his mind, and he knew that nothing, no one, could have kept him from seeing her again. No one except David.

David broke into his reverie. "I trust that the Kestersons were not too overset by the little incident with the balloon?"

Colby frowned. "It has been two days since then, David. I wondered when you would get around to expressing your concern over her."

David looked sheepish. "It's not that I wasn't concerned. I have had too much to think about. The *Gypsy* was nearly destroyed when we crashed up on the hillside. Since I knew you were looking after Topaz, and I knew that she had not been seriously injured, I decided she was in good hands. I did speak to her, if you remember.''

''Then you haven't heard that her guardians have betrothed her to Lord Throckmorton.''

''The devil you say! Arthur Ringwald!'' David pushed back a lock of hair from his forehead. ''She could have done worse, I suppose. Arthur is a pudding cake, but flush in the pockets and already into his title. God help the man, though. Topaz will have him under her thumb before the ink is dry on the marriage contract.''

''And where does that leave you?''

David looked surprised. ''Did you think I intended to marry her? Not likely! I could never afford to take care of her. She's used to the finer things in life.''

''But she loves you, I think.''

''Of course she does,'' David said with a mischievous grin. ''How could she not?''

''Then you intend to continue seeing her?''

''I seem to have very little to say in the matter. She follows me like a lost sheep. Whenever I'm at the field working on my balloon, she appears, she and her little abigail, Sally. That's not to say I discourage her. Topaz is amusing, and a good sort, considering that she's a female.'' He crossed his legs and sat sideways to the table.

''Why all the questions, Peter? You sound strangely interested in my morals. Or is it Topaz who interests you?'' he asked with a sudden keen expression in his eyes.

''Topaz? Don't be absurd. She is an upstart. A rebel child. Why would I be even the least bit interested in a chit who is so determinedly outrageous?''

David nodded. "Why indeed. But I must say, brother of mine, that it has been months, maybe even years, since I've seen that look of moral indignation or...or something...on your face. I wonder if you are protesting too much."

CHAPTER FIVE

ARTHUR CALLED FOR TOPAZ promptly on the night of the Kennilworth party. She had to admit that he cut a dashing figure among the well-dressed party-goers. His coat was made of the finest cloth and his high starcher was arranged in the latest style, *en casade.*

And, to give him credit, he looked upon her with equal approval. As well he might, she decided. After all, Amethyst and Emerald, as well as Lady Udora, had spent the better part of an afternoon making certain that she was at her best. "Everyone will be watching you now that news of your betrothal has become known," Udora had said.

They finally settled upon a green Flanders lace gown embroidered with pink-and-yellow flowers and darker green leaves. The bare-shouldered bodice revealed rather more bosom than Topaz felt comfortable showing, but they assured her it was the latest style. Nevertheless, she added a brilliant pink feather boa for the sake of modesty.

It occurred to her that Lord Colby had seen more of her by the simple act of undoing her gown than this *décolletage* revealed. But that had bothered her far less than exposing this less intimate glimpse to Arthur. She was hard put to understand her own feelings.

Aunt Prudence was more than pleased when Topaz added the feather boa. Prudence had agreed to attend the party, with Major Vonnegut as her escort, only because Topaz was in need of a chaperon. The major wore a magnificent white cutaway overlaid with silver braid and beaded with pearls. Prudence, as always, wore tombstone grey.

The moment the butler announced the Kesterson entourage, everyone turned in their direction. The admiration and envy Topaz saw in their eyes was quite understandable. She and Arthur did make an attractive pair, and Arthur was considered one of the Season's most sought-after catches.

Then, of course, there was still the gossip that surrounded Prudence's return from the Colonies after having been sent away nearly eighteen years ago. One rarely outlived the scandal of giving birth to a merrybegotten child.

Topaz made an effort to smile when their hostess greeted them.

"So you've gone and done it, have you, Arthur? You're a lucky man to have landed one of the Thackery Jewels." Lady Kennilworth had obviously emptied her precious gems chest for the occasion. She glittered, from the top of her diamond-sprinkled hair to the toes of her jewelled slippers. Her beringed hand fluttered over to rest on Arthur's arm.

"What a splash these girls have made this Season," she said, then pursed her lips into a pout. "But I do so regret that it wasn't my dear niece, Abelia, whom you chose. Had she been selected to carry on your line she would most certainly have died of pleasure."

Topaz flashed a wide smile. "My goodness. We can't have her doing that, now can we?"

Lady Kennilworth laughed, albeit rather weakly, and turned her attention to the major. "Such a pleasure to see you again, Major Vonnegut."

He bowed over her hand. "The pleasure is all mine, my lady. I believe you have met Miss Prudence Thackery, recently returned from the Colonies?"

"We have indeed met." Lady Kennilworth's frigid smile barely disturbed one wrinkle on her face. "Well, do find yourselves something to eat. Or you may prefer to dance or join the others in the card room." She laughed giddily. "Such a crush! Can you imagine so many people coming to my party? I confess, I know less than half of them by name."

Arthur chuckled as she walked away. "Needless to say, she must have collected names from the official register. No wonder she doesn't know her guests." He smoothed his prematurely thinning hair across his scalp. "Never could understand why the number of people attending was the measure of success for this sort of party."

"I've heard that some matrons even go so far as to dress their servants as guests to make their party look more sought-after," Topaz said. "But nearly everyone here looks familiar." Her gaze travelled round the room, then came to rest on the two men who had just recently arrived. She caught her breath. There was no need for her to hear their names when they were announced. She knew who they were.

Arthur stared coldly across the room. "What the devil is Colby and his young pup of a brother doing here? You can be sure they weren't invited."

"Why ever not?" Topaz wondered aloud. "David is a fascinating man, and Lord Colby is...is quite presentable," she said for lack of a safer description.

"But they're not our sort. Neither of them frequents the better clubs or participates in games of chance. Nor are they ever invited to the parties of the Upper Ten Thousand. They're outsiders, my sweet. Better to stay away from them."

Still, no sooner had Colby and David arrived than they were surrounded by matrons set on making an alliance for their daughters. Topaz was unaccountably annoyed. She was about to respond to Arthur's unwanted advice when a quelling glance from Prudence stopped the words before they were spoken.

Prudence lifted her quizzing glass. "If they approach you, my child, just give them the cut direct."

"I'll do no such thing. David is a good friend. Neither could I insult his brother by such an offensive action. The least we can do is behave in a civil manner."

"Then perhaps we should take our departure before an untoward incident occurs. You see! He's looking at you. The older one! Didn't I tell you! I vow they will descend upon us in minutes."

The major looked amused. "My dear Prudence, there is little those two could do to compromise Topaz, considering that the room is crowded with people. We've only just arrived. It would be an insult to Lady Kennilworth if we were to leave so early."

"Humph. The only reason you refuse to leave, Major Vonnegut, is that you would miss the attention you receive from the widow ladies who have been hanging on to your coattails from the moment we arrived."

The major grinned. "Are you jealous, my dear Prudence?"

"Don't flatter yourself, sir. I was only commenting on the fact that because you insist on dressing like a peacock you always manage to attract the hens."

"A little colour might work wonders for you as well, Prudence. And why not? You've no call to be in mourning. Bishop's blue or pistachio green would complement the beauty you try so hard to hide."

Prudence blushed. "Your opinions do not amuse me, sir. I suggest we search out the refreshments lest we become rooted to the spot like one of Lady Kennilworth's shoddy rubber trees."

Major Vonnegut, agreeable as always, directed them toward the refectory where a long table was laid with all manner of cold collations.

For some reason Topaz had lost her usually healthy appetite. The salmon mousse tasted pasty. The chilled pheasant in almond aspic was anything but chilled, and the apricot tarts were tough and flavourless.

Additional tables were arranged end to end so that the party-goers could be seated while they enjoyed their food and conversation. Most of the tables were well filled, but Arthur directed them to one that was nearly empty.

They seated themselves in a row, with Prudence and Topaz in the middle. Topaz leaned forward to see if she recognized anyone at the other end of the long table. Lady Breckenridge, everyone's favourite, was seated beside Lady Cowper. They both smiled and waggled their fingers. Lady Breckenridge then looked at Arthur and inclined her head in a more formal greeting. She was attractive for an older woman.

Only once had Topaz set eyes on her sisters, who had arrived together with their fiancés in another carriage. But to be truthful, she knew she was not looking for them. It was Colby she wanted to see, and David, of course. Only because she had never seen them dressed in formal attire, she told herself. It was nothing but curiosity.

When they appeared a few minutes later, she was taken completely by surprise. David and Colby, accompanied by the Albright sisters, were headed directly for her table.

"Can you believe it, Aunt Prudence?" Topaz whispered. "Cornelia and Althea Albright have already set their caps for David and his brother."

Prudence squinted at them. "Serves the gels right. They're dressed like a pair of hoydens with nothing above the waist left to the imagination."

David waved to Topaz. "Aha. There you are. We were wondering where you had got to."

Althea shot him a murderous look, which he apparently didn't see. Cornelia, her purple turban slightly askew, plopped down in a chair between David and Colby.

Colby silently complimented himself for the way he had slipped unobtrusively into the chair directly across the table from Topaz. Lucky for him, Cornelia Albright was an amiable chit. He hadn't wanted to make a scene, but he would have, if necessary. At the same time he cursed himself for his weakness in wanting to sit where he could face Topaz without turning his head. It was as if she had cast a spell over him. This strange compulsion was like a fever burning inside him.

Even David, usually so intent on thoughts of his balloon that he was unaware of anything else, had noticed his brother's moodiness. Colby had tried to laugh it off, but the mood prevailed. Now, seeing Topaz so close but still beyond reach, Colby was reminded that he had no claim on her and never could have. Because of David, of course. Arthur Ringwald was little more than a temporary annoyance who would never succeed in tempting Topaz to his bed. She was too intelligent to waste her life on a gamester like Arthur.

Seeing her like this felt like a knife being twisted in his side. He watched as she speared a piece of sausage and popped it into her mouth. Her lips glistened from the broth, and when her tongue darted out to lick them, Colby squirmed in his seat.

Topaz pushed the food around on her plate and then selected a bit of cauliflower. He watched, fascinated.

It didn't take her long to realize he had been staring at her. She put her fork down and leaned forward. "Are you not dining this evening, Lord Colby?"

He glanced down at his nearly full plate and hastily collected his wits. "On the contrary, Miss Thackery. I am quite enjoying myself. You must try the Russian caviar," he said, reaching across the table with a square of toast on which he had spread a liberal quantity of the delicacy. She blinked twice, then steadied his wrist with her hand while she took a small bite.

Her eyes had opened wide when she touched him, but as she chewed, her nose wrinkled and she leaned back in her chair. "I...I am not certain I find it to my taste. It is very new to me."

"Indeed. But one can easily acquire a taste for new things," he said before placing the remaining bit of food in his own mouth.

Prudence gasped at the subtle implication, but Topaz continued to watch him, and he could have sworn that she was as aware as he was of the mystical connection between them.

He had been shaken by a surge of desire when her fingers grasped his wrist. He knew by the way her pupils dilated that she had almost certainly recognized his need. Not only that, but he sensed that she had, for one brief moment, responded in kind. Perhaps the response was only one of curiosity, but he chose to believe otherwise. Then Arthur, curse the day he was born, said something to her, and her attention was drawn elsewhere.

Cornelia Albright was fortunately so engrossed in her food and the conversation between David and Althea that she was oblivious of the undercurrents between Colby and Topaz.

He fastened his gaze on Topaz's averted face and concentrated as hard as he could to reclaim her attention. Then, as if on command, she stopped in midsentence and turned to face him.

"Did you say something, Lord Colby?"

He exhaled slowly. "I was wondering if you had seen the gardens. The Kennilworths' gardener is quite famous for his roses, so I'm told."

"Not as yet. But I adore roses. If these are a sample," she said, motioning towards the centre-piece, "then I would love to see the rest of them."

Arthur extracted a bit of pheasant from his teeth. "The garden is sure to be damp, what with the rainstorm we had this morning. Make short work of those slippers. Maybe we'll have a go at the dice, eh what? And I hear tell there's a high-stakes game of Faro going on in the card room.''

Colby gave Topaz a hooded look, and her gaze lowered as a bright flush appeared on her cheeks. Colby was captivated by the picture she made, and he ached to know what she was thinking.

Arthur took one look at her, then put down his fork with more than his usual authority and gave Colby a hard stare. ''Come, Topaz. Since you appear to be finished, I think it is time we moved into the card room.''

Topaz was startled by the suddenness of Arthur's suggestion. Indeed it left no room for refusal, although she attempted one. ''Must we? Aunt Prudence and the major have hardly tasted their food.''

Prudence shot a scathing glance at Colby and stiffened. ''I am certain you will be quite safe with your betrothed, Topaz. It is considered quite proper to allow you some time alone. The major and I will join you in a few minutes.''

Arthur rose, and there was little Topaz could do but follow his example, for he was already standing behind her chair. She looked across at David and the two Albright girls, who were involved in a spirited conversation, then, reluctantly, at Colby. ''If you will excuse us.''

Colby rose and David belatedly followed suit.

David stepped backwards in order to see her better. ''I trust you've saved a dance for me on your dance card, Topaz. With Arthur's kind permission, of course.''

Arthur started to protest, but Topaz quickly cut in. "Most certainly, David. A country dance?"

"Perfect."

Topaz expected Colby to make a similar request but he remained silent, which made her more than a trifle irritated. All evening he had been sending seductive signals across the table. Now that he had a chance to act, he seemed to choose the role of the reluctant suitor. She shot him a scornful look, but he appeared unrepentant.

Still, something in his eyes told Topaz that his reluctance was only temporary. He would appear again when she least expected him. She was wondering what it was about him that gave her little *frissons* of excitement whenever he was near, when Arthur took her arm and directed her toward the games room.

The card room was even more crowded than the dining hall. Arthur looked round the tables with growing interest. "I say, there's a bit of everything, isn't there? Would you care to try your hand at Hazard? If you don't know how to play I can teach you in a moment."

"No, thank you, I..."

"See here, it's quite respectable for a lady to play at cards in a private home, you know. Otherwise I wouldn't have suggested it."

"You are most considerate, Arthur, but I prefer to watch."

"Indeed?" He looked round the room and apparently noticed the table where two rows of cards were laid out in front of a series of red-and-black compartments. "I say, what have we here? Perhaps I'll try my hand at Rouge-et-noir. I won a small fortune at Fielden's on Bennet Street last month.''

He smiled and patted her arm. "With you standing behind me to bring me luck, I'm sure to break the bank.''

There were more than a few women indulging themselves in the pastime of cards. Lady Gresham, dressed in bright purple, was having a run of luck. Lady Baldridge had also amassed a pile of chips at another table. Her excitement had drawn a crowd of onlookers who cheered each time she threw the dice.

As for Arthur, he could not have been more wrong when he said that Topaz might bring him good luck. So quickly was he losing his blunt that he began to hint that Topaz had jinxed him. The dealer had just begun to lay out the cards for the *noir* row when Freddie Grenville approached and whispered something in Arthur's ear.

"You don't say!" Arthur exclaimed, and rose from his chair. "Deal me out, Bledsoe. I'm through with this game for tonight.'' He turned to Topaz. "Freddie tells me there is an E.O. table in Lord Kennilworth's study. I've decided to have a go at it.''

"That's a wheel game, isn't it? I thought they were illegal.''

"Just so. But we won't tell anyone, will we?''

"I've never played at Even-Odd.''

Arthur shifted uncomfortably. "And this isn't a good time for you to start. I wouldn't want to get you in trouble, Topaz. Not the way your luck is running tonight.''

"My luck! But I haven't yet begun to play.''

Arthur looked impatient. "You know what I mean. Run off now and keep Prudence company. I'll be gone only a little while. That's a good girl."

He gave her a little shove toward the doorway where Prudence and the major had just entered. Prudence looked distinctly relieved to see her.

"Where has Arthur gone off to in such a hurry?"

"It seems there is a private game in the study. I think he feels that I've brought him bad luck in the way the cards fell tonight."

The major chuckled. "I say! Found the E.O. wheel, did he? Mark my words, your fiancé will rue the day. Lord Kennilworth is famous for weighting the wheel to favour the house odds."

Prudence frowned. "Are you saying that these people are making money in the guise of entertaining their guests?"

"It's hardly unusual, my dear. If one chooses to gamble, one must be aware of the risks."

"Humph. Utterly despicable. I trust there will not be gambling at the Taggarts' in Brighton when we spend next weekend there."

The major was about to answer when Colby signalled for attention. "Forgive me, Major, if I am interrupting." He turned to Topaz. "I see you are temporarily without escort, Miss Thackery. I recall that you expressed an interest in seeing the Kennilworth roses. May I have the honour of showing them to you?"

Prudence drew herself up to her full stature and pinned him with her gaze. "I think not, Lord Colby. The gardens are far too deserted tonight, thanks to the provided evil of gambling. I prefer that Miss Thackery remain where there are other people present to protect her good name.''

Colby nodded. ''I am certain you are correct, Miss Thackery. Then perhaps Miss Topaz will honour me with a dance? I believe the music is about to begin.''

''Indeed not. Surely you know that my niece is betrothed.''

''But I'm not *dead,* Aunt Prudence. I'll only be away for a few minutes. Tell her it is all right, Major.''

He cleared his throat. ''Put me in the middle of it, would you, you minx? But in all truth, Prudence, I believe Topaz will be quite safe with Lord Colby. He is, after all, a gentleman. Am I not correct, Colby?''

''You have my word on it, sir.''

''Good enough.''

Topaz knew it was a mistake the moment she lifted her eyes to meet Colby's heated gaze. She felt mesmerized by the current that flowed between them. Drawn not quite unwillingly by some force that was new to her, she placed her hand on the arm he offered and allowed him to take control. He led her up the curved stairway to the ballroom on the next floor.

Strains of a waltz drifted toward them, seducing them by the richness of the melody played by a dozen violins. Topaz tensed. She glanced quickly up at Colby, but before she could protest, he patted her hand.

''Don't worry, Topaz. I wouldn't dream of asking you to waltz with me. I know that we haven't requested permission and I would not willingly subject you to further censure.''

He had apparently read her mind. Rather than pleasing her, however, the subtle intrusion had the opposite effect. She thrust out her chin. "You need not take responsibility for my actions, Lord Colby. I have a mind of my own. I am quite capable of making my own decisions. Furthermore, I do not remember having given you permission to use my first name."

He smiled. "I must admit, had it not been for your decision to ride in my brother's balloon, we never would have met and I would not be enjoying this party. As to your other concern, considering the intimate glimpse of your person that reckless decision afforded me, I feel I have the right to call you by your given name."

"Only a beast would bring up my temporary indisposition when David's balloon fell to the ground. Besides, I had no control over the situation. Had I been awake you would never have had the opportunity to lay your hands on me."

"Then I am indeed most grateful that you were unconscious," he said softly, "for that brief glimpse is one I shall treasure for the rest of my life."

Topaz was so shaken that she could do little more than stammer. "I—I believe, Lord Colby, that you have been reading too many romantic novels. Or perhaps you have been shut away too long in the country."

"I think you may be correct, at least about my having kept to myself for too long. I have decided to make up for lost time."

They entered the ballroom with its hundreds of candles shining from a dozen crystal chandeliers. The waltz continued as three score or more couples whirled about the room in a fantasy of brilliant colours and flashing jewels. Colby ushered Topaz to a velvet-covered bench and waited for her to be seated before joining her. Their arrival did not go unnoticed. More than one speculative comment was hidden behind lace fans.

Topaz made it a point to ignore the gossips. "So you've decided to make up for lost opportunities. And why, if I may be so bold, are you wasting your time with me? I am no longer available, as my family would hasten to remind you."

"Your *family* . . . and not you?"

She felt the heat rise in her face. "You know what I mean."

"Of course. The question is, do you?"

"Your insinuations are most despicable, sir."

"I agree, and I must apologize. Suppose we leave it at this. Because, as you so correctly remind me, I have played the hermit for far too long, it occurs to me that what I need is a woman of breeding on whom to practice correct social behaviour."

"And you choose me!" She was so shocked that her voice rose despite her attempt to keep the conversation private.

"Now you've done it. You've caught the eyes as well as the ears of every gossip-monger in London. There will be no escape from their witches' brew if you continue to raise your voice."

Topaz took a deep breath and spoke in a near whisper. "Are you trying to tell me that you are going to risk my reputation while you learn to become proficient at seducing rich and beautiful young debutantes?"

"Who better to learn from? After all, you are well-bred, very popular among the Upper Ten Thousand, and you are betrothed, are you not? You have no need to fear being left on the shelf while you assist me in this worthy endeavour. Nor have you anything to fear from me."

Topaz looked puzzled. "How is it that you make it sound so sensible when I know that it is anything but!"

His smile was enigmatic as he stood and offered his arm. "The waltz has ended. I believe this is our dance."

"But I..." Before she could assemble her thoughts, he had swept her onto the dance floor and they were caught up in a stately quadrille. The tempo changed for each of the five movements, and Topaz was forced to concentrate lest she step on her partner's toes. Nevertheless, it was clear to her that Colby had caught the attention of most of the eligible females on the floor... not to mention several who were not quite so eligible. Lady Ferris, for one, who was well into her thirtieth year and had a brood of five children. When Topaz saw her casting her eyes at Colby, she gave her the cut direct.

The dance was exhilarating, but Topaz couldn't help but wonder what it would be like to be held in Colby's arms as they floated around the room. So enthralled was she that Topaz was hardly aware the music was ending. It was only when the square re-formed and Colby returned to her side that she became attentive. He bowed and thanked her for the dance.

"You looked bemused, Topaz. Of what were you thinking?"

"I... I was thinking about Arthur, of course."

"Forgive me if I don't believe you."

"I beg your pardon!"

"Don't be so quick to anger. I have noticed one thing about you. When you speak of your betrothed, a small frown creases your forehead. There was no frown on your face a moment ago. I saw a look of pure pleasure."

"You have quite an imagination, sir. You would do well to keep your impressions of others to yourself, considering that you are not a successful judge of character."

He bowed and smiled. "Thank you. I stand corrected. Shall we consider that Lesson Number One in your campaign to reform my social behaviour?"

Topaz was flustered. "You assume too much, Lord Colby. I have not agreed to become your tutor."

"But neither have you refused. And," he hastened to add, "I trust that your generosity will not permit you to do so."

Topaz felt the heat rise in her face. She suspected that he was playing a game with her, but she wasn't quite sure enough to give him a proper set-down. "I think perhaps it is time you returned me to my chaperon," she said, giving him a quelling look.

"I would far prefer to share another dance with you."

Topaz was appalled. "You can't be serious. You know very well that to do so would severely compromise my reputation."

He looked amused. "Aha! Lesson Number Two. Then shall we seek out Miss Prudence Thackery? I believe I see her with Major Vonnegut on the far side of the ballroom."

Colby offered his arm, and since she could either accept it or be left standing alone in the middle of the dance floor, she accepted it with a forced smile. As they wended their way toward the spot where Prudence and the major were standing, it was more than apparent to Topaz that people were talking about Colby's attention to her. To her surprise, Prudence, as well as the major, beamed at them.

"What a lovely pair you made on the dance floor, my dears," Prudence said.

Colby bowed to her. "You are most kind, madam, but the credit goes to Miss Thackery, who would make a beggar look like a prince. Having met you, I'm sure she must have inherited some of those qualities from your side of the family."

Prudence, for the moment, looked taken aback, but she managed a pleased smile. "You are too kind, sir, but I take no credit. Topaz, though often willful, has a kind and generous heart."

"Generous, indeed," Colby agreed. "She has just offered to tutor me in the fine art of being a gentleman."

The major guffawed. "Having seen you in action tonight, my boy, I hardly think you require such training."

"I'm sure she spoke in jest," Prudence added.

Topaz turned her shoulder to them and shot Colby a withering look. She knew it would be useless to point out his fracturing of the truth. "If I indeed made such a ridiculous offer, sir, I most certainly withdraw it. Now, if you will excuse me, I must return to my fiancé."

She wasn't aware that she had frowned, but Colby suddenly reached over and drew his finger firmly down between her eyebrows and across the tip of her nose.

"Is that a frown I detect, Miss Thackery?"

"Not at all, sir. I merely have something in my eye."

"Indeed." He moved closer and cupped her chin in his hand. "Let me have a look."

She stepped back quickly, alarmed by what his touch did to her. "Thank you, but it has quite gone away." She steadied herself on the arm of a settee. "And please, do not let us detain you. I believe that is Miss Pendleton waving to you."

"So it is," Colby said, then bowed and walked toward the smirking debutante.

Topaz was more annoyed by his quick departure than she cared to admit. To make it worse, she was not quite sure whether her annoyance stemmed from anger, or from embarrassment at having been abandoned so abruptly.

CHAPTER SIX

TOPAZ WAS BEGINNING to feel like a buffleheaded schoolgirl. She had to do something to get the situation between herself and Colby under her own control. His charm, if one could call it that, had begun to eat away at her composure.

She searched the room for Arthur, but he was nowhere to be seen. His absence was increasingly irksome, in spite of the fact that she had no real wish to be in his company. She did, however, notice David coming toward her with a twittering female clinging to each arm.

Topaz resisted the childish desire to stamp her foot. During all the time when she had been slipping away to see him and his balloon, he had made not the least effort to attend a social function with her. Now that she was betrothed, he had managed to come out of the woodwork and dance attention upon the first pair of dandizettes who happened to cross his path. It wasn't fair.

Of course, in all fairness, she had never invited him to a party, reasoning that he would not be made welcome. But then he had never mentioned the fact that his brother was a marquess. Under those circumstances he would have been most welcome.

When he was able to extract his arm from one of his admirers, he greeted Topaz with a wave of his hand. "So there you are. I wondered where you had got to."

"Yes, I can see that you called in reinforcements to search for me."

He grinned. "I believe you know Miss Fortisham and Miss... Sorry. I don't recall your name."

"Lassiter," she provided. "Priscilla Lassiter."

"Yes, I have met them both," Topaz said, with an emphasis that implied they were green girls straight from the country. "And I am sure that they will excuse us. I wish to speak with you, David."

Both women gave her a cool stare but they acquiesced and moved to stand some distance away.

Topaz fastened him with her gaze. "Now that you've become the reigning buck about Town, I suppose I am no longer welcome to ride in your balloon."

"You will always be my choice for first mate, Topaz, but it will be some time before I can fly again. I've hauled the envelope back to London, and it will take me days to sew the rents in the silk."

"I'm very good at needlework. I'll come tomorrow to help you."

"Do you mean it? I thought perhaps Lady Udora wouldn't let you out of her sight."

"She will be having tea with Lady Breckenridge. I can manage to get away for a while. You aren't expecting anyone else, are you?" she said, staring pointedly at the Misses Fortisham and Lassiter. "Look! They're waiting to snap you up the moment we're finished talking."

"Don't be waspish, Topaz. It doesn't become you. I know you don't care tuppence about me beyond a casual flirtation. Then, too, I've seen that look on your face. It's my brother who has you dancing to his tune."

"Don't be a twit, David. You know very well that I'm betrothed to Arthur."

"At least Arthur thinks so."

"Did I hear someone mention my name?" Arthur enquired.

Topaz whirled round. "Must you do that? You startled me."

"I heard my name mentioned. What was it you said?"

Topaz grasped at the first thing that came to mind. "I was just telling David that the cards were not favouring you tonight."

"Indeed, but Lady Luck led me to the Even-Odds wheel. I chanced to win a few coins despite the tight way in which the wheel was set."

Topaz surveyed him with a dry look. "It seems that Lady Luck is ready with her favours when I am not there to watch."

Arthur shrugged. "Gambling is a man's privilege. I've never believed that a lady should partake of the sport. What is your game, David? Hazard?"

David inclined his head. "I would prefer to risk my life than my money."

Arthur apparently recognized the snub, even though he was not always so astute. "Yes, so I've heard. Your own life, not to mention the lives of others. Come, Topaz. Shall we go upstairs to the ballroom? I'm sorry I neglected you. I wouldn't want to leave the party without your having taken a twirl on the dance floor. I know how much you love to dance.''

Topaz was about to tell him that she had already had her twirl on the dance floor, but for once, she took time to think before she spoke. Lady Udora would have been impressed.

The orchestra was just returning for another set when Arthur led Topaz onto the dance floor. A half-dozen squares were being formed. Arthur chose a place for them across from Lord Bancroft and his lady, Yvette, who had become known as the Lark of Lyon for her lovely singing voice. The other corners had gone to Miss Handsford and Lord Darber, and Lord and Lady Phelps.

Just before the music began, Topaz caught a glimpse of her sisters, who along with their fiancés were part of the square at the far end of the long room. They were laughing and enjoying themselves as no one else in the room seemed to be. But they were in love, Topaz reminded herself. And she was not. Life would be easier for her if she could fall in love with Arthur. Easier for everyone. She would have liked to please Lady Udora by making this a love-match.

Arthur was exuberant, if not skilled, at dancing the quadrille. He whirled her around with such enthusiasm that she was quite breathless. But not too breathless to notice that Colby had entered the ballroom . . . quite unattached. He wouldn't remain so for long, Topaz thought disgustedly, because Charlotte Haverford and her odious aunt Agatha had just accosted him.

Arthur, apparently unaware that she was distracted, swung Topaz over to her next partner, but she missed his hand and was sent crashing into a Grecian urn, sending it catapulting from its pedestal to the floor. Fortunately it didn't break, and the other dancers managed to continue with only a slight interruption.

When the music finally stopped, Arthur looked down at her. "A trifle heavy footed tonight, are you, darling? I suggest we walk a bit and forgo the rest of the set." He offered his arm. "I say, isn't that Lord Beasely over there? Let's go and chat with him for a bit."

They were stopped a number of times before they reached Lord Beasley's side, but when they did, the two men greeted each other like old school chums. She watched them as they discussed with gusto a card game they both had witnessed at White's club. Arthur was by far more handsome than Beasley. His features were rounded and smooth, not craggy and pitted, as Beasley's were.

Colby's face, on the other hand, had sharply chiselled lines that gave him a look of barely leashed power. *Colby!* Why had she suddenly begun comparing everyone to Colby? In the brief time since she had met him he had become like a sliver of wood buried just beneath the surface of her skin: annoying, irritating and constantly drawing her attention. As he had even now. It was his fault that she had knocked over the Grecian urn. She tried not to look at him, but it was beyond her control.

COLBY HAD LOST SIGHT of Topaz for a few minutes during the confusion that followed the incident of the plaster urn. When he finally saw her, she was standing next to Arthur Ringwald and another man near the French doors leading to a balcony.

Colby commanded her to look at him, and by a miracle, she heard the silent message. She turned and their gazes met across the crowded room. He held hers for only a fraction of a second before she turned away, took Arthur's arm and laughed up at him in response to something he said.

Colby cursed his evil luck. Why was he placing himself in this position? The world was full of young, beautiful women. If tonight was any indication, he could pick and choose among them as he pleased. *With one exception,* he bitterly reminded himself.

Unfortunately, playing the role of a profligate blood or, at the very least, a dandy, had no appeal for him. Town life, with its sharp divisions between the rich and the poor, left him feeling unsettled. At best, one was never far removed from the squalor, nor from the ever-present stench of open sewers. In contrast, country air was fresh and pure. Moreover, he made a valiant effort to see that his people were well housed and had the means to grow ample food for their tables.

At the same time, he felt the personal urgency to produce an heir. Otherwise David would be next in line for the title, and he had made it clear that he had no interest in preserving the line. Much as he loved David, Colby knew he could never forsake the sacred trust handed on by the generations of Colbys who had gone before him.

He lounged against a wall that was adorned with an enormous tapestry depicting a Bacchanalian revel. He wondered what it would be like to share such a feast of the senses with Topaz. As if propelled by an invisible current of air, he straightened, adjusted his cravat, and angled his way through the gathering of people on the dance floor.

A quick look assured him that Arthur Ringwald was still deeply involved in conversation with the man in the green velvet waistcoat. Topaz feigned interest in the conversation but she was obviously not a part of it. Colby was acutely aware that her glance constantly sought him out across the room. The knowledge heated the blood in his veins.

She must have sensed that he was going to approach her, because she blinked rapidly and once again grasped Arthur's arm. He looked a little annoyed by the interruption, and brushed her hand away.

At last Colby reached the place where the trio was standing. Topaz glared at him, the two men ignored him until he clicked his heels, bowed and addressed Arthur. "Lord Throckmorton. May I request the pleasure of a dance with your beautiful fiancée?"

"Wh...oh, yes, go right ahead."

Topaz started to protest but Colby had already taken her arm and was leading her onto the floor.

"Of all the unmitigated... Colby, this is outrageous! I have already danced with you this evening. I'll be the object of scandal."

"I was under the impression that a little scandal was of small consequence to you. From what I'm told, you have gone out of your way to flout Society's rules."

"But I am betrothed now. I have reformed."

"And happily so?" Colby smiled. "I think not."

"My happiness is none of your concern. I must do what I think best. One could not ask for a more eligible fiancé than Arthur."

He captured her gaze with his. "One could, you know. With all you have to offer, you could afford to choose. Besides, you are still very young. Do you really look forward to spending the rest of your life with a man such as Arthur Ringwald?"

She lifted her chin and he was entranced by her composure. "You are beginning to sound like a schoolmaster, and not a pleasant one at that. I'll thank you to escort me to my chaperon, Lord Colby. Prudence is standing just over there."

He took her hand once again. "Prudence and the major seem to be enjoying themselves. They deserve this time alone."

"What are you suggesting? That there is an attraction between them? How utterly absurd."

"If you say so. But come. The couples are already in place for a country dance. Leaving now would only create a greater scandal. Perhaps no one has noticed that we danced together earlier tonight."

The violins began with a particularly lively tune called "Milkmaids in the Meadow," and the dancers were immediately caught up in a series of allemandes that swung them from partner to partner.

Colby watched, fascinated, as Topaz sparkled with excitement. It was clear that she loved to dance. He silently thanked his mother for insisting that as a boy, he religiously attend his dance tutor and practise the steps whenever he had an opportunity. Much of his skill he owed to Regina Smythe, who was always an available and willing participant.

The dancers were all quite breathless when it ended. Topaz fanned her face a little too vigorously, but she looked bewitchingly pink cheeked. "That was delightful," she exclaimed. "The best dance I've had tonight. Thank you, my lord."

"It is I who thank you, Topaz. It is by far the best dance I have ever had!" He looked up in time to see Prudence thundering toward them like an ominous grey cloud. "All pleasure aside, I fear that we did not go unnoticed, as I had hoped. Your chaperon approaches."

Topaz sighed. "So I see."

Prudence, followed closely by the major, came to a halt just inches from Topaz. "Just what do you think you are doing, miss? Have you not yet brought down enough scandal on the House of Kesterson that you must further compromise your position by making a spectacle of yourself?"

Colby stepped forward and bowed. "My apologies, Miss Thackery, but I fear the fault is mine. I gave Topaz little choice in accepting another dance. I insisted that she dance with me, and rather than make a scene—as we are doing now, I might add—she obliged me."

Topaz looked up sharply. "He did nothing of the sort. The fault is mine. Had I not chosen to dance with him, I would only have needed to walk off the dance floor. It is that simple."

"I would never have allowed it," Colby said. "The truth is, you had no opportunity to leave without making a fool of yourself."

"I most certainly did. If you think you can tell me what I can and cannot do, you are most definitely all abroad."

Prudence, turning first from one to the other, looked properly confused. "Do you mean to tell me that *both* of you accept the blame?"

"Not at all," Topaz said. "He is simply attempting to save my reputation."

The major cleared his throat. "Interesting. Quite interesting, I must say. But as it stands, Prudence, we are ourselves creating something of a scene by discussing this in public. May I suggest that we continue this at home? It is rather up to her ladyship to sort the matter out, is it not?"

Prudence glanced round her and noted the curious looks being cast in their direction. "Yes, I believe you are correct, Major. Come, Topaz. It is time for you to leave."

Colby inclined his head in acknowledgement. "I would be only too willing to explain everything to her ladyship."

"I think not," Prudence said with an icy glare. "You have already done quite enough."

It was only later, after they had gone, when he looked across the room and saw Arthur chatting with his cronies, that Colby realized Topaz and Prudence had forgotten all about Arthur, who for his part seemed oblivious of their disappearance.

Topaz did not think about her fiancé until they arrived home. The major was about to help her down from the carriage when she straightened, nearly striking her head. "Oh, dear. What have we done? We've gone and left Arthur to cool his heels at the party."

"So we have," the major agreed. "Perhaps it would be wise to send a message that you were tired and took the opportunity to return home. Would you like me to take care of it for you?"

"Yes, if you would be so kind. I *am* quite fatigued and shall immediately retire to my room."

"Not until you face her ladyship, you won't, my girl," Prudence said through pursed lips.

The major patted Prudence on the shoulder. "Dear lady, do listen to your heart. Let the girl snatch what pleasure she can before she must embark on a loveless marriage. Surely you can understand her feelings."

Prudence blushed. "You are not to interfere in what is none of your affair, Major. Thank you for escorting us to the party and seeing us safely home. Now you may go."

The major stuck his thumbs in his waistcoat. "Don't try so hard to be unpleasant, Prudence. We all know it is only an attempt to hide your true feelings. I think you are quite taken with me."

"Wh-what an absurdity!" Prudence sputtered. "Do be off before I lose my temper."

He took her hand and pressed it to his lips for a fraction longer than was strictly proper. A flush began at her neck and crawled slowly up her face, but she seemed too stunned to pull away.

"I bid you good-night, ladies." As he turned, the major gave Topaz a broad wink. "You and Colby looked well paired on the dance floor, Topaz. It wouldn't surprise me if this was not the last you heard of him."

Topaz shook her head. "You couldn't be more mistaken, Major. Colby has no affinity for the kind of lives we lead."

"Hmm. Perhaps. On the other hand, I doubt very much if it was the party that drew him."

Prudence shooed the major out the front door and pushed Topaz toward the stairs. Apparently the major's remarks had made an impression because Udora was not summoned. Maggie, whom Udora considered a friend as well as her personal maid, met them on the stairs.

"So, 'tis home early, is it?" she said. "Have a bout with Lord Throckmorton, now did you?"

Prudence, obviously irritated by Maggie's impertinence, had second thoughts. "It is not for you to question us, Maggie. Be so good as to inform her ladyship that we wish to speak with her at once."

Maggie tossed her mop of copper-coloured curls. "I'll not be doin' that tonight, Miss Thackery. Her ladyship has the megrims and I vowed not to disturb her."

"Well, I never! Then see to it that Miss Topaz is made ready for bed. I shall speak to you later. You might tell the new girl that I would like some bricks warmed for my bed tonight, and perhaps a pot of chocolate and biscuits brought to my room."

"Yes, madam." Maggie looked sideways at Topaz and wrinkled her freckled nose. When they were alone in Topaz's bedroom, Maggie went to the armoire and withdrew a robe and nightrail. "The old hag. It will take more than 'ot bricks to warm the likes o' her."

"Hush, Maggie. She might hear you. You know these walls have ears. Besides, Prudence doesn't mean to be so disagreeable. She's lonely, I think. The man she loved left her with child, even though she followed him all the way to the Colonies. And then when her daughter was fourteen, she ran away from home and Prudence never saw her again.''

"Well, listen to you now. If I didn't know better I'd think 'twas Amy who was pleadin' 'er case. Wot's 'e done to you, anyway?'' Maggie asked as she began undoing the hooks at the back of Topaz's gown.

"Arthur?'' Topaz voiced her question to their reflections in the dressing-table mirror.

"Not 'im!'' Maggie said, giving her a quelling look. "The other one. Colby. You 'aven't been the same since the night 'e brought you 'ome in disgrace.''

"Of course I'm the same.''

Maggie snorted and Topaz looked down to avoid meeting her gaze. "Well, if I've changed, it's to be expected, isn't it? After all, I've suddenly become betrothed.''

"But you ain't goin' to marry 'im, now are you?''

"What a strange thing to say. You know I have little choice in the matter. Especially with the way Lady Udora has been acting these days.''

"Aye, so you've seen it, too?''

"Of course. When we first met her, she was carefree and giddy as a schoolgirl. She used to spend hours telling us about the pranks she and her friends played on some of the stuffy old matrons. Now she rarely smiles and keeps to her rooms more than she goes out. What's happened to her, Maggie? Is it because she took on the responsibility of our come-out? I know it isn't trouble between her and Bently.''

Maggie reached for the brush and began to comb out Topaz's hair. "Don't be too sure. She's not as open with 'im as she used to be. Nor with me, for that matter."

"Maybe it has something to do with Aunt Prudence being here," Topaz said.

"Aye, an' you could be right there. Your aunt is sour faced enough to curdle the cream."

"Well there's not much chance she will soon leave us. Not, at least, until she finds her daughter. And that doesn't seem very likely."

Maggie tied a ribbon round Topaz's hair to match the nightdress and patted her head. "Quite the sly-boots, aren't you? You changed the subject without answerin' my question."

"I've forgotten what you asked. Besides, I have a favour to ask of you. You're the quickest one with a needle in the house. Come with me tomorrow and help us mend the rents in David's balloon."

Maggie guffawed. "I'd as lief stick myself in the eye with a hot poker. You know what 'er ladyship would say if she caught me 'elpin' you get close to that David fellow. She's sure you have some kickshaw notion about runnin' off to Gretna Green with 'im."

Topaz swung round in her chair. "I'd never do that. I don't love David. I don't even think of him that way." She stood and kicked off her slippers. "If you help me, I'll give you that purple promenade gown you've been coveting for so long."

Maggie gave her a scathing look that spoke louder than words.

"All right." Topaz sighed. "The amethyst necklace that matches."

Maggie snorted.

"And the earrings."

Maggie smiled. "Wot time tomorrow do we leave, then?"

"I knew you'd have your price. I shall give the things to you as soon as we get back from the park."

"Keep them, miss. I just wondered 'ow much you wanted to see 'im again."

"Oh, go boil some water or something. I have had enough nonsense for one night."

THE ENTIRE FAMILY had gathered for an early breakfast the next morning, thanks to an edict from Bently. Amy and Emerald looked envigorated in spite of the fact that they had remained at the Kennilworth soirée far into the night. Unlike Almack's, which unfailingly stopped the music at the stroke of eleven, no matter who was still dancing, private parties sometimes went on through the night.

Udora looked as though she had been to one of those strenuous routs. Bently, however, looked top of the trees for so early in the day. Prudence, hovering in a grey puddle at the end of the table, cast repeated glances at Topaz. It occurred to Topaz that Prudence had yet to divulge the fact that Colby had twice danced with Topaz the night before.

Looking first to make certain that everyone's plate was filled, Bently stood and tapped his fork against his crystal goblet. "Attention, everyone. I have news."

"Good news, I hope," Topaz said, glancing quickly at Prudence, who frowned and shook her head.

"The best of news. I've booked passage for Udora and myself aboard the *Flying Swan*. We shall embark in September, after the weddings take place." He bent down and placed a kiss on the top of Udora's head. "I have heard you say more than a dozen times how much you want to visit the Indies, my dearest. This is my gift to you in return for making me the happiest man on earth."

Udora's hands flew to her face. "Oh, Bently, what can I say? I love you more than..." Suddenly she burst into tears, pushed back her chair and rushed from the room.

Bently looked astonished. "What did I say? I've never seen her cry."

Amethyst put her hand on his arm and patted it as if she were soothing a child. "I think it must be because she is so very happy, wouldn't you say, girls?"

Both Emerald and Topaz murmured something unintelligible, and Bently nodded. "Yes, yes, I suppose you are correct, but I must go to her. If you will excuse me."

Emerald adjusted her spectacles on her nose. "I, for one, think it's a splendid idea, Bently. Lady Udora is sure to agree."

Amy nodded her approval. "It has never been a secret how much Lady Udora cherished her freedom to travel. By the end of September the three of us will be married and settled in our homes. Her ladyship won't have a care in the world."

"Rubbish! There's something else going on," Topaz said, pushing her plate back from the edge of the table and rising. "Excuse me, please. I've quite lost my appetite. I'm going for a drive. I need some fresh air to clear my head."

Prudence also rose. "Wait. I shall go with you."

"Never mind. I'm taking Maggie as chaperon."

DURING THE SHORT RIDE to Green Park Topaz had time to feel more than a little shamed by her abruptness with Prudence. After all, she had not gone running to Udora with the latest scandal. She deserved some credit for that. But Topaz could not afford to take chances. She had to be given the freedom to visit David while he worked on his balloon.

Maggie leaned forward as the full-top cabriolet came to a stop. "You guessed wrong, miss. 'E's nowheres in sight."

"Don't be a goose. I can see David from here. There he is in the fustian coat."

Maggie snorted. "It weren't 'im who I was talkin' about. It was the other one, the tall one. 'Is brother."

"Colby?"

"Aye. And don't look so surprised. I know 'ow your mind works."

"And you are out of yours, Maggie. Do try to be civil for once."

Maggie laughed. "A girl deserves *some* fun, now don't she?"

Topaz ignored the question and hopped down from the vehicle, at the same time calling a greeting to David. It did not take Topaz long to realize that he wasn't alone. The Misses Fortisham and Lassiter, along with their abigails, had also come to share in the needlework. She smiled in spite of her disappointment. Leave it to David to make the most of his charm. She couldn't quite discern what it was that made him so likable. It was only when Topaz posed the question to Maggie, that the reason became clear. Maggie nodded her head wisely.

"'E just plain likes ladies, is all. 'E treats them the same if they're countess or char girl. And 'e 'as a ready smile for each o' them."

All four women worked for two hours at mending the silk until David called a halt and invited them to share a light repast. He had laid out a picnic of cheese and bread from the bakery and opened a container of sweetmeats. When they were seated on the rug beneath the shade of an oak tree, he sat down next to Topaz.

"I thought you would be here sooner. I was beginning to worry."

Topaz lifted an eyebrow. "As it happens, I was delayed because Bently wanted the family to breakfast together for a change. I am surprised I even crossed your mind, considering your present distractions."

David chuckled. "I've recently been blessed with generous friends. Another day or two and the Gypsy will be as good as new. But what a pity," he said, filling his glass with punch. "Had you arrived a bit sooner you would have had the opportunity to see my brother."

"Colby? He's left, then?" Topaz asked, her disappointment showing in her face.

"I only have one brother," David said drily. "And I have to admit he surprised me by coming here." He lifted an eyebrow. "Do you suppose it could have been because I happened to mention to him that you would be here today?"

Maggie, who was seated nearby, allowed a smug smile to spread across her face.

CHAPTER SEVEN

TOPAZ TARRIED with David and his friends far longer than she should have. He had casually mentioned that Colby might return that afternoon, but he failed to appear. Consequently, it was late when she and Maggie arrived back at Kesterson House. They were immediately summoned to the library, where Lady Udora, along with Prudence, awaited her.

Udora pointed to a chair and said nothing until Topaz was seated and had begun to squirm. "Don't fidget, Topaz. Have you learned nothing from the hours I spent training you to behave like a lady?"

"I'm sorry, my lady."

"'Sorry' appears to have become your favourite word of late. Unfortunately it no longer has any meaning where you are concerned. Apologies apparently come so easily to you that you no longer hesitate to make yourself fodder for the scandalmongers. Thanks to this latest incident, you've replaced even Lord Shipley and the infamous Annabel Rice as the popular subject for gossip."

Topaz shot a questioning look at Prudence, who almost indiscernibly shook her head.

Udora put down her needlework. "No, it was not Prudence who provided me with the facts concerning your most recent fall from grace. The news of your having danced a second dance with Lord Colby has become the latest on dit among the ton. You seem determined to bring disgrace down upon our heads, Topaz, and I simply do not know how to deal with you.''

Topaz started to apologize, then caught herself just in time.

''So you've nothing to say for a change. I wouldn't have expected you to be silent, Topaz. Of the three girls, you are the most outspoken. I wonder,'' Udora said. ''Is it because you are adopted that you are so difficult in comparison to the twins? Perhaps your character can be attributed to the kind of people your own father and mother were. One can only speculate as to what they were like.''

Both Prudence and Topaz gasped. Topaz was too hurt to speak, but Prudence confronted Udora. ''I'm sure you did not mean that the way it sounded, Udora. It was most unworthy of you.''

Udora looked stricken. ''I . . . I was merely thinking aloud. I shouldn't have been so thoughtless. I'm sorry, my dear Topaz, if I have offended you. You know very well that we all adore you.'' She laughed somewhat weakly. ''I rather suspect that I was thinking of my own tendency to be wilful, and how the trait was probably passed on to me by my father.''

Topaz nodded, resisting the urge to massage her hands, which had suddenly grown as cold as ice. ''I understand. Please, do not distress yourself. I was, after all, a foundling. Heaven only knows what my mother and father were like before they abandoned me. They . . . they could have been criminals or even worse.''

"Do not say such a thing," Prudence said. "There could have been many reasons for them to deny you their name. You mustn't judge them."

Udora rose and came over to place her arm around Topaz's shoulders. "You are a Thackery now, my darling girl, and that is all that matters. But along with the name, you must accept a responsibility to protect it from gossip. Soon you will be married and you must also protect your husband's name. It is to that end that you must learn to abide by the rules of Society. Do you understand?"

"Yes, my lady. May I go to my room now?"

"First you must promise me one thing. That you will never again slip away to Green Park, or any other place, to be with David Endicott."

Her first thought was to refuse, but seeing the evidence of pain in Udora's eyes, Topaz slowly nodded. "Yes, if I must, I give you my word."

"Very well. Then if the two of you will excuse me, I believe I shall retire. It has been a long day."

Prudence and Topaz were silent for several minutes after Lady Udora had left the room. At last Prudence broke the silence. "My dear girl. I wish there was something I could do to ease your pain. You look so bereft that it makes my heart ache."

"There is nothing, thank you, Aunt Prudence. But why should you care about what happens to me? I have not been very kind to you since you arrived here from the Colonies. I have, at times, been rather cruel. Especially when it comes to criticizing your clothing."

Prudence shrugged. "With good reason, I fear. I know that I am quite out of step with fashion, but I cannot bring myself to change, no matter how hard I try. As to the other . . . I drove my own daughter away from me. Perhaps the good Lord sent me here to live with you and your sisters to teach me the error of my ways.''

Topaz rose, grasping the arms of the chair to steady herself. ''My sisters? For the first time in my life I am uncomfortable thinking of them in that way. Perhaps I have sisters of my own. Or brothers. And a mother and father.'' Tears formed at the back of her eyes and began to spill down her cheeks. ''All of a sudden I feel completely alone in the world and I need something to hold on to.''

''Then hold on to *me,*'' Prudence said, putting her arm around Topaz's shoulders. ''And don't talk nonsense. You have a family. You were *chosen* to be a part of it. That surely must mean something to you.''

''It did . . . until now. I wish I could talk to David. He has a way of sorting things out.''

''You know you can no longer do that. You cannot go running about, now that you are to be married.''

''I don't know how I shall survive without my freedom. I promised David I'd help him tomorrow. He will think I have deserted him.''

''You could write him a letter. I will see that it is delivered. I will see to it in person.''

''Would you, Aunt Prudence? Would you really do that?''

''I will take it to him tomorrow.''

COLBY, HAVING MISSED Topaz, had, with considerable determination, not returned to Green Park that afternoon. Dawn the following morning found him pacing the floor of the library at Ridgeview in a zealous effort to rid his mind of thoughts that plagued him—thoughts of an adventurous young woman who approached life with such enthusiasm that it amazed him.

He had been so sure that he would encounter Topaz when he stopped at Green Park on the pretext of seeing David. But she wasn't there. To consider himself disappointed was a vast understatement.

"Disappointment" was a word that Colby was not used to using. It had been his custom for years to do pretty much as he pleased, to spend most of his time in the country because he liked overseeing the crops and looking after his growing flock of sheep. His tenant farmers thrived because they worked as hard as he did. He trusted them and they never let him down. Here at Ridgeview he was in control of nearly everything but the weather.

But this was a new experience. What he most wanted from life was out of reach, completely beyond his control. "Double damnation!" he muttered to no one in particular. Must he wait here, pacing the floor, while he let life pass him by? Or would he do something about it? He slapped his hand against his thigh, then strode quickly to the bell-pull. It was nearing the noon hour now. Given fast horses, he could be in London in no time.

JUST AS HE EXPECTED, David was at the field by Green Park where he had erected a tent to protect himself and his balloon from the weather. Colby's senses quickened when he saw the women seated on a blanket under the tree, a huge circle of red-and-yellow silk spread over their laps. Now that he was about to see her again, he nearly panicked. What would he say to her? *Break your engagement to Arthur, Topaz, because I want to marry you?* She would laugh in his face.

Or would she? There were times when she looked at him with such longing in her eyes that it kindled a fire in his blood. He hadn't just imagined the way she watched him. But she was young. Young girls were wont to be in love with the idea of love. Although David denied it, she more than likely gazed at him in the same way. She certainly risked her reputation to visit him as often as she did.

He drew a deep breath to steady himself as he alighted from the carriage and strode toward his brother where he sat on the grass near the women.

How shall I greet her? Colby pondered. *Good morning, Miss Thackery. What a surprise to see you.* No. Perhaps...*Ah, Topaz, how charming you look this afternoon*... or, *So, Topaz, what mischief have you brought with you today?* Colby scowled. Double damnation! Better to take it as it comes.

Their backs were turned toward him as he approached, but David saw him first. "Colby! I didn't expect you. Come and join us. What brings you in from the country?"

The other ladies turned to smile up at him and his heart sank. Nevertheless he managed a token bow. "Good morning, Miss Fortisham, Miss Lassiter. I see my brother has enlisted your help with the needlework."

They giggled, and made some inane response he was too unsettled to comprehend. Instead, he looked round for some sign of Topaz or her carriage.

David, more astute than usual, shook his head. "Sorry, old man. I'm afraid you are not in luck. Miss Prudence Thackery came round with a letter for me. Here it is." He dug into a satchel. "Read it if you wish."

Colby took the letter and went to sit down in the shade of another tree. There was something mystical about holding the paper in his hand. He could smell Topaz's fragrance on the heavy linen paper, visualize her seated at a desk, pen in hand, touching the holder to her lips as she struggled to find the exact words to express her feelings.

"My dear David," the letter read. Colby could almost hear her voice repeating the words.

It pains me to tell you this, but Lady Udora has, at last, reached the end of her patience with my untoward behaviour. Beginning today I am forbidden to see you ever again. Were it not for the possibility that her ladyship is ill, and I might add, refusing to admit it, I would not hesitate to disobey. You know how much I have enjoyed flying up above the crowds. But I cannot bring myself to cause her ladyship further discomfort. For that reason I must refrain from doing the things I most enjoy. I do thank you for all that you have shared with me and wish you the greatest success in your endeavour to follow in the footsteps of your esteemed idols, the Montgolfier brothers and Mr. Brown.

Ever your grateful friend,
Topaz Thackery

With shaking hands, Colby brought the letter to his face, inhaling deeply as if to hold her essence forever in his memory. He was thankful that he had moved away from the others. God help him, he wouldn't have been able to contain his sorrow.

It was nearly ten minutes before David came over to join him. "I'm sorry, old man," David said, squatting down beside him. "I would have thought she might have added a word or two about you."

Colby forced a smile. "Why on earth should she? The girl is betrothed. She's got what she wants."

David shook his head. "We both know better than that. Since the minute she met you she has gone out of her way to question me about you. My God, Colby, she all but spit in Society's face by having a second dance with you at the Kennilworth party."

"I gave her no choice, other than to make a scene. I forced her to dance with me."

David snorted. "No one forces Topaz to do anything she doesn't wish to do."

Colby lifted an eyebrow. "You see? You've won my argument for me."

"You mean her betrothal to Arthur Ringwald? There's another reason for that, you can be sure. Perhaps it all goes back to her refusal to unsettle Lady Udora. Seems that her ladyship is not quite up to snuff."

"I wish I could believe it was that simple."

"You'll never know unless you ask the girl, now will you?"

A dim flicker of hope began to burn in Colby's chest. He smiled. "I believe you have a point, David. Perhaps I will do just that."

David grinned and slapped him on the back. "Good. I can use another expert seamstress in the family."

Colby shot him a quelling look. "Judging from the way your female friends have been watching you, I am certain you will always have a willing supply of helpers."

"At least for another day. Both young women have agreed to attend the Taggarts' house party at Brighton, which begins on Friday."

"Indeed?" Colby's voice indicated that he was not even mildly interested.

David sighed. "Have you forgotten that the Thackery Jewels will also be in attendance?"

"*Indeed!* As a matter of fact, I *had* forgotten."

"Then I suggest that you make it a point to see that you are among the invited guests. Lady Taggart, along with her retinue of card-playing biddies, often comes to the park at the fashionable hour of five."

"At which time I shall be there myself. In the meantime, I must attend my tailor. I have ordered several suits of clothing to augment my wardrobe."

David laughed. "And about time, I hasten to add. One must use all the ammunition one has to catch a wary bird. You might also consider buying another neckcloth or two. The one you're wearing is a bit outdated."

Colby took one look at his brother's grass-stained breeches and chuckled. "Spoken like a man who is devoted to sartorial excellence."

He left a few minutes later to make his way to his Bond Street tailor. Later, as he drove down Piccadilly, he chanced to recognize Lady Taggart and her friends entering Hatchard's bookshop and he ordered his driver to pull the carriage to a halt.

The shop was nearly empty. Colby saw the women thumbing through a sketch-book of country houses and gardens. Instead of approaching them directly, he went round behind a shelf of books and came toward them on the other side.

"Oh, beg pardon, ladies," he said after nearly colliding with them. "I was so immersed in this book that I did not see you." He bowed. "And I fear that is quite inexcusable, considering how fetching the two of you look."

Lady Taggart smiled broadly. "Lord Colby. How nice to see you again. It has been such a long time. My niece, Victoria, said that you had honoured Society by your presence at the Kennilworth soirée."

"I believe it was long overdue, don't you agree?"

"Yes, indeed. Although I am told that your house at Ridgeview makes a lovely hideaway from the hustle and bustle of the Season."

Lady Pendergast, not to be ignored, took the book from his hands. "And what does a handsome young lord from the country read to pass the long evenings? Oh, my dear, how brilliant you must be. Garrison's treatise on medieval tapestries."

"Far from brilliant, Lady Pendergast. In truth, I have read the book a dozen times, for lack of more recent works. I have decided to go to Brighton in a few days, where I am told that Donaldson's circulating library has an excellent collection on the subject."

Lady Taggart raised her lorgnette. "Brighton? How convenient. I wonder, would you be inclined to join us for a small gathering at my home there this Friday? The house party will last through Sunday."

"Thank you, I am truly honoured, my lady, but I'm afraid not."

"Surely you can take a few days away from your work to enjoy the water. I've hired bathing machines for our use, and I warrant it will be a vast relief from the unseasonably warm weather we have suffered these past two days."

Colby appeared to ponder the question. Then he inclined his head. "Yes, since you put it that way, I believe I will accept. Thank you for your kind invitation, Lady Taggart."

She positively glowed. "The pleasure is mine, I assure you."

He bid the ladies good-day, and as he walked away, Lady Taggart was overheard to say, "Imagine! What luck. Now I'll have no trouble at all in persuading my niece to join us."

THE KESTERSON HOUSEHOLD spent the better part of a week preparing for the house party at the Taggart residence, located in the fashionable section west of the Steyne. The rambling stone building boasted fifteen bedchambers. Because of the large number of overnight guests, Emerald, Amethyst and Topaz were crowded into one small room. Prudence and Sally shared an adjoining bedroom.

Topaz was less than happy. "I don't know why I had to come along. I'm sure I'll find nothing to occupy my time."

Amy turned from hanging her reticule on a hook in the armoire. "Oh, but there's so much to do. There are walks along the promenade, and with so many guests, there is sure to be music and dancing in the evening."

"That's all very well for you and Emerald. You have your fiancés to keep you company, but I am sure that Arthur will seek out a game of chance. I will be forced either to stand and watch Arthur play at cards or go off on my own." Topaz kicked off a slipper and it flew across the room. "Probably the latter. He thinks I bring him bad luck when I watch him gamble."

Emerald tilted her spectacles and looked at Topaz over the top rim. "I'm told there are two perfectly lovely lending libraries, Fisher's and Donaldson's, where the most delightful people gather to exchange views."

Amy clasped her hands together. "Lucy Campion said there's to be bathing tomorrow in the Steyne."

Topaz was mildly interested. "That's something, at any rate. But nothing like swimming in the river at Amberleigh. I'm told that everyone is forced to use bathing machines."

"Of course," Amy said. "One wouldn't want to be seen in such a state of undress." She giggled. "But I'm told that there is always a group of cheeky young bucks who ply their telescopes with great enthusiasm."

"Then I shall be forced to keep them entertained, won't I?" Topaz said, raising her skirt well above her knees. "I warrant it will be more fun than anything else that takes place here during the next three days."

Emerald gave her a quelling look. "You are determined to court disaster, aren't you?"

"Perhaps. But why not? I am, after all, an orphan. One cannot blame the Thackerys for my misbehaviour."

Prudence came into the room just in time to hear the remark. "Topaz, my dear, you are an intelligent girl. It doesn't become you to feel sorry for yourself." She removed her shawl and laid it on the *chaise longue.* "The butler has informed me that Arthur and his mother have arrived. He will be waiting for you in the music room."

"So soon? But we've only just got here."

"Do try to be a little more enthusiastic. I caught a glimpse of him, and he looks quite handsome today."

It occurred to Topaz as she reached the lower floor and enquired of a footman as to the location of the music room, that Arthur always looked well turned out. If only she could love him!

She hadn't bothered to change her frock. It was slightly soiled from the nearly six-hour coach ride but it would do. Unfortunately, Lady Throckmorton had seen fit to wait with her son for Topaz to come downstairs.

She raised her lorgnette. "I see you've only just arrived, Topaz, and haven't had time to change. You must forgive us for making it sound so urgent, but Arthur was eager to greet you."

Topaz dropped a curtsy toward the well-endowed woman whose hennaed hair was pulled into a fat braid round her head. "How pleasant to see you again, Lady Throckmorton." Arthur raised his head from the newspaper he had been scouring and rose to welcome her.

"What ho! Glad you're here, Topaz. This should be a jolly good weekend. I understand there's to be a race tomorrow at the racecourse. Prinny's horse will be a contender, so there's sure to be a good crowd."

"Well I'll leave you two children alone to enjoy yourselves," Lady Throckmorton said with a mischievous smile. She wagged her finger. "Now you be very good."

Arthur chuckled after she left. "She's dashed fond of you y'know. I don't s'pose I should be telling you this, but she's buying the Clawswell house down the street from hers. Plans to give it to us for a wedding present."

"That monstrosity?" Topaz demanded before she could catch herself, but then decided to be honest. "It...it rather looks as if it was meant to be a prison."

"It is a little grim, but I warrant you'll do wonders with it. Besides, it's close to mother so you can run over there any time you want to."

"How comforting," Topaz said, but her sarcasm went unnoticed. She was about to continue when the library door opened and Colby entered the room.

"Oh, hello. I didn't realize the room was occupied."

His expression was so guileless that they had no choice but to pretend to believe him. Nevertheless, Arthur gave him a cold stare.

"What the devil are you doing here, Colby? I didn't think you travelled in our circle."

Colby, with his squared jaw and lean, muscular body, made Arthur look soft in comparison. "I try not to go round in circles, Throckmorton, but as it happens, our family was rather close to the Taggarts at one time. Lady Taggart was kind enough to invite me to join the house party this weekend.''

Topaz watched him intently while the two men exchanged guarded thrusts. Everything about him seemed mild-mannered... until she met his gaze. Beneath that innocent facade she sensed an intensity, a simmering heat that was all but ready to ignite.

She would have to have been a complete ninny-hammer not to know that he was pursuing her. For a man who was known to prefer the uncomplicated life of the country, he had certainly begun to act the man about Town. And it seemed to have begun when they first met at Ridgeview after David's balloon crashed.

The knowledge brought heat to her face, and she felt a rush of anticipation that thrilled her. If only... She had a sudden vision of being carried in his strong arms over the threshold to Ridgeview, and it appalled her to realize how appealing it was. But it could never be. She was already betrothed. Besides, Udora would never allow it even if she weren't.

Topaz had learned that the Colby family had a reputation for not being willing to play Society's games. Although they were respected for their lineage, they were, in spite of their rank, outsiders.

Except for his mother, perhaps. And she was a woman unto herself. A little like Lady Udora, Topaz thought, save for the fact that Lady Colby was only on her third husband.

"Oh, do pay attention, Topaz," Arthur said in a quarrelsome voice. "I asked you if you would like to go for a stroll in the gallery. I promised Willingsly we'd meet him and Lady Bonniface there."

"I think not, Arthur. I haven't had time to settle into my room and change my costume."

"Oh, very well. I will speak with you later, then."

Colby straightened. "Since I'm on my way to my room on the second floor, I'll be glad to escort you to your own room. This house is like a maze when it comes to finding your way about."

"See here..." Arthur began.

"Why, thank you, Lord Colby. You're very kind, but I am quite capable of finding my way."

Colby nodded his agreement, and they all emitted a collective sigh, albeit for a variety of reasons. Topaz dropped a curtsy that was intended to serve both gentlemen, but her gaze lingered longest on Colby. She couldn't help herself. He had bewitched her.

CHAPTER EIGHT

THE REST OF THE GUESTS had arrived by late afternoon and, at dusk, were ready to attend a concert on the grounds of Brighton Pavilion. A number of chairs had been placed in strategic positions, close, but not too close, to the Regent's excellent German band.

Visitors and local residents came in droves to hear the music of Beethoven, Bach and Haydn. So many attended this rare evening concert that the chairs were soon filled and the younger people spread rugs on the grass for informal seating.

Arthur escorted Topaz to a spot to the right of the bandstand and near a hedge that enclosed a garden. "This should be adequate, my love. One wouldn't want to get too close to the tuba. It makes a dreadful noise."

"Will the Prince be here, Arthur?"

"No. Unfortunately, he has a toothache and found it too uncomfortable to make the journey. I assume that is why the concert is being held at night, rather than the afternoon, as is the custom. When Prinny is in residence, the band also entertains while he and his guests are dining."

Topaz tried to spread her skirt around her, being careful to conceal her ankles. It was nearly impossible, considering the narrowness of her skirt.

They were soon surrounded by other young couples intent on enjoying the outing. Freddie Grenville and his pretty young friend, Amelia Harding, sat on the rug next to Arthur, who had to draw his feet in to keep from bumping the people in front of him. Arthur and Freddie were soon immersed in conversation, while Amelia traded *on dits* with her neighbour to the left.

Topaz fidgeted in an effort to find a comfortable position. Leaning backwards, she encountered a hard shoulder. "Oh! I beg pardon. I didn't realize..."

"No need to apologize, Topaz. Feel free to lean on me."

When she saw to whom she was speaking, she stopped short. "Colby! I might have known it was you. You seem to appear no matter where I chance to be."

He smiled. "Does that include your dreams?"

"Don't talk rubbish! You are too forward, sir."

"I spoke only in jest."

"Did you indeed? And I suppose you are going to tell me that you chose this particular rug by accident?"

"Most definitely not. I searched carefully until I discovered where you were seated."

"But why?" she asked, surprised by his honesty. "Are you pursuing me?"

"Pursuing you? I'm sure you would never permit it, would you? Well, would you?" he persisted as he tried to capture her gaze.

She momentarily turned away. "You speak such nonsense, Colby. I find it quite impossible to take you seriously." Seeing that he was holding something behind his back, she inclined her head. "What is it you have there?"

"A rose. I brought it for you. Look, all the thorns have been carefully plucked away."

"More than likely you stole it from the rose garden. I can smell their fragrance coming from just beyond the hedge."

"Then you reject my humble offering?"

He looked so wounded that she had to smile. "Oh, do give it to me. Now that you have stolen it, it would be a shame to let it go to waste." He handed it to her, and for an instant, their fingers touched. She quickly pulled away, afraid that he might feel the excitement she knew must surely be reflected in her touch. Tucking the rose into the deep V of her bodice, she looked to him once more.

"Thank you, Lord Colby. But you really must behave yourself. People are beginning to look at us."

"So they are. They must find our conversation disturbing. Just lean back and be still."

They find it disturbing! she silently mused, then consciously resisted the urge to take advantage of his shoulder as a leaning post; resisted for all of three minutes. Then, slowly, she allowed herself to sink back against him. It was ever so much more comfortable. His shoulder was warm, strong and steady.

If Arthur might have objected, she never knew it, because he was oblivious to everything but his conversation with Freddie.

It was during a brief interlude while the musicians refreshed themselves that Arthur turned to Topaz. "I say, good luck. Freddie Grenville and his family have invited us to share his box at the races tomorrow afternoon. I've told him we will be glad to attend.''

Topaz leaned forward and busied her hands with her reticule. ''Really, Arthur, you should have consulted me before making plans. I have already made arrangements to go with my sisters to bathe in the Steyne.''

''Surely the races would be more exciting. Really, my dear, I insist that you accompany me. How would I explain it to the Grenvilles if I arrived without you?''

''It hadn't occurred to me that you would owe them an explanation.''

He smiled and touched two fingers to her cheek. ''You have much to learn, but I am more than willing to teach you.'' He sneezed, then sneezed again. ''What abominable luck! There must be a rose garden just beyond the hedge. Roses make me sneeze, you know. I regret that we have no choice but to leave.''

For a brief instant Topaz considered tossing her rose over the hedge, but on second thought, she pulled her shawl more closely about her, successfully hiding the gift that lay hidden close to her heart.

Arthur continued to sneeze long after they returned to the house. His eyes reddened and his nose had begun to run. Even the prospect of a spirited game of Hazard could not entice him to join the festivities.

He blew his nose for the tenth time in ten minutes. ''Sorry, my love, I'm afraid I'm in for it. I'll be obliged to spend the rest of the evening with a hot plaster stuck to my forehead. And tomorrow, too, unless I miss my guess.''

''How awful for you, Arthur. Is there anything I can do?''

"Nothing," he said, then sneezed twice before he could continue. "Look here, I feel wretched about tomorrow, but I am sure that I shall be quite unable to take you to the races."

Topaz patted his arm. "I've no doubt that I'll survive the disappointment. Shall I ask the maid to send a pot of tea to your bedchamber?"

"Capital suggestion." He bowed and brushed a kiss onto the back of her hand. "I'll say good-night, then."

"Good night, Arthur. Sleep well."

It was with an acute sense of guilt that Topaz went in search of a maid to look after Arthur's needs. Yet she felt as if a burden had fallen from her shoulders. To be free of him for a few hours was like inhaling the first warm breezes of Spring after a long, cold Winter. How then was she going to feel when she was married to him, living in the same house with him day after day? And the nights...

It was with difficulty that she tried to rally her suddenly downcast spirits. She wandered from card room to salon in search of something to relieve the megrims, but in spite of her efforts, she felt isolated from the rest of the house guests. She had hoped to find her sisters, or even Lady Udora or Aunt Prudence, but no doubt they were still enjoying the concert. Arthur had dragged her off in such a hurry it was unlikely that anyone had seen them leave.

At last her footsteps led her to the small music room, where she heard the soothing strains of a concerto. A cozy fire burned in the grate, and Colby was seated at the pianoforte. She watched for a moment before she entered.

"Why don't you join me, Topaz?" he asked without looking at her.

"How did you know it was I?"

"I knew you'd come."

She forced a laugh. "Truly, now. You cannot expect me to believe that."

"Can I not?"

He stood and turned toward her. She was astonished when the music continued to play.

"H-how did you do that?"

He laughed, and the sound of it made her tremble. "It wasn't the piano you heard. It was the music box. There, on top of the piano."

"Oh. The light is so dim that I thought it was you...." The intensity of his gaze was not concealed by the semidarkness. Instead, his eyes seemed to take on a glow that pierced her to her very soul.

He turned and gave the key to the music box a few turns, then moved close to her and held out his hand. "It would be an unpardonable sin to waste such wonderful music. May I beg this dance?"

She laughed, and her voice shook. "Colby, you are a dangerous man. What would I tell my guardian if she found us dancing the waltz? And once again I am unchaperoned."

"We'll think of something," he said, taking her hand in his and pulling her close.

"I cannot imagine what." Topaz sighed, allowing herself to melt into the warmth of his embrace.

There was a breathless pause as he whirled her about the room, holding her at arm's length. But when their eyes met, he drew her closer. She could have sworn she felt him shudder. Then he drew a long breath and they came to a halt, still in a close embrace.

He looked down at her and his eyes darkened as he said, "You could tell her that I love you, Topaz. That I will never love another woman the way I love you. That you have taken pity on a man who dies a bit each day, knowing that you are betrothed to another."

"Oh! Oh!" Her hands flew to her mouth, but he gently removed them and bent to kiss her softly on the lips. She started to protest, but he kissed her again and again. Not the violent kisses she might have expected from a man so virile, so strong, so determined to pursue her, but kisses so tender and loving that the feelings they ignited within Topaz went deeper than passion.

He laced his fingers in her hair and pressed her cheek to his chest. "Forgive me, my love, but I have wanted to do this since the moment I carried you down from the ridge to my house. I think I knew then that I loved you."

"Colby, I . . . I cannot . . ."

"Hush." He lifted his head and kissed the tip of her nose and her forehead. "You must break your engagement to Arthur Ringwald, Topaz. You cannot destroy yourself by marrying someone you despise."

"I don't despise him," she responded tremulously.

"But do you love him?"

"I have promised to marry him."

"You didn't answer my question. If you can swear to me that you are in love with Arthur, then I vow to step aside and stop pursuing you."

Topaz moved away from him, both to give herself time to think and to put some distance between them.

Being so close was to be drawn into the centre of the storm.

With the width of the pianoforte between them, she once again faced him. "What is it you want from me, Colby?"

He leaned forward, placing his palms flat on the highly polished instrument. "I want everything! All that you have to give. I want your mind, your heart and your body... and I want your children to be my children."

She laughed shakily. "Does this mean you wish to become my protector?"

"Protector? What utter nonsense. If you were free to accept, I would ask you to become my wife." He strode round the desk and swept her into his arms. "Double damnation, Topaz. You know we belong together. I love you and I think you love me. I want to marry you."

It was the naked desire on his face more than the words he spoke that was her undoing. The hopelessness of it all closed about her, and she burst into tears. With more strength than she knew she possessed, Topaz broke away from him and darted from the room.

Colby was stunned. He cursed himself for his own impatience. Given time he could have persuaded her. Now he had blundered ahead like an unlicked cub and he had frightened her off. At length he became aware that the music box had run down, that the music had stopped. He tried not to dwell on the similarity to his own state of mind.

THAT NIGHT Topaz barely slept, but to avoid any discussion, she had pretended to be asleep when the twins came up to their room. The following morning the three girls spent an hour gossiping in their bedroom and then went downstairs for a leisurely breakfast. Emerald and her fiancé, Lord Milford, had agreed to meet Lord Chafford at Donaldson's lending library. Lord Farrencourt, Amy's fiancé, had promised to attend a cricket match along with Lord Paxton, thereby leaving Amy without plans. By early afternoon, Amy and Topaz had joined those who wished to make use of the bathing machines provided by their host.

There was only a small crowd waiting at the water's edge. Children watching the horses pull the bathing machines or playing with pails and shovels while their nannies conversed a safe distance away.

Amy, her face glowing with happiness, pointed to one small cherub. "Isn't he adorable? I wonder if my children will look so sweet. Egan promised that we could have as many as I want." She carefully adjusted the string on her bonnet that the gusting breeze had blown askew. "Has Arthur talked to you about children?"

Topaz gave her a quelling look. "He will want a son, of course, but Arthur rarely speaks about anything save card games and horses. It is fortunate that he has a considerable fortune, or gaming would be an impossibility and he would have nothing to live for."

"I suppose it does make it difficult for you. What a shame that you chose to accept Arthur's bid. Granted, he is considered a catch, but not for you, Taz. Definitely not for you."

"Really, Amy, you know I had no choice in the matter. If Lady Udora had not been looking so peaked of late, I would never have agreed to the arrangement."

"Of course. But it's not too late. The banns have yet to be published, and there are plenty of other men." She laughed and nodded in the direction of a wall several yards away from the water line. "I venture to say quite a number of them are watching us with their telescopes."

"I promised Emerald I'd give them a thrill," Topaz said, lifting the hem of her skirt a good two inches and kicking at a seashell. A cheer went up from the dozen or so young blades who were lucky enough to see the flash of ankle.

Amy gasped. "Topaz, what's got into you? You've become so reckless these past few weeks. Of course you always were a little wild, but this is different. It's as if... Oh my," she said, lowering her voice. "Did you see him? Lord Colby is among the lookers."

Topaz glanced up, then regretted it immediately. It was true. Even from this distance one could hardly mistake those broad shoulders.

She grasped Amy's arm to urge her forward. "I've no wish to speak to him. He has already caused me enough trouble."

"Trouble? What do you mean trouble? He hasn't... you know, touched you or anything of that sort?"

Topaz wrapped her arms about herself before responding. "He...he told me last night that he loves me."

"Dear heaven! So that's what made you pretend to be asleep when Em and I came to bed after the concert. I knew that something had changed." She stopped a few feet from a bathing machine and patted the horse's nose while Topaz shook sand from her slipper. "You must remember, Taz, that many men speak of love, but only a few will speak of marriage."

"*He* did." Topaz scooped up a handful of sand and let it sift between her fingers. "He said that if I were free to accept, he would ask me to become his wife."

"Oh Taz! What did you tell him?"

"Nothing. What could I say?"

Amy nodded, and a few curls bounced free of her bonnet. "I know. It is easy enough for him to say it now that you are safely betrothed. Some men do that, you know, simply to start an *affaire de commodité.*"

"Not Colby. He means what he says."

"Of course that's what you want to believe, but…"

"Oh, do be still, Amy. I'm not in the mood for advice. And look. The bathing machine is empty. A dip will be refreshing."

"I'm not at all certain I want to try it, but I will, providing you go first. And do be careful. The water looks very rough today."

"Oh, don't be a ninnyhammer. You know I learned to swim like a fish at Amberleigh."

"All right. But please, do try not to disgrace us."

They were helped up the three steps and into the square wooden structure that had been mounted atop a framework of four large wheels with a tongue to which the horse had been hitched. Once the girls had changed into cotton caps and long-sleeved shifts that covered them from neck to toe, the horse was backed down the sandy slope and into the water. Topaz watched with growing excitement as the water level rose to the edge of the open doorway. The dippers, two old women dressed completely in black, waited to assist her from the machine and hold on to her as they allowed her to immerse herself in the cool water.

"'Old on, Meggie. There's two of 'em what's come in one box."

"It's all right. You may help my sister into the water," Topaz said.

"Aye, there's nought but two of us dippers."

"No matter. I can swim. We shall be quite safe."

Amy came to stand beside Topaz. "I'll just watch for a..."

But she had no chance to finish. An errant breeze caught a red ball that a child had been playing with and drove it with considerable force against the horse's flank. The horse snorted, reared on its hind legs, then lunged forward, dragging the bathing machine out of the water and up onto the sand. The force of the motion threw both girls forward, facedown into the water.

The dippers managed to grasp Amy, but Topaz was momentarily dragged down and away by the current and weight of her shift. For a single instant she panicked as she felt the rolling motion of the water, so unlike the mild current of the river at Amberleigh. Then pleasure overcame her fear and she allowed herself to experience the wonder of becoming one with the sea.

Her foot encountered something, and she held her nose and plunged down to pick it up. Her fingers had barely found the seashell when someone began dragging her to the surface.

"It's all right, don't fight it. I'll save you."

The sudden attack had surprised her so much that she gagged on a mouthful of sea water. She began coughing and he pounded her none too gently on the back.

"Do you mind, sir!" She coughed. "You are breaking my spine."

Instead of responding, he picked her up in his arms and carried her out of the water. "A blanket, please, someone. Hurry."

"Colby! Just what are you doing?"

"I'm saving your life, you idiot. Hold still while they bring a blanket."

"Put me down. I'm not cold."

"But you *are* very nearly naked. The water..."

"Yes, so I see." She wanted to laugh. The wet, clinging cloth did little to hide her secrets, but it was plain to see that it bothered him more than it did her. He seemed to go to great lengths to keep his gaze averted. It was an amusing, yet at the same time touching, gesture.

She couldn't help but wonder what Arthur would have done under the same circumstances. It didn't matter. Arthur was never there when he was needed. That was his worst flaw, she decided. Was Amy right? Should she end this farce of a betrothal? And what would it do to Lady Udora if she did?

She felt a stab of conscience. While she was here in Colby's arms with her hand grazing the back of his neck and his breath touching her face when he chanced to look down at her, no one else mattered. She slipped the seashell into his hand as a token of the moment they had shared.

Someone arrived at last with a blanket to conceal her state of undress. It occurred to her when he set her on her feet, that Colby, too, might have benefitted from something to cover himself. His damp clothing clung to him tenaciously, outlining the muscles and sinews of his lower body. He caught her looking at him and gave her a threatening scowl.

After that they were surrounded by people, and in no time she and Amy were whisked back to the Taggarts' house. Colby apparently succeeded in finding his own means of transportation.

It was fortunate that the house guests were occupied with activities that kept them away from the house for most of the day, but Topaz and Amy knew it was just a question of time until they, along with Colby, became the latest topic of conversation. After changing her clothing, Topaz accompanied Aunt Prudence and Lord Kesterson downstairs to the sun room.

Prudence pulled her grey shawl closely about her. "It does appear, my dear girl, that trouble is your middle name."

Lord Kesterson, stroked his moustache. "And now you are having serious thoughts about ending your engagement. Don't dissemble. I can see it in your face, Topaz."

"You know me so well. I would end it in a minute except for the effect it might have on Lady Udora."

Bently looked grave. "You know, my dear girl, that Udora and I want very much for you to settle down, but at the same time, we would hesitate to force you into a marriage with someone whom you detest."

"I know that. I . . ." She started to say more but Colby stepped into the room and she was suddenly conscious of her less-than-perfect appearance. Her gown was presentable, but her hair, still wet, was tucked beneath a blue mob-cap.

Colby took one look at the three of them, then stopped. "Oh, I beg pardon. I hope I'm not intruding, but I was eager to see if Amy and Topaz were all right."

Topaz met his gaze and for a moment she found it difficult to breathe. "I...yes. We are both quite safe."

"Thanks to you, Lord Colby, or so I understand." Bently rose, stepped forward and offered his hand. "Lady Udora and I both owe you a debt of gratitude."

"It was nothing, I assure you. I am relieved to find that they suffered no ill effects."

Topaz noticed that he had changed into fresh clothing and another pair of boots. He looked more appealing than ever with his hair still damp from the ocean and, his cheekbones a bit pink from the sun.

The conversation had turned to Lady Udora's health. Colby looked concerned. "I trust you will extend my good wishes to her for a quick recovery."

"I will indeed. No doubt she will make an appearance later in the day. Her physician assures me that she will, in time, be her usual cheerful self."

"I'm gratified to hear it. If you will excuse me, then, my lord, ladies."

They acknowledged his courtesies, and both Bently and Prudence smiled warmly until he turned and left the room. Topaz had not smiled. The expression on her face was one that he found difficult to describe. She loved him. He knew it deep in his bones. And he rejoiced in the knowledge that she would make the decision that would set her free to marry him.

Once outside the doorway he remembered that he had left the seashell Topaz had given him on the table. He started to return for it but decided to wait for a lull in their conversation. He hadn't intended to listen but their voices carried down the hallway. Topaz was speaking. "Is it true, Bently? Will Lady Udora be better in a few days?"

"I truly hope so, Topaz, but until then, I feel that we must be circumspect about breaking your betrothal to Arthur. Perhaps you should wait a few days to tell her. Coming to Brighton has been most unsettling to her."

"Brighton? Why would she be disturbed about visiting Brighton?"

Prudence sounded surprised. "Well, Brighton was where you were born, of course. She was concerned that it might give you cause to start wondering about... about things."

"But I... I thought I was born in Coventry."

Colby abhorred eavesdroppers, but he was unable to tear himself away. What was it they were saying? How could Topaz have not known where she was born?

Bently sounded uncomfortable. "Actually, my dear, you were born in Brighton, at the convent. I assumed you knew. Shortly thereafter you were taken to the orphanage at Coventry, where the Thackerys adopted you."

Adopted! Colby felt as if his entire world had suddenly collapsed. He was too stunned to hear the rest. "God in heaven," he murmured softly. "Don't let it be true." For if it were... then how could he offer for her hand in marriage? Above all, the Colby line must be kept pure. It was his own father's dying wish. And his father before him. They had prided themselves upon their ability to trace their ancestors in an unbroken line. How could he, for the sake of a burning passion, marry a woman whose line began with her? It couldn't be done. It couldn't. Pain tore at his gut.

He pushed himself away from the wall and all but ran from the house. He needed air. Space. He needed to walk. But not even the pungent scent from the sea or the bracing wind could clear his mind of the torture that kept fermenting in his brain.

How long he walked he didn't know. Was it by accident that his footsteps led him to the gates of the convent? He had driven by it many times in the past and often felt a twinge of sympathy for those unfortunates who were given away for adoption. His own upbringing had been strict, but he had a family, a sense of pride in who he was... and a name to call his own. He reached over to open the wooden gate, but it was locked. An iron bell was attached to a rope pull, but he was unable to face the truth of Topaz's heritage, whatever it might be. Instead, he turned and walked away.

TRY AS SHE MIGHT, Topaz was unable to extract further information about her background from Bently and Prudence. Neither admitted to knowing the identity of her natural parents, or even if they were still alive. But for the first time in her life it began to matter to her what kind of people they might have been. She didn't like them—of that she was quite certain.

The more she thought about it, the more she wanted to know. It was only fair, wasn't it, that she be able to tell her children about their grandparents? Perhaps, she thought... perhaps I am the daughter of a prince, or even a duke. Perhaps he had an affair with a commoner and could not admit to it. Alone now, in front of the fireplace, she watched the fire flare for a moment before the logs collapsed in a shower of sparks, like her dreams.

Perhaps, she thought, I am really the daughter of a fishmonger and a pickpocket who met his end on the gallows. But if that were so, they had done their best by her... by giving her away the day she was born. She couldn't have asked for better parents than the Thackerys, nor could she even begin to comprehend life without her sisters.

Sisters. Were there blood sisters and brothers she didn't know about? Perhaps she could learn something from the convent where she was born. They always kept records of births and deaths. And it was not far away. Colby would take her. She could always count on him.

She was about to reach for the bell-pull when the major came into the sun room. "Ah, Topaz. I'm pleased to see that your latest adventure caused no serious harm. Indeed," he said, pirouetting her around, "you look quite radiant. Could it be that your young Lord Ringwald has finally piqued your interest?" Seeing the look on her face, he cleared his throat. "No, I fear not."

"Major, have you seen Colby in the last hour?"

"As a matter of fact, I have. I chanced to walk by his room and saw him packing. I believe he intends to return to London shortly."

"But he can't . . . he wouldn't . . . he couldn't." Topaz shook her head. "Please. You must excuse me. I must see him at once."

"Then you'd best hurry. It may already be too late."

In her eagerness to find him, Topaz took the wrong corridor, not once, but twice. When she finally found the stairway, he was on his way down, followed by a footman carrying his satchel.

"I've been looking all over for you, Colby. The major tells me you are leaving. Did you intend to leave without so much as saying goodbye?"

There was no doubt as to the measure of pain in her voice. He waved to the footman to take the bag to the carriage, then he came the rest of the way downstairs to stand next to her. "I'm sorry, Topaz. A . . . a matter of some urgency came to my attention and I fear I have no choice but to return to Ridgeview."

"You . . . look so distraught, my lord. Is there anything I can do?"

"There is nothing anyone can do, I'm afraid."

"I'm so sorry. When will I see you again?"

"I don't know. Something has happened. . . . I will write to you in a few days."

"Peter . . . I . . ."

He was touched by her use of his given name, but he shook his head. She stood waiting for him to break the silence, until he finally spoke. "You said you were looking for me. What was it you wanted?"

"Oh, nothing of importance. I wanted you to accompany me on an errand. There is a particular convent that I wish to visit and I prefer not to ask my family to go along."

"May I ask why?"

She shrugged. "Something to do with my adoption. I have only today learned that Brighton is my true birthplace."

"Then you only recently learned that you were adopted?"

"Oh, heavens, no. I've known from the beginning. It is common knowledge."

"I see."

His distance made her feel uncomfortable. Any other time he would have found some excuse to touch her. But he was different this afternoon. Was he already regretting his impetuous declaration of love? She straightened her shoulders and looked him directly in the eyes.

"Something is wrong, Colby. I would like an explanation."

"I'm sorry. I need time to think."

"Very well. Forgive me for delaying your departure, sir. I wish you a safe journey."

Before he could respond, she turned and walked toward the stairs. She was on the second landing before she heard the door close. When she looked back, he was gone.

CHAPTER NINE

IT WASN'T DIFFICULT for Topaz to locate Sally. She had been asked to look after Lady Udora's needs while Maggie was nursing a chest cold. Topaz found her in the sitting room adjoining the Kestersons' bedchamber. Sally looked up from the burgundy manteau she had been brushing.

"Was there something you wanted, miss?"

"Yes. I need you to accompany me on an errand."

"I don't see as 'ow I kin leave now, what with 'er ladyship feelin' so poor."

"I have already made arrangements for Aunt Prudence to look after Lady Udora, should she awaken. Come along. All you need is a shawl to ward off the chill." When Sally hesitated, Topaz gave her a little push. "Oh, do hurry. I'm asking you to ride in a gig, not a balloon. The Taggarts have been kind enough to let me borrow it for a few hours so that I may visit the convent."

"Oh, miss! I knew that you were discomfited, but I had no idea you were thinkin' o' goin' into seclusion."

"Don't be a pin-wit. I..." They were halfway down the stairs when Topaz saw Colby looking up at her. Their gaze met and she was, for the moment, stunned.

"So you've come back. Did you forget something, my lord?" she managed to say at last.

"No. I remembered something." He stood with his hands locked behind his back, a serene smile upon his face. "It was a quotation my brother often repeated when I reminded him of our family heritage."

"Yes?" Topaz asked, feeling distinctly bewildered.

"Yes. It was by Thomas Arnold and it goes something like this. 'If you let in one little finger of tradition, you will have the whole monster—horns, tail and all.'"

"I'm not sure that I understand."

"It doesn't matter. One day, when we are old and married and sitting in front of the fire, I'll tell you all about it. For now, I believe you asked me to take you to visit the convent."

Sally began to bluster, but Topaz took his extended arm. She felt enveloped by the warmth of his smile. "I am very glad that you have returned, Lord Colby," she said, gazing up at him. "Shall we go?"

There was little Sally could do but mumble as she followed along behind them.

The convent was a cheerless place. Its grey stone walls were unrelieved by flowers or trees. The windows were curtainless, and there was no sign of children playing on the grounds.

Surprisingly, there was an immediate response when Colby tugged on the bell-rope. A bacon-faced young woman dressed all in black enquired as to their business, then ushered them into a crowded but orderly room that served as an office.

"I am Sister Mercy. My superior, Mother Verity, is at prayers now, but perhaps I can help. The records of births are all contained in these books." She lifted three of them down from the shelf and blew the dust away. "As you see, they go back many years. Unfortunately, we shall have to look through them until we find the year for which you are searching. You said eighteen years ago?"

"Yes." Colby responded. "May I assist you?"

"That would be very nice. Oh, look. Here's Mother Verity now." She introduced them to the tall, spare woman whose skin was so tightly drawn that Topaz wondered that it didn't crack.

Sister Mercy placed the books on the table, then nodded to Mother Verity. "Lord Colby and this young lady have come to search our records for a baby born some eighteen years ago."

Mother Verity inclined her head. "I see. She opened the second of the three books. "I believe this is the correct book. Yes. And what was the name of the mother?"

"That is just the problem," Topaz said. "I don't know my mother's name. But I do know the day of birth. It was May seventeenth."

Mother Verity opened the journal to that specific date. "Yes, it was a Thursday."

Colby was looking over the woman's shoulder when Topaz noticed a sudden change in the woman's attitude.

"I'm sorry. There is nothing," she said, closing the book with a snap that caused dust motes to fly into the air.

"Are you sure? Less than a week after I was born, I was taken to the convent in Coventry. Then, shortly thereafter, I was adopted by Quentin and Marion Thackery.''

"I am afraid that you have wasted your time, my dear. There is nothing here for you.''

Colby stepped in front of Mother Verity. "Would you mind, Mother, if I had a look? It's possible that you might have missed something.''

"I really would prefer that you do not, my lord. The books are old and fragile, and much of the information is confidential. I regret that I cannot help you. Now if you would be so good as to excuse me?''

"I have infinite respect for old documents, madam. I promise I shall be very careful.'' He reached for the book, and there was little she could do to avoid handing it to him.

"You see, the page is empty. Only the date, I'm afraid.''

"And a number...144. What does it mean?''

"It merely signifies that there were no births on that particular day...and...and the number of the woman who recorded the entry.''

"Hmm. I see.'' Colby thumbed briefly through the journal, then closed it and handed it to the nun.

"May I see?'' Topaz asked.

Colby gave her a telling look. "There is nothing more to see, Topaz. I believe we have learned everything there is to know.'' He smiled brilliantly and bowed to the nuns. "I noticed the chapel as we came in and couldn't help but admire the beautiful woodcarvings. Would you mind if we had a second look? I would like to leave a small donation in memory of Miss Thackery's parents.''

"Most kind of you, my lord. We have duties to attend to, but you are free to view the chapel as you wish." She emphasized the word "chapel" and made a show of closing the door to the office firmly behind her.

It took Colby less than ten minutes to satisfy his aesthetic needs before taking Topaz's arm and guiding her from the building. She could hardly contain her anger.

Once they were outside, Topaz jerked away from him. "Why did you let them go? You know they weren't telling the truth."

"Of course I know they were lying. But there was nothing to be gained by confronting them. We could hardly resort to using brute force."

"But the answer was there. I know it was. It is something to do with the number. You saw how Mother Verity hesitated when you asked her to explain it. And what about the blue dot that followed the number? Why didn't you enquire about it?"

"I didn't need to. I think I already know the answer." He took her arm once again. "Come. I think they are watching us. I saw a face behind the ivy over the office window. We don't want them to begin to wonder."

"But we must go back and settle this."

"Not now. Trust me. Allow me to help you into the gig." Sally followed her with alacrity and settled herself against the hard seat. When Colby climbed aboard, Topaz became adamant.

"I must go back, Colby. I simply cannot leave without having accomplished something." Topaz knew that her face was red, and she was fast losing her

temper, but it didn't matter. "Lord Colby, I demand
that we return and face them."

He answered by slapping the reins and starting the
horse off at a brisk trot through the open gateway.

"So you have nothing to say? Then stop the gig and
get out," Topaz commanded. "It was I, after all, who
borrowed this contraption. It should be my decision
as to when I return."

"Do calm down and listen to reason."

"Don't try to placate me. I demand that you stop at
once."

"You are having a tantrum, Topaz," he said, leaning down to kiss her on the mouth. "Now hush and let
me take care of you."

Sally let out a shriek, but one look from Colby quieted her.

Topaz was shocked into silence. It was a simple kiss,
a brush across the lips, yet it had the desired effect of
calming her nerves. But one look at Colby's face told
her that he was also suffering some inner turmoil.

He stole a quick glance down at her and then looked
away. "I promise you this, my darling. I will find the
answer, no matter what the risk. The truth lies in the
convent office."

"But how can we persuade the nuns to hand over
the information, and what do you expect to find?"

"I am not quite certain as yet. I think the number
refers to a page in a book. And I believe that the blue
dot indicates a thin blue book that stood on the top
shelf. If you noticed, there were other numbers with
either a red or blue dot alongside them. I suspect that
the books contain information that was kept confidential."

"Information such as the name of the women who gave birth to the children?"

"Precisely. And one way or another, I shall have a look at that book."

"She didn't lock the office," Topaz said at once. "And I noticed that a window was left open. We could come back tonight after they've retired and..."

He groaned. "I might have known you'd suggest something of that sort, Topaz. But it's far too dangerous to consider. I will find a more conventional means of getting to the truth. Just leave it all to me."

"Aye," Sally murmured. "You won't get an argument there! 'Tis only a fool what would break into a sacred place."

Colby gave Topaz a hard look. "You haven't said anything. You *will* let me take care of this, won't you?"

Topaz hesitated, then gave him a dazzling smile. "I couldn't leave the situation in better hands if my life depended upon it," she said.

He settled back as if satisfied, and Topaz slowly let out her breath. It wasn't a lie, was it? Shading the truth a bit, perhaps, but she could not let the matter rest without making some kind of effort to get to the truth herself. She could climb in a window as easily as the next person. At Amberleigh she had found that almost no tree was too difficult for her to master. And there was an ivy trellis fastened to the building alongside the window. It was sure to hold her weight for the short distance from the ground to the window. But it had to be tonight. Heaven only knew if or when the family would ever return to Brighton.

When they arrived at the Taggart residence, Topaz instructed Colby to drive round to the rear entrance. He raised an eyebrow.

"You've no wish to be seen with me?"

"It's not that. Well I suppose it is, in a way. You know how the gossips prattle on, and I am, after all, betrothed to Arthur, but I would prefer not to be seen arriving here."

"And just how long will you continue the farce of your betrothal?"

"Only until I'm sure that Lady Udora will not be harmed by the news."

"Pray God it will be soon."

As it happened, Lady Udora, just coming out of the library, met Topaz as she started upstairs. "Oh, there you are, Topaz. Prudence and I were just talking about you. Where have you been? Someone said you had gone off in the gig."

"Sally and I went for a short drive. Brighton has some lovely old buildings as well as the magnificent view from the Steyne." She took off her shawl and folded it into a neat square. "You're looking ever so much better, Lady Udora. The change of scenery seems to have agreed with you."

Udora patted Topaz's hand. "That and having all three of my girls betrothed. Your young man was looking for you a while ago. He said that you might find him in the card room if you should wish to see him."

"It is very doubtful that he would even notice me. And gaming holds no interest for me."

"I can well understand that, but your fiancé should certainly merit your attention. You must be careful, dear. I know that your association with Lord Colby is one of mere friendship, but the gossips are beginning to wag their tongues. It is most fortunate that he decided to return to London this morning."

Topaz was on the brink of admitting that Colby had not left after all, but Udora had already changed the subject.

"Was Sally able to shake the wrinkles from your blue gown? If not, she will have to press it in time for the party tonight."

"The party?"

"Yes, of course. At Breckenridge House."

"I had forgotten. Would it be all right if I decide not to attend? I am feeling rather exhausted after all the excitement."

"Don't be idiotic, Topaz. You cannot be tired. Besides, this is Lady Breckenridge's first party since her husband passed on. She is so looking forward to opening her house to the festivities. She made a point of inviting a number of young people. We all must go, no matter how reluctant we are."

Topaz mentally calculated the distance from the convent to the house on the Steyne that had been pointed out to her. It was even closer than the Taggarts' house, a definite advantage. Climbing through a window dressed in her party finery could, however, pose a serious problem. That is, unless she wore a pair of men's breeches beneath her gown. Fortunately it was cut full enough that they wouldn't show. A pair of boots tucked away in the corner of the carriage could be exchanged for slippers at the very last minute.

To say that Sally was appalled by the news that she was to accompany Topaz on a midnight foray into the convent was a gross understatement, but a generous bribe soothed her nerves. Maggie would have gone along simply for the adventure.

Topaz had assumed that the three girls and their fiancés would travel the short distance in the same coach, but Arthur was late in putting in an appearance. When he finally arrived downstairs, he looked handsome and dashing as always. He dropped a satin-covered box into her lap.

"Just a token of my esteem, my dear. You have my permission to wear it tonight."

Topaz touched the catch on the jewel box and opened the lid. Inside was a necklace studded with large amber stones interspersed with pearls. The whole effect was heavy-looking and rather gaudy.

Arthur gave her a fatuous smile. "Here, now. Let me fasten the catch for you."

"Oh, dear. What can I say? This is too much, Arthur. Far too much. I can't possibly accept it from you until . . . at least until we are married."

"Of course you can."

"I'm sorry. I truly cannot. Er . . . don't I recall your having said that your mother's birthday is in a few weeks?"

"Two, to be exact."

"Then why don't you save the gift for her? I know how much she adores amber."

"I suppose I could. But I promise to make it up to you once we are married. And may I say how lovely

your hair looks tonight and how attractive you are in
that particular shade of blue?"

Topaz was afraid he would notice that her waist and
hips were not as slender as usual, thanks to the pair of
breeches she had borrowed from a footman. Sally refused to wear the other pair, saying that if she were to
be sent off to gaol, she was not going dressed in men's
clothing.

They arrived at the Breckenridges' without further
delay or complications. Topaz was impressed by the
subdued grandeur of the house. Light glowed from
almost every window, while torches lining the walkway provided a warm greeting for the multitude of
guests who mingled on the grounds and on the side
veranda.

Lady Breckenridge greeted them just after the butler announced them. "My dear Topaz, how pleased I
am that you have arrived. And you, Arthur. Your
mother has been looking for you." She lowered her
voice to a whisper. "I'll warrant she's just a bit angry
that you didn't ask her to ride over with you and Topaz."

Arthur pulled at the front of his waistcoat. "'Pre-
ciate the warning, my lady. I'll have to go chat her up,
smooth things over, don't you know."

"I believe you'll find her on the veranda. Go on if
you wish. I'll look after Topaz."

Topaz studied her hostess with a casual eye. Even
now Lady Breckenridge's eyes showed the effects of
having cared for her husband for the months preced-
ing his death. She was an attractive woman, young-
looking despite her expertly coiffed white hair. Her
moss green gown was studded with hundreds of small

pearls at the bodice and scalloped hem. Around her neck she wore a double strand of emeralds and pearls set in a gold filigree chain.

Sally tagged along behind as they walked down a corridor to the salon. Lady Breckenridge took Topaz by the arm. "The gossips have it that you are quite a daring young girl. Is this true?"

"I never thought of myself as such, my lady. I must confess, however, that I would far rather ride in my friend's balloon than spend a day shopping on Bond Street."

Lady Breckenridge laughed. "I do believe you are an adventurer. Something we'd all like to be if we had the courage, I rather suspect. By the way, there was another young man enquiring after you this evening. He is also a guest at the Taggarts' house. I know I've seen him before but I confess I forgot to ask his name."

"Lord Colby? What did you tell him?"

"That you had not arrived but were expected momentarily. If I were Arthur, I'd be most concerned about this rugged-looking young man." There was a twinkle in her eyes when she said it, but Topaz recognized a serious undertone in the woman's voice as she continued. "People do talk, you know, my dear. If marriage to Arthur is what you truly want, then you might well be advised to use caution."

"Thank you, Lady Breckenridge. I know you mean well, but at this moment, I really don't know what I want."

"I think you do, my dear girl, but you've yet to admit it to yourself." She lifted her fan from where it dangled from her wrist. "Now then, here we are. I believe your sisters are over there just beyond the fernery.''

The evening dragged on forever. Arthur attached himself to Topaz, causing her to feel smothered. At the same time, Udora, Prudence, Bently and her sisters looked on with approval now that Arthur had finally begun to pay her the attention she deserved. They ate, they danced, they gossiped, then repeated the procedure over again.

Topaz searched in vain for a single glimpse of Colby, but when she finally spotted him in the crowd, he was dancing with Lady Taggart's niece. Worse yet, he seemed to be enjoying it. Devil take the man! As the hour grew late, she worried that Arthur would never leave her side. Then inspiration struck. She begged him to take her for a stroll in the conservatory. Once again the roses did him in and he was forced to be driven back to the Taggarts' house.

''Arthur, do you mind terribly if I stay a while longer? Lady Breckenridge has hired some jugglers to entertain her guests and I would hate to miss it.''

''As you wish. I shall send my driver back for you as soon as he leaves me at the door,'' Arthur replied between bouts of sneezing.

''You are far kinder than I deserve,'' Topaz said, feeling qualms of conscience.

The pangs of guilt lasted only until he was out of sight. Then the excitement of what she was about to do drove everything else from her mind. She made her excuses to her hostess, then informed Udora that Arthur was ill and she would see that he returned safely to the Taggarts'. Since it was already well into the evening, she would not return. Udora saw the logic in that and gave her permission for Topaz and Sally to leave. For one dreadful minute it appeared that Prudence would choose to accompany them, but Topaz insisted that Udora needed her more than she did.

It took the driver less than twenty minutes to make the round trip. Topaz and Sally met him a few yards from the front entrance, Topaz wearing the borrowed breeches. If he looked surprised by Topaz's appearance and her order to take them to the convent, he was wise enough not to say anything. He did, however, protest when she told him to wait in the carriage some several yards down the street from the main gate.

A stern reprimand silenced him, and she mentally thanked Udora for teaching her how to maintain control of a situation. She only wished she had as much control over her racing pulse.

Sally was no help at all. She had started to reach for the bell rope at the gate when Topaz grasped her hand. "Not that! Do you want to warn them that we are about to break in and steal their records?"

"The gate's closed. Ain't no way for us to get inside."

"Yes, there is. I noticed a small door off to the side. Yes! Here it is." She lifted the latch and pushed it open to a loud creaking of hinges. "Double damnation!" she said, stealing Colby's favourite expletive.

"Blimey! 'Tis enough to wake the dead. We'd best go before they come after us," Sally said, backing away.

Topaz grasped her arm. "Not until I get what I've come for. Look, there's the window. We shall have to climb up the trellis just a little way in order to reach it."

"Not me. I'm not puttin' me foot on that rickety contraption." Sally's voice had risen. "'Er ladyship would kill me if I fell and broke me neck."

"Be still. Someone is bound to hear us. Very well, if you are going to be so henhearted, I'll go alone, but I hate to think what her ladyship will say if she learns you failed to properly chaperon me."

"All right, I'll come, but it's you what has to answer for it if we get caught. I'll say you forced me to do it."

"Good. I'll give you a hand up once I am over the window ledge, but not a word when we get inside." Sally made some whispered remark but Topaz ignored it. She was already feeling for a third foothold on the wooden trellis as she pulled herself upward.

A sudden noise alerted her, and she froze against the building. "Somebody's comin'," Sally whispered. She was right. Topaz heard it, too, but she was in no position to take flight. All she could do was wait. It didn't take long.

Sally's thin shriek was stifled almost before it had begun. Topaz looked down to see the shadowy figure of a man with his hand over Sally's mouth as he held her in a tight grip. She struggled against him and succeeded in kicking his shins. Topaz heard a soft grunt and then an exclamation.

"Release her at once," Topaz ordered in a controlled whisper, "or I'll be forced to deal with you myself."

"I look forward to that," he said, looking up at her. "Good Lord, what are you wearing?"

"Colby, is that you?" Topaz demanded, ignoring his question.

There was a muffled oath and then he spoke. "Did you expect someone else?" He appeared to reach down to massage his leg. "You are wasting your time at that window. I have already tried it and it's locked."

"Locked? Why would they do that? The least they could do is trust people."

Colby chuckled. "Jump down. I'll catch you."

She did so, so quickly that he was not quite ready for her. He reeled slightly before he regained his footing.

"What happened? Didn't you think I would jump?"

"I expected you to offer a token argument." For a moment he held her in his arms, enjoying the warmth of her and the elusive scent of violets that lingered in the air.

"I believe you might put me down now, Lord Colby. I am quite capable of standing."

"More's the pity."

"You were right, the window was locked. What can we do now?"

Sally was breathing rapidly. "Wot we do now is make like a cat what was chased by a dog."

Colby said calmly, "This is not the time to panic. I have everything under control. While you were viewing the statuary in the chapel this afternoon, I took the opportunity to apply a bit of hot candle wax to disable the latch on a rear door. I think you'll find that it opens quite nicely. But if you prefer to climb another trellis, there is one just around the corner."

"Sarcasm is not one of your more endearing traits, Colby. Shall we try the door?"

"If you insist, but we must be quiet."

"Lead the way," Topaz said, taking Sally's hand—more to keep track of her than to comfort the petrified girl.

The narrow doorway, three short steps down from the walkway, was almost hidden by ropes of ivy that clung to the wall of the fortresslike convent. The odour of damp earth was heavy in the air and the moss-covered stones were slippery beneath their feet. Colby led the way into the musty storage room, then whispered for them to wait there while he opened the door to the chapel.

Topaz could hear Sally's teeth chattering. Something rustled behind them, then seemed to move to the other side of the small room.

"It's just a rat," Topaz said, hoping to convince herself as well as Sally.

"That's it!" Sally exclaimed. "You kin do wot you want, but I'm not goin' to stay 'ere. I'll wait in the carriage." Before Topaz could say a word, Sally had run outside. The door swung shut behind her, and as suddenly darkness descended, Topaz felt danger encircling her like a black shroud.

CHAPTER TEN

"COLBY, WHERE ARE YOU?" Topaz whispered.

"Over here. I've found the doorknob." He succeeded in opening the door, and they were rewarded with a glimmer of light from the sconces that held flickering candles, on either side of the altar.

"Sally has abandoned us," Topaz said.

"Just as well, I'd say. She makes too much noise. The office is this way," he said, taking her hand.

If she had thought the convent was eerie during the day, it was doubly so at night. Topaz had often roamed the halls and passageways at Amberleigh alone and in semidarkness but she had never been afraid, nor had she expected to be afraid now. But when Colby reached for her hand, she was surprised by how comforted it made her feel. She followed him without hesitation.

He found the office with no difficulty, and they were relieved to discover that it was unlocked and unoccupied. He closed the door behind them. "Double damnation. They've moved the candles."

"It's all right. I have candles in my reticule," Topaz said as she handed one over to him and fumbled in her bag for the matches.

"Good girl. I should have thought to bring candles myself. Where did you get them?"

"At the Taggarts'. I stole them from the candelabrum at the top of the stairs."

"I might have known." He paused as if getting his bearings. "Everything seems to be in place. Yes, there's the journal I'm looking for," he said, reaching to the top shelf for the blue leather-bound book.

As he turned the cover, Topaz leaned close. "Page 144 wasn't it?"

"Hmm. Yes, here it is. 'Born here this seventeenth day of May, the year of our Lord 1800, to one Anne Marker: a female child.'" Topaz heard the excitement rise in his voice.

"This has to be your record, Topaz. Didn't you say you were adopted from St. Agnes's Home for Foundling Children in the town of Coventry?"

"On the thirtieth of May."

"That's it, then. It's the only birth listed for a week before and two weeks after that date."

"And everything fits. Yes, yes, I...I think you must be right. Anne Marker," Topaz mused. "My mother. I can't believe I finally know her name. But who is she and where can I find her?"

"Well, we've no way of knowing that at the moment, but perhaps you can learn more about it in Coventry." He put his finger to his lips. "Shh. Listen. I think I heard voices. We'd best hurry." He returned the book to the shelf and grasped her hand. "Quick, blow out the candle. Let's try to retrace our steps."

After the warm glow of the candle, the darkness was even more intense until he opened the door a crack to listen. Pale light and the sound of conversation filtered to them from the chapel. He leaned close and whispered in her ear.

"If we stay near the wall, I think we can pass by them without detection. The draperies will hide us. Are you game?"

She nodded and squeezed his hand. Being with Colby had turned this into an adventure. If she had been forced to do it alone...well, it didn't bear thinking about. The voices of a man and woman grew louder as she and Colby inched their way along the wall. His hand tightened on hers, and when he stopped, she bumped into him. He steadied her, then bent down to whisper.

"I think they're coming this way. We must hide. Here, in the niche behind this statue."

"There's not enough room."

"We've no choice." His tone was terse as he ducked behind the stone figure and pulled her in against him. In his haste, he had all but knocked the air from her lungs. Her back was to him, his arm holding her closely about the waist.

Somewhere along the way, the man and woman must have stopped, because the voices grew no louder. But they were close by. Too close to take chances, Topaz thought when she detected their darker silhouettes against the grey shadows. She felt her heart thudding behind her ribs. She wondered that the sound could not be heard. Colby's breath moved the fine hair at the back of her neck. She was acutely aware of the warm, hard length of his body, the clean male scent that was so peculiar to him, and the innate power in his broad shoulders and muscular thighs. She could have stayed there forever, she thought whimsically.

And it seemed that they might. Colby tried without success to steady his breathing. He knew well enough that it wasn't the danger of being discovered that caused his pulse to race. The real danger lay in his physical awareness of the girl he held against him.

He was only dimly aware when the voices became muted and then ceased altogether. The soft closing of a door somewhere in the distance signalled a logical end to his torment and his bliss.

Topaz turned her head in an effort to look up at him. "They have gone, have they not, Colby? It is safe for us to leave, isn't it?"

He murmured. "Much safer than staying here."

"What was it you said?" She turned her head once again, and he grasped her chin in his hand and bent his head to kiss her. He felt her stiffen, then relax, and then, glory of glories, lean willingly toward him as she had never done before.

"We shouldn't be doing this," she murmured against his mouth. He silenced her with another kiss. He held her face gently, and when he lifted his mouth from hers, she turned her head and pressed her lips against his open palm. The sensation sent waves of heat coursing through him.

The knuckles of his hand that clasped her round the waist grazed the undersides of her breasts, and he longed to cup them in his hand. Only with great strength of will was he able to restrain himself. He bent his head once again to kiss the soft spot just below her right ear. She shuddered.

"Colby, please. You are destroying me," she murmured. "I have never felt so..."

"I know, Topaz. Neither have I. Come, we must go before...before those people return." It was not what he had meant, but it was a good reason to hasten their departure.

It was several moments before she was willing to leave the comfort of his arms. Then, with a sigh, she leaned forward, saw that the way was clear, and led him out of the shallow alcove. It took them considerably less time to leave the convent than it had taken them to enter. Sally was pacing the ground outside the wall.

"Well, it took you long enough, I'd say. I was near to sendin' for 'elp."

Topaz patted her shoulder. "I'm glad you didn't. Everything is quite all right, as you can plainly see."

"Humph. Seems to me you sound a little odd."

"Nonsense. I'm merely out of breath from the excitement of it all." She shot a glance at Colby and smiled. "Come along, Sally. Get into the carriage. And if you breathe one word of this little adventure to anyone..."

"Cross me 'eart, miss. Your secret's safe wi' me. But just so's I know what it is that I'm not to talk about, did you find out who your mum is?"

An almost imperceptible shake of Colby's head warned Topaz to be silent. She sighed. "No, Sally, I still don't know who my mother is."

And it was true. All she had was a name. The woman could have borrowed any name to conceal her identity and no one would have been the wiser. If there truly was an Anne Marker, would they ever find her? And, indeed, was she still alive?

WHEN TOPAZ AND SALLY got back to the Taggarts' the guests were just returning from Lady Breckenridge's party. Topaz had donned her gown quickly, but the timing could not have been worse. Lady Udora was just handing her manteau over to the butler.

"Topaz?" she enquired, looking more than a little apprehensive. "Have you only just arrived? I thought you left the party nearly an hour ago. And where is Arthur?"

"He has already retired to his room. Did you enjoy the party?"

"If you are attempting to change the subject, don't waste your time. But yes, it was a lovely party. Lady Breckenridge has a talent for making her guests feel comfortable. What a pity she had to lose her husband."

"You look very tired, my lady. May I see you to your room?"

"Thank you, but Bently will return in a moment. He is still conferring with our driver. Now then, Topaz, where have you been?"

"I . . . I went for a short drive—with Sally as chaperon, of course."

"At this time of night? Really, Topaz, that is quite . . ."

"I know. Perhaps I shouldn't have, but I've been very unsettled of late. Tell me, Lady Udora, do you know the name Anne Marker?" Topaz watched her closely for some reaction, but she appeared merely to ponder the question.

"No. I cannot say that I do. Is she someone you met at the party?"

"No, the name was mentioned—" She was interrupted when the door opened and Colby came into the entrance hall. He paused when he saw them, then regained his composure and bowed in their direction. Udora inclined her head, then turned her attention back to Topaz. Suspicion was clearly written on her face.

"Tell me the truth, Topaz. Were you with Lord Colby tonight?"

"Why, yes, of course. You saw us dancing together at the Breckenridge party. But it was only the one dance, I assure you, my lady." Topaz gave her a dazzling smile in the hope of distracting her.

Udora was not, however, to be deterred. An expression of weariness crossed over her face. "My dear child, what can I say to you to convince you that you are courting disaster? Arthur has been more than patient with your childish behaviour, but you cannot expect him to tolerate it for long.

"I can understand your attraction to Lord Colby. He has a certain masculine appeal that any woman..." She shrugged. "Well suffice it to say that there is no future for you where he is concerned. Believe me, Topaz, the Colby family holds to the custom of marrying within their own class. They have traditionally cared for their own people but have avoided mingling with common folk. Except for David, that is. He is something of a black sheep, but then he will not inherit unless his brother dies before him." Udora squeezed Topaz's hand. "Lord Colby places great stock in family tradition, Topaz. When he marries, it will be to a woman of noble birth. Trust me. I know this to be true."

When it appeared that he was going to approach them, Udora took Topaz's arm and directed her toward the stairs. "I believe I won't wait for Bently after all. Come along, dear. I'm feeling quite drained."

Topaz looked back over her shoulder at Colby, who stood watching them. There was a look in his eyes that she found quite impossible to define.

Sally went along to Lady Udora's room to help her prepare for bed. When Topaz entered her own chamber, Prudence opened the door from the adjoining bedroom. "So you've returned. This time without any unfortunate display of vulgarity, one would hope."

"One would hope," Topaz replied, then was immediately contrite. "I'm sorry, Aunt Prudence. I didn't mean to be so sarcastic. My life is all a jumble and I don't know where to turn."

"Not surprising, after all. Betrothed to one man and yearning after another. You are going to have to make a decision one way or the other, my dear." She looked closely at Topaz. "But that's not all that's troubling you, is it? Are you still disturbed over what Udora said about your being adopted?"

"I . . . I don't want to discuss it. Let's talk about the party. Haven't the twins returned yet?"

"They were enjoying a play put on by some of the people from the theatre. Lady Breckenridge promised to chaperon them, and the major promised to see to their safe return."

"But I assumed the major brought *you* home."

"Humph. What makes you think I would want him to? A man like him, making eyes at the first woman who dances to his tune."

Topaz stopped taking the pins from her hair and watched her aunt through the mirror. "Was it some woman in particular?"

"Yes, indeed. The widow woman in the scarlet muslin."

"Mrs. Mattingly? I wouldn't have thought she was his type."

"Flashy, that's what she is, with her *décolletage*." Prudence turned to gaze out the window. "Sometimes I wish I were more like her. Carefree, full of laughter and joy."

Topaz was pleasantly surprised. "You could be, you know. Even with your hair pulled back like that, you are still an attractive woman. If you let Maggie curl it for you and arrange it in a more stylish fashion, I'd warrant you would become a changed woman. So many men would chase after you, you would have to beat them off with a stick."

She was rewarded with a smile.

"Dear child, you do have a vivid imagination."

"Why don't you start with your clothing, Aunt Prudence? I remember when Lady Udora first came to live with us. We three girls had been quite unsupervised for many months and had taken to wearing the same dresses for days on end. I once went two months without combing my hair."

Prudence turned round and watched as Topaz ran the brush through her cascade of silken curls. "I can scarcely believe that. It's true, then? What happened to change you?"

"Lady Udora took us in hand. Burned every last stitch of our clothing so that we were forced to wear the new things she had bought for us. And we weren't allowed food until we bathed."

"I can see how you must have suffered." She chuckled.

Topaz smiled at the attempt at humour, a gesture so unlike her aunt. She turned round to face her. "Would you like me to burn *your* clothing, Aunt Prudence?"

Prudence sat down beside her and gave her a hug. "I do not think that will be necessary. But you're right, my dear child. I think perhaps it is time for a change. I have grieved long enough for the daughter I came here to find. Indeed, most probably will never find. But I'll not brood. I intend to begin to enjoy life."

"I know someone who is going to be pleased to hear that."

"Surely you don't mean the major."

"I most certainly do. I suspect he was trying to make you jealous tonight."

Prudence blushed. "Not very likely. Why would he choose me when he has a dozen ladies at his beck and call?"

"Why does anyone choose anyone? Why can I not love Arthur the way he says he loves me?"

"He's not right for you. It is as simple as that. A woman knows. Just as I knew when I ran away to the Colonies."

"Ran away? But I thought the family sent you into exile."

"They would have done, but I beat them to it. And all because the man I loved was not the man my family chose for me to marry."

"But you never married him, your daughter's father?"

"No, more's the pity. He died soon after the ship reached port. Perhaps if he had lived my daughter and I would still be friends, and I would not have come back to London to look for her."

Topaz took her hands. "I've never told you this, Aunt Prudence, but I am very glad you came back. And I pray that you will find your daughter one day soon."

"In God's time." Prudence hastily brushed a tear from the corner of her eye. "But what are we going to do about you? It is that Lord Colby who has caught your eye, is it not?"

"Yes. He is helping me find out who my real mother was." Topaz again took her aunt's hand. "Tell me the truth, Aunt Prudence. Do you know who she is? You were close to my parents back then, before..."

"Before I left in disgrace? Don't be shy, girl. I finally came to terms with what I considered the shame of it all, and I decided it was the way it was meant to be. Not that I would do it the same way twice, you understand, but I did the best I could and I learned from it.

"As to your question. No, regretably, I have no idea who your parents were. All I know is that you were adopted when you were two or three weeks old by my brother, Quentin Thackery, and his wife, Marion. They both loved you very much."

"Do you know the name Anne Marker?"

Prudence seemed to run it over in her mind. "No, the name is unfamiliar."

"Anne Marker was my mother."

Prudence gave her a sharp look. "How do you know this?"

"Colby and I went to the convent and discovered the information. But that is all I know. I'm so afraid I'll never find out who she is . . . or was."

"I suppose the answer might lie in Coventry," Prudence stated cautiously.

"Yes. I have thought about that. Somehow I must convince Bently and Lady Udora that we need to spend some time there."

"Perhaps I can help. A good dose of country air might be just what Udora needs to put the colour back in her cheeks. Besides, she's been missing her cats since she sent them back there to live. I'll try, but convincing her won't be easy with the weddings coming upon us so soon."

"Would you? Thank you, thank you, Aunt Prudence." Topaz hugged her impulsively. Prudence stiffened for a moment, as if unsure what to do. Then she put her arms around Topaz's shoulders and embraced her.

The twins took that precise moment to arrive with more than their usual exuberance. Prudence excused herself and went into the adjoining room.

Amy flopped down onto the silken bed cover and kicked off her slippers. "You should have been there, Topaz. The jugglers were marvellous, and after that there was a trained dog that jumped through hoops. It was dyed pink. Do you suppose the dye will make it sick?" she asked, suddenly concerned.

Emerald pushed her diamond-studded spectacles, a gift from Lord Milford, onto the bridge of her nose. "You are such a goose, Amy. I knew you would make a fuss about the poor dog. His owner advised me that they used beet juice to dye his fur."

"You might have told me sooner so I didn't have to worry," Amy pouted, then quickly turned her attention to Topaz.

"What a hum it is that Arthur's not up to snuff. It's so tiresome having him sick. We were planning to ask the two of you to be partners in the lawn games tomorrow, but I suppose the grass might disagree with him."

"I think Arthur and his friends are hoping to arrange a card-game tomorrow. I promised him that I wouldn't interfere."

Emerald began the process of undoing the hooks on the front of her gown. "He isn't very attentive now that you are betrothed. Doesn't that worry you, Topaz?"

"Not at all. I prefer it that way." She drew a deep breath. "The truth is, I expect to tell him tomorrow that I cannot marry him after all."

"But you can't!" Amy protested. "Lady Udora would be devastated."

"We have taken her illness into consideration. However, she was feeling much better tonight. I am sure she will be all right. I've waited this long to tell her only because she looked so ill."

"We?" Emerald enquired with a sly grin, then nodded. "Yes, her colour was much better this afternoon. Tomorrow would be as good as any time to tell her, but I warn you, she won't be happy about it. Nor will Arthur's mother. I cannot wait to see her face when she hears the news.''

All three girls smiled, but then Amethyst pressed her hands against her face. "Stop this. We mustn't make fun of Arthur's mother."

"Even if she does ride a broomstick to the park every day," Emerald added. They all burst into laughter.

Emerald walked over to the dressing-table to comb out her hair and, as she picked up the brush, she saw a sheet of paper with some writing on it. "What is this?" she asked. "Anne Marker?"

Topaz took the paper from her hand. "Anne Marker is my mother."

"What?" the twins asked in unison. After that the questions flew like bats from an old barn, and Topaz had to be careful not to say too much. Emerald wouldn't talk, but Amy, in her own sweet way, was incapable of keeping a secret.

"I don't suppose either of you has ever heard the name," Topaz said. They hadn't. "Nor has anyone else, apparently. But I plan to find out who she is…or was. After we get back to London, I am going to persuade Lady Udora to spend a few days at Amberleigh so that I can question the nuns at the orphanage in Coventry. You mustn't say anything to her, though."

Amy jumped up. "But we *cannot* go to Coventry next week. Lily Farrencourt is giving a party for me."

"And I have promised to help Milford choose the new draperies for his house so that it will be ready for me after we are married," Emerald said.

"There's no need for the two of you to come along. Prudence promised to stay behind to look after you if

I can convince Lady Udora to go. I just don't want the two of you trying to dissuade Lady Udora from making the trip."

"All well and good—" Emerald's nose wrinkled "—but *Aunt Prudence?* She is sure to have us all wearing black bombazine and covering our hair by the time you return."

Topaz grinned. "I think you might be in for a surprise where Aunt Prudence is concerned."

"What do you mean?" they chorused.

"I'll not say another word. You have to wait and see." They were still attempting to pry the secret from Topaz long after they had tumbled into bed.

Sleep came reluctantly to Topaz, and even then it refused to linger long. She woke at six o'clock and saw that the sun was shining. Behind the house, overlooking the sea, was a tiny hillside that was covered with wild daisies. The urge to walk among them became so intense that almost before she knew what she was doing, she had struggled into her clothing and gone downstairs. The house was silent, save for those unfortunates who were required to rise at dawn to do the work of a busy household. She slipped out the door without being noticed.

Or so she thought.

Colby's heart wrenched at the sight of her skipping along the garden walk toward the headlands. Her silver hair, unconfined by pins or mob-cap, floated behind her in the brisk breeze coming off the sea. The blue shawl she had flung across her shoulders made her look like a forget-me-not among the daisies. He stepped off the veranda and followed her. He knew he shouldn't, but he did. He couldn't help himself. It was that simple.

He found her leaning against the ruin of a marble column that might once have been part of a gazebo. Surprised, she turned quickly when she saw him.

"Colby! What are you doing out here at this hour?"

"You sent for me, didn't you?"

"Sent for you? No... I—"

He moved very close to her. "No, what I mean is that you were thinking of me and you wished that I were here beside you. Well, here I am. All you have to do is wish, and I'll be there."

She laughed and the silvery sound of it seemed to be tossed about on the breeze. "Then I think I had best wish for you over there by that rock. You are far too close for me to preserve my dignity."

He stepped backwards until he was some distance away. "Is this better?"

"'Better' is not the word I would choose. Safer, perhaps."

He took four footsteps toward her. "Are you not safe now?"

"I suppose I am."

He moved two steps closer. "And now?"

"Yes, but..."

Once again he was close enough that he could reach her if he stretched out his arms.

"Please don't come any closer, Colby. You know what happens when we stand close to each other."

"And you know why those things happen, Topaz."

Her face took on the rosy glow of the morning sunshine. "But we mustn't permit them to. Not until I break my engagement to Arthur."

"When will that be? You know that you are driving me mad with waiting."

"Today, I hope. After I tell my guardian. Lady Udora is feeling much better, and I believe it will be safe to tell her of my plans."

"Then let it be soon." He bent down to pick three daisies. "May I come near enough to give these to you?"

"I . . . yes, of course." She reached for them, but he ignored her extended hand and came closer, so close that he saw her pupils widen, then contract.

He held her gaze by the force of his own, then, touching the daisies first to his lips and then to hers, he tucked them into the front of her bodice.

She reached her hands out to him and he grasped them between his palms. "Colby, I've said it before, but I have never meant it more than I do now. You are a dangerous man."

She would have said more, but a sudden movement in an upstairs window caught her attention. "Someone has seen us," she said. "I must go."

CHAPTER ELEVEN

TOPAZ DID NOT KNOW who had been watching them as they stood there so close together, but she knew that if she stayed a moment longer she would once again be lost in his arms. She traced a fingertip across his hand. "Forgive me, Colby, I must go."

She had no more than reached the safety of her bedroom when Sally came charging in. She threw open the draperies with obvious pleasure over the twins' protests.

"'Ere now, stop yer grumblin', for it won't do a bi' o' good. It's packin' we 'ave to do, and you're not to dawdle."

"Who told you that?" Emerald demanded, sitting up so abruptly that her book fell to the floor. "What has happened?"

"We're going 'ome, that's what. 'Er ladyship is took bad again and 'is lordship wants to take 'er 'ome."

Amy rolled over onto her back. "Is it serious? Will she be all right?"

"She says so. Me, I dunno. The doctor was 'ere after dawn and said as how it was safe for 'er to travel."

"Then I must get word to Farrencourt. He was expecting to take me to visit the Pavilion today."

Emerald retrieved her spectacles from the night-stand. "And I must send a message to Milford. We were to attend a gathering at Castle Inn this afternoon."

"And I need to tell…" Topaz stopped, for it wasn't Arthur whom she wanted to advise of their change of plans, it was Colby. Fortunately the twins were too excited to notice.

Sally took one look at her and stepped back. "'Ere now, wot's this? Dressed already without no one to do your 'ooks an' eyes?"

"I couldn't sleep. But I need you to do my hair, Sally. You do it up ever so much better than I can." It didn't take much flattery to keep Sally from noticing the obvious. Topaz rescued the daisies from the front of her gown and tucked them into the folds of her shawl.

It would still be hours before most of the house guests were about. Lady Udora chose to forgo food, but the others went down to the breakfast room to fortify themselves for their journey.

Colby, who had followed Topaz into the house at some distance, had already filled his plate at the sideboard and was seated near the end of the long table. Topaz stopped behind his chair while the rest of her family were occupied with selecting their food.

"I am afraid I have to continue my charade a day or two longer. Her ladyship is not feeling well and we must leave for London directly."

Before he could reply, Bently took a chair across the table from him. "You're an early riser, Colby. What brings you downstairs at this time of day?"

"I often rise at dawn, Lord Kesterson. My house is in the countryside and I like to ride early in the morning before I begin working on my drawings for the boats that I hope to build."

"Ah, yes. I heard you have a talent for shipbuilding."

"Topaz told me of her ladyship's setback. I hope she soon returns to good health."

Topaz took a seat next to Bently. "I wonder, Bently, if a few days in the country would benefit Lady Udora's health. She enjoys the fresh air, away from the smoke of London, and I know she misses her cats."

"I've wondered about the same thing. I must ask her physician if she is well enough to make the journey. As a matter of fact, I would be most eager to spend a few days at the farms to see how the lambing has gone, as well as the repairs to the bridge after the heavy rains we had during the Spring."

Colby seemed interested in the subject of sheep-breeding and Topaz successfully ignored the rest of their conversation. She had plans to make. The first one was how to convince Lady Udora that she be allowed to accompany them to Coventry.

As it turned out, it wasn't difficult at all. Udora was feeling ever so much better by the time they reached the house in London. When Bently broached the subject of visiting the farms, Amberleigh and Pheasant Run, Udora was intrigued. For a moment she demurred, agonizing over the work that had yet to be done to prepare for the weddings in September, but when Prudence offered to take over, Udora willingly agreed. They were to leave in three days. Topaz had hoped for an earlier departure, but Udora insisted that they remain in London for their regular Wednesday evening "at home."

For Prudence's sake, and to avoid thinking about Colby, Topaz decided to take over the task of making the "at home" a memorable evening for both the family and their guests. Keeping it a secret proved to be a rather significant obstacle, because her sisters were still in the habit of sharing their adventures. It was less difficult to evade Lady Udora because of the countless tasks that had to be finished before the family left for Coventry the following day. Topaz waited until everyone had left the house to pursue their various errands before she took Aunt Prudence in tow.

"Whatever are we going to look for in the attic?" Prudence demanded with a touch of her old stuffiness.

"Wait and see. Luckily for us, Lady Udora never discards anything. You are as tall but smaller than she is, and I am sure she has a number of lovely gowns tucked away in a trunk under the eaves."

"But I..."

"Don't worry, no one will recognize them. Then, as soon as we can go to a modiste, we shall have you fitted for some gowns of your own."

"It's not that I am embarrassed to wear Udora's cast-offs. I only hope she won't disapprove."

"I can promise that she will be only too happy to have you properly clothed," Topaz said with undue emphasis. She covered her mouth. "I'm sorry. I didn't mean to imply..."

"No need to apologize. Is that the trunk to which you referred?" Prudence asked when they reached the top of the narrow stairs.

"Yes, and there may be something in the armoire, too, I think." She lifted the lid after blowing away the dust. The scent of lavender and cedar wafted up from the layers of tissue paper, silk and velvet.

"Look, Aunt Prudence. What a lovely shade of green! Oh, but the skirt is too full. Quite *démodé*. It could be altered, but I want something for you to wear tonight."

"So soon? I'm not sure I am quite ready to be . . . transformed so quickly."

"No better time than now. The major has left his card, so I know he will be in attendance."

Prudence blushed. "I do hope we are not making a mistake. I do not wish to look foolish."

"Leave it to me. Maggie promised to help with your hair, and I can trust her to keep a secret, for a while, at least."

They finally selected a Clarence blue gown, deceptively simple in cut, but adorned with elegant little ruffles of Brabant lace, a sort that had been much employed during the reign of Queen Elizabeth and had enjoyed recurring popularity ever since.

"The fit is nearly perfect," Topaz said. "Except for . . ." She made two cups with her hands. "Her ladyship is a little fuller than you. I think we can correct that with a bit of cotton wool."

"Really, Topaz! You are outrageous."

Seeing the change in her aunt, Topaz grinned. "And you are quite beautiful, Aunt Prudence. Here, drape this Paisley shawl around your shoulders."

"I want to look at myself."

"No. Not until you have had your hair curled and it is time to go downstairs."

"I shan't know how to behave."

"Why, the same way you always behave."

Prudence shook her head. "I suspect I will never act in quite the same way again. Not that I did anything wrong, you understand, but already I feel different." She lifted the cashmere shawl to her cheek. "The colours! The glorious colours. It's like being clothed in a rainbow."

Topaz gave her a hug. "You look wonderful, Aunt Prudence. I wish your daughter could see you now."

It was the wrong thing to say. For a while, at least, it put a damper on the day. By evening, however, Prudence was visibly shaking with excitement.

Emerald was the first to notice that Prudence was on edge. "Is something wrong, Aunt Prudence?" she enquired.

Prudence stole a look at Topaz, then shook her head. "Nothing at all. I'm merely a little nervous about tonight's gathering. I am told we are expecting quite a number of visitors."

Emerald shot a look at Topaz, who had to make an effort to keep her excitement from showing. But Emerald was not easy to fool. "I'm sure something is going on. Is it because both Arthur and Colby have left cards and expect to be here tonight?"

Topaz felt an added rush of pleasure. "Colby will be here? I had no idea."

Emerald looked at her from beneath lowered lashes. "Then I suppose you will want to change into something more fetching than that tired sprigged muslin.

Good enough for Arthur but not for Colby, eh? Balancing two beaux at the same time will bring you nothing but trouble."

"If you recall, Arthur was never my choice. Now, why don't you go find your own fiancé and stop plaguing me?"

Emerald shrugged her shoulders in a gesture of resignation, turned and left the room with a sly smile and a flutter of her fan.

When the bedroom door closed behind her, Maggie appeared from the adjoining room, curling tongs in hand. "I thought she'd never go. Sure an' if you want me to do Miss Prudence up right, then we'd best get to it while there's still someone left for 'er to get dressed up for."

"First she must change her gown," Topaz ordered. "Between the three of us, she will be ready in no time."

Maggie gave Topaz a quelling look. "Easy for you to say, miss, since you're not the one what's usin' the curlin' tongs."

While Maggie worked her magic with Prudence's hair, Topaz selected, then discarded, a dozen costumes before deciding what she wanted to wear. She finally chose a gown of burgundy velvet, split down the front to reveal a pale pink underdress. The square-cut neckline edged with amethyst-coloured beads and pearls framed her face and echoed the amethyst-and-pearl comb that held long curls to the back of her head. She pinched her cheeks to bring up the colour before going to the next room to oversee Prudence's metamorphosis.

The change was astounding. Only when Maggie was finished did they allow Prudence to view the miracle. She took one look at herself and all but fainted.

"Who is this woman I see looking back at me?"

"It's you, Aunt Prudence. I told you that you are beautiful. It just took Maggie to prove it to you." Topaz gave the abigail a hug. "Maggie, I vow I'll find some way to repay you."

"And you may be sure I'll remind you of it. Now go on wi' you before McMasters closes the door on the last visitor. I've got to rest me feet."

Topaz grinned. "Rest your feet in Timothy Grodin's lap is what you really mean, don't you, Miss Slyboots? But don't worry. I won't breathe a word."

Maggie gave her a withering look, then shooed them from the room.

THE SALON WAS FILLED with their usual group of Wednesday night visitors plus a few newer acquaintances. Lady Udora always provided background music for her guests. This time she had hired a woman to play the harp. A footman serving sherry and arrack punch was trailed by Alice, a young maid, who carried a silver tray of sweetmeats and frosted grapes.

When Topaz and Prudence entered the room, a sudden silence surrounded them. The hush grew and spread across the room until, save for the music, there was complete silence. Even the harpist was so startled by the unexpected quiet that she struck a discordant note.

Prudence looked up at Topaz with uncertainty in her gaze. Topaz reached over and whispered, "Smile, Aunt Prudence. This is your come-out."

Still no one spoke. It was the major who saved the day. He pushed his way through the crowd, stepped in front of the two women and bowed deeply. "Ladies, I cannot find words to express my admiration. The two of you grace the room with your unequalled beauty."

He offered his arm to Prudence. "May I?" She looked at Topaz as if asking for permission. Topaz nodded, and for the first time that Topaz could remember, Prudence's face was wreathed in smiles.

Then, as if a signal had been given, everyone flocked round Prudence and the major. Topaz managed to back away, only too glad to be out of the main crush. What she really wanted was to be alone. But Arthur found her, and for the next half hour, he danced attention upon her. He seemed only a little disappointed that she would be leaving for Coventry on the morrow, though he told her that invitations had been sent out for a party his mother was planning for a few days after the Kestersons returned from Coventry.

His face was pink with anticipation. "She has invited all of London for the party in our honour."

"All of London?" Topaz asked with considerable irritation.

"Well, only those of consequence. There would be no point in inviting the others, would there?" He bowed and kissed her hand. "Now, there's a good girl. Go and talk to your guests. I must speak with an old friend."

Topaz watched him greet Lord Overfield with enthusiasm. Then her eyes scanned the room for Colby. But as it happened, Colby did not put in an appearance. Both Amy and Em remarked upon the fact later that night when they had retired to their rooms.

"What happened, do you suppose?" Emerald said. "Has he decided not to pursue you after all?"

Amy slipped her fan from her wrist and laid it on the dressing-table. "One could hardly blame him. He has been courting scandal for weeks now, just by turning up wherever Topaz is. He could not have made his feelings more obvious. I think he should stay away altogether and let Taz get on with her wedding plans."

Emerald sent her a scathing look. "What wedding plans? You know very well that Taz will never marry Arthur."

"Of course she will. He is so handsome... and so rich!"

Topaz threw a pillow at Amy and hit her squarely in the back. "If you admire him so much, you may take him as a lover once you've provided Farrencourt with a son."

"Topaz!" Amy all but screamed. "That is disgusting. How can you say such a thing!"

"I'm sorry. Please. If Colby turns up here while I am in Coventry, will you tell him where I am and when I shall return? I confess, I'm finding it hard to leave, now that the day for our departure has nearly arrived."

Emerald hugged her adopted sister. "Of course I'll speak to Colby. You can count on Prudence, too. She is bound to be your slave, considering the change you have wrought in her."

"Just don't let her slip back while I'm gone," Topaz pleaded. "She's really quite a good sort, you know."

Amy nodded. "I have always thought so. We shall look after her, and I know the major will help us, too."

A short time later, Sally and Maggie came in to help them prepare for bed. Topaz lay awake for nearly an hour after they left. It hurt more than she could admit to anyone that Colby had stayed away tonight of all nights. He might have suspected that she would be soon departing for the country and it could be another week until he could see her again.

AMBERLEIGH, the Thackery family's country house, and the adjoining farm, Pheasant Run, owned by the Kestersons, basked in the afternoon sun like two well-fed and much-loved felines. Bently's skill at farming had turned Amberleigh into a thriving community of contented workers.

Mrs. Kragen, the housekeeper who had been at Amberleigh for nearly twenty years, took one look at Udora and pressed her hands to her face. *"Ach de lieber!* Vot have zey done to you? You look tired, my lady."

"It's nothing serious, Mrs. Kragen. Nothing your good dumpling soup and a dose of fresh air cannot cure. My goodness, you have kept the house bright and shining."

"Not like ven you came here za first time, no?" They all laughed to remember how hard Udora had worked to bring order out of the chaos of a motherless home and take over the rearing of the three girls.

Mrs. Kragen handed Bently a piece of folded paper. "Zis is a message zent over from Pheasant Run, m'lord. Just today it came."

"Hmn. I see." He turned his head toward Udora. "It seems that I have a gentleman waiting to see me about the new breed of sheep we introduced last year. I suppose I had best go over and see what he's about. Will you get some rest while I'm gone?"

"Of course, dear. Topaz and Maggie will see me to our room." She brushed a kiss across his cheek. "Hurry back."

Topaz looked at Maggie and they both smiled. Such intimacies were less common in London than they were here at the country house. It was a good sign.

Udora retired to the bedroom suite directly under one of the large glass-domed ceilings that gave Amberleigh its name. The room was flooded with sunlight broken into shards of gold by the many-faceted panes of amber-coloured glass.

She sat down on the edge of the bed. "I shan't be able to fall asleep with all this light."

Topaz sat down next to her. "Would you like to move to another room?"

"Not at all. I love this room. I only need rest, not sleep. Stay here and talk with me for a while."

"I remember other talks we've had in this room. What would you like to talk about?" Topaz asked as she sat down at the foot of the bed.

"Whatever concerns you. This foolishness with Colby, to begin."

"It isn't foolishness, Lady Udora. I love him. I've loved him since the moment I saw him riding his horse down from the hill, his black cloak flying out behind him like some dark avenging angel."

Udora's eyes widened. "How strange. The first time I saw Bently it was under very similar circumstances.

He looked so strong. Threatening, but at the same time, compelling. So unbelievably male."

Topaz smiled. "Exactly! He wants to marry me."

"Then he has said so? He knows, of course, that you are adopted?"

"Yes. It must have come as a shock to him, but I believe he has come to terms with it and has accepted my dubious past."

"Surprising, considering his family background. It's quite impressive, you know."

"It's not his family I care about. I want to marry him, my lady. I . . . I've decided to break my engagement to Arthur. We could never be happy together."

"Ah, yes. I suspected as much, but I wanted you to make the decision yourself."

"I would have told you sooner, but . . ." She shrugged and hesitated before continuing. "Colby is trying to help me discover who my parents were."

"Indeed?"

"Yes. My mother's name was Anne Marker. I can't tell you yet how I gained this information."

Udora gave her a knowing look. "I rather suspect I would prefer not to know. Anne Marker? You questioned me earlier about that name."

"I thought perhaps you knew about her. As yet that's all she is, a name. I want to go to the orphanage here in Coventry to see if they can tell me more."

"I rather thought you had an ulterior motive in coming to Amberleigh. I'll go with you, if you like."

"No. I'll take Maggie. You need to rest." Topaz drew her knees up to her chin. "You know how much we've all worried about you, my lady. Is there something that you haven't told us about your condition?"

Udora drew a deep sigh. "I suppose you will find out sooner or later. But I must ask you not to say a word to Bently. I'm looking for the perfect time to tell him. But we've grown so close, you and I…and I need to confide in someone before my condition becomes obvious."

Suddenly the truth dawned on Topaz. She sat up straight. "You're going to have a baby!"

"H-how did you know? I've been so careful to hide it."

"I didn't until now. I guessed. Little things you have said have begun to fall into place. But aren't you happy about it?"

"I confess I am, or would be if I didn't hesitate to tell Bently. He's so intent on planning our voyage to the Indies after the weddings in September."

"And you have always said you hated the drooling and mess that goes along with having babies."

"Yes, but it's different, isn't it, when the baby is your own."

"I suppose it is. But is it quite safe for you? You've had your thirtieth birthday…."

"Indeed I have, but I am healthy and strong. The doctor tells me that once the first few months have gone by I will feel quite well. But you must promise not to tell Bently."

"You cannot keep this from him for much longer."

"I know, but I must find the right moment to break the news to him. It will all work out as it should." She closed her eyes. "Run along now, dear, and let me rest. Thank you for our little talk. I feel ever so much better.''

"So do I. I shall look in on you later to see if there is anything you need.''

Topaz wandered around the sprawling house and gardens of Amberleigh for more than an hour before she could decide what to do. There was still time for her to visit the orphanage, but, for some reason, she was reluctant to do so. On a whim she had the stable-boy saddle a horse, and she went riding along the edge of the river until she came to the deer park that divided Amberleigh from Pheasant Run.

Beyond the low hedge she could see the spires of the Kesterson house as well as the enclosure that contained the breeding fowl. She was tempted to go there but was reluctant to disturb Bently when he was discussing farm business with a guest. She felt fragmented, like loose stitches pulling their way through a knitted sweater. She missed Colby.

BENTLY WAS NOT in the best of moods. His conversation concerning the advantages and disadvantages of the new breed of sheep was somewhat terse and to the point. Finally he faced his guest from across the table in the library at Pheasant Run.

"Now, then, Colby, what is it you really want? You didn't come all the way to Coventry just to discuss sheep. You're pursuing my ward, Topaz Thackery, are you not?''

"I must admit that I am,'' Colby replied. "I love her and I very much want to marry her.''

"Awkward, isn't it, considering that she is already betrothed?''

"Awkward, but not impossible."

"You know that she is adopted. Given your family background, that must surely be a serious consideration."

"It was, but it no longer matters. Topaz loves me, and I know that I can make her happy." He drew a deep breath and leaned forward. "Perhaps she should be the one to tell you, but I grow impatient. It is her intention to break her engagement to Arthur Ringwald as soon as Lady Udora is well enough to withstand the shock."

Bently frowned. "Only Heaven knows when that will be. I am deeply concerned about her." He stroked his chin. "Very well. If this is what Topaz wants, I have no objection, but there is one thing I must insist upon. You must agree not to see her until she is completely free of Lord Throckmorton."

Colby felt the sweat bead on his forehead. He stood and walked to the window, pushing aside the drapery and staring out at the rolling hills and fields. Then he turned toward Bently once again and clasped his hands behind his back.

"With all due respect, my lord, I cannot promise not to see her. I love her too deeply to spend a minute longer than necessary apart from her. But this I do vow, sir. I will not compromise her virtue nor harm her in any way."

A slow smile spread across Bently's face. He rose and thrust out his hand. "Well done, my boy. Exactly what I wanted to hear. For if you had agreed to my request, I would have questioned the depth of your feeling for this girl. When the time comes, both Udora and I shall be happy to welcome you to our family."

Colby was moved by the man's sincerity, even more so when Bently invited him to remain at Pheasant Run as a house guest while the rest of the family stayed on at Amberleigh.

"And of course you will join us for meals," Bently added.

"It will be my pleasure, sir."

"Good. I'll have my housekeeper show you to your room and let you get settled in. In the meantime, I have to visit some of my tenant farmers before I return to Amberleigh. I will instruct my stable master to have a saddle horse or the gig at your disposal whenever you wish to go ahead. Please consider this your home while you are here."

Colby was understandably surprised by his host's graciousness. Alone in the elegantly furnished suite of rooms that were to be his for the next two days, he paced the floor. Would Lord Kesterson tell Topaz that he was here? Would she think it presumptuous of him to have followed her? He knew that she was enamoured of him and played with the idea of marrying him, but she was so young. Was it merely a passing infatuation?

"Double damnation," he said to no one in particular. "I've got to get out of here." Then he remembered that Topaz had spoken of Kesterson's stable of blooded horses, and he decided to see for himself. Twenty minutes later he was astride a glossy four-year-old chestnut, riding toward a grove of trees that looked serenely inviting.

He saw her before she saw him. His heart thudded in his chest as he slowed his horse to a walk, then dismounted and tied the reins to a tree. Topaz was seated on a rock beside a rushing stream. From time to time she bent down to ripple the water with her fingers. Colby wanted to hold the memory of her forever, but more than that, he wanted to hold her in his arms.

A sound must have disturbed her horse for he nickered and shook his head. Alerted, Topaz looked back over her shoulder. Then, seemingly dazed, as if attempting to arouse herself from a dream, she rose and turned toward him.

"Colby? Is that really you?"

He held out his arms to her. She paused for one heart-stopping moment and then lifted her riding skirt and ran toward him. The force of her body drove him backwards a pace or two, but he regained his footing and buried his face in her hair. All his doubts were swept away by the impact of their embrace. "I couldn't stay away from you, my darling girl. Forgive me, but I had to come after you."

CHAPTER TWELVE

TOPAZ HELD ON to him as if she would never let him go. "I am so glad you've come, Colby. I have missed you dreadfully." She turned her face to brush soft kisses against his throat, his cheek and his chin. Then her lips pulled at his lower lip, sending searing flashes of heat through his body. When he moaned, she kissed him full on the mouth, and the sweetness of her desire left no doubt in his mind that she wanted him completely, as much as he wanted her.

Colby drew upon the last of his strength to pull away. "Dear God, Topaz, we must stop this before I do harm to you."

She gave him an angelic smile and kissed him again, then murmured against his cheek. "The only harm would be in stopping now. Don't you know how much I need you?"

"I feel it in every inch of my body and in the way it cries out for you. But I gave him my word."

She leaned back, surprised. "Who?"

"Lord Kesterson. He has given us his blessing."

Her eyes widened with pleasure. "You told him? And I told Lady Udora! She, too, gave us her blessing."

"But I promised Lord Kesterson that I would not harm you. Surely we can wait a while longer, Topaz. I have already waited for you all these years."

Her gaze dropped to the ground, then she looked toward the horizon. "I suppose. But I am so afraid I shall lose you. There are so many young ladies who vie for your attention. Even your housekeeper, if that's what she really is," Topaz said with a mischievous expression.

Colby smiled at her spark of jealousy. "Regina is a friend, too. Her parents were content to take care of my family, but servitude never appealed to Regina. She has always had ideas above her station."

He lifted Topaz's chin and looked into her eyes. "You have no need to be concerned about Regina, my dearest. I've made arrangements for her to go to Paris to be tutored in the art of French pastry. She has a passion to learn more about it and eventually open her own shop. She's a bright young woman and she has a will to succeed. I promise you, Topaz, Regina will be gone by the time we announce our betrothal."

"It's for the best, I think, even though she was kind to me," Topaz said. "I'm pleased that you consider her feelings. And I must be considerate of Arthur. Before you and I create a scandal I must gently break my engagement."

Colby grinned. "So that's what you have in mind for us, a scandal?"

"Only if you wait too long to lead me to the altar."

"There is not much chance of that. We can still be married in September, if that is what you wish."

"What will your mother…and David say about our betrothal?"

"They will be happy for us. I promise you that."

Topaz sighed. "Then I suppose we had best return to the house, where I can be properly chaperoned. Otherwise, I simply cannot promise to be on my best behaviour."

He bent down and kissed her quickly, without attempting to hold her. "Since Lord Kesterson has invited me to supper, I shall still be able to see you."

UDORA'S FOUR CATS, which had come to live at the farm rather than be subjected to the rigours of life in Town, had been brought up to the house for her pleasure. Bently's cat, Snowball, had taken to meeting Udora's cat, Ulysses, in the milking parlour and was presently heavy with kittens. When Topaz and Colby entered the library, Snowball, along with Udora's four cats, was sprawled in front of the fire.

Bently was sitting behind the desk, a pile of papers spread out in front of him. "Ah, there you are, Colby. Welcome to Amberleigh."

"Thank you, sir. May I say what a pleasure it is to ride such an excellent mount as your four-year-old chestnut."

"That would be Jericho. Glad you took him out for some exercise. Hello, here comes Mrs. Kragen with the sherry. Will you join me?"

Topaz helped herself to a square of toast topped with pickled herring. "Here, Snowball," she crooned. "Here's a treat for you, love."

Mrs. Kragen nearly dropped the tray. "*Mein Gott*, don't be giving her fish in her condition. I varned zat new girl not to zerve fish."

"Why ever not?" Bently demanded.

"For her ladyship's zake, of course. Her in her condition. Yust the smell vould bring it up before it got all za vay down."

Bently laughed. "You have it wrong, Mrs. Kragen. The cat may be in a *condition,* but her ladyship has an *illness.*"

"Humph. Call it what you vant, m'lord, but nine months is a long illness."

Topaz drew a sharp breath. One look at Bently's face assured her that he had not missed a beat in the conversation. He slowly put his glass down on a nearby table, got up and strode to the fireplace with his hands locked behind him. Topaz started to say something but he waved her into silence. Mrs. Kragen left the room, taking along with her the offending plate of fish. Colby looked bewildered.

"We shall talk about this later," Topaz said softly.

Bently turned and pinned her with his gaze. "Then it is true. Udora is expecting a child?"

"Yes. It's true. But she..."

"Why haven't I been told?"

"She...she was not sure of your reaction. I only learned today that she is *enceinte.* She wanted to tell you, but the time was never right. Especially now...the trip to the Indies, and all."

"How could she...? Never mind, not a word of this to her, do you hear?"

He looked so shaken that Topaz was about to attempt to console him when Lady Udora entered the room. "Ah, here you are, my dears. Sorry to be so late. I fell asleep." She stopped short. "Lord Colby? What are you doing here?" She looked genuinely embarrassed. "Sorry. I did not mean to sound ungracious. You caught me by surprise."

He rose and bowed. "You have every right to be surprised. As it happens, I am spending a few days at Pheasant Run to learn more about this new strain of sheep. Lord Kesterson has agreed to sell me a pair of his breeding stock." He finished his sherry and set the glass down on the tray.

"You look well, my lady. The country air seems to agree with you."

"That and seeing my beloved cats. Welcome to Amberleigh, Lord Colby."

"Thank you, my lady."

Bently cleared his throat. "Colby, Topaz. I wonder if you would excuse us for a little while?"

"Certainly," Colby said, offering Topaz his arm. He inclined his head toward Lady Udora and they left the room. Topaz stopped just outside the library and left the door open a crack. She put her finger to her lips.

Colby gave her a quelling look. "Never tell me you intend to eavesdrop," he whispered.

"Very well, I won't tell you."

"What a minx you are! What are they saying?"

"Bently has just put Snowball onto her lap. Lean close. You can hear, too."

Lady Udora said something they couldn't hear. Then she apparently spoke to the cat. "What a hussy, you are, Snowball. We no more than leave you alone at the farm and you run about seducing my Ulysses. Yes, Ulysses. I'm talking about you. I thought your rakish days were over."

Bently chuckled. "It must have been Snowball's white fur coat. I remember one of the first times I saw you, Udora. You were wearing a black cape with a white fur collar and hood. I found you extremely bewitching."

"Indeed? How sweet of you to say so, Bently. But don't think you can fool me. What was it you wanted to say that made you send the children from the room?"

"Children?" Topaz whispered. "Really!"

Bently seemed to have moved about the room before he answered. Udora sounded unsettled. "Please, Bently, you are beginning to worry me. Is it bad news?"

"The truth is, it is very good news from where I stand. The problem is how to introduce the subject." He stroked his chin. "What concerns me is how you are going to feel about it when I tell you."

"Now I really am worried. Please, have out with it."

"Very well. Here it is. Now brace yourself, darling. The truth is . . ." He drew a loud breath. "I am going to have a baby."

"You are *what!*" The cat let out a shriek and jumped to the floor. As if on signal, all five cats, tails held high, burst through the doorway and scattered in all directions.

"Oh, Bently! I'm so sorry," Udora wailed. "I suppose Topaz told you."

"No. I learned quite by chance. But *sorry,* my dear? Surely you don't mean that. I am quite thrilled by the news."

"Thrilled? But I th-thought . . ."

"On the contrary, my love." He was holding her in his arms now and they were kissing. A moment later he lifted his head and without looking in their direction, said, "You may come in now, Topaz. One would hate to have you strain your ears." Topaz ran toward them and enfolded them both in her arms.

LOOKING BACK on their trip to Coventry, Topaz had to think of it as a success. She was closer both to her guardians and to Colby than she had ever been. But the question of her parentage had not been resolved by a visit to the orphanage. Although the nuns were most cooperative, they had given her little information beyond what she already had acquired. The search was beginning to look hopeless.

To top off her feeling of disappointment was the reminder that the family was expected to attend the Throckmorton party the night following their return from Coventry.

"Would it not be kinder of me to break my betrothal to Arthur today instead of allowing his mother to spend a fortune on a party to celebrate our betrothal?" Topaz enquired of Udora.

"My dear girl, the money would already have been spent. The invitations have been sent and the acknowledgements received. You know what that entails. What you must do, I believe, is tell Arthur of your decision before the toasts are drunk to your happiness. That way people will only wonder if something is amiss. Of course it will all be clear when they read of the dissolution of the betrothal in the newspapers."

"I suppose you are right, but I would far rather stay home."

"One cannot do that, can one?"

ONE COULDN'T, OF COURSE. They would all attend the gala. Amethyst and Emerald were delighted by the opportunity to show off their new gowns and to spend an evening with their fiancés. Prudence had worked furiously with the seamstresses to have a new gown ready for the soirée. She glittered radiantly, and the major seemed unable to drag his gaze away from her. Udora looked reborn in a somewhat fuller than usual gown of Devonshire brown that brought out the red-gold of her hair. It would be some time before her condition would be noticeable and she would consequently be forced out of the public eye. "Certainly not until after the weddings," she said with considerable determination.

As for Topaz, she wore the dress she had been saving for such an occasion. An ivory-and-turquoise creation studded with tiny diamonds and pearls. Because Colby would be there and for no other reason, she thought, pleased by her reflection in the mirror.

When they arrived at the Throckmortons' residence the streets surrounding the house were already filled with score upon score of carriages that had delivered eager guests to the party. Kesterson directed his driver to take them to the front entrance, then find carriage space in the rear, which had been reserved for the guests of honour.

If they expected to be greeted with Lady Throckmorton's usual display of suffocating enthusiasm, they were wrong. Even before the butler had an opportunity to announce them, she and a bewildered-looking Arthur, herded them into the library.

Lady Throckmorton lifted her lorgnette. "Miss Prudence Thackery, you and the girls may join the others if you wish. I desire to speak to Lord Kesterson and Lady Udora."

The girls looked at one another and shrugged. Prudence, accompanied by the major who had just joined them, shepherded the three girls toward the ballroom.

"Not you, Topaz," Lady Throckmorton said in an icy voice. "I also wish you to remain behind."

She motioned for them to precede her. Once inside the room, she closed the door with care. "Sit down, all of you. I have something to say."

Udora started to interrupt but Lady Throckmorton motioned her into silence. "There is no graceful way of introducing such a painful subject, so I shall be straightforward. It has come to our attention that Miss Topaz Thackery is not a Thackery at all, but was adopted by Quentin and Marion Thackery when she was a baby."

"Yes?" Udora asked during the brief but heavy silence.

"Yes! *Yes?* Is that all you have to say? Why did you not deign to mention that she was a misbegotten child before my son agreed to marry her?"

Bently put his hand on Udora's arm to calm her before she could vent her feelings. His voice was deceptively mild. "We made no attempt to conceal the fact that Topaz was adopted. In truth, it was common knowledge among the Upper Ten Thousand, or so we assumed."

"Not as common as you might have thought, Lord Kesterson. As it stands, under the circumstances I cannot allow my son to commit himself, or the family name, to one who is quite possibly of low birth."

There was dead silence in the room. Lady Throckmorton's face remained frozen. Finally Udora spoke.

"Arthur? Have you nothing to say about this?"

He shrugged and dug the toe of his boot into the rug.

Udora drew herself up to her full height. "Then let us put an end to it. Suffice it to say I have no wish for my ward to be connected to a family whose views are so narrow-minded that they cannot see the pearl for the oyster shell." She fluttered her fan. "May I ask whom you have told of your decision?"

"Only a few people. My solicitor, a close friend or two, but if it is your wish to keep this confidential, you know better than I that scandal cannot be prevented."

"*You* may consider it a scandal," Udora said smoothly, "but we consider it a blessing. One that we had not counted on."

"Really! If you choose to be so haughty, then it might be well for you to bid us good-night here and now, rather than subject yourselves to further censure."

"No, Lady Throckmorton. I rather think we will stay until the very end. It should be quite interesting. Bently, my girls and I have many friends here, as you will soon come to learn to your great disadvantage."

Udora rose to go, but at that moment there was a knock on the door and Prudence entered along with

Lady Breckenridge. Lady Throckmorton looked shaken.

"Do forgive me, Lady Breckenridge, but I fear this is a private conversation."

"On the contrary, please come in," Bently said. "I am sure you will find it very interesting that her ladyship has decided to void the betrothal contract between her son and Topaz. It seems she was unaware that Topaz is an adopted child."

Prudence raised both eyebrows. "It was never a secret." She looked sideways at Lady Breckenridge, who gave a slight nod. Prudence continued. "I believe we can shed some light on the situation if you will permit us to speak."

Lady Breckenridge stepped forward and took Topaz's hands in hers. "I had hoped for a more opportune time to tell you, my dear child, but when the rumours began circulating this evening... Well, the truth is, I cannot withhold the truth from you any longer. It was I who gave birth to you and later, most reluctantly, gave you up for adoption. I am your mother."

Topaz stared at her, flooded with feelings that threatened to overwhelm her. "But you... you can't be."

"I know this comes as a shock to you. I should have told you long ago. My dear daughter. How I have longed to tell. So much that..." She spread her hands. "But I was afraid you would hate me for giving you up to another woman."

And then it dawned on Topaz. Lady Breckenridge was putting on an act. Her ladyship's first name was Elizabeth, not Anne. Topaz smiled and nodded. "I could never hate you, Mother. I only wish we had known each other before."

Lady Throckmorton, looking more than a little shocked, clasped her hands and gave an exclamation of joy. "How perfectly marvellous. Then all this has been for nothing, my dear girl. One could not have asked for better family connections. The wedding will, of course, go on as planned."

Topaz stiffened her back and lifted her chin. "I think not, your ladyship. I shall announce tonight that the betrothal is ended."

"How absurd! Tell her, Udora, that she is being childish. Tell her that she cannot court ridicule by allowing herself to be ruined by such a silly whim as revenge. That's all it is, you know, a wish for revenge."

Udora clasped her hands over her heart. "And what a sweet and wonderful thing it is! Come, my darlings, I hear music. I am certain some of us feel like dancing."

Arthur followed them for a few paces. Topaz, in a fit of conscience, turned to him. "I am sorry if this distresses you, Arthur. We both know we were completely unsuited to each other."

"I dare say you are right. Don't fret. There are other chits who would kill to take your place." He shrugged and closed the door after her.

Lady Breckenridge clasped Topaz's hand. "I heard what he said. It appears you are lucky to have done with him. I wonder, dear, if we might speak in private?"

"Yes, I would very much like that." Topaz was about to say more when Colby strode quickly toward them with a slight frown on his face.

"There you are, Topaz. Are you all right? I have heard some puzzling rumours about your being held in disgrace, and it occurred to me that I might be the reason." She smiled up at him and he apparently guessed from the radiant glow on her face that she was happy.

"Everything is as it should be," she said. "That is, if you still want to marry me. As of a few moments ago, I am free to do so."

"You cannot mean it!"

"But I do. I have broken my betrothal to Arthur." She laughed. "Well . . . first Lady Throckmorton renounced me, then she took me back, and then I renounced Arthur."

He pressed her hands between his and bent to kiss them. "If I have my way, we shall announce our betrothal tonight."

Topaz saw Lady Breckenridge watching them. "Colby, I owe a debt of gratitude to Lady Breckenridge. She has gone so far as to tell a falsehood in order to save me from embarrassment. I need to speak with her alone for a moment."

He looked surprised. "Can you not share this with me?"

"I would prefer to tell you later, but if you insist . . ."

"No. I defer to your judgement. But don't be long. I fully intend to dance with you this entire evening."

"You are a rascal and a scamp, and I adore you. But go away now. I shall meet you in a few minutes near that ghastly statue of the hunting dogs and the dead fawn." He reluctantly released her hand and she turned to follow Lady Breckenridge into a small reception room.

"My lady, before you explain, I must tell you how generous you were to save me from humiliation. I realize, of course, that you could not possibly be my mother. Her name was Anne Marker. Yours is Elizabeth, is it not?"

"So you've heard of Anne Marker. How, may I ask, did you obtain this information?"

"Illegally, if you must know. And I prefer not to discuss it because it involves someone dear to me."

"That would be Lord Colby, I suspect. No, there is no need to affirm or deny it. He is a worthy young man, one whom I have come to know and admire." She motioned Topaz to sit down next to her on the sofa.

"In answer to your question, Topaz, yes, my name is Elizabeth. Elizabeth Anne Marker Severenson. I was telling the truth when I said that I was...am your mother. Or at the very least the one who gave birth to you. Marion Thackery mothered you in a way that I could only dream of doing. She loved you as if you were her own. And to her I owe my undying gratitude."

Topaz was more unsettled than she had been in her entire life. "You...my mother? But...why? Why did you give me away, like some old dress that you no longer wanted?"

A spasm of pain crossed Lady Breckenridge's face. "It wasn't like that. I had been forced into a marriage to save my father from losing his home...everything he owned. We were a close and loving family. My mother's whole life revolved around our home and possessions. Only I had the power to save them."

"But that's no reason . . ."

"My husband would never have married me if he had known about you and that you were the gift of a very brief affair I had with the man I loved."

"Quentin Thackery?"

"You knew he was your father?"

"No, I merely guessed. We were so much alike."

"It was difficult for him to keep it a secret, but he owed it to his wife. That was all we could do to repay her for her goodness. I never saw him again. But I saw you from time to time, unbeknownst to your family. And I could not have been more happy when I heard that Udora was to become your guardian. I hope you can forgive me for what I have done to you."

"There . . . there is no need for forgiveness. I forgave you a long time ago." She took Lady Breckenridge's hands in hers. "Thank you, my lady, for caring about me. I have always loved you, deep in my heart."

"And I you." She drew a ragged breath. "Well, my dear daughter. What do we do now?"

"I don't know. I don't even know what to call you now. Must we keep it a secret to protect your reputation?"

"The devil take my reputation. I would love to shout it from the rooftops."

Topaz grinned. "I use those very same words. Lady Udora often scolds me for it."

"Then I shall have to reform."

"No, don't. I like the thought of being like you. But as to telling everyone, perhaps we should consult with my guardians before we say too much."

"Of course. I should have thought of that."

"But I must tell Lord Colby. I plan to marry him in September, and nothing should be kept secret between us."

"September? Could you not wait a few months to give us time to become acquainted? Travel together, perhaps?"

"September is not soon. If it were up to me I would ride to Gretna Green and marry him tonight."

Lady Breckenridge smiled. "But of course. Even I can remember the fires of passion. Your father and I were like that. But to be honest, I did come to love my husband, in my own way. He was a gentle man, good to me and good to my family."

"I'm glad."

Lady Breckenridge stood up. "Would it be asking too much to let me hold you in my arms just once before we go out to face the world?"

Topaz smiled and walked straight into her arms.

A short time later they summoned Lord Colby and proceeded to inform him of all that had happened. Lady Breckenridge gave them her blessing and accompanied them to the salon, where the rest of the family had gathered. Later that evening, when the toasts to the happy couple should have been drunk, Lord Kesterson announced that by mutual agreement, the Throckmortons and the Kestersons had chosen to dissolve the contract between the two families. Nothing was said about the fact that Topaz and Colby would be married in September, but it was clear to everyone who saw them together that theirs was a love that bound them closer than any contract ever could.

They linked arms as they strolled round the room, acknowledging the greetings of their friends and carefully avoiding the questions and stares of the overtly curious. The twins, Emerald and Amethyst, sparkled with excitement as they cornered Topaz and Colby to congratulate them on being united at last.

Udora and Bently, seated in comfortable chairs beneath an old tapestry depicting scenes of courtly love, looked round the room with undisguised pleasure. Udora saw Prudence, dressed in soft green velvet, standing close to the major as they shared laughter with Lady Jersey and Lady Cowper. Udora leaned toward Bently.

"Have you noticed the gleam in Prudence's eyes since she has taken to wearing decent clothing?"

"Indeed I have, and may I say that the gleam is reflected in the major's glances? I think they may have a *tendre* for each other. She certainly has changed since the day she arrived in London."

Udora had a trace of tears in her eyes as she reached for his hand. "Speaking of change, my darling Bently...can you believe that all this has come to pass? Our three precious Thackery Jewels, once so slovenly and troublesome. Now they shine more brightly than gemstones."

"They owe it all to you, Udora. Just as I owe you my happiness. Even more so, now that we are going to have a child."

She looked up at him with adoration in her eyes. "And what a child it will be! We work together very well, Bently. I have never been so happy in my entire life." She turned her head to look across the room. "And speaking of happiness, just look at Topaz and her young man. Have you ever seen anything so perfect?"

"Only when I look at you. I wonder where they are going?" he said as he saw Colby take Topaz by the hand and lead her away from the throng of people.

"I'm afraid to guess, knowing Topaz as I do. She is quite likely to lead him astray."

"Should we send a chaperon after them?"

Udora shook her head. "I may not trust Topaz to control her passions, but I trust Colby. Let them be."

COLBY WAS WELL AWARE that they were without doubt being watched as he whisked Topaz onto the balcony that overlooked the garden. But he did need just this brief moment alone with her.

She seemed nearly bursting with excitement as she all but flung herself into his arms. "Is it real, Colby, or is this only a dream? I'm so dreadfully afraid that I'll awaken only to find that it's all over—evaporated like the morning dew."

He bent down and kissed her softly on the mouth. "If it is a dream," he murmured against her hair, "I pray that we shall sleep forever."

"Forever...what a wonderful word, now that I know you love me as I love you." She looked up from lowered lashes. "Must we wait to...you know?"

He chuckled softly. "I'm afraid we must. I want this marriage to be perfect from the very beginning. And much as I want to take you to bed and make passionate love with you, my sweet Topaz, I cannot allow myself that luxury."

"But September is so far away. What are we to do until then?"

"Speaking for myself, I shall be thinking of all the wonderful things I want to teach you about making love."

She stood back and looked up at him with a mischievous twinkle in her eyes. "I've always been told, my lord, that I have a wonderful imagination." She pulled his head down and kissed him slowly, brushing her mouth back and forth over his lips. "Perhaps I can invent some interesting ideas of my own."

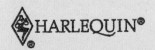

MILLION DOLLAR SWEEPSTAKES (III)

No purchase necessary. To enter, follow the directions published. Method of entry may vary. For eligibility, entries must be received no later than March 31, 1996. No liability is assumed for printing errors, lost, late or misdirected entries. Odds of winning are determined by the number of eligible entries distributed and received. Prizewinners will be determined no later than June 30, 1996.

Sweepstakes open to residents of the U.S. (except Puerto Rico), Canada, Europe and Taiwan who are 18 years of age or older. All applicable laws and regulations apply. Sweepstakes offer void wherever prohibited by law. Values of all prizes are in U.S. currency. This sweepstakes is presented by Torstar Corp., its subsidiaries and affiliates, in conjunction with book, merchandise and/or product offerings. For a copy of the Official Rules send a self-addressed, stamped envelope (WA residents need not affix return postage) to: MILLION DOLLAR SWEEPSTAKES (III) Rules, P.O. Box 4573, Blair, NE 68009, USA.

EXTRA BONUS PRIZE DRAWING

No purchase necessary. The Extra Bonus Prize will be awarded in a random drawing to be conducted no later than 5/30/96 from among all entries received. To qualify, entries must be received by 3/31/96 and comply with published directions. Drawing open to residents of the U.S. (except Puerto Rico), Canada, Europe and Taiwan who are 18 years of age or older. All applicable laws and regulations apply; offer void wherever prohibited by law. Odds of winning are dependent upon number of eligibile entries received. Prize is valued in U.S. currency. The offer is presented by Torstar Corp., its subsidiaries and affiliates in conjunction with book, merchandise and/or product offering. For a copy of the Official Rules governing this sweepstakes, send a self-addressed, stamped envelope (WA residents need not affix return postage) to: Extra Bonus Prize Drawing Rules, P.O. Box 4590, Blair, NE 68009, USA.

SWP-H1294

MEN MADE IN AMERICA

Fifty red-blooded, white-hot, true-blue hunks
from every State in the Union!

Look for MEN MADE IN AMERICA! Written by some
of our most popular authors, these stories feature fifty
of the strongest, sexiest men, each from a different state
in the union!

Two titles available every month at your favorite
retail outlet.

In December, look for:

NATURAL ATTRACTION by Marisa Carroll
(New Hampshire)
MOMENTS HARSH, MOMENTS GENTLE by Joan Hohl
(New Jersey)

In January 1995, look for:

WITHIN REACH by Marilyn Pappano (New Mexico)
IN GOOD FAITH by Judith McWilliams (New York)

You won't be able to resist MEN MADE IN AMERICA!

Where do you find hot Texas nights, smooth Texas charm and dangerously sexy cowboys?

Crystal Creek reverberates with the exciting rhythm of Texas. Each story features the rugged individuals who live and love in the Lone Star state.

"...Crystal Creek wonderfully evokes the hot days and steamy nights of a small Texas community...impossible to put down until the last page is turned."
— *Romantic Times*

"With each book the characters in Crystal Creek become more endearingly familiar. This series is far from formula and a welcome addition to the category genre."
— *Affaire de Coeur*

"Altogether, it couldn't be better." — *Rendezvous*

Don't miss the next book in this exciting series. Look for
THE HEART WON'T LIE by MARGOT DALTON

Available in January wherever Harlequin books are sold.

Harlequin® Historical

LOOK TO THE PAST FOR
FUTURE FUN AND EXCITEMENT!

The past the Harlequin Historical way, that is. 1994 is going to be a banner year for us, so here's a preview of what to expect:

* The continuation of our bigger book program, with titles such as *Across Time* by Nina Beaumont, *Defy the Eagle* by Lynn Bartlett and *Unicorn Bride* by Claire Delacroix.

* A 1994 March Madness promotion featuring four titles by promising new authors Gayle Wilson, Cheryl St. John, Madris Dupree and Emily French.

* Brand-new in-line series: DESTINY'S WOMEN by Merline Lovelace and HIGHLANDER by Ruth Langan; and new chapters in old favorites, such as the SPARHAWK saga by Miranda Jarrett and the WARRIOR series by Margaret Moore.

* *Promised Brides,* an exciting brand-new anthology with stories by Mary Jo Putney, Kristin James and Julie Tetel.

* Our perennial favorite, the Christmas anthology, this year featuring Patricia Gardner Evans, Kathleen Eagle, Elaine Barbieri and Margaret Moore.

Watch for these programs and titles wherever Harlequin Historicals are sold.

HARLEQUIN HISTORICALS...
A TOUCH OF MAGIC!

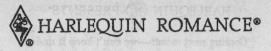

HARLEQUIN ROMANCE®

brings you

More Romances Celebrating Love, Families and Children!

We promised in December, after bringing you
The Nutcracker Prince and **The Santa Sleuth**,
that we would have more wonderful titles in our
KIDS & KISSES series. True to our promise, in January
we have the wonderfully warm story **No Ties**
(Harlequin Romance #3344) by Rosemary Gibson. When
Cassie goes to work for Professor Adam Merrick, she finds
not only love and marriage, but a ready-made family!

Watch for more of these special romances from favorite
Harlequin Romance authors in the coming months:

February	#3347	A Valentine for Daisy	Betty Neels
March	#3351	Leonie's Luck	Emma Goldrick
April	#3357	The Baby Business	Rebecca Winters
May	#3359	Bachelor's Family	Jessica Steele

Available wherever Harlequin books are sold.

HARLEQUIN  PRESENTS®

Coming next month—we can't keep it under
wraps any longer! Our new collection of intriguing and
sensual stories...

Everyone Has Something To Hide

Something which, once discovered, can
dramatically alter lives.

The Colour of Midnight by Robyn Donald
Harlequin Presents #1714

"I'm Stella's sister...."

And Minerva wanted to know why—with everything to live
for—Stella had chosen to die. The only person who might
be able to give her an answer was Nick Peveril, Stella's
husband. But he wasn't the conventional grieving widower.
Nick had a secret—but then, so did Minerva....

Available in January wherever Harlequin books are sold.